A CONDUIT OF LIGHT

A CONDUIT OF LIGHT SERIES
BOOK ONE

CHELSEY ANN TOMPKINS

This book is a work of fiction. Names, characters, places, and plot are the product of the author's imagination. Any resemblance to actual events, locales, or persons, living or dead, is coincidental.

Copyright © 2023 by Chelsey Ann Tompkins

Cover design by Storywrappers

Editing by Muddled Ink Editorial Services

Interior map art by AEKCreates

All rights reserved.

No part of this book may be reproduced in any form or by any electronic or mechanical means, including information storage and retrieval systems, without written permission from the author, except for the use of brief quotations in a book review.

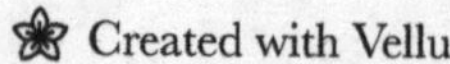 Created with Vellum

for my little loves, W & V
may you find your dreams and chase them

PRONUNCIATION GUIDE

Characters:

Ash'Arah— ASH-ARE-UH

Geyrand— (HARD G) G-AIR-AND

Heimlen— HIGH-M-LEN

Karus— CAR-US

Moira— MOY-RUH

Revich— REV-ICK

Clairannia— CLAIR-AWE-NEE-UH

Figuerah— FIG-AIR-UH

Sylva— SILL-VUH

Pompeii— POM-PAY

Places:

Arcaynen— ARE-CAY-NEN

Hyrithia— HIGH-RIH-THEE-UH

Viridis— VER-IH-DIS

Conduits/magic:

Medicus— MEH-DIH-CUS

Iumenta—EYE-YOU-MEN-TAH
Agricola—AH-GRIH-COLA
Lapis— LAP-IH-S
Rhyzolm— R-EYE-ZOLM

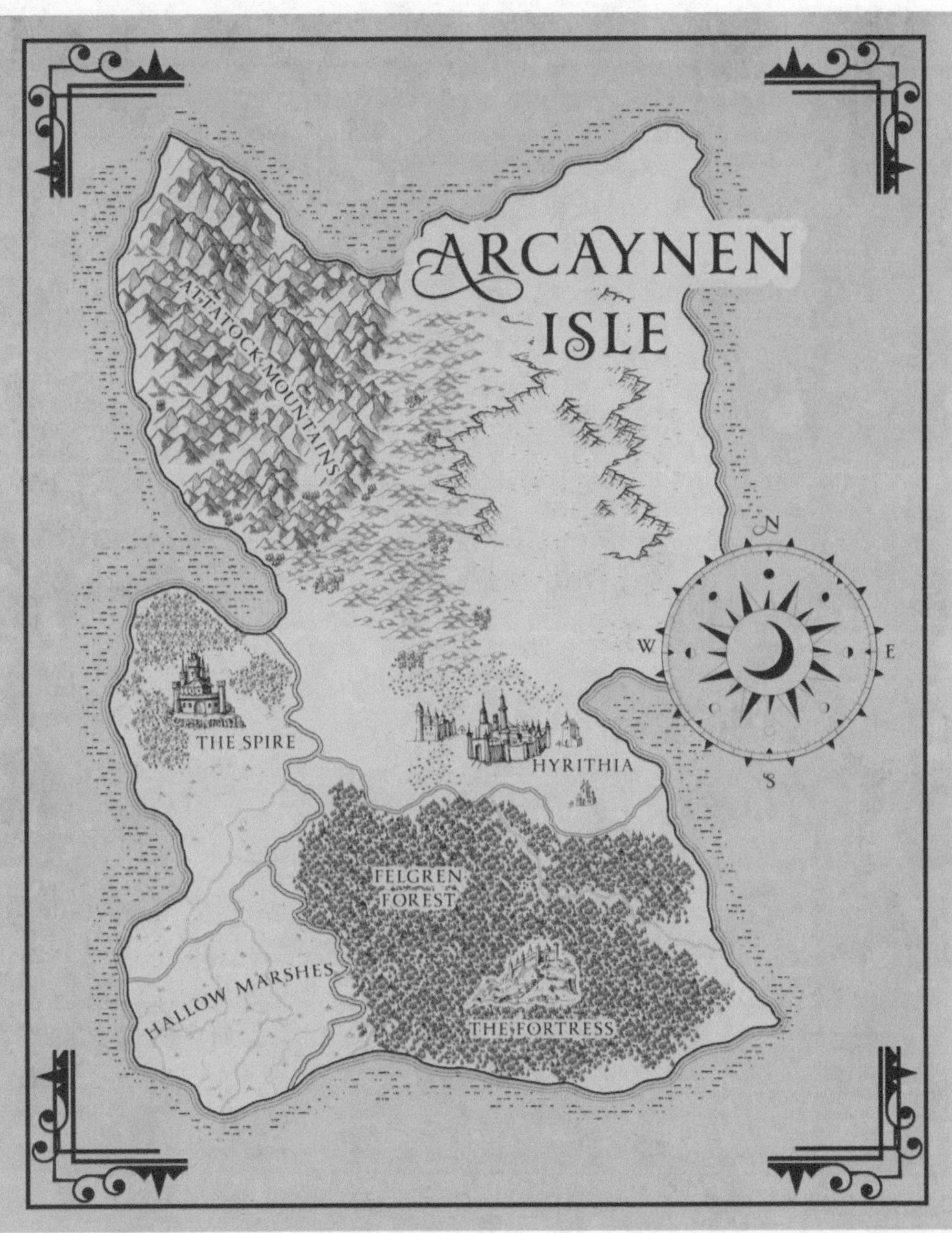

ARCAYNEN ISLE
ATTATOCK MOUNTAINS
THE SPIRE
HYRITHIA
FELGREN FOREST
HALLOW MARSHES
THE FORTRESS
N
W
E
S

PART ONE

CHAPTER I
ASH

Taken. Stolen. Denied the choice to stay or go—whatever she wanted to call it, the outcome was just the same.

Ash'Arah would be whisked away as payment while the evening sun lay drowsily upon the distant horizon. The scent of spring wove through the air to kiss her face, playing with the loose strands of her dark braid.

She recognized the irony, of course. The sun was leaving her home and so was she. But it would return shortly, and she would not.

She closed her eyes and grinned. A madwoman, perhaps, but the insanity of the future she was forced to face was taking hold in her heart, and the only other option was to panic.

Ash thought she'd be stolen away in the middle of the night. She thought the Baron would come when the moon was already high in the starlit sky and the entire exchange would be a secret, hidden from the people of Hyrithia.

That was not the scene that played before her. The Queen had amassed her guards in their finest, and she would be taken in waning sunlight for all the people to see. Those same people who had suffered so greatly would see the cost of their cure.

The royal guards stood in rows wearing their full Hyrithian armor. Silver plates gleamed on their shoulders and torsos. The deepest of blue silk draped elegantly across their chests. A pattern of thistle had been embroidered lovingly through each one. Ash would know—she had taken her own needle and thread to some of them.

She could feel the eyes of her people, hear their stilted whispers, as they gathered to witness the price to be paid to the Savior of Hyrithia. As she finally stepped out of the castle's shadow, her worn shoes scraping along the dusty path, she searched for the ones she loved. Her eyes stung, but the hollow heart residing in her chest refused to let the tears fall in this moment of her last goodbye.

My last goodbye for now, she reminded herself.

She was determined to return one day. After she had proven to the Baron of Felgren that she was worthless to him, she would find her way back home.

When the Black Fever claimed its first victim, the medicus conduit assigned to his case was baffled. She had never seen such a disease in all her years of service to Hyrithia. The man inflicted had been old, loved, and died three days after his fever started. The tips of his worn fingers had turned black with a dark filigree of lines that coursed down to his wrists. Her conduit magic had done nothing but ease his pain.

Mystified, the same medicus conduit met another case just a day later. It was a young mother this time. She had the same high fever, the same blackened fingers. There was no connection that could be made between the two victims, and as news of the ailment began to spread, a dark cloud rained panic across the great city of Hyrithia, coursing as wildly as the disease.

Ash had done what she could.

All her life, she had been unsure of the extent of her channeler power. She did not know if she was prone to medicus magic or not, but her presence and the words she whispered to the victims in the castle seemed to ease their pain—if only for a short while.

The disease moved randomly, infecting someone in one household and no others, before jumping across the city to inflict itself there. The seven medicus conduits of Hyrithia had met with Queen Rina, and though Ash had not been present, she saw the rage in the Queen's eyes as she left the meeting, storming across the castle halls to the guard's tower to send yet another message across the grasslands to Felgren Forest.

To Baron Heimlen's forest.

Some channelers, like Ash, were trained there before becoming true conduits. When they passed the trials and were given their conduit title, they were allowed to begin their professions anywhere throughout Arcaynen Isle, using their magic siphoned from Felgren Forest for the good of the people.

But unlike Ash, they were all given an Offering.

A choice.

Each channeler either made the decision to leave their homes and train or they refused. If they declined, they were willing to live their lives as channelers only, using what magic they possessed until it inevitably died, leaving their bodies without the proper understanding of how to harness more power from the forest.

It was rare to refuse an Offering, but it's exactly what Ash would have done. She had no desire to pursue the extent of her power, and no Baron could change her mind—of that, she was certain.

On the ninety-first day, after thousands of lives had already been lost, the Prince fell victim to the Black Fever's rampage through the city. Ash remembered being called to his side in the dead of night, the realization of his fate pounding through her chest as she clasped her closest friend's hand, tracing the mass of blackened veins and the dark tips of his once unmarred, elegant fingers. Prince Philius was her brother in all but blood and she poured everything she could into willing him to live, for him to survive even though no one else did.

The Queen's face that night had been pained. Her usual mahogany skin looked tight and sickly on her face as she gazed at her only son, the future regent of Hyrithia, the sole path to a female heir, laying on his bed, fevered and tossing in anguish.

Her dark eyes, brimmed with tears, landed on her ward.

Emotions crossed her face that Ash could not identify in that moment.

Now she knew.

She understood that the Queen had made her decision as her only child grew weaker by the hour.

It was either her son's life or her ward's ability to choose her own future.

Ash would be payment for the cure that saved the city, and though the details of the negotiations were never discussed, it didn't seem to matter now.

She became a willing prisoner. She could make this sacrifice if it meant the disease was cured, the Prince would live, and if it meant that Hyrithia would survive; the home she had loved and never planned to leave.

Her heart thrashed in her chest as she continued her path forward, leaving her home behind for an indeterminate amount of her life. It hammered and writhed while her stomach soured, some last attempt her soul would make to resist what she felt forced to do by circumstance.

"My ward, Ash'Arah, is presented to Baron Heimlen of Felgren Forest on this evening as payment for the cure of the Black Fever." The Queen stepped forward from the line of royal guards and presented her hand toward Ash as she continued. "Let it be known that an official Offering was not given on this day and that this woman would choose to decline if she had been presented with one. She leaves for the Fortress in Felgren on my will alone." She paused and finally met Ash's emerald eyes, tears falling down her face. "And it pains me greatly to ask it of her in payment for the life of my son and the lives of my people."

Ash's gaze drew to the row of lumens across the stream and the viridescent portal, open and humming to the right of the wolf-like beasts. A dark figure stood there, dressed in a variation of a conduit's clothing. The man's dark cloak hung heavily down his wide shoulders and his light tunic was immaculate under his pressed black vest.

The Baron Heimlen, she presumed, her captor and the Savior

of Hyrithia. He was the only one powerful enough to cure the disease and the man she was determined to convince of her obscurity.

"Ash."

The harsh whisper of her name forced its way into her distracted mind and she turned to see Geyrand's familiar figure. He had always looked the part in his full royal guard armor, the glint of the sun radiating from the smooth metal, causing a celestial glow to surround his freckled face.

She rushed to him, clinging tightly to his chest, inhaling the soothing scent of mint and chalk, two ingredients in the powder guards spread on their clothes before donning their full armor—a scent she knew well.

She pulled back to see his pale face, holding it in her hands and smiling wide, thinking of all they had shared as childhood friends and eventual lovers.

"Thank you for the memories. I won't forget them. I won't forget you."

She raised up onto her tiptoes, running her hand through his red curls, and kissed his forehead, her last goodbye to the man she cared for deeply, but could never learn to truly love.

She turned to leave but was pulled back into a kiss. His hands held her face to his. His lips were trembling, full of a secret he had been keeping—the truth of his heart told too late.

A cough nearby startled them from their words unsaid, and before she could turn again to go, he grabbed her hand and pressed his lips to her knuckles. His amber eyes did not leave hers until she broke their gaze with her shaking body turning to the future that lay before her.

Her steps must have taken days to complete. Her feet were leaden in her worn leather shoes. Her simple frock must have been weighted as it brushed across the dirt path.

She crossed the stone bridge to her waiting captor, setting her gaze on the lumens. There were easily two dozen of them, massive beasts with jaws the length of her arm, a monstrous beauty about them.

She wasn't sure when she made the decision to do it. It was an impulse, one last rebellion against what she was forced to face. Before she processed the possible danger of it, she was letting go of her handkerchief in the gentle breeze and watched as it floated lazily in front of the giant wolves, their black noses twitching at the sight and scent of it.

All at once, they broke their stance, interrupting the stillness in the air. Great howls echoed through the dusky set of the sun and the beasts pawed at the ground, digging at the small piece of her she let fly free.

"Your monsters are well trained, but even the slightest scent can break them." She smirked at the Baron, standing confident and tall beneath him, poised and ready for their unspoken battle.

"My dear," he chuckled, his black eyes admitting just a hint of silver, the lines of his aging face creasing into an amused grin. "*You* are hardly the slightest of anything." He turned and gave a short whistle, commanding the pack to resume their position. "Shall we?"

Baron Heimlen's black gloved hand reached out for her to take and as she did so, her appearance was transformed. Her slippers turned into tall leather boots, her dress to fine silk. The garment was a dark green, hued like the trees that grew only in Felgren. It fell across the center of her chest, her neck and shoulders exposed while sheer green fabric clung down her arms. The gown held tightly to her torso before spilling out from her hips, black beads adorning the front in a dizzying pattern that began at the crest of her chest and wound down the length of the garment, cascading into what looked like a tangle of vines, ending at her feet.

Her long length of dark hair, the color of a wood owl's wing, was pulled up into a tightly woven bun, fastened with an emerald-studded comb.

The last adornment to appear was her conduit ring. It formed seamlessly around her right forefinger as a simple band of silver before a many-faceted teardrop emerald bloomed as the single stone upon it.

"Interesting," Baron Heimlen murmured, still holding onto her hand, his eyes alit with curiosity.

Refusing to ask what he meant, she turned her head to take one last look at the castle and the life she had every intention of coming back to. She would return in time and this would all be a memory, a tale to tell the Prince's future children before they drifted off to sleep in their nursery.

She moved back to face the Baron and pulled the ornate comb from her hair, tossing it to the dry earth. Her locks cascaded down her open back, a contrast to her pale, porcelain skin in a shimmer of bronze, enhanced by the last goodbye of the fading sun.

"The more you try to bind me, Baron, the less of me you'll have."

He laughed then, a rich tenor of amusement altering his countenance as he nodded to her, and she took a step through the portal.

CHAPTER 2

KARUS

S pring had finally come—life anew and the endless cold rising to a spark of warmth once again.

"Another one gone, look—there!"

I nodded, looking down at the little faerie as she spoke, her long, sage fingers pointing across the sea of spring's evening dew at yet another tree in Felgren that had not made it through the winter.

"At least we only found six of them today, much better than yesterday, and at least they don't all have the look of death about them."

I pulled on the sleeves of my dress, suddenly chilled. "In a way, Moira, they do. Imagine being deprived of all that nurtures your soul. Wouldn't that make a part of you die, too? Wouldn't it forever change you?"

The tiny faerie bowed her head as her fluttering wings held her off the ground. Moira had been so elated to see spring arrive once again, but all I could now see was nature forgetting what it had done to itself.

Well, I wouldn't forget the cold winter. It had been a harsh and long one. Many of the ancient trees of Felgren Forest did not make it to see spring at all. Too much had died, and I wondered as we walked back to the Fortress, if the forest would ever be the same again.

I hoped so.

"C'mon, Karus." Moira tugged on the fabric of my dress. "We don't want to be late." She zipped by me, her little wings fluttering so quickly, they were difficult to see in the waning sun except for the glint of iridescence that could transfix the eye and mesmerize the soul.

That's one thing faeries do well. All their tricks and games were successful because of their gorgeous exterior and mysterious smiles. Moira was different, though. She had been my friend and companion here for…I didn't know how long. The little thing stood no higher than my knee, but she was the best kind of friend. She was always watching out for me in the forest and getting me back into the Fortress when it was time. My mind tended to wander, my thoughts often cloudy and undisciplined, never focusing too hard on one thing for too long.

Except, of course, for the forest. Even in that dreadful winter, I could feel Felgren striving to survive, to hold together what was left of itself until the sweet spring could awaken it yet again. The leaves of the swaying trees shined viridian in the orange glow of the sun, and the birds sang the sweet song of spring's arrival. I closed my eyes and felt the spirit of the forest once again. I felt the magic that flowed through its roots. It embraced me as I walked its dirt floor.

I inhaled deeply to soothe what else was troubling me. Something that I could not name. The breath worked. For a few moments, at least.

We traveled back in silence. I assumed we both were listening to the music of the life around us. Moira spent most of her time in the Fortress with me these days, but I knew her fae heart belonged in the forest with her fellow-kind.

We took a new path back, and I was careful not to disturb the newly grown richness around me. Carefully, I stepped over fallen logs, laden with soft moss, and tiptoed around new ferns and old, unfolding their leaves to greet us. My white, gauzy dress flowed lazily behind me as I ducked under yet another fallen tree.

As I reached out my hand for balance, it brushed something smooth and hard in the coarse, mossy bark. I stepped back from under the tree and searched for the anomaly. It was tucked into the wood, whether forced into it or placed there lovingly, I did not know. All I knew was that it was unnatural.

I glanced under the tree to see that Moira was well ahead of me, but I couldn't just leave it there. I pulled at the withering bark and pried the oval stone from the tree. Smooth and imperfectly shaped, I traced along the black lines adorning the green whole of it.

I felt something then as I placed the stone into my palm, its cool surface mirroring my chilled touch.

A bond.

But more than that, it caressed a sort of embrace around my heart that was so foreign…and yet…I felt as if I knew it well. Of course, I knew it. A sharp clarity nestled into my mind for a moment, and I wondered why I had ever forgotten—

"Kar-us!" Moira called from some distance ahead. "Keep moving or we'll never make it back in time!"

A threat I had heard many times before, I quickly pocketed the stone and continued on my way.

I didn't admit to Moira what I had discovered as I caught up to her frenzied wings. I wasn't sure why, but if this stone was a gift to me, a gift from the forest, I wanted to keep it to myself.

At least, until I understood it.

The Fortress loomed ahead of us, impossible to miss as dark and brooding as it was in the forest of life. The weight of its inanimate high towers and ancient parapets seemed so out of place among the living trees swaying in the evening breeze.

In the winter, it was different. It felt as if the Fortress was the origin of the cold, unforgiving weather, but now that spring had arrived again, the forest seemed to be pushing back. I noticed the creeping ivy winding around the stone staircase, desperate to claim all in its path. I pointed at the vine and a swirl of my magic lazily guided the greenery upward, twisting further toward the Fortress.

We entered through one of the many smaller doors, this one leading straight into the bustling kitchen. The oven was warm and welcoming as I snagged a fresh biscuit from the cook's tray, downing it in three mouthfuls. If the cook saw me again, she didn't say anything this time.

The Fortress was booming with activity today. New faces rushed up and down the stairwells. Some old faces were mixed in too, but somehow more of them than usual. The Baron had little care for who completed his tasks as long as they were done and in a timely manner.

He was searching for something and wouldn't let anyone get in his way, least of all me, so I kept out of his presence as much as possible.

I liked it that way. I was free to roam the Fortress and surrounding woods, was fed good food, given good company in Moira, and I slept in the warmest bed, fire crackling low in the hearth each night. The only thing Baron Revich asked of me was this meeting at the end of each day. I suppose to him, it was a way to check that I was not getting into trouble or wandering off. I was a part of his fortress, and I was somehow his responsibility—whether he liked it or not.

"How are you today, Karus?"

That was always his first question, but hardly much of one.

He gave me a small grin as I closed the door to his study where he stood at his massive oak desk, sorting through papers, flipping open books, and jotting down notes.

I observed the top of his head as he bent, black hair pulled back and tied at the nape of his neck in a green silk ribbon that complimented his warm, sandy skin.

He glanced up at me when I failed to answer, his black eyes boring into mine.

"I am well, thank you."

He stood to his full height, barely taller than me, but for a woman, I was quite tall myself. He was toned, though his vest was sagging slightly, too large for his medium frame. I wondered why he didn't just have it taken in by the seamstress.

"Tell me about your day, Karus," he mumbled, continuing his sorting of papers and books.

"Moira and I walked through the forest," I stated as usual, but felt the urge today to continue. "It is anew with life from the spring sun. The leaves of the trees waved to us in the breeze and the crocus are blooming in fields of purple and white. You should really go and see—"

I realized I had moved away from the heavy wooden door frame more than I usually did during our short meetings. My boots were silent on the woven floral rug, and my voice halted as I wondered why I had stepped so far into the room.

My presence startled him when he realized how close I was, and he quickly dropped his papers and quill next to the ink pot. His features this close were handsome, but not absurdly so, and I observed that he couldn't have been much older than me. His jawline clenched and his lips pursed as he gazed at my face. His eyes flickered across my figure rapidly, his expression impossible to understand.

He sank down in his black leather chair and rubbed his mouth as he spoke slowly, carefully. "And what did you find in the forest, Karus?"

This was always his last question before his dismissal. I always assumed he was hoping I would find what he was looking for as I strolled around the forest. My hands had been steady by my side, but now itched to hold the stone heavy in my pocket.

"Nothing, Baron." I recited my usual reply, this time a lie, "I found nothing."

His obsidian eyes narrowed as he watched me trying to steady my breath. I felt as if I stood before him for hours, our eyes locked and bodies still. We were two people who spoke every day, yet spoke of nothing. I wondered in those moments who he was. I knew little of him except that he brought me here as he brought all the others here, searching and consumed by whatever it was he was looking for.

For a moment, I wondered if what he was searching for was the stone that weighted my pocket. But it couldn't be, and I almost laughed out loud at the thought of the mighty Baron Revich searching for a small stone embedded in a dead tree.

"Baron Revich, the new channelers are waiting." We were interrupted by Pompeii, the Baron's Overseer to the Fortress.

The Baron let out a deep sigh that filled the room with its weight, and he stood, turning away from me to look out of the glass-paned window, spanning floor to ceiling behind him. The sunlight was kept out of the Fortress as much as possible, but here, in his study, it streamed in without hindrance, catching on his sharp features and furrowed eyes.

"You may go, Karus."

I backed away from his desk, hardly able to keep my gaze from his brooding figure. Pompeii gave me a weak smile as he held the door open and gestured toward the dining room.

"Please, Karus, go get something to eat. You look a little worn from your wanderings today." He smiled again, the glint of it never reaching his eyes as he quietly stepped back into the Baron's study.

As I headed toward the dining hall, stomach growling for more than just one biscuit, I saw the new channelers in the entryway, huddled together, green formal clothing enveloping them, their faces nervous and weary. They would be here fresh from their homes after their Offerings, ready to train as conduits. They saw me pass and I gave a quick smile and wave.

I hurried on to the dining hall to fill my plate and rushed upstairs to my room in the tallest tower. Moira would keep me company this night and fill my head with sunshine before I drifted off into the quiet stillness of slumber.

CHAPTER 3
ASH

The first thing Ash noticed was the contrast. It was a juxtaposition to have such a dark, dimly lit fortress stuck right in the middle of a blooming forest full of life. Though, a few tangles of greenery seemed to creep closer as she climbed the dark, moss-covered steps, her ridiculous black and pine dress snagging behind her.

She took her sweet time climbing the stairs, too. After all, if Baron Heimlen expected her full compliance, he wasn't going to get it.

The looming iron-leaded doors were pulled open by a middle-aged man in an emerald servant's uniform. His honey eyes were lined in black kohl and his brass buttons gleamed in the candlelight provided by the massive chandelier hanging in the foyer.

"Welcome, channelers. Please step inside and we will get you seated for dinner."

She studied the two young women beside her. They were already at the base of the steps when she had stepped out of her portal. They couldn't have been much older than Ash's twenty years. They were shivering together, not surprisingly so, considering the lack of cover from the dresses they wore. One wore a shimmering emerald gown with thin sleeves hanging off her delicate shoulders. The other was draped in a tulle dress the color of the sea when it foams on the shore, her muscular arms showing through the sheer drapery. Their eyes were bright with curiosity and nervousness as they surveyed the foyer and its expansive ceiling.

The Fortress surprised her. It was completely black, not only the facade but inside as well, its walls just as dark and dreary. Even the wood was some of the darkest she'd ever seen. As she gazed about the tapestry covered hall, she found herself in the middle of it, admiring a vase of purple crocus on a dark wood table.

"Welcome to Felgren, Ash'Arah."

She jumped and turned quickly, knocking over the vase in doing so—the man's hands already catching the ornament before it fell to the floor. He grinned, never looking away as he steadied the vase back on the table. His smile irritated her immediately. Wide and genuine, she fought any inkling to return it, instead crossing her arms as she looked him over.

Wavy black hair that hung to his broad shoulders, deep-set eyes under straight black brows, and a strong chin formed the features of what she might usually consider an attractive man. This, however, was not a usual situation.

He took his eyes from hers, glancing behind his shoulder at the servant in green who was guiding the other two women through a door.

"My name is Revich, your most humble of Barons." He winked and grinned, bowing slightly.

"Just Ash," she grumbled, eyes narrowing as he raised back to his full height. "You can call me Ash for the short while I am forced to be here."

She'd always hated her full name, and she certainly didn't want anyone to hear it now. She put her hands on her hips and spoke bluntly, "I thought there was only *one* Baron of Felgren." She paused to look him up and down. "And," she continued with a smirk, "you're definitely not him."

He scoffed lightly. "Give it a chance, Ash, before you decide to hate me and this place forever." He turned again to hear the servant clearing his throat and gesturing inside the door the other two women had already entered.

"And you're right. There is usually only one Baron at a time. I am Baron Heimlen's successor, running things here while he healed your city."

"Baron Heimlen is…unwell?" She had no idea the old Baron was training a successor, but knew Barons reigned in Felgren until their lives gave out, their power passing to the man they chose to become their heir.

A flash of worry crossed his face. "We don't need to discuss that now. This is a night of celebration! Besides, it takes years to train the new Baron." He flashed yet another full smile. "And, thankfully, I'll be here the entire time you are here. We get to work together—you and me."

Ash's eyebrows furrowed. She didn't understand why he chose to be so informal in their conversation but wasn't about to show that it bothered her. "Like I said, I don't plan to be here long, Baron Revich. You can count on that." She turned from him and walked swiftly to the open door the servant was still holding.

It led to a dining room, grand, opulent, and glittering with accents of gold. Ash may not have grown up with royal blood, but she had been around enough of the royal family to see how well the rich and important people of the isle lived.

The two other women, however, were in absolute awe. They gazed up at the shining chandelier, gold with copper leaves winding around each arm in mimicry of the ivy she saw winding up the staircase to the Fortress.

Once they were seated, Baron Revich strode quickly to the head of the excessively long table and raised his goblet, nodding to the other women and winking once again at Ash, his excitement hardly restrained.

"Welcome, channelers, to your new home. I am Baron Revich, future successor to Baron Heimlen. I hope your stay here at the Fortress is a productive one and that you find your place within its halls." He gave them a wide smile before continuing, his voice echoing in the vast hall. "Please, fill your bellies tonight and get good rest. We start training tomorrow morning."

At that, he raised his cup and took a long drink. The two women awkwardly grabbed their glasses and did the same. Ash crossed her arms and glared, unwilling to follow along. Her defiance would continue as long as necessary before she convinced them to let her leave.

Just as Baron Revich sat down, his servant in green appeared to whisper in his ear.

"Please excuse me, there is something I must attend to. Enjoy yourself and I'll see you in the morning with Baron Heimlen."

At that, he swiftly left the room with his servant on his heels, and as the door closed, one of the girls giggled in delight.

"I'm so excited I don't know if I could eat a thing!"

Ash noticed it didn't seem to stop her from piling on spoonfuls of yams and a giant turkey leg on her plate.

"I could certainly eat this food!" exclaimed the other, reaching first for what looked like warm rolls and honey butter.

"My name's Clairannia," the first one said, mouth full of potato. Her black hair had fallen loose from the intricate braid piled up on her head. Wisps framed her golden oval face and fell into her dark, almond eyes. Ash glanced down to her delicate hand, curious about her conduit ring. Five brilliant rubies were tucked into a golden band, sparkling diamonds gracing the sides of each one.

"Figuerah," the second replied before reaching out her hand to shake Clairannia's. Her dark skin was tattooed with symbols of the lunar phases and her hair was swept up in a similar fashion, though much thicker and with a reddish hue to her many braids. Figuerah's ring was an elegant tangle of orange and yellow stones that wove together in an unintelligible pattern above a golden band. They both turned to Ash in unison and expectancy.

"Ash," she stated, picking up a slice of ham, juices spilling onto her plate. She might as well not starve while she was here.

"Nice to meet you both!" Clairannia sputtered between bites.

"Where are you two from?" Figuerah asked, brown eyes darting between the two of them. "Baron Heimlen found me in the Attatock Mountains. I lived in a tiny village. It was such a surprise when he showed up!" She stopped chewing and took a gulp of wine, shaking her head as if still in disbelief. "We knew of him of course, but I'm the first he's ever trained from our village, and we weren't expecting it. We didn't even have time for the ceremony, barely even the Offering."

Figuerah gleamed with pride, causing Ash to wonder for the hundredth time how she could possibly belong here.

"I'm from the Spire," Clairannia chimed in. "There's been hundreds of us taken. My ceremony was as grand as they come." She paused and glanced down at her exuberant gown, the emerald straps laying elegantly off her small shoulders. "Well, not as grand as this gown or this place. But still very beautiful."

They again turned expectantly to Ash.

"Hyrithia."

She tried to suppress her amusement at their surprise, a knowing grin lighting her face.

"But…Hyrithia is off limits." Clairannia set down her fork, a piece of turkey thigh still speared. "According to the Treaty, channelers from Hyrithia cannot be taken. It would start a war if that was done."

"There was a…compromise," Ash answered, unsure of how much she was allowed to tell anyone. There had been great secrecy about the Black Fever infecting the people of Hyrithia in case trade was deemed too dangerous to risk from other parts of Arcaynen. "It doesn't matter now," she said, taking a sip of wine from her cup. "I'm here, and there isn't going to be a war. Though, I doubt I'll be here for long."

"Are you sure you're telling us the whole story, Ash?" Figuerah calmly asked across the table. "Doesn't history tell us that none of the Barons have taken someone born of Hyrithia for centuries? Not since the Treaty? Not since…"

They all knew the stories of the Baron who slaughtered five channelers after their Offerings. He had gone mad, though the history books had never detailed why. After that, to prevent an all-out war, the Treaty was made. Different regions could decide if they would allow their citizens to be given an Offering. Hyrithia was the only one to decline, and so, it was impossible to be born in Hyrithia and be trained as a conduit.

Yet, here she was.

"The Treaty didn't matter in my case." Ash sighed and leaned into her high-backed chair, ridiculous in its ornate black tassels. "Life and death were on the line."

She gazed upward at the twelve-pronged chandelier glinting gold in the flickering candlelight. She remembered the cries of joy, altogether in one glorious sound throughout Hyrithia.

One spell. One single spell from Baron Heimlen and all was cured.

She remembered watching from the door of the Prince's room the moment it happened. Her legs felt glued to the floor outside of his chambers knowing her fate and his were tied.

One would stay and one would go.

His eyes had fluttered open, his breathing had stabilized. The gasp and cry of the Queen was heart-wrenching as she clasped her only son in a mother's embrace and wept into his black curls.

Ash had felt relief, and yet, the dread had begun then. If the cure worked, she was to be given freely. No war, no fighting, no chance at refusal.

"Where are you going? You don't even know how to get around the Fortress!" Clairannia exclaimed as Ash rose to leave the dining hall.

"I'll manage."

And she left, unwilling to discuss her past or future the very day she had let go of them both. Back straight, eyes forward, with her stomach writhing in her belly, she pulled open the dining hall doors and stepped back into the foyer.

CHAPTER 4
ASH

The Fortress was enormous. And *black*. So much dark stone, dark wood. Bits of greenery were laid here and there, and Ash wondered who had decided on that feature. It almost seemed out of place in the windowless abyss.

She began with the massive spiral staircase, countless stone steps leading to the tallest of towers. If she was going to leave here as soon as possible, she was at least going to have good stories to tell. No doubt the Prince and Geyrand would be begging her for details someday.

She climbed and climbed, holding onto the stone rail, counting seven landings before exasperation got ahold of her, and she decided to just make up a number beyond.

Few people were moving about. Servants, she assumed, as they were carrying bed linens or lighting candles in ornate iron sconces along the winding walls. They were channelers, all of them, using their magic to complete their tasks, no conduit rings on their fingers. Her eyes narrowed as she watched an older woman dust the frame of an enormous painting on what must have been the twentieth landing. Her magical essence flowed from her wrinkled hand, a steel gray, controlling the cloth in gentle strokes around the painting.

As a spectator, she watched the woman at her work, hundreds of questions forming even in her exhaustion.

Was this woman a channeler brought to Felgren to train in her younger years? She knew some channelers did not pass the conduit trials and she did not see a conduit ring on her finger. Channelers were people with the use of magic but lacked the ability to harness it in more specific ways. More times than not, they eventually lost their magic completely.

As Ash watched from the stairs, the old woman's silvery glow gave out, her dusting rag falling with a slump to the stone floor.

Tears swelled in the woman's grey eyes and she slowly bent her body down to retrieve it.

"Can I help you with that?" Ash stepped closer, unsure of her own role to this woman.

She looked up, smiling warmly at Ash, her pale skin crinkling with the fine lines of long years. "A kind heart keeps the Blightress at bay."

Ash smirked, not expecting to hear one of the many proverbs of her childhood. "I think that one has always been my favorite." Ash moved forward, picking up the cloth and holding out her arm for the woman to regain her footing.

The woman sighed heavily, "My eyesight is not what it used to be. And, I suppose, my magic, too." She took ahold of Ash's outstretched arm, then looked up at the exceedingly large painting. "I never did like this one," she spoke softly, her gaze landing on the subject of the portrait.

A young man stood atop a broken tree trunk, his gaze directed just beyond the painter.

Ash gasped in recognition. "Is that...a young Baron Heimlen?"

"Good eye. This was painted when he was chosen as successor to Baron Thalius, back before even I knew him, and I'm one of the oldest remaining channelers here." She smiled dreamily at the portrait. "But it does not capture the Baron I knew back then. It does not capture his vulnerability. Or his kind eyes."

Ash could sense it—admiration, possibly love in her expression as she gazed at the younger version of the man who had bargained for her. "Do you know Baron Heimlen well?"

"Yes, I know him. He came for me many years ago, just as he came for you. He brought me to the Fortress and taught me to use my magic." She chuckled, "That was back when there was hope for me. But the trials…I just couldn't get through them. And here I am now, decades later." She smirked at Ash and whispered, "At least I got to stay. At least I didn't have to go back in shame." Again, she beamed up at the portrait's subject.

"May I ask how long you've been here…"

"Sylva. Nice to meet you, dear. I've been here seventy-two years now."

Ash narrowed her eyes at the woman. With white hair thick and loose around her shoulders, cheeks flushed with warmth, but skin pale as moonlight, she couldn't have been older than eighty herself.

Sylva cackled at Ash's confusion. "You'll find time works differently here in Felgren. Seasons are long, years linger. Baron Heimlen himself has been here over one hundred years. You'll get used to it, dear. But you'll return to your home and find it very changed. Prepare yourself for that." She bent down to gather her supplies.

"And how long has Baron Revich been here?"

"Ah, so you've met the young Baron, eh?" She held a sly smile as she hobbled toward the downward staircase. "He arrived a few years ago now. I couldn't tell you exactly how many. Baron Heimlen is in need of a successor, and he found one." She began her descent down the winding staircase. "The top, Ash'Arah. You'll find yourself at home up there, dear." She gestured upwards where Ash could see several more floors to what must have been a parapet and a final level to the tower.

Ash nodded to her newfound acquaintance, more questions swimming through her head than when she'd started her climb.

Sylva had known her name as well as Baron Revich. This truth disturbed her, hinting that finding her way back home quickly would be harder than she'd originally thought if she was already being spoken of in this desolate place.

She sighed, taking one more glance at the portrait on the landing before grabbing ahold of the black stone railing and continuing her long ascent to, hopefully, a place of rest.

CHAPTER 5
KARUS

The morning sun was up, welcoming the forest to a new day, but I could not see it. Someone had closed the shutters to the single window in my room, and light from the dawn crept through the slats, begging to be released.

I glanced around my cramped quarters for a stool. The pin at the top of the slanted window was difficult to reach, even with my long legs. Moira usually opened it for me.

Most mornings I awoke to find her sitting on the window's ledge, eating some kind of berry or nut she'd found while I still lay sleeping, waiting patiently for me to wake.

I reached from my chair to pull the pin and sunlight—glorious sunlight—streamed through the window in unapologetic indulgence. Spring truly had arrived, and I was grateful for it as I basked in the rays.

On the tips of my toes, I saw trees—the tops of thousands of trees. The length of their branches reached for the warmth of the sun as I did.

I loved Felgren. I never wanted to leave it.

I sat at my humble vanity, gazing at my reflection in the dingy mirror atop of the dark wooden desk. My hair was always so striking, even to me. Broad streaks of white contrasted atop brown strands the color of the pecans Moira sometimes found and brought for me.

I had never seen another person with hair like mine. There were servants I had seen in the Fortress, their heads sprouting white and gray wisps, but never such a differentiation in color as what I pondered before me.

I took my bristled brush and combed through the tangles a restless sleep had brought and studied my reflection. My eyes were dull, even in the morning light, but the lashes were dark as ever. My cheeks accentuated my pale complexion in a subtle pink and lips wore a soft red hue, the cupid's bow pronounced upon my face in a sultry V shape. I admired my lips—the shape of them fit my features well and added more character than any other part of me.

I painted them red each morning with a concoction Moira made for me. She knew so much more than I did, scouting the forest for the blood-red demorte flower, which was so hearty, it could grow even in a harsh winter. Perhaps that's where Moira was. The blooms must have been rebelling against the frost, growing strong, red, and lovely.

I finished painting my lips and began to dress. Something heavy fell to the wooden floorboards as I wrestled with the long sleeves of my favorite white gown.

I picked up the green stone I had somehow forgotten about and felt the joy it had given me the day before. I closed my eyes and filled my lungs slowly as the sense of a deep bond came again, flooding my body, and I grinned ear-to-ear as I examined the rock in the morning light.

The black veins swirled continuously along the hardened jade polished stone. It was smooth and cool in my hands, heavier than it looked to be and a memory returned to me.

There was a small clearing in Felgren, yellow wildflowers spread through the tall grass, and me—straddled across the back of a lumen, its white patches of fur blinding in the afternoon sun. I laughed in reverie brod spread my arms wide, feeling free and loved.

Loved. I remembered feeling loved.

"Karus, you're awake!"

I jumped, startled in my memory by the lilting sound of Moira's voice coming through the door of my room. She was gasping, carrying a small woven basket full of fruits and cheese.

"Is that a cinnamon bun I smell?" I grinned, placing the stone in my pocket, rushing over to help with her bounty.

"Cook saved you one, but wanted me to remind you to eat the fruit first and blah, blah, blah." Moira displayed her sharp-toothed smile and pulled out a sticky, cold bun, a sweet glaze smeared atop its light brown center. Moira licked her fingers as I took my prize to my bed and sat down to devour the treat.

"I thought you'd be out picking demorte."

"I haven't seen new blooms yet. Here, have some water."

I gulped the cold beverage eagerly, unsure of when I last drank and muttered a thank you.

Moira fluttered around the room, picking up lost hosiery, bits of paper, and books. She returned them to the stack in the corner of the room, and she sang in a playful tune as she worked, poking at the embers of the dying fire in its hearth,

"So long as you keep to your bed at night,
She will not harm you, she might, she might.
Don't let anger in your heart or your head,
Her darkness will find you and you will be
    dead.
The Blightress may find you and you will be
    dead."

I found myself humming along to the song, absently picking at a square of cheese and swaying my hips.

"She sounds awful, this Blightress. We still don't know what angered her, do we?" I spoke absentmindedly as I pinned my long hair back into a half plait, some of the white strands falling across my face in typical defiance.

"Karus…?"

I turned, pins sticking out from my lips, and looked at Moira who had spoken so seriously that I wondered if something was wrong.

Moira stared at me, wings beating furiously behind her tiny frame. She only did that when her heart was beating fast. Her dragonfly wings tended to follow its rhythm.

I blinked, confused at her tone and flustered state, my mind a whirl of chaos in the sudden change between us.

Shaking my head, I took the pins from my mouth and set them on the vanity, resigned to whatever state my hair was in, and desperate to change the mood.

"Can we ride today? I'm sure the channelers won't be training with the lumens on their first day, and I haven't seen Parvus in so long." I gave her my best warm smile and reached into my pocket to palm the stone.

"Yes, we can ride today." She nodded, glancing out the window at the patch of gray looming in the morning sky. "But I don't like the look of those clouds. You know how the lumens smell after a good rain."

"Well, we'd better race the storm then."

And with one last bite of a soft yellow pear, I pulled on my boots, ready to discover something new.

~

"Hello, handsome," I whispered to the lumen nuzzling my ear and giving me a lick in return.

Parvus was the runt of the pack, but strong in his affection. He licked my ear again with his enormous tongue, the size of a dinner plate, and I felt pieces of hair rip from my head. I placed a saddle on his back and buckled it tightly before climbing on. Rauca whined behind us, wanting to come along as usual. I whistled for her to follow as we shot out of the cave, Moira flying ahead, her iridescence sparkling in the few rays of sunlight slitting through the trees.

The pounding of enormous paws over dirt and undergrowth sounded in my ears as the wind rushed past my head. I recalled the memory that came to me that morning as I had held the green stone. I felt the memory's pull and a familiarity with my surroundings, though they looked quite different since that long winter.

"Moira!" I shouted ahead, not taking any time to slow my beast. "I know where we could go!" I turned Parvus to the left over a fallen trunk and off the rocky path. I heard Rauca follow close behind and she let out a long howl in playful excitement to be led away from our usual ride.

I glanced back to see Moira following, her face free with giddy joy. Her first love would always be the open air between the tall trees. I think I played a close second.

We flew through the bushes and ferns, the lumens never slowing, even in the difficult terrain. Branches snagged at my dress and pulled on my hair as I ducked and dodged through the thick of Felgren, but I led Parvus deeper still, unwilling to give up on this trek, this strange memory that loomed before me.

We ventured on for ten minutes at least, the memory growing stronger as we neared the clearing. I pulled Parvus to a halt as we entered the glade. He panted heavily and Rauca slid up beside him seconds later.

"How did you find this place?" Moira asked as she flitted up near my shoulder, her breath steady and hardly panting in spite of the long race through the trees. Faeries may be small, but they are unfazed by the vastness of Felgren.

"I…I'm not sure. It was like a pull. As soon as I was on his back, I just…wanted to get here."

She flew ahead, gazing in awe at the splendor of yellow blooms amidst the grassy plain, bees buzzing lazily in the sunshine. A stark white quiphit popped its head up among the grass and sniffed the fresh air, its large black eyes and tall ears turning quickly toward the lumens.

I had just enough time to slide off his back before Parvus and Rauca dashed after the rodent, eager to hunt it down.

"It must have been born this winter—its coat is pure white," I assumed, walking into the tall grass, my fingers trailing along the tips of the flowers in greeting.

We watched as the quiphit burst ahead of the lumens and dove into its hole in the ground—the lumens digging at the entrance furiously.

"Come, Karus," Moira giggled conspiratorially. "Let us sing in the sunshine and twirl until we fall—or the rain does."

She took my fingers in her hand and led me to the middle of the field, her crystal voice resounding through the open air, beautiful, and enough for me to join in on the duet, each of us taking a part;

> "If my heart could,"
> "I would see you more,"
> "Than twice a day."
> "Than twice a night."
> "But I have not the strength."
> "Nor do I, my love."
> "So I will see you at dawn."
> "So I will see you at dusk."
> "Said the sun to the moon."
> "Said the moon to the sun."

We laughed in delight of our song and collapsed into the wild-flowers, gazing up at the graying sky, the first drops of rain speckling our faces.

MOIRA AND I ATE COLD HAM AND HARD CHEESE FOR LUNCH underneath the long cover of trees, watching the stormy clouds pass, opening the sky back into a haze of blue.

We spent our morning telling stories, mostly from Moira, and laughing at the soaked lumens as they chased more quiphits across the field.

When we arrived back at the lumen den late in the afternoon, Parvus and Rauca drank deeply from the stream near their home, and I stayed with them while Moira wandered ahead toward the Fortress. I gently combed their damp coats full of thistle and twigs leftover from our ride on the off-beaten path. I sang to them the song we echoed through the clearing. The lyrics had come to me sudden and all at once when Moira began the lines of the sun.

Parvus licked my cheek, leaving a wet slop of water across my face. I laughed delightedly, wiping the mess away with my sleeve. I said my goodbyes and headed back down the path toward the Fortress.

I heard Moira speaking quietly to someone after a bend just ahead of me, and I stopped to stay out of sight as her next words came as an ineffective whisper, "She's not ready."

"You've been saying that for a long time, Moira."

"Well, it's still true, *Revich*. She's not ready. *Stop. Asking.* I will bring her to you when it's time."

"You just rode with her to the clearing, you said she sang with you knowing every line, and last afternoon, she spoke to me more than her usual few words at our meeting. What more evidence do you need, *faerie*?"

"Just because we see signs of her memories returning does not mean she's ready to hear the truth, *human*."

Baron Revich sighed audibly, his voice softening. "I don't want to lose what we've gained. Spring is changing her. She has memories we need to bring out, Moira. We need her to remember. We must find—"

"Do you really think I need a reminder of what's at stake here?" Moira's voice was full of ridicule as she interrupted. "Who has been living with her this winter? Who has cared for her like one of my own kind? I hold her memories close too, Baron, and I will tell you when she's ready. You still do not get to make the choices here—you *made* a choice."

"You are cruel."

"You don't know the half of it when it comes to *you*." She paused, her next words softer. "I am speaking to you in honesty… maybe you need to hear it more often."

And with that, I heard Baron Revich turn and storm away, leaving Moira huffing, and myself in utter bewilderment.

CHAPTER 6
ASH

The morning sun was wicked, streaming through Ash's slit of a window in the tallest tower of the Fortress. There were eight rooms altogether on the top floor. Four doors across from each other, and each just as tiny as the last. She knew. She'd peeked into each one. She had chosen the first room, closest to the staircase that had finally ended. She figured she might as well be nearest to the exit.

The Fortress was quiet at night. She'd heard the whisperings of whom she assumed was Clairannia and Figuerah, but no others. Was it just the three of them living up here? And why these rooms? Was this some sort of training?

She could just see it—channelers working their calves night after night, trekking to their quarters, exhausted. She wondered if any of them had rebelled and chosen different rooms, closer to the bottom floor.

Endless questions filled her mind. Where did the servants sleep? Or even the Baron? Well, *Barons* apparently. How strange to be a small part in a transition that takes place once per hundred years or so. She pushed down the significance of this, refusing to acknowledge she might play an important role here.

She finally rose to dress, pulling on two pairs of stockings, cursing the chill in her tower room, her fire having gone out ages ago. She splashed her face in the basin, the cold water forcing her body to wake. A mouth paste made of mint and cinnamon had been left on her dresser along with three sets of channeler clothing.

She had not been allowed to take anything to the Fortress. A ridiculous tradition, honestly. Were channelers really expected to just leave everything and hold nothing of their former lives? She scoffed aloud, pulling on her thick green skirt the color of moss after a harsh rain. She tucked her cream colored shirt into the top band and buttoned her wool vest over her chest. It fit her well, surprisingly so, and she wondered who had chosen the size without her measurements.

The *second* Baron—Baron Revich—had said that they would begin training this morning. She planned to be there, fumbling through any instruction and proving more and more that her place in this world was not in this fortress, not in this forest.

As she arrived in the foyer after the longest descent of stairs that existed in Arcaynen, with sore calves already, she watched a few more servants milling about, getting their tasks done quickly and timely with the use of their magic. She stared as two women, middle aged with features directly opposite of each other, worked together to snuff out the candles in the foyer chandelier. With their magic flowing from their fingers, they guided the bell-shaped tool all around, the smoke from the snuffed flame drifting lazily upwards.

"Good morning, Ash. I hope you slept well." The man in green livery strode up to her, a warm smile across his sharp features. He had used kohl to line his honey eyes again, the line of which angled upward, almost meeting the edge of his full brows. His face was long and ended with a well-trimmed beard and mustache. The ends of it curled ever so slightly, which gave him a look of being constantly amused. His hair was long in a salt and pepper bun atop his head, natural curls gracing the sides of his tanned face.

He bowed slightly to her. "My name is Pompeii, Overseer in the Fortress, manager of conduit trainings, and right-hand man to...

both Barons currently." His smile was enchanting, and he seemed well aware of the effect it could hold on a willing participant.

"What an impressive list of duties," Ash said sincerely. "I hope to lessen them soon as I don't plan on staying here long." And with that, she nodded to him and headed toward the enticing smell of the dining room.

When her back was turned, she inhaled slowly to calm her nerves. The rudeness of her short retorts and manners were getting the best of her.

This wasn't who she was.

The Queen had taught her to withhold her temper, to remain polite at all times, even though she had been jilted often growing up with royalty and without a title herself.

"*Ash'Arah*," the Queen would chide after, once again, Prince Philius had been invited to a celebration she had not. "All you need in this world is yourself. If you know who that is, you can do anything. You can *be* anything. Control your anger, child."

"I cannot *be* anything. I cannot be royal or born into great wealth. I cannot choose my company. I cannot even choose my own name. I will never belong in those places with those people." Ash had been no older than fourteen, laying on her corner bed in the room next to Prince Philius. She'd stuffed her face into a velvet pillow, unwilling to let the Queen see her tears hot with anger and her fists tightening on the sheets.

"Ah, but you are here, are you not? It is true. Your past has been defined already. That cannot change. But your future is yours. And you are the only one who can wield it. And whether you choose to do that sobbing angrily into a pillow or finding something productive to do, is up to you."

The Queen had laid a hand on her back then, patting it softly before leaving her to calm her emotions.

Ash was lost in her memories, hardly paying attention to the food she consumed when Clairannia and Figuerah stepped into the dining hall.

"Good morning!" Clairannia was dressed in the same clothes that had been laid out for each of them.

"Did you sleep well?" Figuerah inquired with a hopeful smile.

She was gorgeous. They both were. Another reason Ash really didn't belong here. Ash's beauty was simple, but both of these women held features written about in sonnets across centuries.

Clairannia had attempted to pile her hair in the same fashion it was last night—a decent attempt, and Figuerah's hung long with tight braids cascading down her back. Pinned away from her face, her dark hair was full and lively.

Ash nodded, thinking again of what the Queen had told her about needing no one, about independence and the strength she had to be her own friend.

The problem was, she liked Clairannia and Figuerah from what she had seen of them. She had few female friends in Hyrithia, always running around with Prince Philius and Geyrand instead. She wanted to connect with these women. She had met few people like her, channelers or conduits. She was curious about their lives, how their power had shown itself, and what line of conduit magic they planned to pursue.

Ash's own magic had shown itself early. After her traumatic birth that left her mother dead and her father's whereabouts unknown, the Queen took her into her castle as a playmate for the Prince. She could bear no other children and worried her infant son would grow up lonely. Ash loved to hear the story of her Awakening and would beg for Queen Rina to tell it before bed each night when she would sleep on the chaise in the Prince's rooms.

"Once there was a small girl, only as tall as a prickly shrub, but twice as fierce as one." She always began the story the same way, but the details would change. "And she could do something very special. She could channel magic from Felgren Forest. But, being barely able to walk, she wasn't good at it yet. One day, the little babe was playing in the Queen's gardens with her son. Her son was a handsome little fellow, just months ahead of her in age, but with a princely opinion of himself already. The little girl was playing with her favorite toy—a little wooden figure in the shape of a lumen, howling up to the moon. Suddenly, the Prince snatched the beast from her tiny, chubby fingers and ran away, laughing with his prize."

"And she was angry!" Ash would say in delight for where the story went next.

"Yes, child, she was angry. As furious and ferocious as the Blightress I'd say, because in that moment, her little round cheeks grew red, and her little chubby fists tightened, and suddenly—"

"Fire!" The Prince would shout and giggle from his four poster bed near the hearth.

"Yes, darling, fire. The Queen's favorite pear tree burst into flames, burning through the fruit and lush green leaves faster than anything that could naturally occur. And it wasn't until the Queen saw the little girl's face that she understood the origins of the crime. The Queen picked her up and brought her into the castle kitchens where she sat her on a stool and told her—not for the last time—'Anger that rests in boys' and girls' hearts, will call the Blightress to their rooms in the dark'."

Ash would then pull her blanket higher up under her chin, thinking of the Blightress entering the Prince's room at night to punish her for her temper.

"And so, the little girl, with much help, learned to control her magic so that it was a helpful thing in the castle. She learned to start fires in the hearths and helped to regrow the pear tree. She became the Prince's best friend and playmate and the Queen's favorite little girl." The Queen would then kiss the top of her head before going to the Prince's bed to do the same.

"What conduit magic do you wield, Ash?"

She blinked out of her childhood memories, not aware that the girls had been speaking.

"I'm not sure. I've never been a very good channeler. And I have no desire to become a conduit."

Clairannia choked on her steaming tea and Figuerah smiled faintly. "I'm sure you just haven't seen what your magic can do," she stated warmly. "The Barons will help, you'll see."

Clairannia tipped her head to the side, eyes narrowing slightly. "If you don't want to be a conduit, then why were you brought here from Hyrithia of all places? Something is amiss with your story."

Ash laughed at that. Amiss was one way to describe her predicament. She studied Clairannia's features across the table—straight, thick black hair, angular, deep-set eyes the color of freshly turned earth with dark lashes. Her lips were small and expressive across her face as she stared right back at Ash, seeming to study her as well.

"Maybe you should just give this training a chance," she started. "After all, it's such a rare thing to be here. I can name dozens of channelers back home who would give their left leg to be where we are now and—"

"As I said," Ash interrupted what seemed to be a chiding speech forming, "I am not blessed with strong magic, and I don't plan to be here long. The Baron can be wrong sometimes. I met a channeler last night, working here as a servant. She told me she never made it through the trials, and so, she stayed on to help as she could. That's not me. When the Barons discover my uselessness, I'll leave and travel back to my home in Hyrithia with just a strange story to tell."

"Oh, I love strange stories." Baron Revich's voice entered the dining room suddenly as he strode briskly to the front of the table. It seemed he was always in a hurry.

"Please tell it, Ash, before we begin training." He grabbed an apple from the bowl of fresh fruits in front of him, tossing it into the air and catching it with one hand before biting into the flesh as eagerly as a child eating sweets. As obnoxiously, too.

Ash sneered and spoke, "Once there was a young woman, magic-less, powerless, yet independent of spirit who was stolen away to a magical forest at the pleasure of sadistic, powerful men, only for them to discover their mistake in taking her. And she was quickly sent back home never to be bothered again where she lived the rest of her days as she desired, alone and happy. The end."

Their reactions to her story were worth anything she had endured here so far as Clairannia glanced around the room in shock, Figuerah covered her mouth to stifle her laugh, and most pleasurable of all, Baron Revich began to choke on the fleshy bits of the apple he had so ferociously bitten into, beating his chest with his fist.

"My, my, Ash'Arah, I can see that you live up to the reputation the Queen of Hyrithia foretold to me." Baron Heimlen's rich voice encompassed the dining hall, reverberating off the vulgar amount of gold serving pieces on the table.

Ash jumped in her chair, having not heard or seen him come in while she addressed Baron Revich's nonchalance quickly and with that spirit Baron Heimlen had been warned about.

She swiftly rose from her seat and met his gaze across the table, her fists wringing her silky verdant napkin. She cleared her throat. "I was not aware you had discussed my reputation with the Queen. I suppose I am unaccustomed to the formalities of a prisoner negotiation."

A ringing clank echoed in the room as Clairannia dropped her fork onto her plate, eyes the size of her tea saucer, mouth agape in disbelief.

Again, Baron Heimlen laughed with fervor at her quick retort. The adrenaline that coursed through Ash's body felt as heavy as lead. She didn't want to be here, like this, deflection after deflection as if she was in a battle for her life. But she *was* here. She took a breath and let it out slowly through her nose, her eyes darting toward Baron Revich to catch his reaction to her insulting remark.

He stared at her still with his gnawed apple in one hand, the other tucked into his pocket, a pained look on his face.

"My dear, there is really no need for your defiance. You belong here just as much as your fellow channelers." He placed his hands on Clairannia and Figuerah's shoulders as he spoke, a great smile upon his worn face as he looked down at them. "Now, let's all finish up and trek to the training grounds. We have much to do in so little a time! Baron Revich, may I speak to you before we begin?"

Baron Heimlen motioned to the opposite door they came in which servants had been darting in and out of. Ash assumed it led to the kitchens.

"Of course," he replied, setting his desecrated apple down on the plate in front of him, taking his eyes off Ash and feigning a smile.

As soon as they were out of earshot, Ash was hit with a stream of questions.

"You didn't tell us you know the Queen of Hyrithia!"

"How could you *speak* to him that way? He is the most powerful man on the isle!"

"And what do you mean magic-less? Do you really not have any?"

"You need to be more careful with your words or you'll end up *worse* than a prisoner."

Doubt filled her head listening to the barrage of commentary from the two women across from her. But what did they know? They had *chosen* to come here. They had chosen this path and this test. And though she felt their words were in earnest and concern, she strengthened her resolve, remembering she had no room in her heart to care. Her path forward was a straight one—leading right out of this impenetrable forest and back to her home.

"Your words are heard but unnecessary. I know what I'm doing."

Silently, they finished their breakfast, and Ash pushed aside the emptiness inside her, ignoring once again the sharp pangs that she knew well from being alone.

CHAPTER 7
KARUS

"What did you find in the forest, Karus?"

Baron Revich's voice was dangerous. It reached across the desk toward me as if in commandment, as if the choice to answer in truth or deception was not my own.

I tilted my head and took a breath about to speak in falsehood for the second day in a row, but I stilled, air lingering in my expanded lungs. *Who is this man and what is his story? How did he come to this position of power, and what does he seek so devoutly?*

His conversation with Moira just hours before filled my head with more questions, my mind spinning as if it were a dancer in the crescendo of a haunting song, on the edge of misstep or perfection.

The eyes of this man were pools. Never in my memory did I see such intensity and earnest as this. Never in my memory had I seen the blackest edge of night creeping into the darkest of waves crashing across the shore. And never in my memory did I have such language to describe them.

I once again found myself closer to his desk, and he stood then to meet me across the surface, placing both hands on the knotted wood as he balanced himself toward me.

I exhaled, the sound of it audible and quick.

"Walk with me." His voice was soft as a whisper and quick, just there for the two of us to bear witness.

He stood straight then, palms leaving the desk along with a line of sweat in the shape of his hands as he quickly walked to the door, opening it wide and gesturing for me to leave the room with him.

I blinked, clearing my mind from its spinning song and wondered how many times he had spoken to me more than those few words he ever did.

I could not remember such a time.

Nonetheless, I found my boots striding quickly to the door, searching for any sign of Moira or Pompeii. This seemed like a secret, this request of his. I remembered what Moira had said. She told him I wasn't ready. Ready for what, I could not produce an answer, but I was too curious to ever let my reluctance around him stop me from this rebellious action.

I noticed him searching too, looking for someone in particular, I didn't know, but the foyer was empty.

He lifted his hand as if to guide my back toward the massive front doors, but it hovered there awkwardly instead, my body tense at the presumption of his touch.

"Quickly," he stated and effortlessly opened one of the front doors as if it were made of tin instead of fortified with iron.

We strode in silence, him in front of me, flexing his fingers in and out of a fist, his pace quick, but quiet.

I kept up at a slight jog, eyes glued to his back, shaking my head periodically in disbelief. In all of my time at the Fortress, he had never taken an interest in anything I said or did. And now, here he was, leading me to somewhere, to what purpose, I couldn't surmise.

He veered to the left onto a less-trodden path, likely one that servants took to gather bounty from the forest.

As I followed, a hint of crimson caught my eye and I mucked through the brush to find a patch of demorte, the bright hue of red a stark contrast to the vivid greenery of the moss and ferns growing nearby.

I began to pluck the petals, thanking each flower in my head for its beauty. It was possible Moira did not yet see this bed of flowers for my lip concoction. Thoughts of preparing it with her tonight were interrupted as I remembered I was not alone.

"Karus."

I could feel his presence standing over me as I stood and shoved the last few petals into my skirt, having left some on each flower, not wanting to take all of its beauty for myself.

"I'm sorry. I was excited to find this flower. You see, Moira makes the petals into a cream and…" I met his gaze and swallowed. "I like to paint it on my lips."

At my last word, his dark eyes, the color of all the black that surrounds the stars, gazed downward at what little hue was left on my mouth.

The Baron raised his hand as if to stroke my face and I closed my eyes, longing to feel the touch of someone.

Anyone.

The absence of his hand was painful, and I thought again of what the stone made me feel when I held it. Such bliss was the feeling of joy, such achingly beautiful freedom from a clouded mind and a heavy heart. I found myself reaching into my pocket once again, my cold fingers wrapping around the green stone.

It was like a wave, the emotions it gifted to me. As if I was standing on a precipice, debating whether to take a step forward or a step back when a warm breeze would swim up from the cliff in my mind, toying with my hair, another reminder that I was not alone.

"What did you find in the forest, Karus?"

Eyes still closed, I could feel the warmth of his whisper on my face.

There, among the trees, as the sun began to nestle into its bed, I felt a balance. My thoughts cleared, the haze of looming shadows whisked away in his breath. The edge of fear for the unknown was drawn from my veins as my heart slowed to a calming pace.

"I found…comfort. A sense of harmony. I…I can't remember the last time I felt so free from the burdens of my mind." I dropped the stone in my pocket and lifted my hands to my temples, as the rush of confusion came back to me all at once, filling my thoughts with a fog so thick, I remembered little of what we were doing there together in the forest.

He touched me for the first time then, gently cradling my hands with both of his as if they were a broken bird, wings no longer able to fly.

Something had changed.

Something was different.

There was an energy pulsing off of his hardened frame and I could almost see the quickened pace of his heartbeat through the layers of loose clothes at his chest.

"What is it you're looking for, Baron?" I questioned, taking my hands from his, keeping them tangled in my skirts at my side, afraid of the sudden heat rising within me. "What is it you so desperately seek out here? So much so that you question me every day with your tired words and preoccupied mind."

He beamed then, the perfection of it stirring more in me than I was ready to accept. He stepped back onto the path leading to the Fortress, his hands buried deep in the pockets of his dark cloak.

"I seek a woman, Karus. A powerful conduit. I believe her magic brought back the spring. And just in time. She is needed. Desperately."

He turned and began his trek back to the Fortress, its newly lit torches flickering in the sun's last betrayal as it left the world in an abyss of dark and cold.

"If you find her," he called without turning his head, "let me know."

I furrowed my brows at his answer and followed a distance behind him, my head throbbing and my hands shaking.

CHAPTER 8
Ash

Ash glared at the patch of newly thawed ground in front of her. Her fingers tightened around her knees, the whites of them as pale as she felt in her efforts to control her magic. She closed her eyes, focused her breathing, and thought of home.

"Good, Ash'Arah."

Baron Heimlen bent down beside her on the ground as she sat still, cross-legged on the hard earth in the same stance as her fellow channelers.

They had been led in a line, marching out to a cleared patch of forest floor half a mile from the Fortress. When they had reached their destination, Baron Heimlen had asked them to sit in a circle and produce a flower.

That was it. That was the extent of his instruction. Baron Revich remained still and quiet for once as Ash, Clairannia, and Figuerah sat foolishly, the choice of wool skirts understandable now, as the cold from the thawing earth met their backsides.

"Focus on the gift of this forest. Listen to her speak your name in unison with the swaying of the trees and the beating of even the smallest quiphit's heart."

He wasn't helping.

Ash peeked through one eye and angered at the small tips of striped, leafy stems poking shyly from the dirt in front of her. Their growth quickened as all of her magic did when she was angry. She closed her eye again and squeezed them both tightly.

She had expected they would be asked to heal a cut from a tree or to move an object at will—something easy she could pretend she could not do, but this? This was proving difficult to feign.

Her name *was* being called, but different, not really the one she knew. She heard it in the wave of the tops of the trees. The flock of sparrows in the pines sang a song of undeniable power that flowed through her skin like sunshine on a cloudless day. She *did* feel the beat of a quiphit's hammering heart as it watched all of them from the bushes to the south of the clearing.

From the moment she had stepped out of that portal and onto the forest floor of Felgren, she had felt all of it. The forest was alive. Even as it awoke from its winter nap, it held more power in its vast wilderness than she knew to be possible. The swaying hum of magic lay silent to all but who could hear its song. Channelers, conduits, Barons —they all could feel it, sense its power, and no matter her efforts to drown the hold, to ignore its pulse, Ash knew they were in vain.

But she thought she could *pretend*. She thought this would be a simple task to lie about the magic coursing through her body. The strength of Felgren seemed to be laughing at her as she looked down once again only to find a bed of violet crocus bloomed before her, their vivid golden center mocking her in a silent hello.

Turning her head to Baron Heimlen, she watched as a subtle grin crossed his face, knowing in nature, and aggravating her already hardened mind. She pursed her lips and kept her emerald eyes on him as the newly bloomed crocus shriveled and limped pathetically to the ground, their lives quick and over.

"How unfortunate," Ash said, sighing. "It seems I could not hold on to the life force of these flowers for long."

She glanced around at Clairannia and Figuerah's attempts at the exercise. Clairannia's eyes were fierce as a cat about to pounce as she studied the tight blooms in front of her. She had managed to produce three tall stems of bright pink tulips, but their buds refused to open.

Figuerah had much better luck as she lightly touched the petals of the purple hyacinth flower before her, a charming grin on her face.

Baron Revich leaned against a nearby tree, silent, toying with something in his hand. At the sudden demise of her flowers, his eyes narrowed, watching Ash with disappointment.

"Unfortunate indeed, Ash'Arah, as you produced the most flowers the quickest of all the channelers here. It's almost as if you are not magic-less, nor are you the prisoner you choose to call yourself."

The chastisement in Baron Heimlen's voice was thick and obvious and her cheeks grew red with embarrassment. Of course, there was no fooling him. He was the bearer of magic after all, the head of all conduits and the most powerful man on the isle. Fooling him would take more than a simple bit of death magic on a bloomed flower. Fear crept through her as she wondered if she could fool him at all.

A delighted squeal broke her thoughts as Clairannia's magenta tulips bloomed in full, dazzling against the droll brown of the frozen earth.

"Well, now that that's settled and you've all proven your worthiness as channelers, let's step back inside. Baron Revich, please escort these women to Viridis."

~

The Fortress lived up to its name—a massive expanse of dark halls and winding staircases. Ash thanked her luck at finding the right staircase the night before that had led to her room. She otherwise might as well have been wandering the channels of an infinite maze, each corridor and hall as confusing as the last.

They traversed the black stone floors with Baron Revich's eerie blue magical orb casting shadows that followed the four of them on their trek to Viridis.

Ash had never heard of Viridis and no explanation was given on their destination, which surprised her, considering Baron Revich seemed to have no problem hearing the sound of his own voice.

Not a single other soul dwelled down the wrought iron staircases or strode through the extensive corridors. For all she knew, Viridis could very well be a dungeon, and she was helpless with no knowledge of her way back to the light of day.

At last, they came to a short stone staircase. It expanded as wide as the dining hall, and at the landing stood two immeasurable doors, black as a starless night with trailing patterns of copper winding up into an incomprehensible abyss above them. Ash could not see where the doors ended and she wondered, not for the first time, if the Fortress was enchanted to look less expansive on the outside than it truly was.

"Welcome to the doors of Viridis. You will spend your mornings here in your training. Don't worry about the journey, you'll manage it yourselves in a few weeks' time. All the channelers do." Baron Revich's grin was ear-to-ear in the flicker of his orb. Whatever Viridis was, he was dying for them to see it. "Figuerah, please step up to the doors and place your palm on the stone."

Stepping closer, Ash saw that in the center of the doors there lay a jade stone the size of a fist with broken lines of black inlaid in its entirety.

"Is that…" Figuerah leaned in closer to study the adornment.

"Rhyzolm," Baron Revich finished. "One of the largest ever found intact. It was placed here centuries ago, thought to strengthen the magic of the doors to Viridis."

Ash had seen rhyzolm before of course, but true to his word, she did believe this was the largest piece ever found. The stone was the rarest on the isle, mined only in the Hallow Marshes to the west of Felgren. It was said that the magic from Felgren's trees washed away in storms to the river capillaries that made up the marshes. New trees then grew from the essence of the forest, their roots growing through stony ground. Occasionally, the magic was imbued into these stones, though not in purity, hence the inky lines coursing through the hard jade.

Every wealthy house on the isle owned at least one rhyzolm as it was fabled to contain magic itself. The rich and royal of the land would keep it near their sleeping children in hopes that the spirit of Felgren would enter their bodies and give them channeler magic. She remembered the piece that the Queen would hang over the Prince's bed at night. In his later years, he wore it around his neck each day. As far as she knew, magic had never come to him, nor did it seem to work on other children. Sometimes, she had observed, the wealthy held on to disproven beliefs, no matter the evidence against them.

"To enter Viridis, you must place your hand on the rhyzolm and speak your name. Speak it clearly. The portal will then open for you to enter."

Figuerah laid her long, elegant fingers upon the stone, grasping it as if to turn the handle of a door and spoke, "Figuerah."

Immediately, a shimmer of green light the size of her body blazed before her, the rhyzolm no longer visible. She stepped through without hesitation before it closed quickly in an intake of breath.

Baron Revich gestured to Clairannia, her face alight with excitement. She spoke loudly at the doors with her hand on the stone, "Clairannia!"

Again, the portal opened before her but adjusted to her smaller sized body, and just as Figuerah, she left instantly to their destination.

Though Ash was unaware of what lay behind those doors in this foreign maze of confusion, she validated her beating heart, adrenaline coursing through her furiously as she stepped up to the green stone, placing her own hand on its cool surface.

All at once she was caught up in her predicament. The longing of home, the excitement of this fortress and this forest, full of the magic she had used since she could walk—it was too much in too short a time. Her heart hammered wickedly in her chest as she looked to the Baron and spoke her name, "Ash."

Baron Revich smirked with knowledge she once again did not possess when her name echoed through the corridor and no portal opened. He chuckled and moved closer. Their bodies inches apart, his orb of light above one hand, the other shoved in his pocket.

"These doors are ancient. Ancient things tend to take on sentience, as you'll learn. It's possible these doors know more of yourself than you do, Ash." He leaned to the side against the doors, looking up at their impossible height, continuing his casual stance and casual way of withholding information she wanted. "When I first tried my name, they didn't let me in either."

"Why? What name did you use?" She lowered her hand to her side, unwilling to stand there stupidly before conscious doors of iron.

"Well, I tried saying my name as it was given to me. '*Revich*' I said and the doors didn't budge. It was Baron Heimlen who laughed then, knowing what I know now and will happily pass on to you."

He raised an eyebrow, waiting for her to question how, but she wasn't about to ask. She'd stand there all morning if need be, knowing her ability to be silent would outlast his. He finally raised his hand to the rhyzolm and in a steady voice spoke, "*Rev*."

Instantly, the portal opened for him, just a few inches taller than herself.

"See you on the other side." And with that irritating wink she'd rolled her eyes at before, he left her there alone in the dark, his light leaving with him.

Cursing, she produced her own ball of light, green in nature as was all of her magic, wondering if he knew she could conjure her own orb or if he didn't care if she couldn't.

She inhaled deeply, half wondering if she should turn around and try to escape, but that thought she forced down quickly. It was more likely she'd be lost in the madness of this place.

Then she wondered if she should try again in the same way and, never being able to gain access to Viridis, would be let free of this place and back to her home in peace.

But she *was* curious. What was Viridis? Why the secrecy and why the ancient, powerful doors that apparently knew more of herself than she did? Her heart was treacherous in her chest as she reached once more for the stone, the sound of her exhale expanding through the empty corridor.

Many names filled her head then. *"Ash'Arah"* was the obvious choice to an outsider, but her disdain for the name meant it could not be the one the doors were listening for.

"Ash" for black powder streaked across the lines of her mother's body as she stumbled to Hyrithia's gatehouse, Ash's emergence into the world very near. *"Arah"*, her mother's name, the only clear bit of speech they could discern from her cries before she left her newborn daughter alone forever. Ash's discontentment for the two words pieced together began as soon as she had been old enough to hear the story of her traumatic entrance into the world. If her mother had lived to name her, she was convinced she would not have been so heartless.

"Dearest"…*"Ward"*…even *"Soot"* came to mind—the tease the Prince had used in their gangly youth for being named from the burnt remnants of a fire.

Nothing fit. No name she had ever heard addressed to her had ever been right. She had wandered all her life alone in a mist of pure circumstance, and yet, just privileged enough to not end up on the streets of Hyrithia in a profession of hardship and hardened woe, and with a name that never once suited her.

"I don't know my name. I…I don't know of one that belongs to me."

Speaking to boundless, sentient doors, she felt ridiculous and humiliated at admitting the truth aloud. And much to her annoyance, the same sort of portal that opened for the rest of them blazed in light before her, just large enough to move through. And so, heart continuing its attempt to burst through her chest, she left the empty passageway and took her first step into Viridis.

~

THE POSSIBILITY THAT VIRIDIS WAS CONTAINED INSIDE THE FORTRESS walls was obsolete. Upon Ash's allowance to enter the sanctuary, the predetermined idea she had of Viridis's use and size were gone from all thought. The light of the soul of the sun spilled across her face, causing her to squint in its persistent nature of warmth and radiance.

Viridis, in the simplest of terms, was a library with a garden at its center—or a garden where books were placed—she wasn't sure which was more accurate.

She stood atop the central landing, her boots gracing white stone, the cracks of which were mended in gold. If the Fortress was a place of inner solitude, Viridis was a place of external exuberance. The two dwellings could not have been more opposite in their appearance, nor in the way she felt inside them.

A vast, open space welcomed her as she gazed in awe down the steps at the enormous courtyard below. The tops of the birch grove swayed slightly in a subtle, harmonious dance. The glow of the sun came from the gold-leaded windows atop of a dome shape which enclosed Viridis entirely. Open halls lined the sides of the courtyard and she tried to count the number of them climbing upward, reaching for the sky. She counted at least ten before her thoughts were interrupted.

"You look good here, Ash." Baron Revich stood next to her, his voice low, his eyes alight in what she could only discern as amusement. "Well, everyone looks good in Viridis…but you especially belong in *this* light."

He did not ask what name she used to enter, and she was thankful, taking the hand he offered without much thought as he guided her down the stairs. She was too enamored with her surroundings to refuse him and concerned she might actually fall.

The massive golden-railed hallways opened to the center with books lining the walls continuously, leaves and vines winding their way through the shelves and trailing down the spines of the manuscripts. Perhaps they were the truest purpose of the place, not the ornamentation to its halls.

Viridis was in bloom. The heady scents of jasmine and lavender floated in the air and the delicate flow of blossoms basked lazily in the light of the sun, the buzz of bees humming as they greeted each one.

She held his hand still, unknowingly, as she observed a flock of birds, the color of a summer sky, flying across the open center of the oasis before her, landing in the tops of swaying trees as green as the newly grown leaves of spring.

"How…how can this place exist? We can't still be in the Fortress."

"Portal magic is rare. Few can use it—it's been that way for centuries. It's said that Viridis was built before the Fortress, and the two were connected by a powerful Baron long ago so that he could properly train his channelers within its magic halls. I read it. In one of these books, actually."

She turned her face to him, an enchanted smile across her lips. His gaze met hers with the same exuberance, his features calm, but somehow deep, soulful. Suddenly aware of their touch, she took her hand from his, color rising in her cheeks.

He swept the hand she had held through his black locks and rested his palm on the back of his neck. "But, to answer your question," he continued, "I think Viridis is alive. Whether it exists because magic exists or vice versa—who knows. I personally spend as much time here as I can. And I probably looked just as you do now the first time I saw it."

She grinned, suppressing a laugh. Viridis, in its unrestrained glory, had lifted her spirits and she couldn't deny her longing to explore its halls.

Soon, settled on a cream silk bench overlooking the first and second levels, Ash opened one of the books she had hoarded in reverence.

She had caught sight of both Figuerah and Clairannia exploring the magical temple, both of them lost in their own minds at its beauty.

Simple Truths of Felgren Forest by Honorah Shrythe was written ten years before her own arrival in the forest and the most recently written book she could find.

Flipping to a random page she read,

"For in my years of training, I never did settle myself to reflect on the origin of the forest. However, after leaving it behind to be of use in my homeland, I have found its origins to be just as fascinating as its power, given to those of us born special enough to wield it."

She shut the book immediately and tossed it aside to restock later. Ash wasn't interested in reading about how special conduits were in this world. Culture had shaped such thoughts throughout society, but to Ash, her magic was just a gift given to her to use as she saw fit. It did not make her better or more worthy of life than anyone else.

The beauty of life, after all, was magic itself.

As she picked up the next book in her pile, its leather cover worn and frayed, *Simple Truths of Felgren Forest* disappeared from her bench with a loud puff of air. She sat upright, searching for the lost memoir when a deep voice sounded behind her.

"Viridis takes care of its treasures. If you no longer wish to read a book, close it gently and ignore it. It will end up in the same place you found it shortly. And it won't leave so haughtily."

Baron Heimlen stood before her, his gloved hand gesturing to the space beside her in question. She nodded and moved her pile as he sat down, a low groan leaving his lips.

"Ah, I see you found Viridis's Conduit Manuscript Hall," he remarked, picking up the top book on the pile. "Each conduit who leaves Felgren writes a memoir of their time here. What they've learned, what they plan to do with their lives—things like that. Some are natural-born writers." He laid the book he had taken, *Conduit Magic, A Magical Memoir*, on the end of the seat and it disappeared quickly as he added, "And some are not."

Ash huffed in amusement and replied, "I thought that one might give an insight as to what magic is really like to wield from a trained conduit. I haven't met many of them."

The Baron raised his eyebrows which were peppered with gray. "I should think the Queen would have wanted you around conduits, helping you control your innate abilities. I know they are rarer in Hyrithia but not unheard of." He tilted his head sideways in question before continuing, "Did Queen Rina allow your use of magic, Ash'Arah? Or was your gift suppressed as I would guess it is to most channelers born within the city gates?"

The insult implied was not lost on Ash and she straightened before answering, "I was of great use to the Queen and her son. Magic had nothing to do with it. And it was *you* who disrupted that life. I was just fine right where I was, thank you."

"I won't apologize for your presence here," he stated firmly, "but I am sorry you are so opposed to it. You are powerful, Ash'Arah. I can feel it. Baron Revich can feel it…Viridis can feel it."

He gestured to the wall of books in front of them across the stone floor. A bit of green vine wafted languidly in a slight breeze, and upon her gaze at its leaves, it bloomed instantly, producing dozens of five-petaled white flowers. The scent of jasmine filled the space between them.

"And, I may have escorted you from Hyrithia, but I was not the one who found you, my dear. My successor is who you can thank for that."

Ignoring the flowers that bloomed at just one glance from her, Ash turned toward the gardens below. Baron Revich was speaking with Figuerah, and his laugh, booming in nature, echoed through the trees.

"Baron Revich did not cure the Black Fever, nor was he there to take me as payment." Ash could feel her indignation clawing up though her chest, but she thought of the lessons she and all children were taught on the isle.

Wrath leads to hate, leads to the Blightress.

She must control her anger or invite evil into her heart.

"Baron Revich has been given a…special task. One of which I believe he has fulfilled. You see," Baron Heimlen spoke, unaware or unconcerned at her anger, as he settled his back against the golden railing, stretching his arms out along the sides, settling down to tell a story.

"A few years ago now, I'm not sure how many exactly—time moves differently in Felgren—I had come to terms with the fact that

I was in need of an heir, a successor to the title of Baron as all Barons before me had found."

Baron Heimlen was a natural storyteller. His eyes, black with hints of gray, seemed to speak with him in their expression. "And so, I left Felgren on a journey that would take me precious months. I could not train channelers in that time, nor could I see to the tasks all Barons must perform in Felgren. Don't worry, you'll eventually learn of those, too."

Ash had just opened her mouth, needing to know more about a Baron's duty here, but closed it quickly at his premonition of her questions.

"He wasn't easy to find, that much I can tell you. He was a broken young man, alone in the world, just growing into himself as it were. I actually almost ran over him with my lumen." He chuckled and brought his gloved hand to his face to stroke his short gray beard. "*Mire* was the name of the settlement, and I do say settlement because it could not truthfully be called a city, nor even a town. The streets were drowning in mud and the people as well. Revich was so frail and malnourished I could have offered him just a crust of bread and he would have come with me. He was a seeker then, of course. Everyone in that place was, spending their hard days digging in the roots for rhyzolm. But it was difficult being young in the profession. You don't have the resources or knowledge of the best places to look. And Revich was even worse off, having no family to speak of and few friends."

"I assume you gave him an Offering then? Though I could also see you grabbing him by the collar and stealing him away to Felgren on the back of your beast."

The Baron sighed this time at her snark, bringing his gloved hands to his lap, bending over them in thought. "You'll have to find a way through this, Ash'Arah, if you are to fulfill your duty here. I can see how fresh it is in your mind, but it's best to get past it as quickly as you can."

He stood then and towered over her as he declared his parting words, scolding as if she was a young child, "You are not leaving Felgren. You are needed *here*. Not in some castle doing the work of a barely accepted ward. Your talents are wasted in Hyrithia. *You* are wasted in Hyrithia. Look around you. I have brought you to paradise. And you can visit any time you like. But you have work to do, and the sooner you move on from your obstinate disposition, one that you insist on alone, the sooner you can face your destiny in Felgren." He turned and stormed away from her, a dark cloud in the place of light.

Ash watched him leave, thankful for his lack of presence, curious at his story of Baron Revich, and wondering just what he believed her destiny was.

She rose and followed her feet down to the central garden of Viridis, wandering the worn paths deep in thought. It was only the day before that she had been taken, but it felt like weeks. And didn't Sylva say time moved differently here? Had it already been weeks outside of Felgren since she had left?

Ash scoffed aloud to herself. Already her mind was accepting her fate here. A betrayal, she felt, since she had never wanted it. But did she *need* it? The truth of it was, Ash had never been more at home than in the forest, or as in this sanctuary here. In her few hours of exploring it, Viridis was a beacon in her heart already and the thought of ever leaving it behind to go back to what she was…it was too heartbreaking a thought to even entertain.

And she *did* feel the pull. The presence of freedom and fate, a sense of belonging and joy. Things she had heard about in stories but never encountered herself.

Surely, they worried about her at the castle. Surely, the Queen wept at the decision she had no choice but to make. They hadn't even been able to speak before she'd been taken. And though she understood her circumstance, Ash couldn't help but feel the sorrow of a woman whose lack of fight had given way to Ash's future gone.

And the pressure of healing a city…she knew how the Queen must be spending her hours meeting with her people, presiding over mass graves of the dead, speaking words of comfort to the living. Hyrithia was cured of the disease, but the loss would linger still.

She was glad to be here at least, in Viridis, to ponder her thoughts.

She sat down on a marble bench, the shape of a giant leaf, impossible detail carved into the hard stone. A lapis conduit must have chiseled it. They were conduits adept at stonework and finding veins of gold and silver in the mountains. She wondered if they also harvested rhyzolm. She traced the veins of the leaf with her fingers, admiring how much work was placed into this one seat in a sea of natural beauty.

"Hello, Ash." Clairannia's voice, light and timid, lifted in the breeze and brought her back to attention. "May I sit with you? Would you like to read any of these?" She came over to the bench, arms full of various sizes and colors of books she was cradling like a newborn babe. "I found these in the Medicus Conduit Hall, fourth level, to the east." She set them down gently and offered a blue-bound book.

"*A Refined History of Medicus: A Conduit's Guide to Healing,*" Ash read aloud from the cover.

"That's what I want to train for. A medicus conduit, I mean. I want to help deliver babies and heal the sick. I've always had an affinity for it." She shyly pushed her hair behind her ears. More of the thick, straight locks had escaped since breakfast.

They read in silence for a while in a sort of truce they had accepted since their strained words that morning. The book was interesting enough, but Ash struggled to pay attention, her conversation with Baron Heimlen and her own dilemma weighing on her mind.

"There you two are!" Their reading was interrupted by Figuerah's deep voice, an echo that belonged among the trees.

"Would you like to join us?" Clairannia's inviting manner was wholesome and infectious as Ash found herself moving over and patting the bench to give room.

"Oooh, what goodies did you two find?" Figuerah asked, picking up *Poxes, Boils, and Papules: A Medicus Guide to Flesh Diseases,* reading the title, and tossing it aside in audible disgust.

Ash laughed at the gesture and agreed, "I was avoiding that one myself."

The book left their bench instantly in a loud slurp.

"Hey! I was gonna read that! Where did it go?" Clairannia's annoyance caused laughter from the other two women as she stood to search under the bench.

"Don't worry, it went right back to where you found it. Baron Heimlen told me that when we are done with a book, we are to place it down gently and Viridis will put it back." She turned to Figuerah. "Maybe more emphasis on the *gently* next time."

She smirked in unison with Ash and apologized to Clairannia, then picked up the next book on the pile and opened to a diagram of the bones in a human hand. "Hmm. Maybe I won't read with you just now. *Definitely* not going the medicus route."

Clairannia closed her book and asked excitedly, "Have you decided which path you'll take as a conduit? Mine is pretty obvious. In the Spire, I was often called to help in the birthing day of mothers. It's the only magic I have a real knack for. That was probably obvious this morning." She rolled her eyes and looked to them for encouragement.

"I thought your tulips were beautiful." Ash closed her own book. "And besides, growing flowers is kind of like birth, isn't it? You grew them and gave them life, helped them reach their potential out of the ground."

"That's a good way to put it, Ash. Your crocus were lovely, too. Do you have an agricola affinity?"

"I-I don't know. Maybe." Ash refused to talk about herself further, so she asked, "What's your affinity, Figuerah?"

"Iumenta. Definitely. Back home, I watched over the sheep and oxen. I milked the cows and goats, made cheeses so divine, I was famous for them." She stood and walked to a tree, calling to the crimson bird singing on one of its low hanging branches. The bird then flew to her outstretched arm and chirped excitedly to her as if in conversation.

"See, I have this connection to all animals." She stroked its feathers gently and then raised her arm to send it off into flight.

"That was amazing! I've never met anyone with that kind of magic!" Clairannia raised excitedly from her seat, clapping at Figuerah who bowed slightly and laughed.

Try as she might, Ash could not help but like these women. Though they came to Felgren with the opposite intention of hers, she could feel their bond.

The hours passed swiftly there in Viridis, the three young women speaking of their homes and hopes for the future. Ash added little to the conversation, but enjoyed listening to their talk of childhood and their lives just before they were given their Offerings. After some time when the sun was high over the glass dome, Sylva came into the courtyard where they were still talking, their laughter and merriment residual on their faces.

"Sylva! Have you met Clairannia and Figuerah?" Ash introduced them to the old woman who was carrying a woven basket with her, its top covered by a wool blanket.

"Good afternoon, I am Sylva. I will be around to help with some of your needs here. I have brought you a late lunch." She set the basket down on the soft grass, carefully laying out the blanket and unpacking their lunch.

"It's nice to meet you, Sylva, and thank you. Please," Figuerah said, bending down next to her, "let us help you with that."

"Would you like to join us? It looks like there's enough food for at least ten people here!"

Out of the basket came crusty breads, hard cheeses, dried meats, strawberries as red as a bird's feathers, and soft, ripe pears. Even a dessert was provided in cinnamon buns and dried fruits. Ash felt her stomach rumble in anticipation and she sat on a corner of the blanket, grabbing a yellow pear and cutting off a slice of crumbling, pale cheese.

"Yes, please join us. We would love to hear your stories of the Fortress. I can tell you're full of them." Ash smiled and scooted to the side, offering her a seat.

"Well, I suppose I could spare a few minutes more." Sylva sat next to Ash and picked up a cinnamon bun. "These are Lia's specialty. She makes them fresh each morning, but doesn't make many, so they can be hard to come by." She bit into the bun and closed her eyes, sighing and chewing loudly.

Figuerah cut the last bun into three and handed each of them a piece.

"How did you come to the Fortress, Sylva? Have you always looked after the channelers who are training here?" Figuerah settled into her spot on the blanket, her plate full of strawberries and bread.

"Well, as I told Ash'Arah last night, I was brought here to train decades ago—just like you."

"Oh, I'm sorry. We don't have to talk about it if it's a sensitive subject." Figuerah's cheeks reddened in embarrassment.

"It's alright, my dear. I have enjoyed my time here as a channeler, even if I didn't pass the trainings and become a conduit myself. You are the first set of channelers I have had the honor of watching over. I mostly tidy up the place, keep it as clean as I can, and stoke the fires. Occasionally, Baron Heimlen allows me to sit in his chambers and knit as he paces and works. He can get into such a state, that man. He says the clicking of the needles and the rocking of the chair help him to think." She sighed deeply and looked off into the distance, lost in her own memories. "I was happy to accept his offer to be your keeper in your time here."

The three met each other's glances and raised eyebrows.

"And…do you know Baron Heimlen well, Sylva?"

Clairannia's elbow shot out into Figuerah's ribs at the question, and Ash looked down to hide her snicker.

"Oh, yes, very, *very* well." Sylva continued to slowly devour her cinnamon bun, her eyes still lost in memory, oblivious to their reaction to the question. "In fact, I have been his closest friend over the years. You see, I was given an Offering early on in his time as Baron, and, though I did not continue on to become a conduit, he made sure to keep me in the Fortress. Instead giving me a different kind of offer." She turned to look at Figuerah then and winked before reaching out to take some berries.

"So, you and Baron Heimlen have…an *intimate* bond you might say?"

Clairannia had given up on trying to reign in Figuerah's candid questions and was instead taking small bites of cheese, watching Sylva's reactions with raised brows.

She laughed and answered, "Yes, you could say that, though intimate in a different way now."

Ash hoped her face hid any sort of surprise at the comment. Though she had spent plenty of her later teenage years stealing kisses with Geyrand between his duties and sneaking off with him on his guard watch, she had never really spoken to anyone about their trysts, nor had she heard much talk of intimacy in her life.

She searched for the mark on Sylva's wrist. It was faded, but there, just below her left palm—just like Ash and all of the adults on Arcaynen Isle. The subtle *l* shape was actually a spell, given by a medicus conduit when a person came of age. It prevented the possibility of any children until two people became companions, the mark leaving their wrists after the ceremony.

"Don't look so surprised, girls, it is common for the residing Baron to take a lover from the channelers he brings. Usually several over his time. But…" she added wistfully, "never does he take a lover for decades like me." She glowed with pride while Ash scowled.

"No doubt Baron Revich will be looking to one of you soon…"

Ash scoffed while Clairannia went pale.

"Well, he'd have to look to these two beauties here if that's the case. I already have a lovely woman back home whom I intend to sleep beside every night when I return." Figuerah took a big bite of her cinnamon bun, the icing sticky on her fingers and made a noise of delight.

"Oh, that is sweet, dear. Of course, you can choose to encourage the Baron's advances or not, but on my advice, it makes your time here much more fun."

Clairannia's cheeks burned red as Figuerah, Ash, and Sylva laughed together at the talk of lovers, the sound echoing up into the trees that swayed with a common fervor.

~

After they had eaten all the food, bellies content, the three helped Sylva pack up the luncheon and spoke their gratitude, saying goodbye to her fondly.

Soon after, they caught sight of Baron Revich entering Viridis through the portal and hustling down the vast stairs, unaware that he had left.

When he reached them with a wide smile, his black eyes warring with the blue they must have originally been, he clapped his hands together, rubbing them heartily. "Well, well, channelers—you look rested and full. A morning in Viridis will do that, even to the most reluctant of hearts." He smirked, his lips curling to the side as he winked in Ash's direction. "Follow me, please, back into Felgren we go."

What was it about his energy that irritated her so? Clairannia and Figuerah seemed to enjoy his infectious spirit, like an excited puppy every time they met him. But as Ash begrudgingly followed the hound, arms crossed, and her happy mood dulled at the sight of him, she couldn't really find a fault in it. Perhaps, she admitted, she wanted thunderstorms and he was clear blue skies. She wanted to mope and resist all enjoyment in Felgren, but had been unable to do so walking Viridis's halls and laughing with the other women.

The Barons, however, were who she could direct her anger to. They were the reason for her cloud, they were forcing her to stay, even though just hours before she had admitted to not wanting to leave. Was she being fair? *Likely not*, she admitted, as Baron Revich led them back down the dark corridors of the Fortress.

Watching his back, her thoughts and memories turned to Geyrand. She'd been around very few men her own age, one like her brother, the other a friend and lover.

Geyrand had accepted her as a friend when they were children as she proved she could keep up with the Prince's roughhousing just as well as he could. As they had gotten older, they began to see each other in a different way, and one morning when she had visited him during his post, she'd kissed him. It led to many more days and nights of secret meetings and awkward, fumbling bodies as most first trysts do. Geyrand was quiet, never saying more than necessary, speaking often with his gestures and subtle manners. He was attractive in his quiet calm, and Ash had delighted in finding him no real challenge to her desires.

But she did not love him. She did not dream of a future with him in it. She had read about that kind of love and heard the story of the Queen's companion before he had died when the Prince was just a few days old.

"We were inseparable, your father and I," the Queen would whisper in the dark to the Prince some nights when he asked about his father. "We had the kind of bond told about in storybooks and song. A love that brings peace and purpose to your heart. One I hope you find, my dearest."

Ash would ponder her words, turning toward the wall in the Prince's room, little fingers tracing the vine pattern painted there. She wanted to find that kind of love, too. Had her parents loved each other like that? Did everyone find a companion to love, or just the lucky ones? But how many times had the Queen told her all she really needed was her own companionship? She never whispered such hopes to Ash in the dark before sleep.

It was possible, she thought, that the Queen had seen Ash's purpose as more of a friend to her and the Prince in the future. Not so much a servant, but not exactly family, either. Not really belonging, but too useful to let leave.

Maybe she was right. Even after Geyrand's intimate, longing kiss at her departure, Ash had felt no more love for him than the friendship she had felt for many years before. It seemed likely she was better off on her own.

"You'll be exhausted tonight." Baron Revich's voice interrupted her thoughts and she blinked in confusion, finding that they had arrived back in the foyer.

"Hmm?" She turned to face him, catching the scent of amber and earth, realizing how close she had come to his body.

"I said, you'll be exhausted tonight, Ash. The first full day is often the hardest, and experiencing Viridis for the first time…" He shoved his hands into his pockets, leaning to the side. "I wish I could live that again."

Ash bit her lower lip, wondering if she should agree or say nothing at all. Instead, she gave a short nod, casting her eyes away from his small smile, turning toward the doors leading to Felgren.

He was just being nice, she reminded herself, feeling foolish for her lack of response. Color rose to her cheeks as he swept past her as if their conversation had not occurred at all, opening the doors and gesturing for the women to follow him into the forest. She sighed and shoved her own hands into her skirt pockets, managing to fall behind—wondering if she'd ever truly have a place she belonged.

CHAPTER 9
KARUS

I traced the letters of my name across the wooden music box.

K-A-R-U-S

The box usually gathered dust on my vanity, but today, as the morning sun greeted me in my sulky temperament, chin resting on my fist, I wondered where it had come from. I always assumed Moira, my only friend, had it made for me, but wood carving, I realized, was not really in her repertoire.

I opened the lid and music filled my ears, though dying out quickly before I rewound the clasp on the back of the box. A familiar song filled my room.

The Sun and the Moon.

The song Moira and I had sung in the glen was so familiar then, like something I had always known, yet didn't know how.

Frustration rose inside of me, and I slammed the lid before huffing, collapsing with arms crossed back in the chair.

It had been weeks of the Baron's mysterious treks out into the forest, and they were wearing on me. Every sunset, I would come back into the Fortress after spending the day with Moira, only to be snuck out again, the Baron's midnight blue eyes alight with mischief, little said from his lips. He would lead the way through the forest, a different path each time, trotting along ahead of me, silent, but aware of my presence all the same.

It was his silence that annoyed me so. Was I not worth speaking to? Was my company so bland that he could not find a single thing to say?

He hadn't touched me again since that first secret outing at dusk, but, I admitted reluctantly, I wanted him to. I wasn't sure if it was his touch I craved or anyone's who could hold me when my mind fell into echoes of darkness and patterns of fog.

I again felt my thoughts slipping away. They often did, but less and less the more I held the stone. The more I changed my routine, following his dark figure out of the Fortress and into the setting sun, the more I was able to grasp my emotions and hold onto them.

I hated dusk. The whisper of it veered closely when we walked, its presence tangible between the sway of the trees, the tops of which soaked every last drop of sunlight before the dark entombed us all.

I would watch in trepidation each time as the sun betrayed the sky and broke its promise to illuminate the very world of which it gave life to. I would stand on the precipice of all-knowing to the obliterating black of night, and as the last sliver of my maker shed the last glimmer of promise to return, Baron Revich would turn around, smile my way, and lead us back home.

A cruel man indeed, I thought as I wound the box again and listened, waiting for Moira's company. She was gone longer these past few weeks, and I wondered if she had yet caught on to our secret walks in the woods.

I didn't know why I looked forward to following him, or why my heart raced each time I entered his study when I used to dread it. He'd be there, looking out of the window to the forest, waiting for me, often pacing. I'd close the door and stare at him. Each time he'd stare back. Sometimes for just a moment before practically racing across the room to leave, sometimes for what seemed like ten minutes, twenty—our gaze confusing to me, but I couldn't just let it go. It was like he spoke a language I did not understand. He wanted something from me, but I could not, in all of my efforts, understand what. Nor could I completely clear my mind of swirling mists and a heaviness.

So, so heavy.

I didn't know why I kept it from Moira. Just like keeping the stone from her, something told me not to say anything, and I guessed Moira wouldn't approve.

Confusion plagued me again and I stood to pace the room, hand reaching for the stone at the bottom of my pocket as it often did now. My mind cleared the moment I squeezed it in my palm. A hush so calming and still rushed through me. I closed my eyes, standing still, the last few chimes of the music box playing slowly through the room.

"Said the sun to the moon."
"Said the moon to the sun."

I shook my head, my body itching to be free of this place. I wanted to be far away from the black walls that silenced everything and held secrets I could not unravel.

It was as if the green stone was the end of a story, a peaceful conclusion that warmed my soul and held my heart. *But how? Why?* I was missing the rest of the story. I didn't have the reasons and I felt myself going mad there, in the tallest tower, if it was all kept from me any longer.

There were two souls that I knew had the answers.

Moira's whereabouts could be anywhere.

But the Baron's? His I could guess at, and so I stood, resolute among my place of rest. I was going to get my story.

I shut the music box and stormed to the door of my room, anger beginning to take hold of my heart with a determination I hadn't remembered ever feeling before.

It felt...*good*.

I pulled the handle to my door and it opened loud and wide, startling Moira who was just coming up the stairs nearby.

"Karus! What was that about?"

"Oh! You're here." My cheeks flushed. Moira was carrying a leaf pouch that she used to gather demorte petals.

"What's wrong? Why are you so…red?"

I raised a hand to my cheeks, assuming they had flushed. "I—never mind. Did you find some demorte?"

Moira's eyes narrowed, but she nodded, fluttering into my room before I closed the door. My anger suddenly fell away, not before curdling into something sour in my stomach.

"You're different, Karus. I don't know why, but you've changed recently." Moira busied herself at my vanity, gathering the supplies she'd need from the drawers and settling down to do her work, the mortar and pestle just the right size for a faerie.

I slumped onto my bed, arms spread wide, looking up to the stones that ran together in endless black, completing the cage I slept in every night.

"I do feel different, but why? Why do I spend my days here in the Fortress, wandering the forest, no purpose, no reason…nothing? I grow weary of it, Moira. I find myself questioning things I did not know to question." I sat up and ran fingers through my white-streaked hair. "Why can't I remember, Moira? What's wrong with me?"

She sighed in a heaviness not befitting her usual self, placing her hands on the pestle and then resting her pointed chin on the long length of her sage fingers. "I don't know if I'm the right one to tell you. I was hoping your memories would all come back at once, you know? But, you seem to be coming back in pieces. All incomplete and out of place." She shook her head and mumbled, "I don't know how humans work."

"*Please*, Moira." I rushed to the vanity. "Help me understand. I am so *tired* of this struggle. I'm so tired of this confusion and forgetting. You have answers. I know you do. I know you can help me, so why won't you?"

"I'm afraid. I'm afraid to tell you about your life. I don't want you to fall back into all shadows, Karus." She fluttered into my outstretched hands and pulled her knobby knees up to her chest, placing her chin on top of them. "I don't think…I don't *know* if you'd make it back out again. And seeing you now…closer to who you were? I don't want to lose that."

"I promise, Moira—my greatest friend—I will listen. I will hold on and just listen to anything you say. I am too awake to fall. I am too needed to leave again."

"*Needed?* Who have you been talking to?" She hovered above my head, her fae wings reflecting in the sunshine streaming in through the window, transferring rainbows on the walls, fluttering at maximum speed.

"Just…" I stood and busied myself with tidying up the space. "You hear things, you know? And I can *feel* it. There's a pressure about my presence every time I'm around anyone but you."

"I *knew* it! I knew he was saying things to you! I'll curse him! By the Blightress, I'll pull his hair out one by one and nibble the tips of his toes at night! He'll never dream peacefully again!"

Moira flew around the room in a rage I had not seen before—from faerie or human alike.

I attempted to repress a laugh. "It's not like that! Settle down! Let me explain before you go giving him anything nasty."

Crossing her arms, she slumped on my bed, her right foot rollicking up and down in impatience and subdued anger.

"He doesn't say much to me," I started, unsure of how to explain our odd excursions. "He told me once, weeks ago, after you had talked to him—that he's looking for someone…and he needs her help."

"You *heard* that? And you didn't tell—"

I cut her off to finish my dwindling thoughts. "I think he must be talking about me. Why else would he pay so much attention to me now that I'm feeling…different? Maybe he just suspects it's me, but I don't even know why he needs this woman. He doesn't talk, Moira, I promise. He doesn't even ask me his questions anymore, just has me follow him out into the forest at dusk to a different area each time, and then he turns around, smiles, and heads home. That's it. That's all he does and has been doing for the past few weeks."

Moira's face was filled with concern and concentration. I could see a million thoughts were racing through her mind all at once and she sighed deeply again. "I'm still going to curse him, even if he *was* right." She met my eyes with hers, which had grown to giant circles on her face, mostly violet in color and taking up the majority of it. "Maybe you don't need to listen. Maybe you just need to…see. There's something I can show you. It might help with your memories, but what if you get worse? What if you go back to—" Tears swelled at the corners of her eyes. "Come on. Let's go. That is, if you're willing to risk it?"

I thought about all I had felt since finding the stone. I didn't want to return to a foggy haze, forced to live my life here in rote memory, my only enjoyment found in walking the forest and falling into a dreamless sleep each night in my tower room.

Moira stared at me, waiting for an answer.

"Take me, Moira. There's no turning back now."

CHAPTER 10
ASH

As the weeks eased by in Felgren, so did Ash's contempt for her situation. As time in the Fortress and the forest waxed and waned each day, Ash's eyes grew brighter. Her laughter returned to her in unexpected ways. Clairannia and Figuerah's stories of their lives before Felgren, her daily rides on her lumen, even Baron Revich's charm and radiant laugher while they trained was causing her lips to slide upwards…slightly.

She could feel herself in the midst of letting go. The freedom given to her was enticing and illuminating as she realized how hidden away she had truly been—how her power had been.

The idea of becoming a conduit was no longer so abhorrent to her. The thought that she could actually use her gifts for more than simple tasks around the castle seemed to fit well with her soul. It was settling in, unfolding into new dreams and new pursuits for her life.

Her anger left in pieces.

Little bits of her hardened shell drifted away in the spring breeze or at the inhalation of the pouring rain that doused the forest floor in droplets that sank to the very roots of the trees that gave her magic—that gave her life.

She'd lie awake at night, her tower window open to the starlight and she would contemplate how she felt, still torn in surprising ways. Her heart, missing the Queen, the Prince, and Geyrand, was in constant battle with her curiosity. The Queen's lessons on self-reliance were challenged every morning when Clairannia and Figuerah greeted her at breakfast. Then again, every time Sylva brought them lunch and stayed to laugh and eat together as old friends, and especially each time she used her magic in Felgren.

Above all, that was what she loved. She spent many hours walking its paths, encouraging its flowers to bloom and the leaves of its trees to unfurl. In that, she felt a purpose. This one much more resonating than what she had tried so hard to convince herself of in Hyrithia. But here it was different. In the forest, she didn't question if she belonged; the truth of it stared her in the face each time she walked out of the Fortress doors and into the wondrous wood, the heart of it beating with hers.

"What do you think grows here in summer?" Ash asked Clairannia and Figuerah as they basked in the spring sun, looking up at the puffs of white swimming lazily in the crisp blue sky. They met in the field of golden buttercup blossoms each day after their morning lessons with Baron Heimlen or Baron Revich.

"You two really need to read from the Flora of Felgren Hall more often," Clairannia chided half-heartedly. "There's an entire row of books just about the seasons here and what grows in each of them."

"I'm too busy in the fauna section," remarked Figuerah. "For example, did you two know that quiphits here are different colors according to what season they were born in?" Figuerah lurched upward. "A quiphit born in winter will have a pure white coat, while one born in the summer will be dark greens and browns to blend in with the underbrush."

"And what does a quiphit in autumn look like?" Ash asked, chewing on a sweet blade of grass, one arm tucked behind her head, resting on her beast's soft belly.

"All brown and gold—just as you'd imagine. I think it's fascinating we get to see the animals here," she admitted, petting her lumen's head and scratching her ears. "I think that's what my memoir will be about before I leave. *The Fascinating Fauna of Felgren Forest* by Conduit Figuerah Attima."

Clairannia grinned in agreement and added, "I think mine will be about the healing plants in Felgren. Already I've discovered new uses for the bark of an aspen tree. There's a whole copse of them not far from the lumen den."

Ash thought for a moment. "*Arcaynen Isle's Best Healing Tinctures: A Guide to Medicine in Felgren Forest* by Conduit Clairannia…wait, what's your second name?"

"It's Lynns. And that title is *perfect*, Ash. You have a way with words." She stretched her arms up, popping them loudly. "What do you think your memoir will be about?"

"Magic language. The use of names of things. Origins and meanings." She stood and brushed the grass and dirt off of her green skirts. "Names are important, after all. Like the title of a story, or the first line of a song—the last line of a poem."

Figuerah grinned impishly and began,

> "So long as you keep to your bed at night,
> She will not harm you, she might, she might.
> Don't let your anger in your heart or your
> head,
> Her darkness will find you, and you will be
> dead.
> The Blightress may find you, and you will be
> dead."

Ash laughed aloud and nodded. "Yes, even nursery rhyme lines are important. Especially the 'dead' part in that one."

Her time in Viridis was spent on the list of materials given to each of them every morning by Baron Revich, but at every opportunity, she headed to the Magical Language Hall. Origins of Felgren, their current course of study, though interesting enough, was all just lore. Myths and legends of how the magic of their world had come to be. But the language of a conduit—that was solid. A foundation for those who could use it to wield more magic or make it stronger.

She had tried out a few of the simpler words for magic enhancement and they had all done what she had intended. Flowers bloomed brighter, their scent sweeter. Water formed into a sphere above her hand and flame burst to life at the end of her finger—a more dangerous spell, she realized, in a library.

She knew her interest in the conduit language had another purpose as well. Still the doors of Viridis accepted her answer of not having a name that suited her. She made sure each morning that she was the last one through the doors, her embarrassment real enough without Figuerah or Clairannia hearing it.

"Well, my fellow lovely channelers, it's time to get back. Viridis awaits us again." Figuerah whistled to her lumen who had run off at the sight of a possible snack and groaned. "Baron Revich is killing me with these leaf exercises." She rolled her shoulders, pushing on the nape of her neck at the tension left there.

The past four days Baron Revich had been relentless.

"Channelers," he'd spout, having led them to a new type of tree each morning with fresh enthusiasm. "I need you to bring me a seven-leaf stem with length being the bottom of your palm to the tip of your middle finger. It must show variation in its color, light to dark green, and it must be fully intact, no notches or holes in the leaves."

That morning he had brought them to an enormous mahogany tree, its foliage far too high to inspect by eyes alone.

The Barons had taught them to feel the trees, not just see them. They had been trained to close their eyes, seeping their way into the heart of each one, asking it for what they sought before it would eventually be brought to them, floating lazily down to their outstretched fingers, encased in their magic.

Ash had watched as Clairannia and Figuerah raised their arms above their shoulders, their magic flickering out of the tips of their hands, as their conduit rings sparkled and shined, willing the tree to give them what they wanted.

Baron Revich's eyes always landed on hers in these sessions, challenging her to show him what she could do. Her stubbornness was insatiable as she'd pretend not to notice. She'd follow the movements of her fellow trainees, even though, without much thought at all, she knew exactly where the branch she was looking for hung every time, with every single tree. She'd pretend to struggle obtaining it, though. After all, the idea of making the Baron wait was a pleasant one.

He'd inspect each of their bounties before nodding and moving to the next and the next until their arms could barely hold upright any longer.

"I wonder, Ash," he had mumbled to her that morning after requesting a willow leaf exactly half eaten by a caterpillar, holding hers up to the sunlight. "You are always last to produce what I ask, yet yours is always the most *perfect*. If you're not careful, I might just think you have the most talent here." He'd winked at her then, his grin lighting up half of his face.

It irritated her beyond rational thought when he did those things, always ignoring her attempts at indifference.

"Ooh, maybe I can find a book about salves in Viridis and make one for our shoulders." Clairannia grinned giddily, bringing Ash back to the present, climbing up onto her lumen to ride back to the den.

"Whew, I'm glad we have a medicus conduit trainee with us, right Ash?" Figuerah had both hands on the side of her lumen's face, the wolf's long tongue hanging happily out the side of her mouth.

"She's certainly proving useful, isn't she?" Ash quipped, Clairannia throwing a twig in her hair.

They raced back to the lumen den, maneuvering their beasts over the underbrush, through the dense trees, their laughter at home in the forest that fed them their magic.

When they entered Viridis one by one, Ash making sure she was last, both Barons were waiting for them on the white marble steps.

Baron Heimlen gave each of them a weak smile, nodding as they stepped out of the portal. But Baron Revich's head was still, his mouth tipped downward in a frown, his gaze piercing in her direction.

She glanced around, unsure of the reason behind his serious demeanor, one she realized she had never actually seen before.

"Ash'Arah, walk with me, please." Baron Heimlen's voice was dull and swift. He turned, heading immediately down the stairs toward the courtyard.

She paused and shrugged, unable to identify his purpose as Clairannia raised a single eyebrow in her direction and Figuerah mouthed, *good luck.*

She could feel Baron Revich's gaze at her back as she hurried down the steps, following the aging Baron, his cloak billowing out behind him. The length of it fell off each stair in turn as he descended into the courtyard. She turned her head to see Baron Revich still, his hands in his pockets at the top of the landing, his expression completely unreadable. She frowned back at him, unsure of why he would look at her in such a way, considering he didn't ever seem capable of it.

Ash and Baron Heimlen walked in silence through the forest of swaying trees and blooming bushes, passing benches and fountains along with an array of exotic birds preening in the glow of the sun, a warm welcome shining through the glass far above them.

She felt as if she was a little girl again, about to be chastised for what, she didn't know. As far as she could tell, there were very few rules in the Fortress—the main one being, of course, that she couldn't leave Felgren's boundaries. But no one had remarked on her behavior otherwise.

As she pondered what she could have done to deserve a personal outing with Baron Heimlen, they came upon a short wooden door. Its hinges were made of black iron and bars of the same material stretched across the old wood, ending in a lock near the handle.

This was the first door Ash had seen inside of Viridis. Even leaving the halls did not produce a door, but a shimmering portal instead, waiting for its patrons to leave at any time of their choosing.

Baron Heimlen placed a leather-gloved hand in his cloak pocket and produced an iron key. Watching silently, Ash stood before the door as he unlocked it with an audible click.

"I wanted to wait longer before taking you here, Ash'Arah, but I am afraid we cannot waste any more time."

"What is it?" Ash spoke, her voice dry in her throat. "What's behind this door?"

"Do you remember what I said about Baron Revich on your first visit to Viridis? About the task I gave him?"

She nodded, remembering how she didn't get to hear the full story due to her impatience with the Baron. She was more willing to listen now.

"I'll cut the story short. Baron Revich was chosen by me as my successor, not only because of his rare ability as a male to use magic, but because of his natural bond to rhyzolm. You see, rhyzolm is coveted, yes, by wealthy people who believe it possesses magic and can make channelers out of their children." He paused and pulled a small rhyzolm from his pocket. Ash took it in her hands, her fingers rubbing the smooth surface.

"It's not true though, is it? Rhyzolm can't create channelers."

"No, it cannot. But that doesn't mean it doesn't have magic. The roots of the trees in Felgren are the heart of the power the forest possesses. And the runoff of water that flows into the Hallow Marshes does contain some of that power. But rhyzolm has another purpose to a Baron." He held out his hand for her to give the stone back and she did so, eager to hear more. "You see, rhyzolm contains Felgren magic. It is embedded into its core and cannot escape unless the stone is broken. But power likes power, and so, for centuries, Barons have used rhyzolm to find the most powerful channelers. The stone pulls us to them. In a way, it is as if the magic of Felgren is calling to those who can wield it." He placed the stone back in his pocket.

"I chose Baron Revich because he was not only adept at finding rhyzolm, he was talented at *using* it. He didn't know he possessed magic until he dug up his first stone, just a boy, and that night he felt its pull in his village. It led him to a small cottage. The family inside the decrepit house was unaware that their son was a channeler. But rhyzolm does not lie, and the story of the young boy who could grow wheat in a marshland trickled from mouth to mouth until it met my ears.

"Usually, a Baron cannot use a rhyzolm to find children channelers, or we might take them to Felgren earlier. Its pull is strongest when a channeler reaches their later adolescence. I was curious about the power of this small child, but more so about the boy who discovered him. And so, I visited Revich often in his village, watching for more signs of magic. The day he turned nineteen, barely younger than you are now, he came with me back to Felgren. His task before him set. He was to train as Baron, but more importantly, find me the most powerful channeler on the isle."

Baron Heimlen's dark, graying eyes bore into hers, the truth of his story and where it was leading evident on his aging face.

"And he found her? In Hyrithia?"

He smiled to one side. "I believe so, though, he is less sure. He tells me you are a contradiction—your obvious love of Felgren at war with your resistance to show us your true power."

She narrowed her eyes in natural offense, internally huffing at the truth of his words. She bit her lower lip and broke her gaze from the Baron to the door before them, unlocked, but unopened.

"You still haven't told me why you need such a powerful channeler. Why you wanted to break the Treaty and bring me here." She straightened, her stance braver than she felt. "What is behind this door?"

Baron Heimlen stepped closer, leaning in to speak softly, "What you are about to see, you will tell to no one. The only people who are aware are now you, Baron Revich, and myself. It will stay that way, Ash'Arah." His authority was unsettling. She was not in the slightest bit used to being lectured by a man, let alone the most powerful one on the isle. A chill crept up her spine and left bumps on her skin.

He opened the door, head turning in all directions, to assure of their solitary presence. She expected the door to creak, loudly, as old doors often do. But this door seemed well taken care of as it opened into a dark stone hallway, the light of Viridis the only one to illuminate its entrance. The Baron nodded for her to enter and she spoke aloud, "*Illuminare*", an enhancement spell she had recently learned to make her orb of green light brighter and pulsing, following the beat of her own heart.

The sound of their footsteps across ancient stone echoed through the narrow corridor, and a heavy scent hung stale in the air that she could not place. They walked for some time, her emerald orb pulsing faster to the beat of her pacing heart until another wooden door, the twin of the last, lay before them. Turning silently behind her to look at the Baron, she took the black key from his outstretched hand.

The lock clicked in acceptance, and, giving a small shove, she was able to push it open, though it seemed to be caught. She stumbled out into an expanse of trees, though at what time of day, she couldn't tell. A haze of mist and darkened shadows loomed before them as Baron Heimlen stepped out beside her.

They were no longer in Viridis.

That much was evident.

Before them lay massive vines, black as dried blood, tangling through broken mounds of moldy earth. They wound up and through the unsettling, dead trees in a portrait of strangulation and possession all at once. Ash covered her mouth and nose to subdue the stench of death as the harsh presence of it stung her eyes and caused them to tear.

A white bloom of fungus lay over the corpses of unknown animals, covering what was left of the bodies in a silent blanket of death. The air lingered thick, almost tangible as she held out her hand only to have the mist around it swirl in mocking waves of frivolity.

The orb of magic she held before her became erratic in its pulse, her fear of where she tread kept in time with the single source of light.

She stepped forward, her feet uneven on the expanse of thorny vines that were caught on the door behind her. "Where…" She turned to the Baron, her face illuminated in the green light, panic emanating from its features. She swallowed, the hard lump in her throat refusing to subdue. "Where are we? This isn't—"

"Felgren." He nodded gravely, stepping closer to her and placing his gloved hand on her shoulder. "You are in Felgren, Ash'Arah. And this…" He gestured to the expanse of decay and embodiment of death before them. "This is the Blight."

CHAPTER II
KARUS

I knelt on the broken ground, my thin, white dress ruined in the decay. I reached out gently to lift the drooping stem of a peony bush, buds closed tightly in slumber, its desire to live evident in the remaining red and green of its stems.

But I saw the Blight.

It was subtle, but there all the same, as its murderous vines crept under the soil and began to wind their way around the base of the bush—as if they were reaching for me.

Moira had brought me to the edge of the diseased forest that lay far, far away from the Fortress—further than I had ever remembered traveling. Rauca and Parvus were whimpering, unsteady and uneasy nearby.

"You see, Karus…I didn't want to show you, but you *must* see it. This is what consumes all of Felgren. This is what you call the Blight." She flew to the top of a mossy outcropping of rocks and sat in a slump, her pointy chin resting in her long fingers, a look of acceptance on her face—an acceptance that I was nowhere near willing to face.

I stood shakily, knees wobbling at the Blight before me. I stepped into the bounds of the decay and the suffocating scent of disease hit me, but I could not turn away. It wasn't all death, I realized, as I moved carefully among the massive vines, smothering everything in their path.

I saw that the vines themselves were fueled in life. It was a sickening energy I could not describe, nor fathom to understand. I followed the base of one where it sprouted from the soil, having a girth larger than my own body and covered in small thorns. I walked beside it, careful not to trip on the tangled growth running in all directions around me. It wound up a tree, oak from what I could discern, and spiraled like the staircase to my tower in the Fortress, scorching the trunk in its wake with lines of black disease slithering out from all sides.

I placed a hand on the oak tree, not possessing the strength to touch the Blight. The tree's life was waning.

Rapidly.

"Karus, let's go. You've seen plenty today. I'll make an excuse to Baron Revich this evening. You don't need to talk to anyone if you don't want to." Moira flew to my shoulder, tugging gently on the long sleeves of my dress.

My voice was soft, but vibrated through my chest as my hand left the dying tree. "Where is he? Where is Baron Revich right now?"

"I don't know. I don't keep track of him or anything. Probably in his study. Why? Are you...*angry* with him?" Her face lit in excitement, her wings fluttering. "Alright, let's go find him."

She stuck her long slender fingers into her mouth and whistled, the lumens howling at the sound and running to the edge of the dying forest to greet us eagerly.

I said nothing as I climbed on top of Parvus, his relief in leaving the Blight evident in his quickened run through the lush forest floor, Rauca ahead.

I didn't even turn back to look.

I feared losing my grip on reality no longer, for wrath was fueling me now.

CHAPTER 12
ASH

Though she'd had much practice in her life, Ash could not stop her tears this time. They streamed down her face in rivulets, slipping together just before dropping off the base of her chin.

"How much?" She choked on her words, sniffing and wiping her face with her sleeve.

Baron Heimlen held a handkerchief to her in silence and she took it, grateful.

She cleared her swollen throat and spoke again, her voice steadying with rising anger. "How much of the forest is taken, and how long do we have?"

Baron Heimlen stepped forward, his boot kicking aside a black vine in the process of smothering the corpse of something large.

"From what I have been able to document, almost nine thousand acres. Spring has stunted its growth—for now." He turned to Ash, placing his gloved hands on both of her shoulders, looking down at her in earnest. "We need *you*, Ash'Arah. Felgren needs *you*. I know you can save it. You *must* save it."

"I don't...I don't know how. What can I possibly do to stop..."

she gestured to the dark wood before them, silent and still, and mumbled, "all of this?"

"I can teach you. Baron Revich can teach you. There is a kind of magic we can try. Only the most powerful of magic users can wield it, and with yours and my magic combined…" He pulled her chin up to look him in the eyes. "We can stop the Blight. Together, we can prevent more destruction, more death." He pulled her to his chest in an embrace as if she was a child, her talents realized and praised.

She stood there still, arms at her side, her mind racing with an impossible task that she surely could not complete.

He let her go and turned back to the door to Viridis. "Come, you have seen enough for now. I do not want your heart weakened by the sight of it." He left through the door, an orb of a silvery light before him.

She followed, taking one last look before closing it and locking it tight. Her steps echoed in the wake of his, her heart hammering in its cage, and her mind a mess of what seemed unachievable and what seemed like fate.

After all, she hadn't been *weakened* among the Blight.

She crossed her arms at her chest, cold at her realization—she had felt more *powerful* because of it.

CHAPTER 13
KARUS

"You're early today, Karus." Baron Revich smiled up at me in genuine pleasure before scribbling something on the open ledger before him.

"*Predictable*," Moira mumbled, rolling her wild, violet eyes upon quickly finding him hiding away in his study and apparent place of rest. A large blanket and pillow had been tossed to the side of a leather armchair.

I gave her a half smile and told her I wanted to speak to him alone, suggesting she ask the cook to bake some extra cinnamon buns for us to scarf down later. I closed the heavy door, turning my back upon it, and stared at the man sitting at his desk in his usual slew of papers, books, and maps.

I saw him every single day, and yet every day he was not out there fighting the Blight. Every moment we met was *wasted*.

He glanced back up to me, realizing I was silent, still standing with my back to his door. "Is…everything alright?" He narrowed his eyes in confusion and dropped his quill. "You look…angry."

"Why don't you ask me, Baron? Ask me if I found anything in the forest." I strode across the room in three steps, my gown a mess of blackened underbrush against the white cloth. "No, don't ask—

you'll take too long. I'll tell you." I slammed my hands on his desk and stood over him, my white streaks of hair falling forward, no longer contained in their plaited prison. He watched me with a strange stillness, as if not daring to breathe.

"*Death*. I found death, and decay, and disease. A *blight*. It's raging through Felgren, and what are you doing to stop it? Why aren't you out there now, doing every *damn* thing you can? Gather every single channeler and conduit—*anyone* who can wield magic and stop it!"

Rage came over me in waves. We had to *do* something. Time was limited by the looks of the growth, and yet, he sat there, every day passing papers from hand to hand, taking me on walks through a dying forest, doing nothing, *nothing* to save the forest I loved.

He stared at me, his jaw clenching as he spoke in a low, dangerous tone. "She told me not to tell you. She said you weren't ready. I see that *faerie* gets to do whatever she wants."

"Don't you *dare* bring Moira into this," I seethed. "*She* has taken care of me. *She* has seen to my needs and *talked* with me. Actually *talked* with me and helped me understand what's at stake. She has said more to me just today than you have in *months*."

"And you think that was *my* idea?" He sprang out of his chair, meeting my eyes with ones so dark, the faintest hint of blue would be lost to anyone else. "You do not *know* what it has been like, Karus! You do not *know* what I have suffered—keeping to a short script of words and questions—the dullest, *meaningless* questions that she has persuaded me to say. Talking about *nothing*, just to keep you from falling further back into that place of shadows!"

"Say them then! Say the words you wanted to say! Let's hear it —all of your *suffering*!" Exasperated, I raised my hands into the air, slamming them back down on the desk between us, pushing my body forward. "C'mon, *Baron*, let it out!"

"*I still love you!*"

If I wanted more anger and argument, I would not get it. His body calmed instantly, the tension in his face and shoulders relaxing the moment his confession left his lips. Confusion and a heaviness I knew well rang hollow in my head as my brows knitted further, my mouth agape.

"I *love* you, and I'm sorry…I'm so *sorry*, Karus." He exhaled quickly, a laugh in his breath as he shook his head in disbelief, bringing a hand up to the back of his neck, rubbing it softly. His eyes met mine, now the color of the first breath a wave takes as it tumbles across the sea. He leaned in close and whispered softly with a conspiratorial smile, "I cannot tell you how long I've wanted to say that."

It's not as if I didn't know what the words meant.

It's not as if I didn't hear them, either, as a short gasping, "*What?*" came from my lips and I stood tall, straight, and still, hands leaving the desk, blood draining from my face.

"I love you. I love you. I love you."

He leaned forward more as if to catch me as I took a step back. His voice was full of confident truth, as if saying it three more times would convince me to stay near. The unfamiliarity of his words held me in a bind as seconds ticked past. I was rigid, caged in a cell of confusion and disbelief.

I shoved my hand in my pocket, feeling for the stone. Pulling it out in front of him, some of my confusion turned to anger once again, but the cool, green surface still comforted me and steadied my heart.

"What is this?"

Shock and relief lit his face in quick succession as he took the stone from my hand and laughed, a single tear rolling down his cheek. He shook his head again and looked into my eyes with an intense pain I did not understand. "I think you're ready to hear what this is, Karus."

Walking around his desk, he pulled the leather chair in front of it, patting at the pillow, eyeing my ruined dress for the first time, shrugging, and then offering me the blanket as well. He held the stone out for me to take, and then, in a few hurried steps, he went to the door and locked it using a black iron key from his pocket.

"You'd better sit down. We'll be here a while."

I rolled the stone across my fingers, feeling so small in this world. He knew what it was, and I knew nothing. He knew of my past, and I knew *nothing*.

It wasn't fair.

He said he loved me, and though I had no way of knowing if it was ever returned, it seemed as though *he* at least believed it was true.

Exhaling heavily, he fell into the chair behind his desk, rubbing a hand on his mouth, looking out the window to the sunlit forest.

"I'm not sure where to—" he began, facing me again.

"All of it. Tell me all of it, Revich." I pulled the blanket across my lap and sat back on the pillow, the stone held tightly in my hand. "Tell me my story."

PART TWO

CHAPTER 14

ASH

"Good, my child. *Breathe.* Channel your magic from its source. You are a conduit in all but name, Ash'Arah. Feel your power reside inside of you. Gather it and send it to me."

Ash peeked one eye open, her knees aching on the hard, wet earth. Baron Heimlen knelt in front of her, one black leather glove touching her shoulder, his other resting flat on the earthen floor. His eyes were closed as hers were supposed to be, so she took the opportunity to look down at their contact.

Beams of silver and green light radiated around her shoulder and his arm, twirling in a sort of strange dance to music only the magic of Felgren could hear. She looked up to see the branches, newly green with the toddler leaves of spring swaying to the same rhythm, a recital few would likely ever see.

She stifled a yawn, even in the beauty and boundless power of Felgren, and admitted what she didn't want to show.

Ash was exhausted.

Her first night in the Fortress was now months past and still spring held on, no promise of summer yet on her cool breezes and rainy mornings. But time moved differently here in Felgren as Sylva had mentioned that first night, and Ash wondered how much time had passed outside of the forest border.

Another heavy sigh escaped Baron Heimlen as he let go of her and sat down on the earth himself, his gray eyes meeting hers in a sort of disappointment only a parental figure can give.

"Your mind is wandering again, my dear." He rubbed the bridge of his nose as he reprimanded her, looking worn himself.

He was a handsome man, and Ash looked him over quickly, thinking about his relationship with Sylva. His wavy hair was cut to his shoulders, almost fully gray but hinting that it was once the color of summer sun. His mustache and beard blended together well in grays and whites against his sun-kissed skin, his mouth set at a perpetual pout that must have been quite becoming and brooding in his younger years. Ash could see how Sylva must have fallen for him easily decades ago when she first arrived at the Fortress. But what she thought was most endearing about his face was the way his eyes could look into yours with kindness, as if he understood your purpose and would share it with you if you'd only ask.

Weeks of training side-by-side had softened her view of him. He had a good reason to bring her here, even if it was without her agreement. He really did believe that she could help—that she was powerful enough to help him stop the Blight, and she was thankful for that purpose.

"I'm sorry. It's just…I miss Clairannia and Figuerah. I miss Hyrithia and I-I'm just so tired." She rubbed her eyes like a child stayed up too late to watch the stars appear.

Their time together was spent in the practice of Cosensian Magic. She had never heard of it and Clairannia and Figuerah had not either when she had asked at dinner one night.

"It's ancient," Ash had told them, whispering, unsure of how much she was willing to say. "There is only one single book in all of Viridis about how to use it and bits of it are hard to decipher."

"But what can it do?" Clairannia had asked, leaning in closer, her whisper hardly one at all.

"What does the book look like?" Figuerah had asked at the same time, a true whisper on her lips.

"Well, it's black and yellowing and I'm not really allowed to touch it, but according to the text and Baron Heimlen, it acts as a way to *combine* conduit magic. If two or more magic users touch, they can store their magic into one person, who can then use it as a sort of…enhanced spell for whatever they want to wield. I told you how the forest is dying to a blight. To restore it, we're going to use Cosensian Magic, working together with twice as much power." Ash had sat back in her tall chair, eyebrows raised, enjoying the view of their excitement.

"But why doesn't he ask us to help, too?" Clairannia had gotten her whispering voice down correctly. "Wouldn't Cosensian Magic be stronger with more than just you two?"

"I asked him that very question, and do you know what he said?" She mimicked his deep voice and sat up tall, wagging a finger, "This magic is to stay between you, me, and Baron Revich, Ash'Arah. It is old and it is more powerful than any other type of incantation. I believe you are strong enough to help me wield it, but I cannot risk the other channelers as well."

"Wow. I don't know whether to be flattered or offended," Figuerah said, returning to her meal.

"You *cannot* tell anyone else about this. I won't be able to train with you as much, but I'll let you know how it goes."

"You are done for the day, Ash'Arah."

The Baron brought her thoughts back to the present away from that conversation weeks ago, and she stood, thankful to the training's end, and stretched, her body popping in several places.

Ash had told her friends about the forest dying, but left out the true details of the Blight. She did see less of them each day but promised to try to join them each afternoon for lumen riding, their favorite pastime outside of Viridis.

"I think I'll head to the lumen den, then," she mumbled, dusting her skirts and rubbing her neck. Cosensian Magic not only exhausted her, it made her sore wherever Baron Heimlen placed his gloved hand to channel their power.

"I want to see you back here after breakfast tomorrow. No Viridis, my dear. You need more practice and fewer distractions.

And come rested. You look as if you could use a good night's sleep." He gave her a half smile then and placed a hand on her other shoulder. "I have confidence we can do this."

He left silently, his black cloak trailing out behind him like a villain in a child's bedtime story, the towers of the Fortress looming tall and dark against the bright green of the swaying leaves and cloudless sky.

She turned toward the other path, leading to the lumen den where she would meet Clairannia and Figuerah in an hour's time. As she trekked through the forest, she thought of how much her life had changed. She missed Hyrithia, but it wasn't the same kind of hollow pain she had felt in those first few weeks away. She had adjusted well—even better than anyone might have guessed she would, herself included.

There was still no word, though, from Hyrithia, and she couldn't help but be disappointed. She wanted to know what had happened after the cure. She wanted to walk the streets to see how the city mourned their dead. She wanted to be reminded of what Baron Heimlen had done. She wanted to see the blackened hands of those who had survived and remind herself that what he had done was worth the price.

Flashes of Prince Philius's fingers flooded her mind. She didn't know if there was magic to return them to their original russet hue, but she didn't doubt he wouldn't want it if there was. Knowing him well, she guessed he would use stories of his harrowing time in the midst of the fever to begin conversations with plenty of women.

Her thoughts returned to the Queen as well. There must be a way to receive letters in Felgren, and though she had not attempted to send any either, she promised herself to ask Sylva that evening.

Walking to the den, she took her time, humming one of her favorite childhood songs before looking up to check the sun for her bearings. If she was on the correct path to the lumens, it should have been descending toward the western hemisphere of the blue sky.

It was not.

She turned around, looking behind her, not recognizing any of the trees, nor the path she had just come from. Puzzled, she turned in full circle, unable to catch sight of anything familiar.

"What's your name, human?" She heard a small voice, high pitched and piercing among the trees.

"Who's there? Show yourself." Ash whipped around in a frenzy, disoriented and frightened. She knew there were many creatures who lived in the forest that did not reside anywhere else on the isle. She thought of the old stories children were told about monsters in Felgren who could speak and probably ate humans at every chance. But those were childhood tales, she reminded herself, and spoke, "Ash. My name is Ash. And it seems as if I am lost."

A light giggle, the sound of it chiming in echoes on the wind, emanated from somewhere behind her. Turning slowly, she saw a small creature sitting on a branch above her head, legs the color of dried sage and crossed at the ankles, swinging lazily up and down, ending barefoot and dirty.

Her hair was not like human hair at all, more like sprouted vines cascading down her barely clothed body. She wore a dress of sorts, most of it made from blades of woven grass and crocus petals that encircled her waist, sitting upside-down in a sort of forest skirt. Her violet eyes took up most of her face and pointed ears stuck out from the sides of her head. She couldn't have been taller than Ash's forearm.

She leapt off the branch, and Ash, expecting her to fall, took two quick steps forward as if to catch her before eyeing the irides-cent dragonfly wings fluttering from her back.

"What a strange name." She flew closer, putting her hands on her hips, leaning in for a better look. "And no wonder you're lost, *Ash*. You've strayed very, very far from the Fortress. You *really* shouldn't let the hideous thing out of your sight. Something might eat you up out here." The creature sneered, her sharp teeth menacing as she laughed that chiming way again.

"What is your name? And…I'm sorry, but I don't know the name of your kind." Ash curtsied to the creature, hoping politeness might lighten the tension.

"Ha! Aren't you an interesting one, *Ashhh*." She drew out her name mockingly and flew around Ash's head in tight circles. "Hmm. Yes, you are very unlike the other humans I've met with your bark hair and leafy eyes."

The little creature grabbed the side of Ash's face, leaning in close. Startled, Ash tried not to move. She was aware that a quick swipe of the hand could knock the little thing down easily, but she was not that careless. Though small, she didn't doubt the extensive abilities this creature had. In fact, Ash was beginning to wonder if she hadn't really become lost by herself at all.

The creature sighed and flew back from her face, rubbing her own as if deep in thought, her long sage fingers tapping her cheek lightly. "I *was* going to tie your hair in hideous knots and send you to the bog monster, but I think I'll let you go…for now."

"What's a bog monster?" Ash wondered aloud, thankful that she wouldn't have to spend the evening combing through tangles.

"I dunno. We've not been properly introduced. But, he's definitely something you'd only like to encounter once." She giggled again and flew back to the tree, twirling on the branch in her crocus skirt.

"I'd like to know your name. So that if we meet again, I can properly greet you." Again Ash stayed polite, though annoyed at the creature's suggestion she meet a monster.

"You couldn't pronounce my name even if you had a thousand years to try." She then let out a deafening screech full of harsh guttural sounds and high-pitched notes that lasted twenty seconds or more.

The little creature looked pleased at Ash's discomfort when she held her hands to her ears.

"See?" She laughed and her sharp teeth glinted in the afternoon sun.

"Yes, I see. I could never say your name. Not in a thousand years. But maybe you have one I *could* say? Names are important."

"I heard the name 'Moira' once and liked it. So, humans call me that. I guess you can, too." She jumped to the next branch up on the tree, then another and another, almost out of sight.

"Wait! Can you help me find the lumen den? I'm still lost!" Ash shouted up to the tree, but the creature was gone, or at least was done with her.

She looked around, hoping her confusion would leave, since the creature who had surely caused it in the first place had gone. But still nothing was familiar, so she turned, and did her best to follow the direction from which she came, hoping to once again see the towers of the Fortress.

As she walked, her hands brushed the rough bark of the trees and the fronds of the ferns littering the sides of the dirt path, her magic flowing from her fingers to greet them. Her thoughts returned to the Blight.

She felt so young, so small. Barely into her twentieth year, she was given the task to save the forest which produced all magic in Arcaynen. She had only just accepted her training here and now she was to not only stay, but heal what was breaking. The pressure of her task and role in Baron Heimlen's eyes weighed on her each night as she lay in her bed, watching the moonlit sky outside of her angled window.

At times her thoughts wandered to Baron Revich. She had seen little of him since being shown the Blight, and yet she couldn't stop thinking about what Baron Heimlen had said.

Baron Revich had doubted her.

She couldn't blame him, really. She had held back at all of the trainings until now, until she understood the importance of what she was brought to Felgren to do. Her own sense of pride longed to show him the truth. She wanted to shake him into acceptance of what she knew she was capable of—what she knew she could wield.

The sound of splashing nearby took her out of her thoughts and she turned down a smaller dirt path. Thinking of the bog monster, she hesitated a moment before pushing on through the tall grasses. If it was real, she hoped it didn't eat channelers in training.

The path ended alongside a small lake, shallow and full of silt, its water a light brown, swirling ripples meeting the edge of the muddy shore, likely due to the ruckus before her.

Baron Revich's back was facing her across the lake, knee deep in the water and bent, black gloves running all the way up to his elbows. She grinned, recognizing his easily identifiable black hair, the color glistening almost blue in the sun, tied back into a knot with a white ribbon.

"Oh, I've got you *now*," he spoke through what sounded like gritted teeth as he yanked on whatever he was holding under the water. "Whoa, easy, *easy*."

Ash hadn't really noticed his muscular frame before, but she certainly did now. His shirt clung to him, wet and thin, the ripple of muscle down his back impossible to miss as he yelled in triumph, finally pulling a massive fish out of the muck and holding it high above him. The fish writhed in protest, causing him to lose his balance and fall back into the water.

She ran forward without thinking, her boots skimming the edge of the lake just as his head emerged from it, his grip somehow still on the powerful beast.

He faced her pushing his muddy black hair from his eyes in one quick motion, before wiping them clean.

She needed to leave.

Quickly.

She turned in a flurry of green skirts.

"Ash?" he called and she stopped, turning back around, a flush of blood creeping up her cheeks.

"Oh, hello," she said hesitantly with a little wave, her breath suddenly short.

She understood exactly why as her eyes flitted across his body, the cotton material of his tunic clinging to him in a pathetic attempt to stay on his toned chest.

He had his hand inside of the coppery fish's mouth, pulling it along as it thrashed in determined resistance to the result of the fight.

"What are you doing out here? Are you lost?" He threw the massive fish onto the muddy shore, some of the sludge splashing onto her skirts. He pulled off his gloves and tossed them to the shore as well, taking a moment to wipe more silt from his face and flick it into the water.

She shoved her hands into her pockets. "I—" She cleared her

throat in an attempt to sound normal. "I was looking for the lumen den, actually. I finished my time with Baron Heimlen this morning and was going to meet Clairannia and Figuerah, but I got turned around."

He listened while he worked, pulling the top half of his hair back and curling it around in a spiral to stay out of his face, his white ribbon long gone.

"I—I suspect it was the little winged creature I found along the path to the den."

Ash cursed at her nervousness. Her heart was beating wildly and something familiar was tugging at her belly as she watched him peel his wet tunic off his torso, the muscle on his stomach defined before cutting into a deep V that fell somewhere below the line of his pants. He quickly replaced his tunic with the dry one he pulled from a sack on the shoreline.

Had she really never noticed?

Of course she had. How could anyone miss how attractive he was? But she had stayed stubborn, even to herself, not willing to admit any kind of attraction to the Baron she found most irritating.

But now? Now her body refused to deny what seemed so obvious.

He chuckled, rolling up his sleeves. "Let me guess—you met Moira."

She nodded, not trusting herself to speak, feeling warm, the palms of her hands sweaty in her pockets. She took them out and wiped them on her dirty skirt as he pulled his legs out of the water, coming up to the shore beside her.

"She's a fae by the way, if you didn't know. A pixie, faerie, they have lots of names. But," he went on, sighing, placing his hands on his hips, cocking to one side, confidence gracing his face, "whatever they're called, they are known for mischief." He looked her up and down, smirking, his lips pulling to one side. "I see you escaped unharmed. Your hair's intact and your boots are still on the right feet." He wiped his brow. "She once told me that if I didn't hop on one foot and clap my hands, she would curse me to never again be able to have happy dreams. She said all of them would be nightmares, and I would never sleep well until I died—only then would I have peace."

Ash raised her eyebrows and laughed. "And what did you do?"

"I hopped on one foot and clapped, of course. I'm not going to risk *that* curse."

His smile reached his eyes every single time. *How does he do that?* she wondered, turning away from the ocean hue of them, reminding her of the shores near Hyrithia on a calm summer day. Again her throat swelled and heat poured through her.

Maybe she was just tired. Or, maybe she was missing something she'd not had in what felt like a *very* long time.

Either way, she felt ridiculous.

They stood together along the silty shore in silence, the giant fish no longer flapping in protest of giving its life, its copper scales gleaming in the sun.

"So…you like to fish?" The words escaped her lips without her permission and no consciousness of them ever even forming in her mind.

"It's called mudfishing. That is a mudcopper fish. When eaten, it can calm the swelling of limbs." He nodded off to the forest trees. "I was good at it growing up. We had mudcoppers in the Hallow Marshes, but not like this. They grow enormous here and are very difficult to catch." He looked back to her, a small smile on his lips. "I've been finding them for Baron Heimlen. His legs ache at night and the fish seems to help." He walked over to the massive mud beast and hauled it into his sack, the fishy tail sticking out of the material as he slung it one-handed over his back.

"You two are…close? Baron Heimlen, I mean, not the fish."

He laughed, tilting his head back in doing so and Ash noticed the dark stubble beginning to show on the underside of his chin and down his neck, his throat bobbing in the sound of his hearty bellow.

"Well…yes. I don't know what he's told you, but he found me in the Hallow Marshes years ago and eventually brought me here to succeed him as Baron—as you do know." Sighing, he nodded for Ash to follow him back down the small path. "I do what I can. The magic of Felgren is leaving him, and so, his spirit is leaving his body, too." He looked back to me, cloaked in seriousness. "I know you've resisted it, Ash, and I understand why, but I hope you really do see why you're needed here."

They reached the dirt path, much wider than the last and Ash moved beside him. "Do you believe I'm the one he's been looking for? The powerful conduit, I mean. The one that…well, *you* discovered, actually." She crossed her arms at her chest, thankful for the cool breeze that swept lazily their way, toying with her hair.

"I don't know, honestly." He stared down at her, though his full height barely rivaled hers. "That's really up to you to figure out. It doesn't matter what I or Baron Heimlen thinks—we needed the most powerful conduit we could find, and this little beauty," he said before pulling a rhyzolm from his pocket, "led me to you. Even as hidden as you were." He winked then, tossing the stone into the air and catching it with ease before shoving it back down into his wet pants, his tall black boots dripping muddy water.

"I don't know if I'm the right one either. But, I promise I'll try. I've…fallen in love with Felgren and I don't want to see its death. The trees, the creatures that make their homes here—the essence of Felgren feels like—like my home now." She huffed and shook her head. "It's like—like thinking you knew what nurtured your soul until you find the real thing, you know? Like waking up from a disappointing dream, to discover you're safe and sound in your own bed." She laughed, pulling her bronzed hair out of her face and to one side. "Does that make any sense?"

Realizing she had taken a few steps without him, she looked back only to see that same look she could not place pronounced on his face. It was the one from their first breakfast together, the one he gave her on the stairs of Viridis before she was taken to the Blight. She narrowed her eyes in confusion and cocked her head to the side, biting her lower lip, wondering what he was thinking.

"Can I—" He hesitated, rubbing the back of his neck with his free hand. "I'd like to show you something. If you want, I mean. But I'd have to show you at night—it only happens then."

She raised one eyebrow and looked at him, a half smile on her face, her green eyes alight in humor. "Oh, really? I don't think it *has* to happen at night. Some just prefer it that way." She winked back at him hardly containing the laughter in her chest at the sight of his embarrassment, evident in his red cheeks and shake of his head.

"No, I mean—I think you'd see Felgren in a different way. I just—"

"Yes. I'll come see it, whatever it is. Thank you." She found herself in front of him and touched his arm briefly. "I'm sorry, I just couldn't help myself. You set yourself up for that one."

He paused, swallowing hard. "Yeah, I think I did. The lumen den is down this path." He pointed to the right at the fork in the forest.

Ash nodded, turning to leave, unsure if she really wanted to.

"And Ash," he called to her as she walked away. "I'll pick you up around ten—if you're not asleep by then."

"Don't worry," she called back to him. "I won't be."

CHAPTER 15
ASH

"So you're telling me, you witnessed Baron Revich, dripping wet—"

"And *shirtless*—"

"*And shirtless*, and you say to him—and I quote, '*So you like to fish?*'" Figuerah laid back roaring with laughter, Clairannia dipping her head onto her shoulder in conspiring mirth, the scene playing out on their lips sounding ridiculous, even more so to Ash.

"I think I would have *died* seeing that," Clairannia spoke first.

"I would have paid a good sum of *money* to see that!"

Ash rolled her eyes, cheeks red as ever. "It wasn't like that! Well, maybe it was exactly like that, but I just didn't know what to say! And I *always* know what to say!"

"I get it. You just didn't know what to say around *him*," Figuerah added pulling up a yellow blossom and twirling it between her fingers.

"I have no problem speaking to him usually. In fact, I've even gone out of my way to be rude, but," she shook her head, placing her hands over her face and mumbled, "I don't know what came over me."

Figuerah raised an eyebrow.

"Okay, I know exactly what came over me, but this is crazy, right? Tell me this is crazy."

"Well," Clairannia's voice flew high. "It kind of sounds like Baron Revich has singled out a channeler…just like Baron Heimlen singled out Sylva."

The girls burst into laughter and giggles, their lumens perking up at the noise. They had gone to the golden field again, resting in the afternoon sunlight, a breeze coursing through the buttercups, playing gently with the loose strands of their hair.

"It's not *like* that. It really is not. I mean, he's handsome and… you know…"

"Incredibly attractive, sexy, a steamy pile of confidence who just happens to be really powerful and well-toned? Are those the words you're looking for, Ash, because I will happily give them to you." Figuerah's grin was contagious and Ash tried to hide hers, leaning back to feel the sunshine, refusing to admit her friend was absolutely correct.

"I swear, Ash, if you do not go with him tonight, I will mope for *days*. Don't you want to? Aren't you the least bit curious?" Clairannia tugged on her skirts, putting her knees up to her chin.

"I do want to go. I…I've been tired, training with Baron Heimlen, but I've also been wanting to see Felgren at night, and not just from the little window in our rooms. It just so *happens* that the 'Oh, So Good-Looking' Baron Revich has offered to take me. Purely a coincidence."

"Three cinnamon buns says they kiss." Figuerah held her hand out to Clairannia to shake on the deal.

"Alright, you're on. I don't think they're ready. I think they'll get there, but—just look at her. She's all resistance to what *we* can clearly see and have for a while now—at least from him." Clairannia took her hand and the two grinned at Ash as she shook her head and placed her arm over her eyes.

She would *not* be kissing anyone.

"Better start hoarding those cinnamon buns now, Figuerah."

"We'll see, Ash. We'll see."

~

Sitting on her bed, the full moon brilliant in the night sky, Ash stifled a yawn. She looked to her pillow and blankets with a yearning to fall back into them and ignore the Baron's soft knock. Maybe he could pick a different night, and maybe she should tell him that.

He leaned against her doorframe, one hand in his pocket, the epitome of what she would call handsome, sexy, and a steamy pile of confidence. She immediately swallowed any thoughts of dismissing him.

A smile raced across his face, his eyes darting across the open neckline of her shirt that exposed her neck and collar bones. "Ready?"

"Yes. Let's go." She shrugged off her exhaustion, curiosity getting the better of her once again. Maybe she could skip breakfast tomorrow and get some extra sleep. Though being hungry would likely cause her to perform even worse for Baron Heimlen.

She tugged on her long, green cloak, the one given to each of the channelers to stay warm when winter eventually came. It was the color of an evergreen, and in the darkness of the Fortress, she might have mistaken it for the deepest of black.

He led her down the never-ending staircase, a few sconces lighting their way, and out through the kitchens, still warm from dinner.

"So, where are we going?" She tugged her cloak tighter around her shoulders.

The glow of the moon, full and massive in the night sky, illuminated the forest in a sort of midday mimicry, the path before them adorned in a silvery hue.

"It's not so much about *where* we're going as it is what we'll see when we get there."

She nodded, stifling yet another yawn with the back of her hand.

He stopped. "Are you sure you want to come? You seem so tired—we can wait for another night if you'd rather go back to bed."

Concern lit half of his face in the pale glow and his features were clear, more pronounced. His hair was down, gentle waves pulled to one side and tucked behind his ear.

"No, no, I'm okay. I think I'll be perpetually tired from this point on until we can cure the Blight."

"I can talk to Baron Heimlen, if you want. I know he's been pushing you pretty hard, but if he does that, it's because he really believes in you." He nodded to a less-trodden path. "This way."

They continued their moon-lit journey in relative silence, Baron Revich glancing back at her often, giving her an encouraging smile each time.

Dammit.

He was incredibly distracting while she tried to enjoy walking in the forest under the moon. She tried to focus on the beauty of the silver leaves, the sound of crickets and frogs singing to their mates, but her eyes continuously darted back to him. Why was he bringing her out here? What were his intentions? And why did she study him so closely as she followed in his footsteps, not caring as much as she should about the first two questions?

Clairannia had mentioned he was obviously interested in her, but she hadn't really seen it—had she been so blind?

A stone of guilt sat at the bottom of her stomach as she thought about how rude she had been on several occasions, even though he had never been anything but kind to her.

No wonder the Queen had told her not to set her heart on anyone other than herself. She must have known exactly what it was like—the distractions attraction held. Ash had been physically attracted to Geyrand, yes, but this—what she felt watching Baron Revich expertly navigating Felgren as if he were privy to its nightly secrets—this was something new.

And it was exciting.

Ash scoffed aloud at herself. How shallow she was, having been determined to hate *both* Barons upon her arrival, and now, here she was, training with the one who took her, and following the one who found her, dutifully walking behind him into the depths of the shadowy forest. The glow of the moon gracefully highlighted the sharpness of his jaw and the cupid's bow of his lips when he turned to check on her progress through the underbrush.

Get a grip, Ash.

"Sorry, did you say something?" Baron Revich stopped and turned back to her again.

"Oh, no, I was just…"—she gulped—"thinking."

"We're almost there, I promise. I won't keep you up too late."

The absolute treachery of her thoughts at such a comment caused her to shake her head in disbelief as scenes she knew well flashed in her mind, indecent and salacious. She had to shove her hands in her pockets in an effort to put her budding energy *somewhere.*

Thankful he couldn't see her flushed face on the dimly lit path, they kept moving through the brush before coming to a copse of trees she had never seen before.

"Where are we?"

"We are at the southern end of the Fortress. You don't have reason to go here, so I'm not surprised you haven't yet." He walked closer to the circle of trees which were arranged oddly, as if in a pattern and not by random design. He unrolled a worn blanket from his cloak and laid it flat on the tall grass, sitting down and patting the space beside him.

"You had that in your cloak the whole time?" she asked, sitting on the blanket but keeping her distance all the same. "How did you fit it in there?"

"Oh, sure, I can fit all kinds of large things in here, though I doubt you're interested in seeing all of them." He winked at her, charming as ever and laughed.

"I set myself up for that one, didn't I?"

"It's payback, what can I say?"

"What are we doing here? Are we waiting for something?" Ash changed the subject quickly, not trusting herself ever again around this man.

"Yes, but not until midnight. We have some time still to wait."

"Why did we leave so early then? It took just a little more than an hour to get here." Ash folded her legs and adjusted her skirts, pulling her cloak tighter around herself, gazing out at the grove of trees.

The shape of how they grew was odd, and if she could fly above their tops, she was sure she'd see a spiral, winding around to a point in the middle. They were growing in a sort of bowl in the clearing, the edges of which were slanting downward and covered in tall grass like the place they sat together now.

"Honestly, Ash, I wasn't sure how steady you would be in the forest off the beaten path." He turned to her, leaning back on his hands, legs splayed out in front of him. "I know you come from the biggest city on the isle and probably haven't spent as much time navigating thicker underbrush. Also, you got lost today, so I figured we might need extra time." He grinned sheepishly at her.

Flushed and ready to defend her trekking skills, she laughed instead.

She let herself laugh.

He had the forethought to add time to their late night outing just to ease her journey of it. Of course, he was wrong. She had spent much of her childhood with the Prince outside of the city walls, getting lost in the grassy hills and running along the sandy shores, climbing the great rocks there, toning her body, growing strong and lithe.

"That was kind of you. It's not necessary to have concern for me out in the wilderness, but I can see why you would. I spent many days of my childhood outside of Hyrithia's walls, getting into all sorts of trouble and also finding my way out of it."

He paused before admitting, "You're not like…like I thought you would be." He furrowed his brows and turned his body toward hers, laying on his side and holding his head up on his hand.

"Oh? And is that a shame?" Ash grinned wickedly down at him, turning her body toward his.

"Just the opposite, actually. I'm more relieved that I was wrong. I worried, after you came here, that having lived with royalty your whole life, you might be entitled, rude, and selfish— unwilling to get your hands dirty and do what we brought you here to do."

Ash smiled genuinely, understanding the assumptions people had about royalty.

"Well," he added, "I guess you were a little rude to me, but that's understandable considering what you were forced into."

Her heart hammered in her chest. His validation of her resistance in coming here was one she had only given herself.

No one had yet given it to her.

She sensed the dull pang of longing for home creep into her thoughts. Again she worried she had betrayed her past in accepting her future. How could she leave the one place she was loved and needed, only to find herself happy in another?

Because she *was* happy here.

She knew it, no matter how often she struggled to admit the words in her own mind. She had decided to stay. And staying meant leaving her past in Hyrithia behind. That was something she was not sure she could yet do. She gazed into the night for some time, their silence easy to adjust to.

"What are you thinking about? You go somewhere else when you're thinking hard." He pulled at a loose thread on the blanket.

"Do I? I guess it feels like that sometimes." She sighed and laid herself down, mirroring his propped hand. "I'm sorry. I…this…" She exhaled sharply and laid on her stomach, holding her hands over her face, debating whether to express her internal conflicts aloud. "It's not easy. I guess that's obvious. I loved my life in Hyrithia. I had a place I belonged, and knowing I was one of the lucky orphans only made me appreciate it more. My mother is dead. My father is likely too, and I could have been tossed into the orphanage, but the Queen took me in as her ward and I will forever be grateful for that. She raised me alongside her son and I got to live a comfortable life." She shook her head. "But I feel so *different* in Felgren. This place…it just has a hold on my heart. Like the piece of me I never knew was here the whole time. And now, I cannot imagine living without it." She laughed and peeked out from her hands. "Does that make any sense at all?"

"Yes." His voice was raspy and he swallowed hard, nodding in assurance of himself or her, she couldn't tell.

"What about you? Care to share any of your own inner turmoil under the moon near midnight?"

His gaze on her was brilliant in the soft glow, and he stared at her that way for some moments. "I'm not sure you'd be interested in my inner turmoil, but I do understand how you feel about Felgren. I experienced something similar when I arrived. It was a sort of calm I had never known until then. I'm so grateful to Baron Heimlen for choosing me. For bringing me to this place and acting as my mentor, giving me the opportunity to be Baron." He sighed heavily and laid back, rubbing his face. "It's a lot. The pressure of becoming a Baron is more draining than I expected. But I know I can be a good one. There's so much *more* I want to do. We can train more channelers, help more people. We can work with the Queen of Hyrithia, the Lady of the Spire, and the Madame of the Mountains. A part of Felgren is sick, but we can cure that. We can make it stronger than ever." He smiled up at her then. "All three of us can."

She nodded, enchanted by his words, his smile, his kindness—all of it. She moved her hand forward to brush a dark wave from his eyes and hesitated. Frightened of her own feelings, she quickly took her hand back, unsure if she should touch him, unable to tell with certainty that he was feeling the same.

He caught her hand before she could tuck it under her, determined to sit on it the rest of the night.

"Look." He sat up, pulling her with him, and she struggled not to focus on her body's welcome to his touch. He entwined his fingers with hers as a glowing ball of light floated lazily toward them. It was lit low, like the dying flame of a candle burned too long as it fluttered onto their clasped hands.

When her eyes adjusted, she saw a glowing white moth, the size of her palm, its fuzzy head searching their hands for a taste of something sweet. Ash smiled brightly in an intake of breath.

"It's a nitor moth. It means 'glow' in the language of magic. See how its tiny scales are illuminated? Each one acts," he murmured, raising his other hand to brush her hair from her lips, "as a conduit of light."

The moth flew from their hands, and Ash watched in glee as it illuminated the world around it, heading for the copse of trees.

He cupped her chin, his hand warm and caressing as he silently turned her face to look behind them.

She gasped at the sea of illuminated wings fluttering gently in the night air, low to the ground and passing their blanket in a languid daze, silent over the tall grass. Her eyes followed the swarm of light as the hundreds of moths joined together and began their dance around the spiral of trees, flying in purposeful patterns up and down the branches, synchronized in their efforts.

"They're so beautiful," she spoke under her breath.

"It gets better," Baron Revich replied softly, close to her, their hands still entwined.

A flicker of blue, hazy light which began on one tree, soon turned into thousands of twinkling blossoms blooming from each branch. The nitor moths then settled in their performance and began to drink heavily, the entire copse of trees alight like the moon itself—her glow a mirror to the one before them.

"The nitor trees only bloom after the moths ask them. And the nitor moths only travel on nights of the full moon. That's why I wanted to show you tonight. I don't know that I'm patient enough to wait another few weeks." His smile was drawn to one side.

Ash shook her head. "I'm glad you didn't wait. I don't ever plan to miss this again." She turned back to the captivating glow before them, her green eyes alight with more appreciation for Felgren and the magic it held for all of its creatures.

"Ash…" he broke the silence with a breathless whisper, "can I…"

His face was close to hers, too close to imply anything other than what she had been longing to do for hours now.

"Kiss me? Why, Baron Revich, I thought you'd never ask." She grinned, her lips lingering above his own, all sense of caution gone as she leaned closer to his warm body.

"It's Rev," he whispered, mumbling the rest on her open mouth, "just Rev."

Their lips joined, their embrace natural and fitting, the weight of her worries slipping away one by one with each caress of his mouth.

She pulled away slightly, their breathing matched in rapidity. As her thumb lightly stroked his cheek, she whispered, "Do you know the cook well? I need her to bake some additional cinnamon buns in the morning."

Confusion lit his face and Ash laughed, head back in reverie at the sight of it, the sound of her joy light upon the breeze as Revich groaned, grabbed her waist and pulled her underneath him, the late hour long forgotten, as two hearts pounded to the same rhythm.

CHAPTER 16
ASH

"That's your fifth yawn this morning, Ash'Arah." Baron Heimlen's tone reeked of rebuke. "I told you to get some rest. You apparently did not."

Ash sat on her knees, both hands flat on the ground. The exercise the Baron had introduced this morning was about attempting to take magic directly from Felgren's forest floor. It was working, but it would have worked better if she'd had the energy to really concentrate on the task.

She pushed her fingertips further into the damp earth, calling silently to the power radiating through the soil. A prickle of magic met her fingertips in a calm greeting, lazily climbing over her fingers, across her conduit ring, and up her arms. But the tendrils of power were thin, often broken—only a shadow of what she knew she could request from the forest if her exhaustion had not weighed her down.

Ash and Rev had kissed under the moon until their lips were red and puffy, holding onto one another, whispering in the dark until they fell asleep, wrapped in their warm cloaks and wool blanket in the glow of the nitor trees.

As dawn broke, Revich woke her, and hand in hand, they

arrived back at the Fortress. Ash stumbled up to her room for another hour of rest, running into an observant Sylva with a sly look in her eyes before tumbling into bed. She had skipped breakfast and knew she'd never hear the end of it from Figuerah and Clairannia when they made the connection of why.

Baron Heimlen sighed heavily for what must have been the tenth time. "What ails you, my dear?" He lifted her chin with a gloved hand and smiled faintly, though it failed to meet his black eyes which were filled with irritation.

Ash could make an entire list of things that ailed her. Hyrithia, the Queen, the Prince, Geyrand, Revich, her role here and the pressure of what she *must* do.

Really, she thought, *what doesn't ail me?*

She looked up to Baron Heimlen, wondering how much of her troubles she could really tell him. Her entire life she had lived without a single soul she could express her deepest thoughts to—the ones that made her question who she was and the extent of her shadows. For how could a soul be understood when it was not your own? How could anyone ever comprehend the words her soul would speak when it was a language only she seemed able to understand?

Not for the first or last time, Ash blew air out of her lips, resigning to the choice of speaking little about her woes instead of speaking the truth of them.

"I am sorry, Baron. Would—would it be alright if…if I spent the day in Viridis?" She bit the bottom corner of her lip, waiting for the reply that didn't come. "I haven't been in days, and I promise to spend my time there in the Origins of Felgren Hall like you've asked. Please, I-I just need a day to my own thoughts, and then I promise to be ready tomorrow." She could hear the pleading in her voice, unsure if he would acknowledge it.

He stared at her in an uncomfortable silence before replying, "You may have your day, Ash'Arah. But first, you will again witness the Blight." He stood and held his black glove out to her, which she took and nodded. "You will be reminded of your *reason* for coming to Felgren, your *reason* for leaving Hyrithia, and your *reason* for your gift of magic. If anything ails you, it should be that you are not doing all you can to stop the Blight."

There it was—the reprimand that stings.

She winced inwardly, the tone of disappointment thick on his tongue with the words of a father-figure finding his daughter to be less than what he believed she could be.

Ash felt immense guilt and uncomfortable with her decisions as they rode silently on lumens to the edge of the Blight—closer to the Fortress than she would like. She had thought of Baron Heimlen as an all-powerful force, the strongest living man on the isle, but she had seen it herself, and Rev had confirmed it—he was aging rapidly. And there she had been, out frolicking with his successor in the moonlight instead of taking her role here to heart and preparing for the day's training.

She felt low, chiding herself the entire way to the Blight, determined to take the day as her own. No distractions, no wandering mind. She would study history, eat heartily, and fall asleep early.

The Blight loomed before them, and she could sense the apprehension in her lumen's gait as he slowed his pace. She rubbed his ears in encouragement.

"Walk into the Blight, Ash'Arah. Take it in."

Baron Heimlen, still mounted on his lumen, nodded to her as she slowly dismounted from hers. She didn't want to be here, but knew it was the price for her choices. She walked to the line in the forest, clearly drawn between life and death. It looked so out of place, especially here, on the edge of endless green compared to the pure dark of it through the door in Viridis.

"Step inside, Ash'Arah." His command was taut, his patience with her running thin.

Warily, she took a step into the mass of black forest floor, rotted fallen trees, and even more corpses of varying sizes that littered the soil as unearthly adornments. The stench of decay was so overpowering, she again had to cover her nose and mouth to reduce the need to retch.

The thick, black vines that spewed from the dead earth wound their way up the trees with small, vein-like ribbons of black almost pulsating as they smothered the life of each one. She bent down, forcing herself to touch one of the Blight's vines, solely to remind herself of her task, her purpose in coming here.

Thump. Thump.

She tore her hand away and stood in shock.

A heartbeat? Had she imagined it?

She turned her head back to the Baron, questions on her lips.

"You see, my dear. It must be destroyed. This"—he gestured to the consuming dark around them—"must be stopped. If the Blight takes Felgren, where do you think it will go next? The Hallow Marshes? Hyrithia? Without us to stop it, it will consume the isle until there is nothing left to consume."

But the heartbeat. Did he not know?

She took a breath and reached down once more. The beat was steady, just as her heart had been a few moments before. The pulse spread through the vine, telling her what she did not wish to ever admit.

"Do…do you know it's alive? I can feel a pulse, a thrumming—like a heartbeat."

The Baron dismounted and walked briskly to her side, a slight limp in his left leg. He bent down to the same vine she had touched and placed a gloved hand across its thorny surface. He watched her face, eyes narrowing in confusion or revelation, she couldn't tell.

"I must continue my research." He rose quickly and with a newly found gait that showed no signs of illness. He threw a leg over his lumen and turned the beast to leave Ash where she stood in the decay.

"Take your day. I expect to hear of your studies tomorrow morning where you will be rested and fed. No more excuses, no more delay, Ash'Arah. Your time to serve your purpose here is coming fast, whether you acknowledge it or not. And you *must* be trained before then. When the season of autumn descends upon us, we will have no choice but to fight the Blight. If it spreads any further beyond that time, it will be too dense to stop. Winter is its time to flourish when Felgren sleeps and cannot continue its battle against the suffocation." He gave a command to his lumen and she lunged forward in haste back to her den.

Ash watched as Baron Heimlen left her there, standing amidst the poison which was killing Felgren, and which would kill everything on the isle if she couldn't help stop it. She shook her head in disbelief at her discovery. The Blight was not only alive, but somewhere it had a heart that could possibly be destroyed.

"THE STRANGEST THING HAPPENED THIS MORNING, ASH."

As if waiting in roguish attack, Clairannia and Figuerah were lingering in the entrance to Viridis, practicing their magic by tossing a cinnamon bun in the air and the other using her magic to catch it.

Flashes of brilliant red sparked from Clairannia's hands while Figuerah's was a luminous gold light, illuminating the dark stairwell before the doors of Viridis. Their colored magic matched the stones of their conduit rings.

"There we were," Figuerah said with a grin of playful mischief, "happily eating breakfast like good channelers do, when who do you think bursts into the dining hall—"

"*Whistling*," Clairannia added.

"Yes, *whistling*, with three fresh cinnamon buns on a plate just for Clairannia and me?"

"I don't care if it was the Blightress herself, please just tell me you kept that one," Ash growled, pointing to the cinnamon bun flying through the air, held tight in a crimson orb, "for me."

"We did, of course, Ash. But..."—Clairannia brought the bun to the plate resting on the stairs—"you only get to eat it *after* you tell us what happened last night. Because we don't think Baron Revich was just being nice."

"How did you even know I'd be here? This seems like an ambush," Ash muffled in reply, ignoring Clairannia's demands and stuffing the dripping iced bun into her mouth, her stomach rumbling at its first food for the day.

"We saw Baron Heimlen storm into the Fortress just as we were leaving for Viridis. He headed straight to his study, and we figured you'd probably head here." Figuerah shrugged. "Well, I say probably because for all we knew, you'd be out in Felgren somewhere with the *other* Baron."

"Baron Heimlen has a study?" Ash asked, licking her fingers.

"Oh, yes, he has one about halfway up the winding staircase, it's a big black—of course it's black—door with an emerald knob. I've seen him go—"

"*Clairannia*. C'mon, girl, let's focus." Figuerah turned back to Ash. "So…what happened?" She sat next to Ash on the black staircase with a golden orb of light above her palm to keep the corridor illuminated.

"Okay. I'll tell you. But don't expect detailed, descriptive narratives from here on out. I can't believe he brought you cinnamon buns." She laughed, the sound echoing in the dark hall. "I did tell him about your bet, but that was actually *later*." She paused for effect. "*After* we had kissed. A lot. We kissed a lot." She absently rubbed her slightly swollen lips.

Clairannia and Figuerah erupted in giggles, their excitement contagious as a brilliant grin lit Ash's face.

"Was it good kissing? I mean, it must have been if it was *a lot*." Figuerah leaned into Ash's space, searching for more information.

"Yes. It was good. Really, *really* good kissing. I think I'll do it again."

Clairannia sighed next to her. "I can't wait to hear where the rest of this story goes. Maybe you'll end up like Sylva, so romantically entranced with Baron Revich choosing you over any other channeler. Or maybe you'll become companions. Oh, that would be *perfect*."

"What? We're not going to become *companions*. Barons don't have companions anyway. You don't need to predict our future, Clairannia, it was just some kissing."

"Under the *moonlight*."

"With a *Baron*."

Ash stood and brushed the crumbs off her skirts, her mind racing to change the subject. Companions were common on the isle, but she didn't know of any in Felgren. She knew the Prince planned to seek one this very year, but she had never given one much thought. A companion, after all, would mean she would have to bind herself to another life, pledging to never break that bond without considerable purpose. And companions often created life together.

She rubbed at the small *liberum* mark on her left wrist, given to her by a medicus conduit after her first bleeding. She was again thankful for the mark, ensuring no children would come from any of her passions with any man. She knew Revich had one, too.

This was all too much to process in her exhaustion, in her fear of the Blight and its unnatural heartbeat, and she found herself standing before the doors to Viridis ready to step inside and spend her day there among the courtyard and books she loved.

"Are you alright, Ash?" Clairannia stepped up behind her touching her arm gently. "We're sorry. We don't mean to tease you too much. It's just possibly one of the more exciting things that's happened to us here so far." She hugged Ash's shoulders, squeezing slightly. "We promise to leave you be in Viridis. Sure, Baron Revich gave us cinnamon rolls, but there's no stopping him. We have a page-long list of books to study today about the Treaty and process of Offerings." She stuck out her tongue but smiled at Ash. "Go on, we'll see you at lunchtime."

Ash could hear Figuerah stand and stretch behind her as she added, "Sorry, love, we really didn't mean to embarrass you. Okay, well, we did, but just in a bit of our own fun." She placed a hand on Ash's back and rubbed it gently—both comforts from her friends warming her heart.

"That's not why I'm still standing here." Ash turned around, hands trembling slightly, shoved in her pockets. It was time to tell them.

"What's wrong? Why aren't you going in?" Clairannia's eyes, the color of the bark of a maple tree, were furrowed and she cocked her head to one side.

"I can't get into Viridis like you. My name doesn't work."

"What do you mean your *name* doesn't work? That's how anyone gets into Viridis. How did you do it before?" Figuerah had her hands on her hips, disbelief on her face.

"I tell the doors I don't know my name because I've never had one that fits." Ash shrugged as if the truth of that statement was coming carefree from her lips instead of loaded with a history of questioning herself and her role in this world since childhood.

An audible scoff came from Clairannia as Figuerah raised one eyebrow high onto her forehead.

"Ash,"—she shook her head and sighed—"you're all kinds of mess, aren't you?"

She nodded, laughing lightly at the perfect truth of it.

"Well," Figuerah added, taking in a deep breath and turning Ash's body around toward the doors, "maybe you should disregard Baron Heimlen's tasks for the day and go find yourself a new one."

CHAPTER 17

ASH

The scent of roses hung heavily in the air as Ash admired a particular white bunch of them growing steadfastly out of a section of books on a very particular subject.

The First Days of Felgren, Felgren Forest: Origin Myths, and one thick one in particular, *Legends of the Blightress: A Collection of Tales Passed Down Through Centuries.*

In true form, Ash first gave her attention to the roses, clumped together as if in competition to see which could meet her nose first. She touched their petals lightly, admiring the soft silkiness of each one and inhaled their scent, eyes closed as if in the presence of that which healed her soul.

She had found from her time in Viridis, that the more she appreciated its offerings, the more at peace she felt. She also noticed that she found the books she was looking for much easier after stopping to admire its beauty.

Smiling, humming, she placed her attention back on her work. Baron Heimlen had tasked her with Felgren origin study. Figuerah and Clairannia had already looked through these books, but were quickly ushered to move on to other histories of the isle.

Furrowing her brow, she turned her head to the side to read

each spine in order, tucking the chestnut strands of wayward bits of hair back into the plait that wound just at the top of her head, the rest of it spilling out among her shoulders. She absentmindedly unbuttoned the top of her cream linen shirt—just to a hint of her breasts, her body radiating a familiar heat since the night before. She'd skipped the traditional channeler vest this morning, opting for comfort over style.

She'd been reading all morning, and she struggled to keep her mind on the task given to her. Concentration was not her strong suit today with her thoughts reeling over her night with Rev. She had no opportunity yet to process them, and things were moving so quickly, she felt she was tumbling down a hole, unable to grab the sides and stop herself from falling.

She felt so young, pining after the heir of Felgren. He was the most obviously handsome man here, who not only was to take the reins of Baron, but had discovered her existence and apparent talent in conduit magic. Which, according to Baron Heimlen, was essential for saving Felgren and the entire isle.

What was she *doing*?

She let her mind race as she traced the depressed imprint of each title. There was no concentrating on her task until she had faced her thoughts and let the stream of them out of her consciousness, like a floodgate no longer able to restrain what rumbled behind it.

Her inner monologue would *not* be subdued.

Revich was a Baron. She started with that. Almost revoltingly charming, a smile that might as well be a plague considering how it seemed to spread to whomever witnessed it. Well built, but not obnoxiously so, he had obviously worked hard in physical labor during his adolescent years.

And his eyes. She groaned aloud and rubbed the space between her own. His eyes constantly reminded her of home. The deep blues of the unabating sea she had walked countless times—just miles from the towers of Hyrithia.

It was strange to see—Baron Heimlen's eyes were typically fully black except for the outer white. No iris could be distinguished most of the time, but she swore she had seen lighter hints of gray on occasion, and she wondered then if all Barons' eyes could change color.

She knew, of course, that Barons had almost fully black eyes, but she was not expecting Rev's. They were most often the deep hue of a dusk sky on the brink of utter darkness. His brows rested black and straight across his forehead and the length of his nose was just right, before giving way to a full set of lips that always curved up slightly in a never-ending smirk.

Ash shook her head in disbelief. The amount of detail she had somewhere hoarded in the recesses of her mind was absurd. But she wasn't done yet as she recalled the waves of his black hair, set at his shoulders, just long enough to pull back into a colorful ribbon. She thought of how she had run her fingers through it the night before and her lower belly ached in a demand she knew well enough.

Most confusing was his interest in her. She had been rude. She had been short, unwilling to give way to a friendship or a relationship of any sort for most of her time here. Yet he desired her? Why?

She mostly understood her attraction to him, yes, but what did he see in her? She knew she was pretty. She had been told so on enough occasions to ascertain that her strong physique and bright green eyes were desirable.

But again, she had been unkind. Ungrateful, unwilling to accept her fate, distrusting—all of it. And rightfully so, she reminded herself. But as her time in Felgren grew longer, and with her introduction to Viridis, her heart had softened along with her determination to leave.

Had he noticed? Had he admired her for it? Forgiven her for her initial behavior toward him? She wasn't sure if she deserved it.

It wasn't the physical attraction that confused her. That she understood perfectly well, and had experienced it fully with Geyrand. But she couldn't help but notice something was different here. And her mind screamed it throughout her thoughts, her efforts to silence such revelations useless now that she had acted on her attraction.

She felt helpless and foolish. The Queen had warned her time and again about keeping her distance from Geyrand. She was well aware, of course, of their affair, as any mother would realize, but how many times had she been told by the Queen, *"Satisfy your desires, but keep your heart to yourself. You are its sole protector."*

Ash had never really stopped to wonder why the Queen was so adamant on her never falling for Geyrand. But she wondered about it now, in the pangs of lust for Revich, her consciousness finally admitting to something deeper than the desires of flesh. A spark that flickered to life recently, whose origins she understood, but whose purpose she did not yet know.

"What is it you're looking for, Ash?"

The voice of the man whom she had just spent an unknowable amount of time thinking about startled her in her incognizant state. She jolted slightly, always easy to frighten, and she turned her head toward him.

Dammit.

She was going to get nothing done if he continued to look at her like that, arms crossed at his chest, sans cloak this time, his black vest striking and coordinated with his dark hair, flowing gracefully aside his face as if he was some marble statue—sole purpose to be admired for its beauty.

Turning back to the books before her, she inhaled sharply, trying desperately to vanquish the rising tides of devotion to this man, two sides of her warring just at his presence, and she was mortified at such admittance.

Settling herself was not easy, but her will won out. She replied in casual flirtation, "I seek a man." She glanced at him alluringly, eyebrows raised in question, a one-sided smirk on her face. "A tall one. But not too tall."

The easiest way out of the truth of her feelings was always the pretense, forever the feigning of confidence in who she was and what she was doing.

"And handsome?" he questioned, sliding his hands into his pockets, stepping away from the marble pillar, taking a few strides toward her, his eyes never leaving her face.

"Oh, yes." She turned back to the shelved books, pulling one out, her heart throbbing in excitement as he neared, her head not able to even comprehend the title. "*Very* handsome."

"And strong? Charming?"

As if he had read her thoughts just moments before, Revich neared her side, his body radiating heat, and Ash swore she witnessed the white roses bloom fuller at his presence.

"Mmhm." She didn't trust her treacherous self to speak. As she swallowed the lump in her throat, opening her mouth to exhale silently, her body protested at still being turned toward the bookcase. She hadn't asked for this when she came to Felgren—hadn't expected it even—but she wanted it.

Badly.

His voice rumbled wickedly, full of honey, smooth and thick, "What about funny and kind? Those traits are important, too, you know." He leaned into her neck, pulling her hair from her shoulder, his lips brushing her skin as a chill ran through her entire body.

She laughed softly and closed her eyes, exposing more of her throat for him to continue his soft trek across it, feeling herself start to fade into the rapture of his touch. She fumbled to make room somewhere on the shelf for the book she had taken and it disappeared instantly, returning to its proper place a few spaces down.

"I do know," she whispered, turning then to meet his mouth with hers, all sense of hesitation long gone as he pulled her head closer to him, leaning gently on her lower half, pushing her waist into the bookcase. She maneuvered one leg out from her skirts and wrapped it partially around him, the invitation to come nearer unspoken but heavy in the air.

His kiss was full of passion, his tongue exploring hers in awe and worship, and she felt as if they were there again beneath the moon in the glow of the nitor trees.

She returned his enthusiasm, pulling him closer, the upper half of her body plunging into the books behind her as her lower half pressed into his.

Ash pulled her head back, desperate for air to fill her panting lungs, desperate to regain control of her mind that was slipping into a place where she could not return to rational thought without a release.

He didn't hesitate, his mouth seeking her neck once again, and she could tell he was slipping, too. She laughed lightly in her gasp of pleasure, seeking control of the very part of her which knew not the definition and uttered sweetly, "If you find him, let me know."

Snickering, he held his head against her neck, his breath hot against her skin, placing one last kiss there before pulling back to look at her. "Oh, Ash, what am I going to do with you."

It was a statement, no implication of question as he held her face, brushing her bottom lip with his thumb.

She kissed it, most of her wishing he hadn't stopped, and whispered, "I can think of a few things."

He cleared his throat, hands unwilling to leave her face. "Believe it or not, I came to find you for a different purpose."

"What a shame, Rev."

He let out a breath, low and harsh from his lips, shaking his head and entwining his hand in hers. He pulled her out from the indent of books they had made on the shelf which righted themselves immediately.

"Come. Clairannia and Figuerah are waiting for you in the courtyard. Sylva has brought lunch."

"Will you be joining us, then?" She walked with him, swinging their embraced hands against her skirts.

"I wouldn't even dare to." He glanced down at her eyes, then to her unbuttoned shirt, her exposed skin flushed with what had been obvious moments before.

"What a relief. I don't think I could sit through the whole thing with you staring across from me like that." She ran a hand down the top of her chest, playing with the next fastened button.

He raked his other hand through his hair exhaling sharply again. "What are you doing *after* lunch?"

"Lumen riding most likely—with the girls."

"Do you think they'd notice if I stole you away?"

She scoffed, still holding his hand tightly in hers as they descended another staircase. "They probably noticed how long it took you to get me. I don't doubt they'd notice both of our absences. *Nothing* eludes those two. Though, I really should get back to studying instead. Baron Heimlen is not at all pleased with me, and I promised to be fresh tomorrow with a clear head and notes to tell of my time in Viridis."

"I'd prefer you leave out *that* encounter." He nodded behind them to where the white roses bloomed fully.

She laughed, tilting her head back and pressing her shoulder to his. "I think I will. But he asked me to study Felgren origins again and I've plenty more to read."

"Again? Haven't you moved on from that subject?"

"I thought so, but maybe he's not satisfied with the number of books I've read so far."

The courtyard loomed near, and it was the first time she'd felt disappointment upon seeing it. He pulled her now messier hair behind her ears and kissed her lips lightly.

"After dinner then—will you come to me?"

"I don't even know where your rooms are."

"Oh, I'd be happy to remedy *that*, Ash," he whispered in her ear and sent her spine tingling as she debated discovering his rooms right now, her growling stomach be damned.

Clearing her throat, she let go of his hand, every ounce of her revolting at the freedom of it. "Alright. I'll see you at dinner then." And she turned toward the forest of trees, beautiful in their steady stance and opposite to her current one.

She could feel his eyes on her back as she walked away, clamping her lips shut with her teeth as she turned to look at him again.

His eyes were still heavy with the desire they had just shared that was not seen to fruition. And she stilled herself to remember— remember his gaze on hers, their story together unfolding quickly, yet still unknown and untold.

CHAPTER 18
ASH

*L*egends *of the Blightress: A Collection of Tales Passed Down Through Centuries* by Layngden Roper lay open before Ash as she rested on her stomach, head held up by one hand, keeping the book open with the other. She was laying across one of the many cushioned benches in Viridis. This one was draped in a midnight blue silk, its legs a dark mahogany and carved into the claws of a hawk.

Belly full, she had explained to Clairannia and Figuerah that her lumen riding would need to wait, and her focus must continue if she was to survive Baron Heimlen's lessons in the morning.

"The entity of the Blightress outdates any other written records on the isle and has fascinated and frightened its people for centuries. The lyrics and rhymes recited in her name are filled with anger, death, and the promise that she will destroy all of which you love.

This author, dear reader, presumes that you do not believe in the bump in the night. He assumes that you have been told such tales and have grown to see them for what they truly are—lessons for children so that they may behave as their parents wish them to.

But that still leaves the question of the origins of the Blightress, who she

*may have been, and what led to her stories so dark and ominous that she is used
today to warn others of their power in their anger."*

This book in particular had caught her attention. She had
always enjoyed the slight bit of fear stories of the Blightress could
instill in her as a little girl, and she continued to wonder at their
origins. The author of the book seemed to imply that the Blightress
was a real person in Arcaynen's history, and Ash began to contemplate her story as she never had before.

She turned the page and continued reading, a warm breeze
running across her face.

*"The first of her stories that I could find in my search pre-dates the Spire,
though Hyrithia is mentioned. It is a short tale, at times difficult to decipher in
its spelling, but the sentiment on the Blightress's deeds are the same:*

*'If not ye wish to be dead out of the gates of Hyrythiah, wander not to the
north of the cytydel where She blackens all life and styls all brything from thy
chest. Her wryath consumes all after the fall of Felgryn from her arms and thy
Bayron sayved us from Her eyvil'."*

A *Baron* saved Felgren? What did she do that needed saving from
and what was this *wrath* the story, and many of the tales she had
heard as a child, spoke of? Fascinated, Ash kept reading:

*"This particular short warning of sorts was found in the depths of the
Hyrithian castle on rolled parchment among ancient records of trade from the
people who lived there at the time. Hyrithia was not yet the city it is now, having
a population of likely less than a thousand people.*

*But here, we see that the fear of the Blightress was being spread, most likely
by word of mouth, and this is the most solid piece of evidence I could find to
prove that she did once exist. This is due to its origins in time as well as its
implication of a direct warning of the Blightress's wrath, rather than a story to
frighten children. However, more questions of her origins and what exactly she
did to have Felgren Forest 'fall from her arms' adds more to the puzzle.*

*Historians of the isle are aware of the first Baron. Though spellings of his
name vary, the most common is Baron Adaynth. It is said he began the settle-*

ment of Hyrithia before traveling to the heart of Felgren to begin training future conduits, using their magic to make the isle prosperous. However, how he came into power is never mentioned in old texts and his own origins are left up to our imaginations. In my research, I have found historians who have detailed his good deeds in books, but I remind you, this book will entail only stories of the Blightress.

After my discovery of the first written mention of the Blightress, I continued my search for the reason of her wrath. The first text implies that she was a keeper of sorts of Felgren—so what caused her fall into darkness, and what lay beyond to the north of Hyrithia?"

Ash paused. Of all the stories and songs of the Blightress she knew, the origins of her anger were never mentioned. The promise that she would take you—kill you even—were always the theme of the tales if you showed the same anger that she had apparently shown centuries before.

Anger was to be suppressed. Anger was an emotion that did not belong in their society. Those were lessons instilled in children since they could comprehend language, and they were lessons taught by the way of the Blightress. What had she done? What caused such anger?

Ash was aware of the commonality in the names. The Blight and the Blightress were too similar to not have a connection. But all disease on crops and flora was called a blight. It's just that the Blight residing in Felgren was unlike anything else growing on the isle, and Ash had not bothered to connect the two until the mention of Felgren being a part of the Blightress's story. *That* was a detail never said in the rhyme and song passed down to children.

Had she caused the disease centuries ago? How could that be possible if it had not grown so full until now? If the Blight had begun with her, wouldn't it have taken over all of Felgren centuries later?

Question after question wracked her thoughts and she wondered what Baron Heimlen already knew. There must be more to the Blight that he was not telling her. Why else would he send her here, to this hallway in Viridis to study Felgren origins? And why was a book solely focused on the Blightress in this section?

> *"I would be lying, reader, to say I was not in fact faced with disappointment at my findings because there were none. In no record was there any mention of how the Blightress lived in Felgren, nor her role there. I will say, however, that I have heard of a place where these questions might be answered. It is said that within the Fortress itself, there resides a library, vast and beautiful, which contains copies of most written books on the isle. The origins of its name meaning 'green' in the magical language as it is called, Viridis. It is my deepest desire to one day walk its halls, but alas, I contain no ounce of magic in my bones, and so, will likely never see my dream come to pass.*
>
> *I have heard said from conduits themselves that books on any magical subject or history can be found there; therefore, if there was such evidence of the Blightress's role in Felgren or the cause of her rage, this humble historian would suggest it would be found within those halls."*

Viridis held evidence of the Blightress's role in Felgren? Ash rubbed her face, her mind racing. This information was all so new, and it seemed as if Baron Heimlen had a true goal in summoning her to this very section.

Did he expect her to find a connection between the stories of the Blightress and the Blight? Could there be a clue on how to destroy the disease based on these stories?

But the Blightress was dead. *If* she had lived at all. Though Ash was now beginning to think she must have been real, living centuries ago when Hyrithia was just beginning to take breath. Could she have created a disease with magic that now spread rampantly through Felgren? Again, the question of *why* rose to Ash's mind, but she pushed it aside, her task now to find more information on the Blightress's time in Felgren as well as information on this first Baron —Baron Adaynth.

She flipped through the rest of the book, looking for more than the stories and songs that she had already heard throughout her childhood, but recognizing most.

There was one rhyme, however, that the author claimed to have found high in the Attatock Mountains that she had never heard before:

> *"The following poem was spoken generation to generation, having never been written in any form. In fact, due to old superstitions, I was not allowed to write it down in front of the old crone who recited it while I spent my time in the Attatock Mountains. It was only later that I wrote it down, for any eyes to witness. Though it does not mention the Blightress directly, it is believed that it refers to her as the image of a woman and her anger are present in the piece:*
>
> *'Without anger, She laughed in mirth.*
> *Without love, She left them bleeding.*
> *Without\hope, She walks the earth.*
> *Without fear, Her heart is fleeting.'"*

Heart? The first mention of the Blightress's heart was here in this book just after Ash had discovered a pulse in the Blight. *That* could not be a coincidence. *Without fear, Her heart is fleeting.* Without fear of what?

Ash closed the book and gently placed it on the edge of the bench. She patted the top of the cover just as it disappeared—right back to the place she found it. *Good,* she thought, she would need it again.

She raced down the stairs of Viridis, questions forming in her mind as she flew, determined now to find the one person in Felgren who was most likely to know the poem—the channeler from the Attatok Mountains.

"Done studying already, Ash?"

"Perfect, you're just in time to help us brush the thistle out of the lumens."

Clairannia and Figuerah were found right where she expected them to be. Both of the channelers were grooming the massive wolves, Clairannia brushing the tail of her white beast and Figuerah too busy calling hers endearments to really be doing any of her work.

At the sight of her, her small lumen, who seemed to be the runt of the bunch, trotted to her side, nuzzling her shoulder for attention. Ash brushed her hand down his long snout, and rubbed his ears.

"Figuerah, I need to speak with you. It's about…the Blightress."

Figuerah popped her head up from snuggling in the side of her lumen and narrowed her eyes at Ash. "The Blightress? Why? I doubt I know any more of the stories than you do. Don't most of them come from Hyrithia?"

"Yes, but those aren't the ones I'm talking about. Tell me if you've heard this one:

'Without anger, She laughed in mirth.

Without love, She left them bleeding.

Without hope, She walks the earth.

Without fear, Her heart is fleeting.'"

Ash brought her eyes back down from the clear blue sky where she had been concentrating as she tried to remember each line exactly.

"How—how do you know that poem? I thought it had never been written down. Did someone tell it to you?"

"I read it. There's a book I found in Viridis containing stories and poetry all about the Blightress. The author said he was not supposed to write it down but did anyway. You've heard it then?"

"Of course, I've heard it. Every child in the Attatock Mountains has heard it. We blame her for everything, the Blightress." She paused, remembering. "It's ridiculous, actually. Any rumble in the earth, any crop that dies, any animal found to be malnourished—we blame the Blightress. And usually, that very poem is recited." She sighed and put her hands on her hips, cocking to one side. "We really need more conduits up there."

"Why do you ask, Ash? Did you discover something in your research?" Clairannia patted her lumen and walked across the path to join their conversation.

"I might have, but I'm not sure. Something strange happened today when Baron Heimlen took me to the Blight. I touched it for the first time and felt a heartbeat." Both of the young women skewed their faces into disbelief and disgust. "But this poem *mentions* a heart. What if the Blight has a heart that can be destroyed and a clue to doing so is in this poem?"

"It mentions the Blightress's heart, not that disease—"

"But what if the Blightress was real and created the Blight? What if she gave it life in Felgren and it now grows due to... due to—"

"Fear?" Clairannia piped in, biting her nails as she usually did when she was thinking hard. "The poem says, 'Without fear, Her heart is fleeting.' What if some kind of fear is powering the Blight?"

Figuerah shook her head. "That's a real stretch, Clairannia. We'd have to assume the Blightress made the Blight and even though they share a name, she was supposed to have lived almost a thousand years ago if she lived at all. Why would the Blight just now be growing in mass? There's no evidence anything like that exists on the isle anywhere else."

"I had the same question, Figuerah, but it might be worth investigating further. Do you know any more stories or poems that were handed down without being written?"

Figuerah thought for a moment, moving a pebble around on the earthen floor. "I can't think of anything right now. Again, the Blightress in our legends is similar to yours, but her anger is not as focused on. She's more blamed for anything that goes wrong in the mountains."

"And in the Spire, our tales focus on not only her anger, but her abandonment of people. We are taught as children that to be alone is to be as the Blightress, never experiencing the joy of love."

Ash furrowed her brows even further. She hadn't realized that stories of the Blightress were so different in the varying regions of the isle.

"Maybe I should go talk to Baron Heimlen about this." Ash closed her eyes and rubbed her face, all of the information she had gained in the last hour swimming in her head. "This might be worth his time now, instead of waiting until morning. And I feel like I'm struggling to keep all of my thoughts together." She peeked her eyes open above her hands. "You know, since I'm so *exhausted* from last night."

Just as she'd planned, her friends burst into laughter.

"Well, if Baron Heimlen is anywhere, he's likely in his study. I've noticed that he's there *a lot*. I know Sylva brings him food and she even brought that tincture I made for him to bring color back to his face."

"You said it's a black door with a green handle? I don't remember seeing it on the stairwell."

"It's in an alcove. Down a short hallway to the right—you can't see it just from the stairs."

Ash and Figuerah looked to Clairannia in question.

"What?" She crossed her arms. "I've explored a lot of the Fortress in my free time. I want to make sure I add enough detail of the place in my future memoir so that the readers can really picture it."

"Well, I'm glad of it, Clairannia. Thank you." Ash turned to leave, patting her lumen one last time. "I'll see you two at dinner and let you know what he says."

IT DID NOT TAKE HER LONG TO FIND THE DOOR, THOUGH HER RUSH through the foyer raised a questioning look from Pompeii. She gave him a short wave and he shrugged in her direction and went about his business.

She remembered the alcove about halfway up the staircase but hadn't seen the door. It was sunk a few feet into the black stone walls —almost like it was meant to be hidden.

The darkness of it made details difficult to observe, but the green glass knob was a brilliant contrast and caught her eye immediately.

She knocked on the door, hoping her intrusion was not going to be met with more reprimand.

There was a slight pause before Baron Heimlen's voice, gruff and low called out, "Yes? Who is it?"

"It's Ash'Arah, Baron. I-I read something in Viridis that I thought you might be interested in knowing now…instead of waiting until morning. Maybe it would help in your research?" Her voice was higher than usual and she began to wonder if disturbing him would only make more work for her.

There was silence for several seconds and Ash was about to tell him through the door that she was being silly, of course it could wait until morning, when it opened.

Before her stood Revich, his eyes twinkling in an attempt at a suppressed smile. He moved to the side, gesturing for her to come into the room.

Her heart skipped a beat seeing him there, several in fact it seemed, and she told herself to show no sign of surprise at his presence in Baron Heimlen's study. Of course he could be there. He worked closely with his mentor after all.

She glanced around the room, absorbing its detail—mostly to deliver to Clairannia later who would likely ask. A dull glow from a lantern at Baron Heimlen's desk was the only source of light. It flickered across his features as she stepped further toward him, her hands clasped tightly.

The black desk took up the majority of the space in the middle of the room, though the wall behind him was lined with shelves and what looked like a workspace. Bottles and flasks were haphazardly strewn across the shelves and large tomes lay open on top of each other along the bench behind the Baron. It was an unkempt space, which surprised her, considering that Baron Heimlen never appeared as an unkempt man.

He sat, looking pale and tired, a journal open in front of him, his quill poised above the paper. Another chair, black as ever, was facing the corner of the desk and she guessed that Revich had just come from it.

"What is it, my dear? What cannot wait until morning?" His voice was lost in its gruffness, sounding haggard and strained.

Ash glanced behind her, her mouth open, about to speak.

"You may say what you wish in the presence of Baron Revich. He is aware of the situation in its entirety."

She shut her mouth, concerned less with what Revich did and did not know, and more with how idiotic she might sound in just a moment.

"I'm sorry to disturb your..." She moved aside, careful not to touch him as the second Baron brushed past her. That infuriating smirk lifted his lips as he sat back down in his seat, propping his elbow on the desk and resting his chin on his fist. His complete attention was on her, eyes alight and taunting in the glow of the low flame. "To disturb your...research," she finished, avoiding Revich's gaze for the moment.

"It is of little consequence, child. Tell me what you have found." Baron Heimlen gently placed his quill on the desk and sat back in his chair, gloved hands folded across his lap, his dark eyes waiting for her to speak.

Ash cleared her throat. "I was reading a book in Viridis on stories of the Blightress."

"Hmm."

The sound came from Revich and as her eyes darted his way, she saw the slight nod of his head and raise of his eyebrows. She pressed her lips together in a tight squeeze, determined not to show amusement.

"The book was in the Origins of Felgren Hall and it contained mostly stories and songs I've heard before, but there was one poem I had not. I found it interesting due to...due to what I felt this morning at the Blight." She wrung her hands in the folds of her mossy green skirt, waiting for a reply.

"And would you recite this poem for us, Ash'*Arah*?"

She was going to have words for him when they were alone again. Revich's voice hung tauntingly in the air, the tease of her full name on his lips, though hopefully not observed by Baron Heimlen.

"Yes, what is this poem? I am not familiar with that book, but I know it is said that the Blightress was a real woman whose origins began in Felgren." Baron Heimlen seemed unaware of the effect his successor was having on her or assumed she was nervous around them both.

She cleared her throat and recited the poem, willing her voice not to shake or make any embarrassing noises.

"Without anger, She laughed in mirth.

Without love, She left them bleeding.

Without hope, She walks the earth.

Without fear, Her heart is fleeting."

Ash dared to look to Revich again, but the teasing nature of his expression had changed to one of confusion.

"I…thought the last line was particularly interesting. It mentions her heart and I thought—what if the Blightress created the Blight hundreds of years ago and…somehow, she gave it a heartbeat? Like…like the one I felt this morning?" Ash's face was beet red even in the dark glow of the room as she cursed herself for sounding so moronic. Speaking her theory aloud to the Barons, it *did* sound like a stretch—just as Figuerah had said.

Baron Heimlen focused his daunting gaze on her face, the silence of the room unbearable. "Baron Revich," he addressed his heir and finally captured his attention away from Ash. "You will go with Ash'Arah to the Blight. I would like your observation on what she speaks of. I expect a report back to me before dinner."

"Of course, Baron Heimlen," Revich replied and stood before her, their eyes meeting. "Shall we?" he added, his arm outstretched toward the door.

Ash turned and opened it, spilling into the dark corridor, skirts cascading around her legs as if they were escaping as well. She sighed in relief to be out of the small, dark office in front of the two most powerful men on the isle.

Revich closed the door behind him and took her sweaty hand in his, a smile about to burst into a laugh on his lips as he led her down the staircase and out of the front doors of the Fortress.

She followed his lead, jogging to keep up with his forever hurried stride.

"I think I might just die of embarrassment," she mumbled as they trekked toward the lumen den to ride to the edge of the Blight.

Not able to contain his laughter any longer, it burst loud and low from his chest as he tilted his head up to the sky and squeezed her hand in reassurance.

"Come, now, *my dear*, it wasn't that bad. Baron Heimlen is harmless once you get used to his stern manner. He can be pleasant and even humorous at times. I know you've seen maybe a glimpse of that before." He pulled her into an embrace, unyielding in his handholding prowess as he brought her knuckles to his lips, his eyes still sparkling in amusement.

She was too tired to resist such a welcoming invitation and she brought her face down into his neck, laughing at her own humiliation.

"The Baron told me what you discovered today, and I am curious to observe it myself." He brushed the hair from her face and kissed the top of her forehead. "Come, the sooner we visit the Blight, the sooner we can leave its horror and take time for ourselves before dinner."

"I'm not at all sure you're taking this as seriously as I am, *Baron Revich*."

"Oh, you are mistaken, my lady. I take it *most* seriously, for the sooner we destroy the disease, the sooner I get to train you all by myself." He winked in her direction as they met their lumens who greeted them with slobbery enthusiasm.

"Hello, handsome." Ash greeted her lumen, his coat shining after his afternoon grooming session.

"You ride *him*?" Revich patted his head, grinning.

"Yes, and who is this?" Ash rubbed the ear of a lumen she had seen but not known the name of as none of the channelers had chosen to ride her. Her coat was patterned in black across her face and back, her legs white as snow.

"This is Rauca. She is his mother."

Ash gasped in delight and gave her a kiss on the nose, which she fully returned. "How charming. She's beautiful."

"That she is." Revich mounted the massive wolf, watching Ash with a sly grin.

They rode together across the forest, Revich taking the lead, and when they arrived at the edge of the darkness, he glided easily from

Rauca's back and hurried to Ash's side, offering a hand to her as she swung her legs off of her beast.

He didn't let go as they neared the Blight, holding her hand tightly in his, his face rare in its serious demeanor as he stepped into the decay, muffling a cough at the death in the air around them.

"It was there." Ash pointed to the spot she had bent to earlier this morning. "I felt the thrumming there, on that vine."

Revich bent down on one knee, taking her with him, unwilling to let go of her as if in fear of losing her to the decay.

He reached out and placed a hand on the surface of the obsidian vine, grotesque in its mere existence, let alone the thorny protrusions that ravaged its woody surface.

He looked to her then, concern and fear crossing his eyes.

She lifted her hand to the surface as well, her heart hammering in her chest. "There, you feel it too, don't you? It's so rhythmic. Like a heart beating at a steady pace. *Thump thump, thump thump.*"

He let go of her hand then, rising quickly, shoving both of his into his pockets. Concern brushed the features of his face into a frown.

She rose after him, placing a hand on his arm. "What is it? I know it's disturbing, but—"

He didn't allow her to finish, pulling a hand from his pocket and placing it on her shoulder, speaking low in the stillness of the decay around them. "I didn't feel it, Ash. There is no heartbeat."

CHAPTER 19

ASH

"That's not funny, Rev."

"I know it's not funny."

"What do you mean you didn't feel it?"

"I didn't feel it. I felt no beat—no pulse."

"How is that possible? It's so obvious. I don't understand."

"Nor do I."

"But—try again. Really focus, push harder into the vine."

He lowered his hand again to the Blight, his face radiating concern—over her ability to sense it or his lack of ability, she was unsure. He shook his head and opened his mouth, speechless. Ash pushed her hand into his, trying to feel the thrum. It was there, clear as ever, pulsating in a steady rhythm.

"But Baron Heimlen—"

"Baron Heimlen did not say he could feel what you do. He told me this morning of your discovery, but failed to mention anything about being able to feel it as well. And I..." he trailed off and grabbed her free hand, entwining his cold fingers in hers as she stared in disbelief, "I cannot feel it, Ash."

She scoffed aloud. That was it then. She had gone mad. The

beat was so incredibly obvious that she could almost see the ripple of it as it flowed along the thorny vine, suffocating the tree it wrapped around.

"Come. Let's leave this place. I know where we can talk. Or not talk. I just…I know a place." He helped her onto her lumen, the wolves eager to leave.

They traveled through the forest as the sun sank lower in the clear sky, its promise to return unspoken in the cool dusk air. He led them to a stream trickling down an outcropping of heavy stone over which grew a massive maple tree, its roots running down the boulders like veins. The sun winked behind the leaves and caused a stained glass effect, and Ash admired the beauty of it, even with the hollowness of her stomach.

Revich led her to a rock, guiding her to sit, her mind racing with questions and feelings of complete insanity. He then scooped the clear water into his hands and splashed his face, wiping it dry in one swift swoop, hand still hanging over his mouth, his dark eyes on hers.

"I…I'm just tired today." Ash laughed with no amusement. "That's it. I'm just very, very tired."

"That's not it, Ash."

"If that's not it, then I'm disturbed. Something is wrong with me." She fell into her hands, struggling not to sob, the blood in her veins cold as she came to terms with the truth she felt was the only explanation.

"That's not it either."

She could feel his gaze and instead of wanting to run from it, she was pulled to it. She wanted to slip into his arms and hear from him that it was alright. That *she* was alright.

But she didn't. Could she trust him? Or would he run to Baron Heimlen at first chance and have her thrown out of Felgren, her magic obviously twisted and unreliable. He had given no indication she could not trust him, but the lessons she had learned about guarding yourself around others seeped in through the waves of her thoughts like ink on paper.

"What can you do, Ash?" Revich had hopped over the stream and was now bent in front of her, gently prying her hands from her tear-streaked face.

"What do you mean?"

"I mean, what makes you so powerful? What led me to find you? Show me." He rubbed a thumb over her cheek, catching a tear as it fell. "Show me what you can do."

She didn't understand the request. Show him what? In Hyrithia she was taught to use her magic for convenience, not for show. And she was never to use it in accordance with emotion, whether desired or intrusive.

It was simple for her. She could flick her wrist and cause a flower to bloom, a fruit to ripen, a bird to take flight to her hand. But she had never explored that power beyond the small tasks she performed for the Queen and the Prince, and she didn't think that was what Rev was asking for. Never had she allowed her magic to move beyond what was necessary, and never had she been asked to show the full power of it—not by anyone.

Until now.

She nodded, standing, taking his hand in hers and wiping at her nose with the other, inhaling fully, filling her lungs with the sweet, cool air. She turned them toward the towering maple tree nestled above the rocks.

An orb of green light hovered over her upturned and outstretched hand. She stared at it, her magic flowing endlessly from her fingertips.

It was so easy.

So simple.

Her magic flowed from the soles of her boots, from the whisper on the wind, from the growth of the trees that surrounded them. It radiated through her. She was its conduit, able to pull the energy and direct it to whatever she wanted.

One moment she wondered what she should try to do, the next it was happening in real time as her thoughts produced the story that unfolded.

The orb left her hand at lightning speed, splashing into the massive maple tree in an expanse of energy. The leaves swayed and absorbed her magic almost as if in an inhalation of breath.

He squeezed her hand tightly, as a whisper echoed on the wind, indistinguishable, yet a language all the same. The leaves on the tree grew darker, greener in the glow of the setting sun and its fruit was grown in mere seconds, as thousands of winged seeds flew gracefully toward them, winding around and around in a twirling dance only to fall still at their feet, in the stream, upon her outstretched hand.

"Ash...how did you..." he reached out and plucked a falling seed from the air.

"That's not the only thing I can do, Rev. And I..."—tears welled again in her eyes, threatening to spill over—"I'm afraid," she finished.

She kept her gaze steady on him as the color around them began to change. The green hue of the magic in her hand became darker, poisoned with what she would do next.

The winged seeds turned brown and decayed into the earth. The leaves of the enormous tree, having been given more life by her hand, were turning to orange, then brown, falling rapidly like glass falling from a shattered window. She watched his face as trepidation crossed it, the tree rupturing down the center of its massive trunk, splitting open wide, revealing what once was spongy wood, now rotting and dark, the boom of the break echoing among the dense forest.

"Ash, stop!" he called out, taking her face in his hands. "Stop!"

The crackle of fire was next, its flames licking their way up the branches until the once living beauty was fully alight, now a charred monstrosity.

She was a monstrosity.

She dropped her gaze, panting, holding onto him for a guide back from the recesses of her mind. Smoke filled the air, the fire no longer able to sustain itself without her.

"You see," she panted, her head pressed into his shoulder, "this is what I can do. This is why the rhyzolm led you to me. And I'm afraid. Afraid of myself. I cannot put my trust in you, Revich. I cannot put my trust in *anyone*. Imagine what I could destroy if asked by the right person. Just imagine what I am capable of. I must rely on myself solely if I am to live freely, without fear of my capability" —she gestured to the broken tree, its skeletal remains black and smoking—"of death and destruction."

CHAPTER 20

ASH

The sound of crackling wood in a fireplace met Ash's ears as she woke from her deep, dreamless sleep. She found herself in a bed fully clothed, her legs tangled in soft white sheets. A heavy blue quilt lay over her chest, warm and thicker than her thin blanket in the tallest tower of the Fortress.

This was not her room.

This was not her bed.

She sat up abruptly, dizzying in the movement. In the low light of the dying fire, she could see well enough. She was in someone's personal chambers and based on the lingering scent of the quilt and what she could remember from their last meeting, she guessed they were Revich's.

First, water. Maybe some food. Then, she could face what had happened and try to remember how she'd ended up here.

Thanking him silently, she moved toward the cup and pitcher on a small table beside her. She poured a full glass and did not stop drinking until she could feel the entirety of the cool water in her belly. She laughed to herself, thankful again, as she reached for a small plate of sliced pear and cheese beside the pitcher.

That man thought of everything.

She stilled her breath, forcing herself to close her eyes and chew, taking the moments to breathe and be mindful of each mouthful.

She couldn't help it, though. Curiosity ruled her spirit and she stood, steadier than she would have guessed, cheese in one hand, more water in the other.

Would it be rude to explore this room? She told herself she would just look around, not open any drawers or read any of the books that lay atop the table.

The room was large, the bed enormous, and the fireplace was the centerpiece. It graced one wall, almost as tall as she was, and a blue, wing-backed chair was placed across from it with a small end table by its side. She slumped down into the chair, tucking her legs underneath her, careful not to spill, the seat too inviting to avoid. She threw another log onto the fire and poked it absently with the iron prong laying against the wall.

She glanced around the room, finishing her meal and drinking more water. She had no idea what time it was, and this room, like most rooms in the Fortress, had no window. She sat still and listened for the ticking sound of a clock. She found it at his bedside table. She had missed dinner, and according to the time, she had been asleep for four hours.

His room was finely furnished with midnight-hued curtains draped across the headboard of his four-poster bed, pulled into a ribbon at each corner. The wood was dark, almost black, of course.

Bookcases lined two walls, connecting at the corner of the room, and they were filled, overly so—some of the shelves displaying two rows of books. The room lacked a writing desk, which surprised her. But perhaps *this* Baron had his own study as well. A door was slightly ajar next to the massive black stone fireplace, and she guessed that one led to a washing room. The other door was at the far end of the chamber and she guessed again that it led to the main areas of the Fortress.

She let her gaze fall to the flickering of the fire, burning with gusto now that it had more fuel to feed it, not unlike her own self.

Remembering the tree, the bloom of it, the fire that killed it, she rubbed her face, thoughts of shame and guilt wracking through her body.

He had asked her. He had asked her to show him what she could do, and she did it.

The lovely *and* the monstrous.

She was well aware that she was capable of more destruction than she had ever let on. Even the Queen was likely not fully aware of her capabilities.

Yet, she thought, head turning, *maybe she was*.

If the Queen had encouraged Ash's solitary life, it was possible she did so out of protection. Whether *Ash's* protection or everyone else's, she didn't know.

Time and again she had been reminded to keep her heart to herself. Not to share such precious things with others because all she needed to survive was to hold her own. Ash had always assumed that was meant to keep *her* safe. To stop *her* from being hurt, but what if the Queen understood more than that?

Ash could only imagine what she might be capable of if her heart was in the wrong hands. If she was groomed to believe something from someone she loved, they could use her as a conduit of power for their own personal gains.

Surely, she would never let that happen. Surely, she knew well enough of herself to know when she was being used and when she was being seen as a path to power rather than a guiding light.

Cursing aloud to herself, she wished she could speak to the Queen. But, as Sylva had said when she'd asked, there were no quick means to get letters to Hyrithia. There were shipments to Felgren from the other cities where trade happened on the outskirts of the forest, but that happened only twice a year. The next shipment was a whole season away at the end of summer.

Was she so easy to break? All of the lessons taught by the woman who was a mother to her, all of the restraint she had practiced in keeping her heart hidden and guarded, seemed to be unraveling at a speed she could not control. Like a ball of wool fallen from a lap, rolling across the room, unspiraling at an impossible rate and freely, no pretense of what it must stay to fulfill a purpose it did not choose.

Rev.

Was he with Baron Heimlen now? Explaining the chaos he witnessed and the madness she felt? How *could* it be explained? She felt a beating heart in the Blight—no exhaustion nor empty belly could be at fault, and she feared that only something awful could account for it.

She must be wicked.

Having always known she held massive power, she had never thought it was in any way wrong. But how could it not be? She was able to burn away life in seconds and make a connection to the very disease killing that which she loved. If that didn't make her a monster, she didn't know what would.

A light knock came from the door and she jumped, lost in thoughts of little self-worth. She pulled herself out of the chair, her legs popping in places from lack of use and opened it slightly.

Pompeii leaned in to speak to her, his peppered mustache ending in the same upward curl as his smile. "Ah, happy to see you awake, Ash. I hope you were able to sleep well. I have brought you some things Baron Revich thought you might need." He nodded to the interior of the room, a request to be let in.

"Oh, thank you, Pompeii. Please—" She turned and gestured him inside, closing the door lightly behind him.

"The Baron requested I look to your needs, assuming you'd be awake by now." He bowed so elegantly in his sharp green uniform, holding out a folded dress.

"Goodness," she lilted, taking the white, gauzy gown from his hands and hugging it close to her breast. "He thinks of everything, doesn't he?"

Pompeii laughed and nodded. "That he does, my dear. I see you found the water and plate of food he requested I bring as well?"

"Yes. Thank you. It was much appreciated."

He gestured to the door ajar to the left of the fireplace. "Please, feel free to change out of your clothes. You have been in them for quite some time now. There should be water to freshen up as well. I will wait here for you to be done but take your time. You can't rush a cleansing of the spirit."

Such a charming smile and way of speaking, Ash thought, as she followed his advice and left for the washing room. It was larger than the one she shared with Clairannia and Figuerah in the tallest tower, and she gasped at the sight of the massive tub in the center of it.

Wishing she had the means and opportunity to sit in steamy hot water for an hour, she instead undressed. Picking up a neatly folded towel, she scrubbed at her face and neck using water from the basin under an ornate, golden mirror. Black ash had settled on her skin in the wake of the fire she had brought forth, and she was slightly embarrassed to see streaks across her face. After wiping it as clean as she could, she used some of the mouth paste from the jar near the basin, its rich peppermint oil erasing the feeling of sleep on her tongue.

Her hair was…untamable at the moment, but she assured herself no one cared. In Hyrithia, your appearance was yours and very little judgment was brought upon it. It seemed that sentiment was common throughout all of the isle. But she fussed a little anyway, pulling out the plait from around the top of her head and using the comb by the basin to brush through the tangles. Wild, but more clean, she left it hanging down, the thought of binding it giving her a headache just to think about.

She stepped into her gown and pulled it up over her shoulders. She looked amiss in the low light of the room, the two sconces on the wall having been lit at some point in her time here. A beam of white against all of the black stone, she stood out like a ghostly spirit in the pitch black of night.

The material of the dress was a light white cotton, hugging her chest and waist with ties before falling heavily around her hips all the way to the top of her bare feet. She was miraculously able to tighten the back, determined not to ask Pompeii for help. The sleeves were shorter than her usual attire, ending in gathered cloth that wrapped just above her elbow as if in homage to the petals on a rose.

She admired her reflection in the mirror, its gilded frame a gold cacophony of leaves that intertwined along its rectangular shape. The dress accentuated one of her best features where her collarbone met her chest and settled softly, the hint of her breasts subtle from the cut of the square neckline.

Inhaling slowly, she held her breath, listening to the sound of something scraping across the floor of Revich's chamber. She opened the washing room door slightly to see Pompeii dragging a cushioned chair through the room, placing it across from the one she had just occupied in front of the fireplace.

"Ah. I am sorry to disturb your peace." He gestured to the chair. "I did not expect it to be so heavy. Baron Revich requested this be brought in as well."

She smiled brightly, convinced the Baron could foresee the future. She would need a chair to sit in when he eventually came to see her.

"It's perfect, Pompeii, thank you."

"Of course, Ash. Now please, if you'd like, rest awhile more." He offered his hand for her to take, leading her to the black chair he had just placed. She sat, aware of the uncomfortable stiffness of this one compared to Revich's.

A flash of green caught her eye on the blue chair across from her. Following her gaze, Pompeii tsked aloud and picked up the object, twirling it around in his fingers. As he brought it toward her, she realized what it was—the rhyzolm. The same stone that Revich had tossed around while walking with her from the pond. The same stone he had used to find her.

"I can't tell you the number of times I've found this the past few years—stuffed in chairs, lying on the floor in the dining hall. Once it showed up in his lumen's mouth and she spat it out into my hand." He held it up to her between two fingers. "Wherever it goes, I know he's been." He chuckled. "For all of Baron Revich's foresight, he can't ever seem to keep a hold of this." He reached down and took her hand, placing the cool stone in her palm.

"How…"—she cleared her throat, her voice hoarse—"how long have you known Revi—the young Baron?"

"We arrived in Felgren around the same time—a few years past.

Every Baron has an Overseer of the Fortress as I am to Baron Revich. Baron Heimlen's man died some years ago, I'm told. We have bonded together in learning all of the ways here in Felgren. I come from the Spire, you see, a land of great wealth, color, and revelry." He grinned ear to ear, snapping his fingers and sending bright purple sparks into the air. "And though I miss home, I could not pass the opportunity to do what few untrained channelers can."

"And what is that?" she asked, looking down at the stone, admiring the black lines coursing through the green whole of it.

"Live out their days in Felgren, of course. I am happy to live here, in this position, transitioning channelers to conduits by taking care of the Baron's needs and helping him with his duties."

He moved to the enormous bed. Brilliant purple magic flowed from his fingertips as he used it to throw the heavy quilt into the air, letting it fall back down on top of the sheets, covering all of the corners.

He turned his head to speak over his shoulder. "He's a good man, you know."

Ash nodded, knowing that full well. Anyone could see he was good. Wholesome, kind, thoughtful. If ever she had searched for someone, it would be someone like him, and knowing that was part of her fear. It would be all too easy to fall.

"Well, I'll leave you to your thoughts. He should be back from his meeting with Baron Heimlen shortly. You've missed dinner, but I could have more food brought up to you, if you wish."

"No, I'll be fine. Thank you for taking care of me, Pompeii." The pear and cheese sat heavy in her belly when her thoughts turned to what the Barons were discussing that very moment. The Overseer of the Fortress nodded and left quietly.

He's a good man, you know.

The implication was not lost on her, and obviously, she was sitting there in his rooms with a new dress, barefoot, hair awry, waiting for him to return. She was no fool—in that moment at least—and neither was Pompeii. It must be accepted then, here, in the Fortress, for the residing Baron to take a channeler as his lover. And his Overseer thought he was doing just that.

Probably because it was true.

Ash sighed and bit her lip, turning the stone around and around between her thumb and forefinger. The flicker of flame from the fire reflected in its smooth surface. She wondered at this small, precious stone. Truthfully, it was the cause of all that had happened to her, and though she was no longer sorry for it, everything was happening so fast. Her feelings toward Rev, his for her, and the question of what was next. The *implication* even.

He's a good man, you know.

It would be easier if it was not true. She would be able to still her heartbeat at the anticipation of him walking into the room if he had been cold, cunning, and rude. She didn't doubt there would still have been some physical attraction, but she knew that would be *all* it would be.

Restless, she stood, pacing at the foot of the bed. Her bare feet were ice cold, but she barely noticed. She tossed the stone up and down, catching it each time with ease.

She could see two choices.

One, she could give in. She could let him take her, body and soul, and be done with the fight instilled in her against such things. She could live out her days in Felgren, her heart in his hands, her body as well, and figure out how to leave later—if she ever *wanted* to leave. But that was all assuming that's what he wanted. He had never said he wanted to love her, but it seemed the suggestion may be there. Then again, it could be he was just looking for a lover to discard when she left or when a new batch of channelers arrived.

Dammit.

Two, she could move on. She could push him away, tell him she was done. Tell him she did not want to pursue anything further and that would be the end of it. She knew that with one conversation with him, he would respect her choice and leave her be.

By the Blightress—she didn't want that.

And this was all assuming he wasn't with Baron Heimlen this very moment, plotting how to get rid of her. Maybe use her first to help with the Blight? *Then* get rid of her? Send her back to Hyrithia as a broken thing, something the Queen could deal with and hopefully not destroy the city in doing so.

He's a good man, you know.

The truth of the statement she did know, yet she struggled to trust it. The mess she was in was only going to get messier.

She tossed the rhyzolm up high, ready to catch it in her off hand, when there was a loud knock at the door. Cursing, she searched the floor for where the stone landed as it rolled into the tip of a black boot.

Revich bent down to pick it up, chuckling to himself before tossing it back to her. She caught it, thankfully, and squeezed it tightly in her hand. "I'm sorry I-I found it in your chair, and then I was just thinking and I was tossing it around…"

He closed the door and leaned against it, eyebrows raised, arms crossed at his broad chest, a teasing smirk on his face.

"And…and I dropped it when I heard you knock." She was saying so many words—far too many words—and she was struggling to catch up to them as they spewed from her lips without her permission. "So then…it…" She trailed off, biting her lips together inwardly, determined not to say another word.

"I'm always losing that stone." He pushed off from the door and slid his hands in his pockets, walking toward her slowly, his eyes catching the flicker of the fire, never leaving her own. "Thankfully, it always finds its way back to me."

He was closer now, standing right in front of her, their bodies only inches apart. "It's the first rhyzolm I ever found, you know." He took her hand and lifted it to his chest. "This stone has been with me since I was a boy in the Hallow Marshes. Alone. Always alone. But when the Baron asked it of me, it led me to you." He laughed softly to himself as she moved to place the stone back in his hand and closed his fingers around it. "I can still feel you when I hold it."

"I'm glad it's not lost then," she whispered, softness returning to her pulse.

He stepped away from her, turning to the fire and lowering himself to the black chair, shoving the stone into his pocket and resting his elbows on his knees, bent forward, clasping his hands. "Please. Sit. We have much to discuss."

He gestured to the blue wing-backed chair, and she swept toward it silently, sitting stiff and upright, hands in the lap of her white gown as if waiting for her dismissal from Felgren itself. *And I may well be*, she thought.

"First, I want you to know that what happened at the stream happened between you and me. Whatever horrific tales your mind has come up with as to what I've told Baron Heimlen about that… demonstration, you can forget. I asked you to show me what you could do and you did."

"I—" she started, but he held up a hand to stop her.

"Please. Let me speak before you say what I can see plainly on your face." He lowered his head and sighed before taking a moment to look back up at her, rubbing his hand across his mouth. "I could not keep him from our discovery in the Blight. I can omit information, but I cannot lie to him. It was what he suspected anyway. He told me he could not feel the Blight's heartbeat either. So—" He pushed up from his seat and began pacing the room, just as she had moments before, rubbing the side of his neck as he seemed to habitually do when deep in thought.

"What's going on here? Are you able to sense a heart beating because you are powerful? Or are you somehow connected to the Blight in a way that is unclear? A combination of the two? Regardless of which one—or even if those two are the only options —I do not believe you are some concealed monster, brought here to destroy us all. So you can take that look right off of your face, Ash."

She wasn't aware she *had* a look on her face.

"The next question is, what do we do with this discovery? Do we continue your lessons in Cosensian Magic? Do we explore your connection to the Blight further, hoping for some better glimpse into how to destroy it? This is what the Baron and I have been discussing for the past few hours while you got some much needed rest here."

"Thank you," she whispered, watching him pace. "For not telling him about what I did."

"*Ash*," his voice came in a rough whisper, exasperated and heavy.

"You do not have to be afraid of your gifts. Not around me. *Never* with me. I see that look you're giving me. I've seen it more times than I'd like. I see you doubt, wondering who you can trust, wondering about your future here." He moved back to the black chair, pulling hers closer. "Because I know you think of your future. I know you must be tormented, unsure of your fate, having all of it lie in someone else's hands, someone else's decisions."

His sigh was weighing, his eyes a swirling mass of black and blue. "Baron Heimlen will be dead by winter. There is no doubt in my mind. His health is fading quickly. And so, he is hard on you. He knows what's at stake, what kind of legacy he will leave behind if he fails to stop the Blight. He is a good man. He wants to stop the death, but he cannot always see the light on the other side, nor what sacrifices he asks of me…of you."

She reached out to touch his hand, and he took hers in both of his with one swift motion, as if needing only that small gesture to go on.

"I have seen you come alive here, Ash. When you arrived, you were hurting, torn from the life you knew, and I am sorry for that sacrifice you made unwillingly. But I will be the sole Baron here in two season's time, and I will not force any more from you. If you help us with the Blight, if you do all you can to stop it or even just hinder its growth in some way, you may leave."

She gasped and narrowed her eyes. "You mean…I could go? Before all the training is done and before the conduit trials? You'd let me just leave?"

"I would, Ash. I see your desire for freedom. I want you to make your own choices, but I do believe in you. I believe you want to see Felgren thrive just as we all do. So, when you have done what you can, you may go if you wish."

She shook her head slightly and stared into his eyes, watching as they turned glassy. He took her other hand as well and squeezed, swallowing hard. "So go. Be great. Be happy and fulfilled. But know this, Ash'Arah—if you leave, you leave a stain. I have scoured and I have scrubbed until I have little feeling left, yet thoughts of you remain. Since the day you arrived, you have not left my thoughts, and I cannot seem to distance my soul from yours. I have accepted it, and I see it not as a loss, but as an answer to the question I didn't realize I was seeking.

"I tell you this not to coerce you, but to steady my own feet. And yes, I am selfish for it. Last night you gave me hope, but I see now that I was looking for it so desperately, I did not stop to wonder if you felt more than…than desire. But I cannot let you make your choice to stay or go without knowing the future I can see. The future I would choose if it was solely up to me." He trembled, holding onto her still. "Our future together if you would let me love you."

She couldn't move.

She couldn't speak.

If you would let me love you.

His words rang in her ears. Was it that simple? All she had to do was commit and let go and she'd be loved by this man? She wasn't allowed to give her heart. She wasn't *meant* to love, or so she had been told.

She had been told many things.

She had been ordered where to go, what to do with her life—even now she still held little power.

But the choice he offered…was it really a choice at all?

Confusion and frustration tore through her body, clawing at the surface and no longer able to dismiss them, she stood. "And yet, you would use me, just as Baron Heimlen does now? What if we destroyed the Blight and it came back? Would I still be free to go then? Will that always be a contingency in your offer of a choice, Revich?"

"That's not fair."

"Of course it's not fair. None of this is *fair.* I have spent my entire life in the service of others. The purpose of my life—of my future—has never been my own, and yet, you come to me asking for my help, giving me a reason to stay, but letting me have the choice to go? How could you be such a contradiction? How could you sit before me offering to love me, offering to give me a choice in a future together when I have been told time and again that I must guard my heart completely? That I must keep myself hidden from the world, only needing myself, my *own* company. You cannot just rip those words away from me. You cannot sit there and confess the very things I have been wanting you to confess. The very things I would lose myself to with another flash of your *stupid* smile."

She swallowed back the tears, struggling to keep herself together, to keep herself from falling apart into the warmth of his chest. She sunk back down into the chair, shaking her head. "Your words tell me it was all for nothing then. The loneliness, the self-preservation I have forced myself to learn…the pain of knowing I could never have *this*. I could never have what you offer…it was all for nothing."

He was kneeling before her then, his hands holding onto her face. "It led me to you. Your life before led my heart to you and I will never see that as nothing. You have become who you are because of it and not ever would I call that nothing. I got to touch you, and hold you, to kiss your lips as they are the very part of the soul my heart resides in, and I would never once utter words to counter that. I love you. You can accept what you were told, you can choose to walk away, you can continue to guard your heart, but you cannot go through your life thinking no one has loved you. Thinking no one has seen your soul, because I have. I see it, Ash. And I love you for it."

He kissed the top of her eyes as she closed them, tears running down her face, all fight from her gone. The chance of locking her heart in the cage she had made for it was gone.

All those words of longing for a choice, and yet she found she had none.

She had fallen, irrevocably fallen.

"I *love* you," he repeated. "These words are yours. And they are words I will speak forever until the day I am forced to stop."

She opened her eyes, her lashes wet and heavy, staring into his. They were the clearest she had ever seen, the color of a calm sea just before the sun keeps her promise to the world and rises once again.

She leaned into his kiss, his lips soft and slow in a question which she returned with her answer. She pressed harder into his mouth, coaxing it to open so that she could feel the full warmth of his tongue on hers. She slid her hands up into his hair as he wound his arms around her waist, pulling their bodies close, their hearts pounding, yearning for something more.

He pulled her to her feet and she did not hesitate, moving her mouth along his chin, his jaw, his neck, slightly rough—the prickly feel delighting her.

"Will you stay with me tonight?" he spoke in a raw rasp and she kissed his throat lightly as it bobbed in his question.

She pulled back, her smile sultry, filled with a promise of the passion they would share. Sweeping his hair from his face, she cupped the side of his cheek and whispered above his lips, "I don't think there's a single thing on this isle that could drag me from your bed tonight."

He was on her mouth then, their passion colliding in a wave of kisses and heavy breaths, all hesitation gone, all thoughts of her power and whether she would stay disappeared with every caress of her back and every tug on his hair.

He lifted her to him, her legs wrapping around his waist, and she pushed harder on his mouth, unwilling to let herself *breathe* without his lips on hers.

He balanced her on his knee as he placed a boot on the edge of the bed, holding her up with ease, grabbing her waist with one hand, pulling at the ties of her dress with the other, his talents revealed in the movement, and she smirked on his lips as she felt her bodice loosen and begin to fall off her chest.

The freedom of it was welcome, her skin longing for his hands, his caress, and she fell back onto his bed, tugging at the sleeves, pulling the white cotton off her chest, pushing it down off her hips, her belly writhing in anticipation of his body over hers.

She pulled her legs out in one quick motion and threw the gown off the bed, stretched out before him, unclothed, unsheathed, and unwilling to look away from his gaze.

He stared down at her, his sharp intake of breath through his nose at the sight of her fully before him excited her and she laughed in bliss of how she affected him.

He began with his boots, pulling them off one by one before moving to the buttons on his vest, his eyes never leaving hers as she lay back on her elbows, one leg crossed over the other, a smirk on her lips, enjoying the presentation before her.

Shrugging out of his vest, he pulled his shirt over his head and tossed it to the heap of clothing piling up on the floor. The sight of his torso, toned, hair trailing down his chest, eventually disappearing into the band at his waistline, was almost too much for her, and she resisted going to him, ready to help in his undressing.

He gave her a half smile as he moved his hands to the button of his trousers. She could see the evidence of his desire for her pressing against them. They fell off his waist and confirmed her thoughts, her lower belly twisting, warm, and almost painful at the anticipation.

"You are so beautiful." She broke the silence, unwilling to let him ever wonder at her thoughts as he stood unclothed before her, the tight muscle of his thighs flexing as he brought himself onto the bed, over her body, their skin not yet touching—hers writhing in the agony of it.

"And you? What does that make you?" He lowered his body onto hers finally, her hips rising to meet with his as she slid her leg up his side, pulling him even closer, her hands sliding through his hair.

Grazing her lips between each thought, he whispered, "You are perfect. Every inch of you." He shook his head in the dark, the low firelight casting his face in shadow. "I cannot imagine how I am ever going to leave this bed again with *you* in it."

"Then don't," she challenged, welcoming the fullness of him inside her, their bodies entwined, moving as one, as the fire died low behind them.

CHAPTER 21
ASH

Rev's touch was light as he stroked a thumb across Ash's lips, rousing her from a deep sleep. She smiled at the gentleness of his caress, sweeter than the raw passion they had shared the night before. His fingers traced the shape of her bottom lip and she kissed them, relishing in the earthy scent of pine.

Keeping her eyes shut, she reached out and pulled him onto her, their bodies bare and warm, pressed together in a lover's embrace. He chuckled to himself as he began those early morning kisses, starting lightly on her temple, across her eyes, down her nose, meeting her lips, his tongue coy and coaxing—asking her to come out and play. She stretched her body along the length of his, pushing her hips into the hardness of him, sliding her belly up his length, an inviting smile on her lips.

Revich groaned lightly at the suggestion and whispered on her mouth, "We have no time for that, my love."

Her eyes flickered open, lips in a pout. "Why not? Neither of us have left this bed. Might as well just keep going."

He laughed, pressing his forehead into hers, his eyes serious. "If we don't leave this bed, I'm afraid Clairannia and Figuerah will break down the door."

"What!" She sat up, pulling the quilt to her chest, turning toward the door out of the room.

"They were here about twenty minutes ago. You were dead asleep, Ash." He laid onto his back, placing his hands behind his head. "I didn't get up to meet them, but Figuerah yelled through the door, and I quote, '*If we don't see Ash in thirty minutes, we're tearing this door down by whatever means necessary.*'"

Ash laughed at the thought of it.

"I believe her. You said you'd see them at dinner, right? And then you've also missed breakfast?" He tsked his tongue and took her hand, pulling her onto his chest. "I'd be breaking down doors, too."

"We missed breakfast?"

On cue, her stomach rumbled loudly, warring with other parts of her body that begged to stay in bed—door and belly be damned.

"Pompeii can bring us something to eat if you'd like. Baron Heimlen is aware of your exhaustion, and I let him know last night that I've given you the morning off from training."

She gasped in mock anger. "You sneaky Baron, you! You *planned* on seducing me—admit it!"

"I figured you needed the morning off even if you didn't fall to my schemes."

They laughed together as two lovers do, bonded in bodies and spirit, tangled in limbs and sheets in the early hours of day, little care given to the world around them.

"You know I have to leave this bed, Baron Revich."

"I don't know that."

"You have to leave it, too."

"You don't know that."

She sighed heavily, her head resting on his chest, unable to see his face, her hands tracing patterns across it. "Wouldn't it be lovely if we had all the time we wanted? If you and I could stay? What if we didn't have to save the world, just each other?" She turned her head to rest her chin on his chest. "Wouldn't that just be perfect?"

He stroked her hair, the flickering light from the fireplace catching in his eyes. "Yes, yes, it would."

She reached up to touch the line of his jaw, hard and defined—such a beautiful feature. "What a future we have together, Rev. I'll let go if you let go. I'll open my heart to you if you give me yours." She grinned. "A heart for a heart?" She met his lips again as he slid his hands to her neck, pulling her closer.

A pounding fist sounded at the door, and they both turned toward it, snickering.

"It's been long enough, Ash. If you're in there, you'd better come out now and let us know you're alright."

She took his hand and kissed the inside of his wrist before hopping off the bed, looking for her long-forgotten dress.

"Be there a minute!"

She pulled it on quickly, fumbling with the ties behind her before she felt his hands pulling the strings, tightening the bodice with impressive competence. He swept her hair to the side, kissed the back of her neck and whispered, *"A heart for a heart."* She turned and cupped the side of his face, smiling in the brilliance of someone falling without reservation.

For, she had none. All of her hesitancy, all of her questioning what she should or should not accept left her thoughts hours ago with each of his kisses, each stroke of his fingertips across her back, each speck of midnight blue that lit his eyes as he made love to her.

She flew to the door, opening it a crack, looking upon two very angry women.

"Good morning," she stated, realizing what a terrible friend she'd been and understanding all of their concern. And she was happy for it. This was a different kind of love, and she welcomed it fully.

"*Ash!* What *happened* yesterday?" Clairannia spoke before Figuerah, who was pacing the corridor, about ready to burst.

"I'm so, so sorry. I'll explain everything. Meet me in Viridis in thirty minutes?" She bit the bottom of her lip, raising her eyes in truce.

"Oh, what's *another* thirty minutes to *us*, Ash? We've just been worried sick all night. And then Pompeii this morning casually drops that we don't need to be because you're with *him*," Figuerah scoffed, nodding at the inside of the room, hands on her hips. "Like that's going to fly. So then we spend our whole morning trying to find this stupid door because no one would tell us where Baron Revich's rooms are, and then when we do find it, he has the gall to just summon his man servant to tell us to leave you two alone—and we were never going to do that—so, yes, Ash, you can have *another* thirty minutes, but you have some explaining to do." She turned in a huff while Clairannia smothered a smile as she backed away from the door, eyes bright with the promise of a good story.

Ash sighed and closed the door, placing her forehead on the hard wood. They had every right to be angry. They had been afraid for her, and given all she had told them about her connection to the Blight, she wasn't at all surprised at their worry.

"That bad, huh?" Revich was out of the bed, pulling on his pants from the pile and buttoning the top.

"I don't think I've ever been so endeared as I am in this moment," she laughed and turned around, looking up with her head against the door frame.

"Mmm. I would bet not."

"Can you really summon Pompeii without seeing him? Figuerah said you summoned him this morning, but we were together the whole time."

"I can. Barons have a wordless connection to their Overseers. It's something we had to practice, but we have it down pretty well now."

"So you can…speak to each other through your minds?" She tilted her head, confused, as she watched him dress. It was almost as entertaining as the opposite.

"Sort of. It's not so much words as feelings. Like a pull to do a specific task. And yes, I was incredibly selfish this morning and had no desire to let go of you yet, so I just called to Pompeii to…give us a little more time."

He pulled on his second boot and walked to her, placing a hand against the door, leaning over her body, his confidence almost unbearable. She glanced to the bed she'd much rather be in.

He followed her gaze, murmuring, "And I'd do it again, no matter how many doors were about to be broken down."

They stood in silence for a moment, their eyes saying more to each other than any words could. He brushed her cheek softly and admitted, "I don't want to leave. I don't want to spend the day wondering if this was real. Second guessing…everything."

She reached up to his neck and pulled herself close, kissing him sweetly. "Then don't." And with a brilliant smile, she turned around and left, leaving his room before she was past the point of being able to.

She stood, back against the door in a large corridor, sconces lit along the walls with one clear direction out of it.

She took a moment to breathe—just breathe. The day before replayed in a flash of scenes in her mind and she exhaled from her lips in one long expanse of air, a reminder of what she had decided and fallen into. She steadied her racing heart and nodded.

She wouldn't go back. She'd never return to guarding her heart so closely. This feeling, this bliss, was worth every ounce of heartache she might feel in the future and she would never give it up.

Not for anything.

The Queen was wrong. She understood that better now. Life was about letting yourself go. Giving yourself to someone, even with the risks that came with it.

He loved her. He wanted her.

And she knew she could never deny the same, so why even bother trying? She wouldn't do it. She loved herself too much to deny that which made her spirit fly free.

Pulling herself away from his door, she began her walk to Viridis, her face beaming, and her heart steady—sure of its keeper.

CHAPTER 22

ASH

Walking through the halls of Viridis, Ash swore its blooms had never been so sweet, never so lovely as in that morning light. On the third floor, she found her friends.

"Ash…you're…you're *literally* glowing." Clairannia put her book down and stood from the settee she had been nestled into, Figuerah laid back on another one, book in her face, foot flouncing in irritation.

Ash looked down at her hands. A haze of her green magic was radiating from her fingers. She raised them to her face in confusion, having never experienced her magic leaving her body uncalled before.

Closing her eyes, she tried to calm herself. She imagined absorbing the light to settle back into her skin, and veins, and fluttering heart. When she looked down again, the glow was gone.

Figuerah huffed and slammed her book closed. She stood and walked toward Ash as it disappeared in a haughty *thwap*.

"*Are you okay?*" were her first words, but before Ash could answer, she was onto the rest. "Apparently, you're okay if you're actually *glowing*. What were you *thinking?*" She began listing things off on her fingers. "First, you tell us you have some wild epiphany about the Blight—that you can feel a heart beating through it, and then you make this insane connection to the Blightress. You run off to Baron Heimlen's study, *promising* to see us at dinner and let us know what happens." She emphasized another finger, on to her second complaint. "*Then* you don't show. So, there we were, worried about what had happened to keep you away from eating dinner because I *know* you love dinner, Ash. I've seen you eat."

She raised a third finger, finally taking another breath. "And *then*, you don't show up at breakfast, either. And we checked your room, Ash. We knew you hadn't slept there. We knew we had to tell someone, so we catch Pompeii at breakfast, and he tells us that you're with *Baron Revich* and we had nothing to worry about! As if that was some common occurrence in your life! Sneaking off with Barons, never a word said to your friends to let them know you were safe and that all of it was in your control!"

The reprimand flowed from Figuerah like a rampant wind, the strength of it unstoppable, her big, brown eyes alight with anger and worry and everything she had felt the night before. Her hair was hanging loosely around her shoulders, some of the braids unpinned as Ash had hardly ever seen.

"I am sorry. To both of you. I see now that I was so caught up in the moment that I—" Ash cut herself off, stepping forward. She wrapped her arms around her friend, squeezing tightly. "I didn't think about how you'd feel. I was being a terrible friend. I promise not to do it again."

Figuerah sighed and wrapped her own arms around Ash, giving in to the embrace as Clairannia rushed over to join the hug as well.

"You'd better have a damn good story to tell us, Ash," Figuerah murmured into her hair. "Considering your magic is leaving your body without you consciously aware of it, I'm guessing it will be."

Clairannia giggled, hopping up and down on her toes.

Ash snorted, pulling back. "It's…something. You'd better sit down."

She told them what had happened—the meeting in Baron Heimlen's study, the trek out to the Blight, Revich's inability to feel a heartbeat. When it came to the part of the story where Ash had destroyed the giant maple tree, she left out the detail where she had burned it to ashes.

"That's amazing, Ash. I bet there are fewer than a handful of even trained conduits who can produce enough magic to cause a tree to fully bloom." Clairannia was chewing on her nails in awe of the story so far.

"I wouldn't doubt that," Figuerah agreed. "I know Hyrithia is a bit sheltered in some of their knowledge of conduits, but Ash…I hope you know—that kind of magic is basically unheard of everywhere on the isle."

Ash bit her lip, thinking. She did know. And it was true, conduits were rarer in Hyrithia, but they did exist and worked peacefully in their place, welcomed even. The truth that those born in the walls of Hyrithia were not ever allowed the chance of an Offering did not stop the people there from *seeing* the magic of Felgren. It just made it less common.

"I don't know why I have this ability. I don't know why I can use the magic in Felgren more than other channelers and conduits. I don't have an answer for that, but I do know that maybe the Barons were right. If I'm this strong, I might really be the one person who has a chance to fight the Blight and destroy it."

"We really hope so." Clairannia put a hand on her arm, smiling warmly. "But really, how did you end up with Baron Revich all night? Did you two…" She smirked wryly and waited for an answer.

Ash put her elbows on her knees, her head in her hands, and blew air out of her mouth in surrender. "Yes. We did." She rubbed her face, smiling fully, the color in her cheeks rising. "I—he—" She shook her head, laughing. "We're together."

"Obviously," Figuerah muttered under her breath.

"I mean we are more than what Sylva said. He told me I can leave Felgren after doing all I can to destroy the Blight. I don't have to stay for the rest of my training if I don't want to. He told me he loves me, wants me to stay, wants to…to have a future here together."

"He said he *loves* you?"

"He said you could just *leave*?"

"I know. It's a lot. And maybe now you can see how all I was thinking about was, well, myself. I'm sorry for causing such a panic."

"*Ash*. That doesn't just happen. I know you aren't up to date in your History of Barons research"—Clairannia pointed to the third floor across the courtyard—"but this is…unusual."

"No, it's unheard of. We moved on from that section last week during your lessons with Baron Heimlen, and there's not a single mention of a Baron ever having a companion. Not one." Figuerah's eyes were narrowed, doubt in her voice.

"I didn't say we will be companions. I said he loves me."

"And wants a *future* together."

"And is *willing* to let you just leave."

Ash's brows furrowed. Companions? He'd never said they could be. He just told her he loved her, told her he'd accept her decision to stay or leave. He didn't say he was willing to commit to her as companions. And if throughout history Barons didn't have companions, why would he?

"I—I think it's okay to take this one day at a time." Ash stood, brushing her white dress smooth. "That's what I'm going to do. I'm going to train as hard as I can. We only have until the winter, and I'm sure the first signs of summer will be coming soon. I'm going to spend time with Revich. I *want* to spend time with Revich. He makes me…"

"Glow?" Figuerah finished and tilted her head to the side. "I know the feeling. And yeah,"—she turned to Clairannia who was beaming with excitement—"I think you should do those things too. We're happy for you, Ash."

"We believe in you," Clairannia added.

"But for our sakes, can you *please* just let us know you're safe?"

Ash nodded and pulled them back into a hug, resting her head on Figuerah's shoulder for a moment, squeezing them both tightly.

And as she walked away to find Baron Heimlen and begin the day's training, her heart full, she wondered what she had ever done to deserve such friendship and love.

~

BEFORE MEETING BARON HEIMLEN, ASH CHANGED INTO FRESH conduit clothing, wanting to look the proper part for her acceptance of her role in the saving of Felgren. She passed Pompeii as she walked to the doors of the Fortress who nodded to her with a sly grin.

She refused to be embarrassed. She didn't care if the entire fortress found out about her and Revich's relationship because there was nothing to be ashamed of. Thoughts of Sylva flashed through her mind as she followed the path to the patch of earth Baron Heimlen preferred to train on.

What had their relationship been like in the beginning? Had he ever confessed his love to Sylva, promising things in her ear and keeping her loyal to him all the while? She hadn't left after all, having failed her conduit trial. And they still spent time together.

She wondered if she could do that. Live still at the Fortress, serving those who resided there, stealing time with Revich as they both grew old with age.

"Ash'Arah. Please, come, we have much to discuss." Baron Heimlen stood before her, hands clasped behind his back, the shadows from the trees around them embracing his dark frame.

"We do. But before we start,"—she stepped up to him, standing tall, her confidence anew—"I want you to know that I'm ready. Maybe I wasn't before, but…I'm committed to this fight. I promise to take it seriously, and with your help, destroy the Blight. And I understand. I understand why you…took me."

He smiled faintly. "I am glad to hear it, my dear. I have been told by Baron Revich that you are aware that this situation is dire, and, though we don't know why you have some connection to the Blight, you are the right one to help stop it." He cleared his throat. "I am also aware of your relationship with the Baron."

She flushed, having just been about ready to tell him herself.

"Though it does not surprise me in the slightest, I hope you do know, Ash'Arah, that Baron Revich is committed to me and his duty here in Felgren. He will continue his role, and after I am gone, he will not fail to continue training conduits and bring magic to the isle as Barons have done for centuries."

"Of course," she murmured lightly, questioning his opinion of their relationship.

"Let us begin then."

Irritation settled into her chest. Was it a slight on her to suggest that she somehow planned to keep Revich from his duties? Was that what he thought of her—a distraction against what needed to be done?

Angry and averse to letting him dismiss her as a tool to be used, she held out her hand as if ready to begin their Cosensian Magic training.

He smiled and clasped her arm in his gloved hand, closing his eyes to begin their connection.

But she was unwilling. Their magic did not flow together as they had practiced before, connecting and entwining with energy of silver and green before bundling into Baron Heimlen to use as he would.

Because she wasn't going to allow it until he *understood*.

She was loved.

She was accepted as a whole—by her friends, by her lover, and by herself. And maybe that was all anyone really needed. She had understood herself better in the last twelve hours than she had her entire life and she wasn't going to stand idly by, her role in people's lives here dismissed by its current reigning Baron, even if he had been the Savior of Hyrithia. Even if he had been the one to bring her.

Instead, she willed the earth to move, pushing her anger not aside as she had been taught on many occasions, but using it to fuel her power.

The mossy ground beneath them rumbled, and Baron Heimlen opened his eyes, confusion littering his face as she stared back at him, silent, displaying her power.

The earth broke, a long crack running through it as a stem rose from the ground, small and thin at first, but quickly growing into the trunk of a tree. Its solid, woody mass grew rapidly around their clasped hands and upward still, leaving a hole in the trunk where she held onto him, her eyes never leaving his face.

"What are you…" the Baron trailed off as he watched the tree bud, then leaves unfurled themselves in a rich dance of spring green before its clumped flowers bloomed in brilliant white.

The buzzing of bees harmonized around them as a full swarm flew to the blossoms, bouncing to each one, drinking their fill on the sweet nectar and flashing away in one loud flurry moments later.

She kept her eyes on him still while he watched in revelation as the tiny blossoms lost their petals, falling to the ground in one last chance to frolic in the shining sun. A bud of fruit began to form at the end of the flower stems—green, to yellow, then to a climax, as red, ripened cherries hung full and heavy.

Ash picked one, excitement running through her veins, as she admired the beauty of the fruit she had willed the forest to produce in her power—in her acceptance of who and what she was. She might not yet have a name for it, but there she stood all the same, loved.

She was truly loved for the first time in her life because she had allowed it. And no one was going to deny it from her.

Baron Heimlen held strong to her arm, his eyes on her face, unreadable and dark. "I see you now, Ash'Arah. I see you now, my dear."

Smiling, he picked a cherry, red as blood, popping it into his mouth, relishing in the fruit of her labors.

Ash braced herself to begin.

CHAPTER 23
ASH

Impatience rose through Ash while she stood on the third floor of Viridis. She had spent the last precious hour of her free time searching the shelves for more books on the Blightress or the first Baron.

She hadn't forgotten about the book she had read the day before, nor had she forgotten her theory on the Blight's origins. They weren't well received by her friends or the Barons, but something was…off. She couldn't put a finger on what, and she couldn't get over the mention of a heart.

Without fear, her heart is fleeting.

It wasn't much to go on, she understood that, but it didn't feel like nothing either.

Baron Heimlen was proud of his protege. She could see it in his face this morning as they trained, his eyes never leaving hers, as her magic tangled with his over and over in practice. But he looked tired, and understandably so, as she felt the pangs of needing rest as well.

Ash had lunch with Clairannia and Figuerah in their usual glen and her exhaustion led way to good stories of their childhoods and quiphit watching—the animals abundant this time of year.

She had been given two hours in the afternoon to herself before another three hours of training with Baron Heimlen before dinner. He had explained to her that Revich would be joining them. He had been sure she was ready for Cosensian Magic with a third.

Her fingers traced over the books, gently brushing the vines that hung from this section, tangled together in knots and dropping all the way to the floor.

Exasperation continually growing in her disappointment, she decided to spend her last hour in her favorite hallway instead.

Illuminare, Excress, Incendo, Nitidus—she had learned all of these magic enhancements from one single book in the Magic Language Hall on the first floor.

Illuminare she had used often, the light of her magic glowing bright and pulsating with the beat of her heart.

Excress was used to enhance the size of fruits or objects, but the magic didn't last forever.

Incendo she'd never really need. It was a way to make a fire grow, not start, and she could already do both of those things, but she had practiced it anyway, interested in the power of her words rather than the power that came easily to her.

Lastly, *Nitidus,* she found useful on occasion. It enhanced the appearance of things, cleaning them if they were dirty, or giving them a polish and shine. She hadn't used it to enhance her own appearance, but she had definitely thought about it, unsure if it would work.

Thoughts of Revich crept into her mind for the thousandth time and she beamed, holding *The Language of Magic, a Guide to Speaking With a Conduit's Soul* by Seraphyn Antynn. She had opened to a page about magical language in the history of love. According to the author, spells had been tried throughout the ages to coerce another into falling in love but all were futile—that type of magic did not exist. A magic user could not use their power to force something like love onto another.

Ash chewed on her lower lip, just at the corner, thinking about Revich. What she felt when she was with him…she couldn't imagine how she had lived without it.

Her thoughts passed to her friends as well. Clairannia and Figuerah had made her time in Felgren bearable in those first few weeks, training with her, going through the experience of a new channeler coming to Felgren. She had grown to love them as sisters and looked forward to talking with them each day.

Her time here had changed in the blink of an eye.

She thought of her refusal to cooperate at first. She thought of how much she had softened since then, loving the forest, loving Viridis, and being loved in return.

Just...*loved.*

She understood now that her relationships in Hyrithia had been but a shadow of the word. She didn't doubt the Queen and the Prince—even Geyrand—had loved her. But her role in that castle was given to her, not taken for herself, and she realized then that she could never have been free within those walls. She could never have been loved fully if she was caged, if her power was used for convenience, never as something great that could create life or bring light to the darkness.

Hatred and fear had led her survival in her first days within Felgren. But now? A chance at happiness, loving those she wished, and fulfilling her purpose here drove her to keep trying. She had found a reason to give her power over to those who could wield it and stop the disease killing Felgren.

Her eyes skimmed over the page, reading words of magical endearments of love.

They stopped over one word, and she whispered it aloud.

All at once, the scent of lilac and roses filled the air. A warm breeze swept past her cheeks, as birds, blue as the sky above her, flew from the courtyard in one flighted symphony. The word echoed in the hallway around her as she spoke it again.

It felt...right. It felt as if this word had been waiting for her here, in Viridis, all this time—waiting for her to read it aloud, to take it in, to realize that she had the power to choose her own self, her own future, her own loves in this world.

And she understood then.

Viridis had given its approval.

She had found her new name—the one that fit her heart fully. The one that meant *beloved*.

CHAPTER 24
ASH

Closing the book and thanking it under her breath, she rushed to the nearby podium, tearing off a piece of parchment that was left there for training channelers to take notes on any of their discoveries or thoughts.

She dipped the quill in the dark green ink and watched in delight as the letters curved over the paper in her own handwriting.

It was lovely.

And it was *hers*. She had the choice to accept it and that was… that was everything.

She blew softly on the ink and folded it into the pocket of her mossy green skirt. She knew who she wanted to tell first. And to get to him before Baron Heimlen showed, she'd have to hurry.

"THIS IS AGONY, YOU KNOW. I HAVEN'T BEEN ABLE TO FOCUS ON A single thing all day with *you* running through my mind as a thorough distraction."

Revich was in the bare clearing Baron Heimlen and she had been training on for weeks—bare except for the cherry tree that now grew there, its fruit still ripe and red with birds of the forest swooping down for a visit.

"This your work?" He raised one eyebrow and nodded toward the tree as she came closer. He was sitting on a large rock covered in moss, one boot up on the stone and one bracing on the dirt floor. He held a carving knife in his hands, and he was working away at a large piece of wood, shavings falling to the ground around his feet.

She nodded and smiled, bending down to meet his lips in a kiss. "I didn't know you…whittled?"

"You still have lots of things to learn about me, Ash." He winked and there it was—that charming smile upon his face and she sighed inwardly, accepting her lack of control around it.

"I wanted to show you something. Before we start." She pulled the paper out of her pocket and handed it to him, her heart hammering.

"What's this?" He opened the parchment and grinned. "Beloved? That's what it means, doesn't it? Don't look so surprised. I've spent my fair share of time in the Magical Language Hall." He winked at her again and placed his carving and knife on the side of the rock.

"It's…I…I want it to be my new name." Cheeks flushed, she felt the need to explain. "I was reading this book and it was talking about how love cannot be coerced with magic, and I just thought of you and the girls and my time here, loving Felgren, loving Viridis. I looked over the page and this word just…"

"Fit," he finished, a dazzling grin lighting his face. He nodded, looking down at the paper. "It really does. It's beautiful. Perfect."

He stood and leaned in for a kiss, taking her face in his hands as she held onto his arms, bliss overtaking all of her senses.

It was real.

The love they shared, the happiness, the sense of purpose. All of it was real and she was determined to never forget that moment, Revich's lips on hers, pulling her closer in stolen moments before their duties must begin.

The sun shone down in the forest upon the two lovers, their

future bright ahead of them, while the first signs of summer whispered on the warm breath of the wind.

IT WAS SEVERAL DAYS LATER THAT SHE LAY IN REVICH'S BED, THE fire the only source of light in the room as the flames licked over fresh fir tree wood, the scent warm and welcoming in the air.

Her body flushed hot, sweat rolling down her chest as she tried to catch her breath. The waves of her release still pulsed through her body as he kissed his way up her belly, stopping at the base of her breast, as he always did, his lips light and teasing.

She groaned in satisfaction, pulling his head up to hers, kissing his face repeatedly before she found his mouth and tasted the heady sweetness on his tongue.

"I have something for you," he whispered on her lips, the sound muffled by her determination to continue their current task.

She laughed against his mouth, whispering back, "Why, *Baron Revich*, and here I was thinking you'd done enough."

He returned her laugh, snickering on her mouth between kisses. Then, finally leaving her lips, he got out of the bed and walked to the shelves of books against the wall.

She admired the view, watching the muscles of his legs tighten with each step he took, eager for him to return.

When he did, he held the rhyzolm in one hand and an object in the other, wrapped in green cloth.

"What's this?" she asked, sitting up, curiosity alight in her eyes.

"I want you to keep this," he said, taking her hand and placing the green stone in her palm, kissing the tips of her fingers before closing them around it.

She beamed at him, knowing what it meant. Understanding that he was giving her a piece of himself that he cherished. That stone was connected to them both, and he trusted her with the keeping of it.

"I'll hold it close forever. I promise." She held the stone to her heart, her overwhelming sense of love and joy pouring into it. She closed her eyes, thanking the stone for bringing her here, to this very moment where she was incandescently loved by its owner.

"And when you're not holding it, I made you something. Something to keep it in—for safe keeping." He handed her the wrapped object.

She set the stone on the bed beside them and unwrapped her treasure. It was a wooden box, polished and shining in the low light. She felt the clasp at the back and wound it before opening the lid. Music met their ears, light and joyful as the tines of the mechanism flicked over the protrusions of a revolving cylinder.

She gasped and looked up at him, the sound lilting through the room. "It's beautiful. You made this? This is what you've been secretly whittling away at this week?"

"Yes. And the song is for you as well. I'm sure you know it—I've heard you humming it before. It's *The Sun and The Moon*. Pompeii made the mechanism inside. He is a gifted artist and learned the skill in the Spire." He swept hair back from her face as she stared down at the box, her mouth still open in surprise. "You love it?"

"I do. It's absolutely perfect."

Closing the heavy lid, she traced the letters he had carved into its top, elegant and lovely.

Her new name.

Karus.

PART THREE

CHAPTER 25
KARUS

Leaning back in my chair, rubbing the finger my conduit ring once adorned, I studied Revich as he took a moment to gather himself. He clasped his hands together tightly, the whites of his knuckles evident and raw.

This part of my story he had struggled through the most, stopping often to find the right words to describe what we had apparently felt together.

What *I* had felt for *him*.

I broke the silence, interrupting his thoughts, with a raspy, "How long?"

He had been staring at the ceiling, struggling to keep his eyes from spilling over with tears. He blinked them away, steadying himself before asking, "How long for what?"

"How long have I been like this?"

He pursed his lips together, his breath heavy, his jaw twitching as he rubbed his mouth, hiding his expression behind his hand. "In seasons? One."

"In years, Revich. I want to know how long I've been like this according to the isle outside of Felgren." My voice was steel—hard and cool as I stared across from him over his desk.

"It's been…seven years, Karus."

Karus.

It sounded different now, coming from his deep voice, now that I knew of its origins. Now that I understood its meaning—understood why I had chosen it.

"Seven…years." I shook my head as it began to swim, thoughts of the life I'd missed—thoughts of the people I had known and had loved flashed in my mind. Where were they now? Where were Clairannia and Figuerah? Where was Baron Heimlen and Sylva?

I pulled at my hair and lowered my head to my lap, eyes squeezed shut, breaths leaving my lungs in rapid succession. Dizziness overcame my senses as I rocked up and down. The pain of recognition, of admittance to the story he had been telling me of my life as Ash'Arah, jumbled in my head like stones in a box.

Scenes played out in detail and I wondered if they were from living them or if my mind was just imagining what they must have been.

I felt his hands on my arms as he pushed my chair back across the floor, gaining access to me, the blanket falling between us.

"Karus. It's going to be okay. You're going to be alright. We can stop. We can stop here and continue another time. You are not alone." He smoothed the top of my hair, bent down close to my face, the nearness of his voice acting as an anchor in my panic and I stopped my rocking, meeting his eyes.

We stared at each other for a stolen moment in time, everything said and unsaid hanging heavily in the air between us.

"I—I want to see Viridis."

He inhaled deeply and let it out slowly, steadying it as he clasped his hand across his lips, watching me closely.

"*Please,* Rev. Take me there."

At the sound of his name on my tongue, his face hardened and his eyes swirled a turbulent blue.

"I'll take you. But then we're done. You need rest. We can continue in the morning."

I nodded in agreement to his words as if I meant to abide by them, as if I was going to just agree to pause what was *my* story.

What was *my* life to learn. I had no plans to ascend lightly to my room in the tallest tower, waiting patiently to hear the rest. No plans to fall asleep in my bed, wondering what he had apologized for, wondering what had happened to cause my internal chaos.

No.

I was waking, suspended in that first moment of consciousness when you stir from a long dream, when all of your thoughts are colliding as you begin to sort them piece by piece.

He was going to tell me *everything* before the night was through. I wouldn't go back to what I had been for *seven years*. I deserved the truth.

All of it.

I prepared myself inwardly with each breath I drew because I already knew this truth: whatever had happened between us, whatever he had apologized for, it was going to be painful to relive...for both of us.

I followed him out of the study when Pompeii appeared, and I wondered if Revich had summoned him. He bowed slightly, waiting to hear a request.

"Please bring Karus some dinner. She will be eating in her room tonight. And start a fire as well." He paused and stepped forward, his voice low and quiet. "We are going to Viridis."

Surprise lit Pompeii's face as he responded similarly, "Do you think that's wise?" He glanced over at me, narrowing his eyes slightly with a question on his face.

"I...I know you." I smiled faintly, recognition pulling from a place, still locked, that held all my knowledge of this life. Something told me Viridis would help open it further.

"Karus." His smile was brilliant in the flickering light of the sconces on the walls in the grand foyer. His eyes pulled upward, aligned with that familiar black kohl coming to a point at the sides of his face.

"We won't be long," Revich dismissed his Overseer and nodded to me. "This way."

I followed, a sense of urgency I could not explain in my heart.

Viridis.

At the description in his story of my life here, I corrected things in my mind. The Magical Language Hall was not on the first floor, but the second. The settees were not carved into the talons of a hawk, but bestial claws, like a monster from a tale of caution and woe, grotesque in their shape and detail carved into the wood.

Revich's blue light adorned the walls, flickering before us as we began our trek to the doors of Viridis.

Had '*Karus*' worked on them? *Ash'Arah*, or even *Ash*, had felt so unfamiliar as he told my story, and I didn't doubt that the name had never fit me properly.

"Did the doors…did they accept my new name? You said they wouldn't accept Ash—did Karus work?"

He chuckled and turned his head back at me as we walked. "They did. You brought me with you the first time you tried. You said, '*If anyone should see this work, it's you. Let me show you that I can actually give a name to Viridis that it will accept.*'"

I nodded and pulled my hair over one shoulder, hands wringing on the skirt of my ruined dress, caked with black earth from kneeling in the Blight this morning.

He stopped abruptly and I almost ran into him, his body solid and warm. "You need to brace yourself, Karus. Viridis…it's not what it was."

"What do you mean? What's wrong with it?"

"The Blight—it got through the small door and…" He furrowed his brows, looking down at me.

Panic shuddered through me, my heart a wild thing, pulse rising rapidly in fear. I grabbed his hand in mine and raced forward, running down the dark halls, dread of what I would find chilling my blood as my feet took me through the right paths to the great doors.

"Karus," I puffed, placing my hand on the massive rhyzolm for just a moment. The viridescent portal bloomed and I let go of his hand as I stepped through it.

I stumbled out of the opening, falling to my knees, catching myself on white marble inlaid with bits of gold, dull and dirty, the stairwell cracked in places.

I closed my eyes, unwilling to look.

I *couldn't* look.

I heard him enter behind me, silent, a replication of the lack of sound that *should* have surrounded me.

I should have heard birds and the light breeze as it ruffled through the leaves of the trees in the courtyard, echoing throughout the golden halls.

I should have smelled the roses blooming full and the air sweet with the scent of a forever summer garden.

I coughed, choking, an unwilling participant in the reaction my body had as I inhaled the scent of decay—of death.

"*No,*" I cried out in pain, softly, as I looked up to witness what I knew would break me.

Viridis was a graveyard.

The Blight grew from every inch of the sanctuary. Its black, woody vines wound through what once were the trees of life. They combed through the halls, breaking through the glass dome at the very top, jutting toward the sky like an abomination reaching out to corrupt all that was good—all that was right, and lovely, and peaceful.

I screamed, tears rolling down my face, anger raging through my body as if my soul itself was a monster rattling its cage. My anguished cry resounded through the halls and the Blight responded quickly.

A creaking and cracking that would forever haunt my dreams echoed through the vines as they grew. They persisted in their deathly embrace over the sides of the bannisters, further up the trees, and curled toward me, slithering onto the stair landing that led to the center of Viridis.

I reached out, my fingers brushing the spongy wood of the monstrous vine slithering toward me. It greeted me in a familiar embrace of a cruel nature, the beating of a steady heart pulsing through it, loud as ever.

CHAPTER 26
KARUS

"This *can't be*," I whispered, unwilling to break my connection to the Blight. Unwilling to let go of what had ravaged the place I loved.

"No!" I yelled, grabbing ahold of the obsidian vine in my hand, the depths of its grotesque hue darker than even the moonless night sky.

The vine was strong, sturdy, sure in its own survival as it sent tendrils of inky death along my hand while I screamed, my rage no match for the perseverance of its soulless life.

Revich's hand grasped mine, his body sheltering me as he wrapped his arm around my waist.

"Karus. Let it go," he whispered in my ear.

I shivered, exhaling quickly, tears rolling down my cheeks. "Tell me it isn't real. Tell me I'm dreaming. Tell me I'm lost again in my mind and I will wake up soon. Please, Revich."

I unwound myself from the vine and turned around to face him, grabbing his black vest, my grip tight as if it was my final threshold before falling into an abyss. "*Tell me I didn't do this*. Tell me the Blight does not grow at my anguish. Tell me…"

He lifted his hands to my face, his gaze deep, searching for something he held precious. He remained silent, the slightest single shake of his head involuntarily given to me in answer.

"It's not true. This isn't real." Fear struck me and pulsed through my body as I stood, turning toward the ruined sanctuary, a dull light cast upon it. I took a few steps forward, unwilling to accept the truth.

I tried to focus my breath in vain, closing my eyes and thinking of the beauty I remembered. Pulling from the depths of me that still held memory of this place, I lowered my head and raised my hands, a sputtering of dark green magic sweeping across my fingertips.

I thought of life—of good, and love, and joy. I imagined all the feelings the stone had given me since I had discovered it in the broken tree all those weeks ago.

I willed Viridis to *live*.

I willed it to return, alive and beautiful, its gardens everlasting, its shelves ever-flowing with knowledge and the peace of discovery.

"Karus! No!"

Revich's voice echoed somewhere in my mind, a dull quiet sound, muted, but bellowing all the same.

I opened my eyes and abject horror greeted me.

I was trying to *save* it. I was *trying* to bring life back to Viridis, and all I had done was desecrate it further.

Before me rose a mass of black limbs and woven branches, pustules large and on the edge of bursting, growing en masse, bundled together on the trunk of the revolting tree as its branches hung low, their fruit black and bleeding.

I stepped back, staring at the monstrosity I had borne.

Revich's hands gripped my arms, almost painfully as he yelled hurriedly, "We need to leave—now!"

I realized the source of his fear as the black fruit pulsed and burst, the fleshy obsidian pulp slapping onto the marble stone in a sickening *thwack*. The splatter then writhed, its strength impossible as it hissed through the marble floor and new growth arose from the destruction, faster—impossibly fast—as Revich pulled me back to him.

The last thing I saw of Viridis was a dozen more trees like the horror I had produced sprouting from the stairwell, the fruit of the first still bursting in succession as I faded into the portal.

CHAPTER 27
KARUS

We fell back into the dark corridor, Viridis's doors mocking us in their silent black stone, the tops disappearing into the unfathomable ceiling above. Revich's blue light was dim, barely illuminating his face.

"It's my fault. I should *never* have taken you. I shouldn't have let you see. Karus…" He pulled me into his arms, repeating my name over and over, his hands brushing my face and hair, rough and shaking as his tears fell. "This is not what you are. This is not your *fault*, Karus. Look at me!" He shook my head and my glazed eyes focused on him.

"This is not you. *Do you hear me?* Do not go back. Do not fade again. *Please.*" He pulled me to his chest, cradling my body with his, rocking gently as he whispered into the dark, "Please don't leave me, my love."

Even with his desperate words, I let myself slip into the most welcome of black where pain wasn't real, and where the truth of what I was could hurt my soul no longer.

CHAPTER 28
REV

I paced outside of her room.

It must have been hours.

It must have been *days*.

I'd been there for days, waiting for her to wake.

I had been waiting for some sign that she was going to get through this and return to where we had gotten to.

She had been waking.

She had remembered, and when she spoke my name…I'm not sure how I held myself together.

The rhyzolm.

She'd found it.

And it must have been helping. Holding it, hiding it from me every time we met. That must have meant she understood it was special. That must have meant she had felt *something*.

Memories of the last time she faded ran through my thoughts, my own personal brand of torture. My own personal ghost of memories, haunting, consuming all of my time, all of my soul.

But I deserved it.

Every single ounce of pain—it was all mine to bear—and the

truth of it was, I knew I did not bear it alone. I knew that she held it still and it was all my fault.

I did this to her. I *lied* to her.

For the millionth time, I tried to go back. I tried to return to that one dusk, that one evening, and change it all.

But I've never possessed that power.

No one does.

And for the millionth time, I wished that I was enough to pull her back from those shadows. I wished that I had saved her from everything.

But I wasn't.

And I couldn't.

So, I steadied myself to wait.

I could do it again, if need be.

I could wait for her forever.

PART FOUR

SEVEN YEARS BEFORE

CHAPTER 29

REV

Her chest rose and fell in a rhythmic balance that Rev tried to imitate with his own breathing. Her head was tucked in close, one of her long legs, bare and lithe, she had draped over his hips at some point in their tangle of sleep together.

Karus.

He shook his head again, in an involuntary way, unbelieving of what he held onto as the fire burned low.

Her face had been a beacon of light when she told him the name she had chosen for herself. Her eyes had glistened like fresh dew on a blade of grass, and everyone had accepted the name so well.

As he stroked her dark hair, he recalled that first night she had come to the Fortress as Ash'Arah or *"Just Ash"* as she had snapped at him.

Gorgeous.

Enticing.

She had been radiating a defiance he had since learned to admire and adore.

Her gown had fit her perfectly in shape and detail—black beads creating a complex pattern across her chest and torso. And that deep green—it accented her eyes like the fabric was dyed with her in mind.

That was one thing he was going to have to get better at. Baron Heimlen had decades of practice choosing channelers with his rhyzolm, giving the Offering, and bringing them to Felgren, adorning them in gowns that fit their character—as was tradition.

She had despised him that night and next morning, unwilling to say even a single nice thing when she was in his presence…until he took her to Viridis. She'd been in awe of the library, the impossible beauty of it clear on her face. She had glowed, stepping out of that portal, and Rev had noticed the magic slide down her fingers as he held her hand for the first time. Her loveliness had been a rival to the courtyard before her, and his attraction to her had only grown watching her light up in the glow of the Viridis sun.

He had hope then. Suppressing his need to know her had been easier when she wanted nothing to do with him, but she had been kind—no quick retorts in viewing Viridis for the first time, no resentment for him on her lips.

He had waited, observing her carefully and keeping his distance as she fell in love with Felgren each day, looking for any sign she was interested in getting to know him better.

Her face had been hot and flustered when she stumbled upon him in the lake. He guessed he had Moira to thank for that.

He'd finally gotten to see her unbarred, and he took his chance, asking her to come with him that night, hoping she would finally let him in where he knew he belonged.

Rev grinned at the memories and kissed the top of her head, his arm having gone numb a while ago, but she was so serene when she slept, he didn't want to wake her just yet.

Baron Heimlen still needed as much care as Revich could provide. The end of his life was nearing, and Rev would do every-thing in his power to help ease his passing. Heimlen had taken him from his loneliness and given him purpose, guiding him into his role as future Baron and sole trainer of conduits for the isle.

There was so much to do. So much still to learn.

But right then?

In that early morning?

He allowed himself to stay.

He told himself all of it could wait just a little longer. Just as he told himself the previous morning and the one before that.

He knew she'd be ravenous if she missed breakfast again. He'd have to wake her soon. She needed her strength. He saw what Cosensian Magic took from her. And though she was doing much better than either Baron had expected, Rev could see her strength wane by evening each day.

He'd gladly moved her into his rooms. He had Pompeii bring everything she needed and she had gratefully accepted, looking forward to having very few stairs to climb each evening before rest.

Well, when they eventually rested.

Rev pulled her closer to his chest thinking of her fervor each night those past weeks. There were moments of blissful clarity between them as well as times of wild passion that seemed to consume his soul and set it on fire.

She had set him on fire, and he would not be doused.

He'd never go back to the loneliness, the longing for someone—anyone who could keep him whole.

Those nights in the Hallow Marshes, he had just been surviving. There had been many women in his bed, but never one that had felt like this.

He brushed Karus's cheek with his thumb, moving to her lips. An unwavering longing sat low in his stomach whenever he touched them. He couldn't say they were her best feature because that would be an insult to the rest of her, but he loved them. They were full and often red, the curve of her lower lip sultry and—

Fuck, he had no self-control.

He leaned in and kissed them softly.

Silently, she stirred and returned his kiss, stretching her long torso along his body in the way that about killed him each time. She lifted her bare leg further up his side, pressing herself to him. He inhaled sharply, roused and flushed with need for her.

He'd always need her now.

He moved swiftly, kissing his way down her neck as she arched her head back into the pillow, her breath coming in short exhales as she tightened her grip on his shoulders, pulling him on top of her body laid out bare on the bed they shared.

She found his hand and guided it to the slick, soft space between her legs, showing him what she wanted without a word.

"You know, Karus," he whispered in her ear as he grabbed her rear and slid himself inside her, relishing in the cry of pleasure he caused from her lips, "I think you'll be the end of me."

He nipped her ear as she moaned in need, arching her back, and exposing her breasts to him. Passing over them with one hand, lingering on each sensitive tip, he trailed back down to the center of her, his thumb starting slow circles to match the rhythm of his thrusts.

He watched her bite her bottom lip in ecstasy, her eyes closed as she began to fall into the pleasure, hanging on to him as an anchor before losing herself in the bliss.

"*Please*, Rev."

He about lost it.

Every single time she said his name, he had to work to suppress his urge to take her to the ground right then and there, consequences be damned.

He fulfilled her request—this time—unable to tease her this morning, his own want heavy and undisciplined as he bent down to her lips. He kissed her with little restraint, pulling every inch of her to him over and over again. She cried out on his mouth, her nails biting into his skin in the swell of pleasure that undid him each time he felt it pulse around him.

He held himself over her, both of them breathless, and she opened her eyes finally to look at him, smiling in her knowledge of how she affected him.

"Don't leave me yet, my love. We have so many memories still to make." Reaching up to kiss him again, her mouth was slow and tender. And he thanked—for the millionth time—whatever power it was that led him to her.

CHAPTER 30
REV

"Need I remind you of the hour?" Baron Heimlen's voice reeked of scorn, a tone Revich heard more and more since he and Karus had become lovers.

"Baron, I apologize. I do not wish to keep you waiting."

He'd do it again, though.

"Then why do you insist on doing so?"

The reason was worth every bit of irritation in Baron Heimlen's voice, though Revich still swallowed some guilt upon hearing it.

He cleared his throat, ready to answer his mentor. "I struggle at times, Baron, to pull myself from my rooms in the morning. I will be early tomorrow to make up for my tardiness today."

"And what of your tardiness last week? And the one before? You are late at least half the time, Revich." Baron Heimlen sighed heavily. The glow from the single lantern on his desk flickered across his worn features, and Rev noticed his cheeks sinking deeper into his face.

He leaned back in his chair as he continued, his tone lighter. "Do not think I do not understand, Revich. You may forget, I was once a young Baron, too."

That caught Revich's attention, having been slumped in the chair beside the desk, very little shame in his previous apology.

"Yes, I remember. The channelers would come to the Fortress. Beautiful women. Occasionally men. But what I remember most was the awe on their faces upon arriving." He chuckled to himself, a smile racing across his face as he crossed his arms. "There was this one woman. Powerful, breathtaking, the dress that mirrored her character left very little to the imagination, and she did wear it well. When I asked her to my rooms a few weeks later, she scolded me for taking so long. Those were wild nights, and yes, late mornings." His smile faded as he looked back to Revich. "But that was all they were. That's all a Baron needs and it's all a Baron can have.

"When Karus has done her duty here, she will be gone. I have no doubt that she will return to Hyrithia, whether a fully trained conduit or a channeler still, I will not live to see. But she will go. Her ties to that place are strong. And the Queen…well, let's just say the Queen plans for her return and will likely be on the edge of Felgren the moment her training is up. With an army behind her."

Revich listened reluctantly. Heimlen was repeating his own fears easily, with little thought, which must make them obvious to everyone but himself.

His mentor leaned in closer, his black eyes littered with gray. "She will *leave*, Revich. You know this. So, take your extra time in the mornings—within reason. And know that though it may ache upon her departure, you will encounter another, in time, who fulfills your needs just as well as she does."

Chills echoed through his body, as Rev tightened his jaw. Heimlen's words were relentless in their truth, something he knew and understood from his first year of training as Baron.

But Karus was *different*.

He was different.

He wasn't interested in quick romances that lasted a year, maybe two, before the channeler-turned-conduit, would leave Felgren, her future on the isle bright before her.

He was only interested in *her*.

In spending his free time with *her*.

He was interested in keeping her—loving *her*.

And though he said he would, he could not see himself giving her up. Of course, she would be free to go, but he often concocted ways he could make her stay in those early morning hours as she slept beside him.

In his bed.

In *their* bed.

"No need to be melancholy, Revich. That day is far from us now. Let's continue. If I remember correctly, we left off at the second trial yesterday. Remind me, is the second trial of medicus or agricola magic?"

"Lapis magic, Baron. The second trial is for stonework."

Baron Heimlen smiled and nodded. "Good, my boy. I see you're ready now. Let's continue."

Revich straightened his back, his jaw set, eyes like cool steel, but his heart beat hollow in his chest, the reminder of a Baron's future echoing in the promise of losing what he knew he could never bear to.

CHAPTER 31
KARUS

"In all the history of the great Barons of Felgren Forest, there have been few who have lived up to the first.

Baron Adaynth founded the conduit trials, and we can thank him many times over today for his work, giving us conduit magic that we use to prosper in our society.

Before his talents, channelers were rarely found, let alone trained in such a way that they could fulfill their purpose and enhance our culture."

Karus frowned and groaned inwardly.

After more searching, she had found another book praising the first Baron in a way that made her recoil. It seemed that many historians on the isle had placed Baron Adaynth in history books as a savior of sorts. And maybe he was, but Karus couldn't help but wonder still about that first book she had read weeks ago claiming he had saved Hyrithia from the Blightress's wrath.

If no evidence could be found as to what had caused her anger or what she had done because of it, why were historians so quick to believe the centuries ago written diaries of the man who had claimed to save them all?

Karus knew those diaries existed because the handful of books she had found about the first Baron had referenced them. But they did not seem to exist in Viridis.

She had scoured the shelves for hours at this point, her eagerness to find them in vain as Viridis either did not contain them or would not give them up.

Could books be taken out of Viridis? She had wondered about this on several occasions, not wanting to let go of her reading and longing to bring her books back to the rooms she now shared with Revich so that she could continue her research.

She had browsed the books on the shelves in his chambers but kept forgetting to ask if they came from Viridis or elsewhere.

She forgot just about everything in those rooms.

There were a few reference books on various stones found on the isle and a few about mudfishing and healing potions.

One book, found buried deep behind three others, was a romantic novel which she had teased him endlessly about before insisting they read it together each night, some of their more passionate moments taken in reference.

She sighed, looking out into the courtyard, the trees waving in response and she closed her eyes, turning her head upward, soaking in the balmy summer sun. A warm embrace enveloped her and she began to hum.

It was the song she had always loved as a child, the one her music box played for her when she soaked her aching body in Revich's enormous tub.

In the song, the moon and the sun confessed their love for each other, each resigning to the fact that they would only ever see each other at dawn and dusk.

It was beautiful, though heartbreaking that two such beacons of light would never meet for more than a few moments before attending to their duty to the world.

"But I have not the strength."

Rev.

Keeping her eyes closed, she grinned, hearing him voice the lyrics to the song she hummed, and her heart hammered in the same way she had by now accepted it always would in his presence. His lips brushed across her temple, and he settled himself behind her, pulling her back onto his warm chest, his arms wrapping around her waist.

"Nor do I, my love," she added.

She could hear the grin in his voice as he pressed his face into her hair and whispered, "So, I will see you at dawn."

"So, I will see you at dusk."

"Said the sun to the moon."

"Said the moon to the sun."

He found her hand and entwined his fingers in hers. "Your summer glow enchants me, my Sun."

"Wait. I thought I was the moon?"

"You are."

"And you're the sun?"

"No, you're the sun, too."

Karus laughed, turning to see his face, his smile mischievous and somewhat reckless.

"Then what are you?"

"I am the sky that holds you." Revich turned her body, pulling her legs over his so that she straddled him, the book she had been reading forgotten and fallen to the floor.

"The sky? But the sun and the moon see the sky all the time."

"Ah, so you've caught onto my schemes. If I am the sky, I get to hold you up forever, never leaving you at dawn and dusk and all that nonsense." He pulled his hands through the hair she had left down that morning in their rush to make it to breakfast. "Your light is too bright for me to ever compete anyway. So, I'll happily hold you instead."

She chuckled, shaking her head. The light breeze flowed through the open hall, playing with his black waves, and she pulled them away from his face, tucking the dark strands behind his ears. "And what about the new moon? When I cannot glow for you, for I am tired and weary. What then, my Sky?"

"Then I'll wait for you and love you still."

She leaned into him, wrapping her arms around his neck, her red lips above his.

"Promise?"

"Promise."

~

"Karus, my dear, your hard work has not gone unnoticed. I see a change in you these past few weeks, and I am proud of it." Baron Heimlen's black glove squeezed her shoulder in the affection of a doting father seeing his efforts in raising his child come to light.

She grinned, happy to be recognized in such a way. A way that she had little experience of before, especially by a father-figure.

"I can feel my purpose here, Baron. And, I want you to know that I have more to give. I…I can feel it."

"Your power is growing, child. Felgren feeds you each day you wake on its soil and gives you its light. Summer has begun, but we still have time."

She hesitated as they walked to their training grounds.

He was wrong.

Her power was not growing, and she was well aware of it. Her power had always been there, ready to use as soon as she could *control* it. Felgren was not feeding her *more* power, but teaching her how to tame what had always been hers to wield.

But something pulled at her power that she did not understand. Her strength grew near the Blight for a reason she could not determine, for a reason she could not research in Viridis. Revich also had not understood as she had tried to explain how the Blight seemed to call to her.

She squeezed the rhyzolm in her pocket. Holding the cool stone gave her comfort and she had been prone to taking it with her each morning and lovingly placing it back in the music box each night.

It was a reminder that she was loved, that she was content. Her heart was held and accepted. With each squeeze of her hand, she'd pour her joy into the piece of Rev she was responsible for, the piece which joined them both.

"You grow quiet? Tell me your thoughts." Baron Heimlen squeezed her shoulder again, an encouragement surely, and yet, she struggled to articulate what poured through her mind.

"I was just thinking…where do you think the Blight came from? I mean, it's been growing for years now, correct?" She looked up to his face as they entered the clearing, waiting for Revich to return from his time with Figuerah and Clairannia in their training with healing spells this morning.

His gaze wandered in the direction of the Blight, its vast expanse of black too far to see from their current position but beating in Felgren all the same. "Have you discovered any other stories of the Blightress, Karus? Ones you have not heard before?"

The question startled her. "I have found very little in Viridis, Baron. Though I have tried. I do not believe the books I wish to find exist there. Viridis…seems to live. It has a consciousness I feel each time I enter its halls, and though I have asked time and again, it has never given me another book on the history of the Blightress. I want to know more about her. I want to know what happened. I believe she was real—I think you believe that, too."

He chuckled and groaned as he eased his body onto a rock, Karus taking his gloved hand to help him. "You are correct. I also believe she existed. And I too feel the same when I enter Viridis." He smiled and shook his head slightly, leaning on one knee as he gazed up at her. "If I hadn't brought you through the portal myself, I might have thought you were born in this forest, Karus. Your keen eye for detail and intuition is not to be questioned, I see. But, as to your search for more information on the Blightress…no. No, I do not think you will find more in Viridis. I believe some manuscripts were taken out long ago. Some books reference them, but they do not show themselves."

"So, books can be taken from Viridis then? Are we allowed to do that? Can I just walk out with them?"

"Yes, to a certain extent. Viridis, as you and I know, is alive, and just as it knows your name to enter, it knows your purpose in its halls as well. And so, by that means," he explained, sending a small wave to Revich coming into the clearing, "if your purpose is clear on why you need the book, I'm sure Viridis would let you have it. Clairannia, for example, might be able to leave with a book about the nerve structure of human limbs, whereas Figuerah would likely never be able to do so."

"But if their roles were reversed..." Karus bit her lip, thinking of her purpose in those halls and what she might be able to steal away for a time.

"Yes, if Figuerah wished to borrow a book about the migration habits of the great Attatok Horned Vintras, she would have no trouble."

"Whereas Clairannia wouldn't be able to do it," Karus finished, a smile lighting her face as she held her hand out to Revich. He took it in his, kissing the top of her head in a wordless greeting.

"Ah, what have I missed? Are we discussing the Horned Vintras? Figuerah should be here then. She is a fountain of knowledge on anything with horns."

Karus laughed, nodding. She was about to ask just what a Horned Vintras was exactly when an ear-piercing scream echoed through the trees. It was high and deafening, and she pressed her hands to her ears, wincing at the pain of it.

"It's coming from the direction of the Blight!" Revich yelled, jerking his head toward the thicket of trees to the north of the Fortress. "Baron, you stay here! Karus, come with me!"

Baron Heimlen nodded, covering his ears as silver wisps of his magic surrounded his hands, no doubt muting the sound. Karus took Revich's outstretched hand, warm and tight in hers, as he led her toward the scream. The echo of it caused massive flocks of birds to take flight above them.

The sound paused for a few moments as they ran toward the decay, Karus cursing herself for wearing her thicker skirts which were more suited for colder days.

"What do you think it could be?" she puffed out, her breath short as she yanked the dark mossy wool away from a particularly thorny bush.

"I have no idea. Be on your guard." He squeezed her hand in reassurance, and they resumed their run through the thicket as the sound began again, closer this time and in short, resonating effects.

Something was in pain, deep in a death rattle. The weight of her worry sat heavy like a stone in her stomach, for she knew that the Blight played a role.

She had little to fear in Felgren, though she understood there were creatures within its boundaries that she never wanted to meet. They tended to avoid humans, however, or so Baron Heimlen had reassured them on their first few outings into the forest. He had said that the smell of the Fortress on their skin and clothes deterred the more dangerous creatures of the forest from interacting with humans.

But the Blight must be killing something. There was no doubt of it in her mind as they finally neared the blackened edge, sweat running down their faces in the relentless summer sun, their hands still clasped despite the slickness of their touch.

The sound had stopped and they stood at the perimeter of the black abyss, the stench of its decay even more pungent now that heat had taken its toll on the rotting corpses it desecrated.

"Do you think…do you think it's dead?" Karus wondered aloud in short breaths looking a few inches up into Revich's eyes as he squinted and scanned the dark.

He shook his head and mumbled, "We might be too late."

She stood at the edge, a cool mist emanating from the dark. It seemed to beckon her forward, an invitation she knew she wanted to accept.

"What are you doing?" Revich pulled on her hand, tugging her back from where she had stepped forward into the abscess of Felgren.

"I'm going in there."

"It's dead, Karus. Whatever it was, the Blight has consumed it."

"We don't know that. We heard its cry just moments ago. It's possible the creature is still alive, but its strength to scream might have left it. We don't have time to argue."

She pulled her hand from his and ambled forward, her pace more cautious and careful as she pulled her skirts to above her knees. Her boots crunched over dead trees and dead creatures, their lives long since consumed.

She scanned the space, coughing in the reeking stench, looking for any signs of movement, her ears asking for any sign of life. The disturbance of Revich's footsteps following her lessened her doubts on her decision and she trekked forward.

The power of the Blight was almost overwhelming. She could feel the distant hum of its pulse with each step she took. Each fall of her boot onto its hallowed ground seemed to accentuate the wicked music of that which only consumed.

That's what the Blight was, after all. It only knew destruction and hunger, never giving way to life, but death? Death was its desire.

She tried to ignore it.

The beating.

But the pulse clouded her mind, and chills ran down her back as she closed her eyes, trying to control her heart, promising herself that she would leave this place. Once she had found the creature or was ready to give up, she would leave the mist.

But panic was overtaking her quickly as the dark surrounded her in a cruel embrace. She felt the mist brush her cheeks, tug at her hair, and pull her inward still.

Thump, thump.

Thump, thump.

The beating of a venomous heart quickened as she marched forward, and she realized then how careless she had been as she lost control, her feet pulling her forward, despite her need to stop. She began to run, wild, as cold sweat dripped down her back. Sparks of green light—her magic uncontrolled—swam with the cool mist in a tangle of familiarity. She whipped her head around, lost, confused…and alone.

"*Karus!*" Revich's voice was distant and distorted, yet harsh in nature. She knew she was in for a scolding, and it would be well deserved.

"I…I can't…stop," she stammered to herself as her feet moved her forward still, pulling her away from what could save her.

A cry of pain, this time muted, as if Karus was hearing it

behind a closed door, rang out to the right of her. Hearing the sound again brought her out of the haze and she shook her head to escape the mist drawing patterns in her mind.

In front of her was a massive fallen tree, and with new determination, she began to climb to the other side, certain the cry came from there. Her fingers found hold in the decaying pockets of the wood, smearing her dress and hands in dark, inky rot.

The long-dead tree lay at an angle, the underside of it a thicket of black vines and impassable. As she lifted herself over, her pocket caught onto a jutting bough and she heard the tear of fabric as she slid down, landing on her feet, her skirts torn and ruined.

There, just on the other side, lay the body of a large beast. Its fur blackened and its limbs were riddled with the vines of the Blight, stabbing into its skin, returning unbroken through parts of its mangled body. It met her horrified gaze with eyes entirely black, snarling, pinned, its fangs dripping with blood and saliva—all sanity gone.

The Blight was consuming it as it wildly attempted to consume something else. The beast lay stretched at unnatural angles and she could see that its massive paws pinned something to the putrid earth.

Not hesitating another moment, she shouted, "*Fulgyren!*"

A shock of green lightning vaulted from the tips of her fingers, striking the beast with enough force to cause it to recoil, its cry low and feral as its tongue lulled out of its mouth and all movement stopped.

She arrived at the body moments later, tangled in vines, and she reached out, lifting its lifeless paw, hoping to find the creature she had come to save.

Her dragonfly wings were crumpled and smeared with black mud, her legs bleeding and at an odd angle, crushed into the rotten soil. But her eyes blinked open slightly, the purple hue glazed over. She picked Moira up, cradling her small frame in her arms.

"*Karus!*" Revich's voice boomed again in the quiet haze, panicked and angry. "Where are you? Karus!"

"Here!" she yelled and turned.

The mist was thick. She could no longer see the tree she had climbed, nor even the body of the cat-like creature as obsidian vines encircled the ground beneath her, groaning and creaking, moving along the black floor like a nest of vipers.

She held Moira close to her chest, her breath coming in short puffs as she chose a direction and stumbled through the thicket, hoping against the odds that she was heading toward Revich and not deeper into the Blight.

Moments later, he grabbed her arm from behind, whipping her around in a frenzy, squeezing her shoulders, grabbing her chin and moving her head up, touching every part of her face looking for signs of harm.

He didn't speak.

Not another word was uttered from his pursed lips, his jaw looking as if it would break in the force he placed upon it. He glanced down finally at the faerie she held, her arms cradling her like a wounded child.

He pried one of her hands free and Karus was left to hold on to Moira with only one arm, his fingers cold and pressing. He pulled her through the Blight with the swift determination of a man full of fear and anger, and she wondered how he knew which way to go. Everything was cold mist and black rot to her as she stumbled to keep up with him.

When they met the forest's edge, he pulled her out first and she almost tumbled to the ground before he caught her, helping her stay upright.

"You don't need to be so harsh."

"Apparently, I do."

He let go of her finally, running a black-streaked hand through his hair, some of the inky decay smearing across his face.

Karus looked down to Moira nestled into the crook of her arm, whispering kind words of promise that she would live. She wished Clairannia was there to help ease her pain. She could possibly even heal her completely.

She did the best she could, mumbling to her magic what she hoped to achieve. Dark green light encircled the faerie's broken legs and ran across her delicate face which looked so innocent now, unlike the wild thing she had encountered weeks ago when she had been lost in the forest. Karus could see her chest raise and lower, and she sighed in relief.

She didn't want to look up. She knew he was angry. In fact, she could almost feel the heat of his gaze on her as he paced the edge of the forest.

"We need to get her back to the Fortress. Clairannia or Baron Heimlen can—"

"You need to understand something right now, Karus," he interrupted, and she finally looked his way, wincing when she saw his eyes. They were black. There were no signs of the deep blue she loved that seemed to change with his mood.

"I'm sorry. I know I went too far. I realized it quickly and I should have waited for you. But I saved her. That was worth—"

"That was worth *nothing*. Do you even realize what happened in there? Do you understand that as soon as you were away from me, the mist poured over every inch of that place?" He shook his head and looked to the sky, cheery and light blue, a contrast to the thunder in his voice.

"I saw it," she stated, her own anger rising.

"And still you persisted. What if you had been lost to me? What if you went too far? Karus, we don't *know* much about the Blight. Very little, in fact, and yet you stroll into it as if a path to your purpose is laid out in gold stone. As if you *own* the damn place! You were careless, foolish, and selfish."

"I was *not* selfish! I went in there to find her! The Blight was taking another life and I couldn't stand the thought of it. You heard her cry—you heard how close she was to death! And I made it out. I'm alive and so are you and so is she and that was worth—"

"It is not worth what you risked!" He stormed to her then in a few short steps and grasped her shoulders, shaking them slightly. "Your life is not worth the risk you took! Do you not yet understand? Do you not yet see what is so obvious?"

He cupped her cheeks, the features on his face struggling to keep calm, pain crossing each one as he glared into her eyes. "You are connected to this Blight. Maybe it wants you. Maybe it needs you—I don't fucking care about the motive, Karus. *It. Can't. Have. You.* It can't have a single damn part of you, and I swear, if you ever do something so stupid again, I will march you back to Hyrithia myself and tell the Queen to lock you up for your own good."

"It wasn't as bad as *that*. You're exaggerating because you're afraid." She moved out of his touch. "I'm *fine*. The Blight is just more powerful than I gave it credit for and—"

He moved behind her then, his body no longer blocking the view to the edge of the Blight.

She inhaled sharply.

It was growing.

Such a strange thing, she thought, suddenly entranced, to see the dark poisonous vines glide languidly over the mossy earth leaving a scorch of black in their wake.

"Who do you think it's coming for?" His voice was steel and short in her ear as he pulled her body against his.

He was right. The vines crept out of their decomposing womb toward where the three of them stood, and Moira groaned lightly in her arm, turning her head, eyes closed still.

"What if it's coming for—"

"It is *not* and you know it. It does not want me or Moira. It comes for *you*. Here's your proof." He took Moira from her arms, gentle, as if taking a child. He wrapped her in his vest, stepping behind Karus, inclining his head toward the vines.

They inched forward still, silent, but steady.

And no—she couldn't deny it any longer.

The Blight was growing.

And it was coming for her.

CHAPTER 32
REV

Revich paced the room.

A withered book lay open in the palm of his hand, his other rubbing the back of his neck, pushing on the tense muscle there, tight as a bow string.

"Incendo." His mumble of magic lit the dying flames anew and in doing so, he could read the tiny script a little better.

> *"And so came the second age of Felgren, life returning to its soil, as if healed by Baron Adaynth himself. There, he trained channelers, those who could wield magic, and made them into true conduits, those who had the knowledge needed to be useful in their preordained abilities.*
>
> *Legend tells us that Baron Adaynth was a medicus conduit. The first, but certainly not the last on the isle.*
>
> *Much of his time was spent creating the trials. Four in total, each one representing the needed skills for each of the conduit types. A channeler would need to pass at least one of these trials to move forward in their path as a conduit and then begin their apprenticeship outside of Felgren.*
>
> *The four women who first trained with Baron Adaynth became the first mentors of the conduits he would produce, and it is said that most of them would continue on to become the first in lineage as the rulers of the isle.*

The medicus conduit becoming the first Lady of the Spire, mentoring future healers. The first iumenta conduit becoming the Madame of the Mountain, raising livestock and connecting with animals of the region. And finally, the first Queen of Hyrithia is said to have been an agricola conduit and no doubt the reason Hyrithia is known for its finely grown grains and fruit trees.

It is unknown what happened to the first lapis conduit. Some sources say she ended up in the Hallow Marshes, her ability to find precious stone leading to the first discovery of rhyzolm.

This tale would fit neatly into the story of the first four trained conduits by Baron Adaynth, but this author wonders, how often is history molded to fit neatly into a box that we all can wrap our heads around? Which of these stories are true, and which were created out of convenience, allowing the following generations the ability to hold onto something that cannot hurt them? Something that is easy to believe and accept with no doubts crossing their minds as they go on with their lives, raising their children, working in their towns, unaware that what they have been told may not be the truth—or at least not the whole of it."

There it was again.

Another author questioning history on the isle.

Revich and Baron Heimlen had found dozens of books by now that seemed to imply that through all the author's research, they could not confirm their findings, only suggest what may have been.

In some ways, it felt to Rev as if his understanding of the world was crumbling. The stories they told all children now had gaping holes and cracks that he had not seen before.

For months, he and Baron Heimlen had been researching Felgren Origins, the first Baron, and anything even hinting at the reason for the Blight. But Viridis had given them little to go on.

"And so came the second age of Felgren, life returning to its soil, as if healed by Baron Adaynth himself."

He reread the beginning line of the book, flipping back once more to the title page, but there was nothing else. The book he held and had read at least twice now, began there, with that line.

To Revich, it was suggesting something. What was the first age of Felgren, and what had caused the need for a second?

Unease tightened his chest as he tilted his head back, lost in thought. He didn't even want to entertain the natural conclusion that Felgren had seen the Blight before. But that was exactly what this book was suggesting, wasn't it? They all knew Felgren needed healing *now*. He and Baron Heimlen had never discussed a possible connection between the Blight and the Blightress.

Then Karus had found that book.

He had felt an immense sense of pride when she had found her way to the Baron's study, claiming the Blightress and the Blight *must* be connected.

And the heart?

That was something else he could not understand.

He too believed the Blightress once lived—centuries ago. But people didn't just hang around for hundreds of years. The longest on record was the eighth or so Baron who lived to a ripe age of 146 in years measured outside of Felgren. Within the forest, it was not quite so long as that, or so it felt to the people who had known him.

Revich sighed in frustration, tossing *To Train a Conduit: A History of the Conduit Trials* by Thalia Lighton to the chair by the fire. It landed atop three other books he had recently pulled from Baron Heimlen's study.

Everyone else had rushed to help Moira. He knew he'd be useless and get in the way, never having been adept at healing magic. Also, his anger and fear with Karus would likely hinder any positive auras they were trying to radiate to the broken fae. Baron Heimlen had arrived with lumens shortly after they had escaped the dark abyss.

Barely escaped.

They had rode back to the Fortress with Karus bursting through the doors calling for Clairannia who was already there, of course, since Revich had used his bond to explain to Pompeii what had happened as soon as the black towers were in his sight.

He sat on the black chair across from the blue one he had

insisted was now hers. Rubbing his hands on his face, he contemplated what he had seen.

Maybe he had known.

Maybe Baron Heimlen had guessed it as well.

But now there was no denying it.

The Blight's connection with Karus ran deeper than her ability to feel it pulsating.

It wanted her.

It wanted her?

But why?

The moment she had stepped far enough away from him that he could not reach out to her, the mist had poured in and she was gone. Fear, panic, all of the ugliness had raged through him and he ran. He ran to where she had been, finding only more death and more darkness. It seemed to have consumed her and when his voice had grown hoarse from calling her name, he heard her—barely.

He followed that voice as if his own life depended on it, because, in reality, he knew it had.

If he had lost her…

If she had gone too far…

He shook his head, anger rising at her recklessness again.

He had more to say to her, more scolding to do, and then he'd likely never let her go.

But that was a folly, he knew—no one could stop her will and trying to would just loosen his hold.

Revich hadn't expected this fear after falling for her. Falling sounded easy, like falling into bed after a long day, or falling into the arms of a lover where you could be safe even if just for a short amount of time. Those things he understood and knew well, but the fear of losing what he loved was sharp and clouded his thoughts at times, muddling his thinking and intentions.

Now that he had found his missing piece, the thought of ever losing her was torture. He'd never be able to replace her, no matter what wise words Baron Heimlen had for him. Therefore, losing her was surely the end of him as a whole.

Fuck.

Why did she go in there so confidently?

His mind raced again about the things he'd like to say to her when he heard a light knock at the door.

"Come in."

She slid through the small opening she gave herself, shutting the heavy door quietly, leaning back against it, biting her lower lip as she always did when she was scheming. She stood there, her hair wild, her skirts ripped and blackened, the whiff of withered life meeting his nose.

"You knock now?"

"I wasn't sure if you had calmed down yet."

"I haven't."

"I figured. But I wanted to change and all of my things are here."

"Of course all of your things are here. You live here."

"I know I live here."

"Good."

"Good."

Revich sat tense on the chair, his head turned over his shoulder so that he could look at her.

He varied between yelling and laughing. He was angry, yes, but she was adorable.

She was home.

There was his piece, his heart, standing at the door, looking as if she'd just survived a battle and yet her presence allured him anyway.

"I'll just get changed then."

She moved toward the armoire they shared, and he caught her hand as she passed, rising finally, turning her around.

"Our discussion isn't done."

"I know that."

"In fact, I think you'll be hearing about it not just from me in the near future. Once Figuerah and Clairannia learn about this—"

"I told them already. And yes, I heard plenty about it from them. She's okay by the way. Moira. Clairannia is truly gifted. We will keep her in my old room for now as she heals. I'll stay with her. It's best Clairannia is near anyway in case she takes a turn…"

Her voice trailed off in her explanation. He looked down at her in distress, recalling her disappearance in the mist and how he had screamed her name over and over again.

She shook her head, reaching up to cup his cheek. "I'm sorry, Rev. I'm sorry, but I'm going to stop apologizing now. And I'm *not* sorry for saving Moira's life."

He opened his mouth to speak, having plenty to say about that faerie and what she was really worth, but she covered it with her hand, the scent of her warming his heart.

"Don't speak. Go back to not speaking for a moment."

He couldn't help but smile under her hand. Her green eyes brightened. "You were there to save me. You got me out. You got *us* out. And we know more about the Blight now. I promise, I will never enter it without you again. I am safe. I am here. We are together. There is no need for your fear, Rev. I'm okay. We're both okay."

She rose slightly to meet his lips and her hands tucked his hair back behind his ears. It was a kiss of assurance. A way to subdue him, as she surely intended.

He kept his eyes open and watched her face as she caressed her mouth over his.

She was right about one thing.

She would never go into the Blight without him again.

Because she was never again going into the Blight.

Period.

CHAPTER 33
KARUS

"**W**hy have you brought me to this dreadful place, Burned Girl?"

Moira lay against Karus's pillow, her iridescent wings splayed out behind her delicate green body. She looked out of place there. The bed was far too big and her makeshift clothes Figuerah had fashioned out of a stocking hung off her shoulders at an odd angle. The material wrapped around her chest and waist in a half-hearted attempt to give her body cover. It was mostly an unsuccessful attempt, and Moira began pulling at the thin material, trying to unwrap what was wrapped around her several times.

"*Ash*. It *was* Ash. My name has changed since we last met." Karus gently swept the faerie's hands aside and helped unravel the stocking from her body. "My name is Karus now." She smiled warmly as she brought the blanket up over Moira's chest, the stocking tossed aside.

"Well, that's eons better. Why didn't you go by Karus in the first place?" Moira sat up, the blanket falling off her chest as she flexed her wings in and out, testing their fluidity.

Karus laughed and shrugged. "I was *given* the name Ash. I *chose* the name Karus."

The faerie scoffed and rolled her large violet eyes mumbling, "Humans are so backwards."

"How do you feel, Moira?"

She crossed her arms and cocked her head. "How do I *feel*? Do I have to answer to leave?" She stood up, stumbling, but catching herself. Her wings fluttered as she lifted off the bed. Her right wing faltered after a few moments and she cascaded down, bouncing and rolling back onto the sheets.

"Your wing and legs were broken. Maybe it's best if you stay here for a few days. We're not keeping you here forever, just suggesting you stay until you have your strength back."

Moira's gaze was venomous as she sat cross-legged, arms folded and teeth clenched.

"Would you like something to eat? I have fruit, meat—some water if you'd like."

"What's that there?" She pointed to the single cinnamon bun Karus had been able to snatch from the kitchens after changing her clothes.

"That is something delicious. It's called a cinnamon bun. It's cinnamon, sugar, and butter wrapped in dough and baked. Then a sticky icing is added—"

"What's butter? I do not know these words, *Karusss*." She hissed her name just as she did on their first meeting. And now that Karus knew she was out of danger, she laughed, the little fae's attempt to be menacing lost in her new environment and situation.

"Just try it. I think you'll be pleasantly surprised." She tore a piece from the bun and handed it to her.

Moira sniffed it tentatively before taking a small bite, chewing loudly. Her eyes raised in surprise, and she heartily took another.

"I want to ask—what were you doing in the Blight? You were so far into it, I almost didn't make it out after I found you."

"I was exploring, *obviously*. Why would anything go in there unless that was their reason?" She narrowed her eyes at Karus, staring at her as if she was dense as stone.

"I don't know, I just thought maybe you knew something I didn't about the Blight and you had another reason."

"I'm sure I *do* know more than you about *That Which Consumes*, but surely even you are not surprised by that."

"That Which Consumes? That's what you call it?"

"That's what *all* the living things in the forest call it. It consumes. Makes more sense than this…*blight* you keep saying."

"A blight is a disease on plant life, so—"

"And does it just disease plants, Karus?" She shook her head in dismay, licking her long fingers. "You humans and your language." She sighed and flexed her wings again. "I suppose, though, that I should be grateful to you. The dark became too thick for even me to notice that it had not yet completely devoured the muri I was examining."

"Muri? That was the large cat creature?"

"Do you know *nothing*? What do they teach you here in this eyesore anyway?" She rolled her eyes and began examining her fingers.

"I suppose I'm a bit behind in my lessons on forest fauna. I'm sure Figuerah knows—"

"The wooded one?" She scoffed. "Do not bring her back in here. She pestered me with so many questions while you were gone just now that I decided to pretend to sleep to escape. I've never met a human so interested in my kind."

Karus laughed heartily. She wished she had been there to see Figuerah pepper her with questions.

A loud knock came at the door. Karus rose from the bed and opened it a crack.

"I came to see how Moira is doing. And I have a few questions for her as well if she's up to it."

Revich stood at the door, his hands shoved into his pockets. It was one of the few times Karus had seen him frown so much in a day and she decided to stifle her grin.

"I'll ask. She's not dressed currently, so you'll have to wait out here while I do it." She closed the door and turned back to the bed. Moira was already out of it, having climbed down the side, holding onto the blankets, now rummaging naked in Karus's old dresser drawers.

"Are you looking for something to wear?"

Moira was pulling out some ribbons and tying them behind her, covering her chest and most of her lower half. She shrugged and climbed to the top of the dresser, the cinnamon bun on the plate next to her, and she began picking off pieces of the icing. "I didn't know you already knew the bog monster."

"What?"

"The bog monster? The thing I warned you about when you got yourself lost in the forest?"

"*Revich* is the bog monster?" Karus's laugh boomed through the small room, causing Moira to jump and flutter in place for a moment before coming back down to continue her treat.

"Of course, he is. Have you actually *seen* him? Rummaging around the forest blindly, jumping into the murkiest waters, causing a ruckus wherever he steps. I made him jump in place for an hour once." She took in another mouthful. "He had to clap, too."

Karus was beside herself in laughter, no doubt irritating the bog monster behind the door. Wiping tears, she stammered, "I thought you had never met the bog monster. That's what you told me. It was something you'd only encounter once."

"Well, hopefully you'd only ever encounter it once. And I didn't really meet him—I didn't even ask his name. I just made him jump."

"Can you really curse someone to never have happy dreams again? Isn't that what you said you'd do?"

She narrowed her eyes, leaning forward. "No, I can't. And don't tell me you actually *like* the bog monster?"

Karus shrugged. "Actually, I fell in love with the bog monster. And his name is Revich."

Moira stuck out her tongue in mock disgust.

"Though, I believe I will never let him live this one down, so thank you for giving him a name. I will use it wisely."

"If you want to love monsters, I have some more suggestions for you."

"Maybe another time." Karus grinned. She was beginning to like this faerie. "He wanted to ask you some questions. I can turn him away if you're not up to it."

"Questions? Sure, I'll answer his questions on one condition."

"And what is that, Moira?"

"He brings me another one of these." She gestured to the top-eaten cinnamon bun, her smile full of sharp teeth, her mouth covered in sticky icing.

CHAPTER 34
REV

"We can work together on this, Moira. You and us. Your kind and ours. What have you learned of the Blight?"

It had taken ages for the cook to make another batch of these damned cinnamon buns—they seemed to haunt him now.

The fae sat quietly, her green hands a mess, the ribbons around her body out of place on her spongy form. He had heard Karus laughing at whatever she had said and that had irritated him even more.

He hated being irritated. It wasn't something he was used to and he sulked the entire hour it took to make the buns. Surely, Lia knew some magic to speed up the process. He knew she had been a channeler in training decades ago, but knew little else about her and thought it was best not to pester the one who made your food everyday.

Moira grinned, her smile so alarming and feral. "Well…let's see. I know, for one, our name for it is much better than yours." She looked up to him casually, shrugging. "Names are important, you know."

"Fine. *That Which Consumes*. What do you know of it besides the obvious consuming it does?"

Karus placed a hand on his shoulder. He was sitting in front of her old dresser, the infuriating faerie on top, dangling her legs over the drawer. He sighed at the gesture and understood it. She was probably right. He was being too harsh to get any information out of her.

"I know that it consumes all it touches. I know that it has grown rapidly in the past fifteen weeks, and I know that sometimes, the things it devours regain life."

"Regain life? How so?"

"Some of the creatures come back to living. You haven't been inside of it much, have you, *Baron*?" She stood and began to flutter off the dresser, the use of his title full of mocking disdain.

"No. We haven't. We've mostly been trying to find history of it, thinking if we can discover its origins, we can discover its weaknesses."

"Weaknesses?" she scoffed, landing and leaning to one side, her hands glued to her hips. "*Light*, you fool. Haven't you discovered yet that light can repel it?" She shook her head in disbelief. "Have you not seen that it grows slowly in the sun? And compare that to a cloudy day? What have you been doing all this time? Huddling around books instead of doing productive things like observing and measuring it?"

Unfortunately, this was one of those times where the obvious seems to strike you in the face. Rev felt embarrassment rising to his cheeks and he leaned on his mouth.

Why *hadn't* they been measuring the Blight regularly? Why hadn't they been observing it each day instead of pouring over book after book, looking for any mention of it?

He did feel a fool now, an aggravated one, stuffed up in this room that was no longer hers, being told off by this faerie of whom Karus had almost been gone forever to save.

He shook his head and bit his tongue. "I will speak to Baron Heimlen, but no, I don't believe we knew direct light keeps it at bay."

Karus piped in, "That must be why I was able to finish off the muri. I enhanced my magic with a lightning spell and killed it."

Revich clenched his jaw. Would this event haunt him forever now? Would his anger rise every time he remembered what had almost been?

"Maybe. But it's really sunlight that does it in. We've been measuring That Which Consumes since it arrived. And that was years ago. Well before either of *you* came. Back when we only had *one* Baron to deal with."

Revich took a moment to gather his thoughts. He stood and paced the small room, which was difficult. "Moira, how many faeries are there in the forest? You're the only one I've encountered."

"I don't think you need to know that, human. But I will tell you —of all of us, I'm the most willing to be civil to your kind. Ever trip on a rock in the forest? Ever step into an orb weaver's web?" She giggled. "Ever find yourself a bit lost and confused?"

Karus folded her arms across her chest, shaking her head.

"We're everywhere, so don't even think about doing anything secretly in *our* forest. Been out under the full moon lately?"

"You saw that?" Karus was doing her best not to laugh, her eyes meeting his.

"I heard about it. The bog monster found a boggy lady and blah, blah, blah."

Revich pinched the space between his brows. "Okay. We get it. You're everywhere. Moira, would you be willing to show us your findings? The growth rate, I mean. Also, the date which you discovered That Which Consumes. I'm sure we can share our discoveries with your kind as well."

The little fae laid back on the dresser, arms behind her head, legs crossed at the knee. "I suppose so. Only because we all currently want the same thing. I'll speak to our growers. They'll have the information you're asking for. I'll tell them you want it gone, too. Maybe that will help your case."

"Is there anything else you can tell us?"

"Probably."

"Will you?"

"Maybe."

Revich looked to Karus, annoyance practically swimming in the air around them both.

"Let's let her rest, Rev. She's had a long day."

He shoved his hands back in his pockets, squeezing them into fists and nodded. "I'll go speak to Baron Heimlen then. Can I talk to you outside, Karus?"

They were alone in the narrow hallway with Clairannia and Figuerah's rooms just a little ways down, though they were likely in Viridis currently.

Karus began to walk with him toward the winding staircase, her questions coming in quick succession out of earshot of the faerie. "What do you think? Is she telling the truth? Does sunlight repel the Blight?"

He'd been wondering the same. "I don't think faeries lie very well. They can distort the truth, if I'm not mistaken, but maybe that's something to speak to Figuerah about or search for in Viridis. I don't know why she would lie, considering her kind also wants to see the Blight gone."

Karus leaned against the banister, the foyer many levels below them. "We really do know very little about it, don't we? This all seems so…daunting. How are we ever going to destroy it?" She shook her head and bit her bottom lip. "Maybe it's time to practice Cosensian Magic near the Blight. Maybe we can start to try using it? Surely there's magic Baron Heimlen is thinking of trying. Why else would we practice so often?"

"Maybe. He and I can go first."

"I'm not a child, Revich. I won't make the same mistake again. Even Baron Heimlen has said—you need me, too."

"Yeah. Yeah, I do."

His words hung in the air, the truth of them flitting across her face.

He stared at her, wanting her, needing to be close to her. He needed to know she was safe, she was his—as much his as she would give.

He'd take it.

He'd take whatever she gave him.

"*Rev.*"

And there it was again. Her voice unfolding smooth and soft.

In a moment she was in his arms, his hands sliding into her hair, their lips pressed together as he inhaled fully.

He could live in this moment.

She was safe.

She was here.

"Karus," he whispered. She broke from his mouth to kiss his jaw, his neck, sliding her hands under his shirt, pulling him nearer. "I need you."

"Then by all means—take me."

That was all he ever wanted to hear.

He pulled her up onto his hips, his mouth back on hers, hard, determined. If he never broke from her kiss, he'd be fine with that.

He led them to a small, dark alcove just off the stairs. He pushed her back against the stone, reaching up under her skirts, pushing aside the undergarments in his way.

He slid one hand down the very center of her, smiling at the slickness which met his fingers. He slid two inside of her, curling them toward him and she inhaled sharply, arching her head back, just as he wanted her to.

She'd become wild. He loved doing that to her.

Her passion was never to be dismissed in these moments. She pulled on his shoulders, his neck, anywhere she could grip, her desire for him pouring off of her in rollicking waves, her pleasure an ocean he'd happily drown within.

He ran circles over her most sensitive center with his thumb, kissing her hard—harder than he usually would.

She met his passion with her own, just as raw and forceful.

Usually by now, she'd be begging him for what she wanted. He loved that. But she resisted. Whether it was due to her strong will or just because she knew what he needed, he didn't have time to wonder, as her hand found her way to the thick of him.

She gripped him softly at first, her hands delicate and gentle.

Their desire consumed their very souls, burning, scorching—two young lovers unbroken and unmarred by the desolation of love.

She held him firm, her strokes quick, the pressure in him mounting, and he broke from her lips, his head leaning back, breath coming in long audible exhales, his chest sinking inward.

She saw her opportunity and took it, pushing him into the corner and pressing his shoulders down.

She was over him in an instant, adjusting her skirts expertly. She slid onto him in one deft motion, the embrace of her body catching him off-guard each time, reminding him of just how powerless he'd become, reminding him he would do anything—anything—to keep her.

She sat still on top of him in some kind of new torture, kissing his forehead, his eyes, the tip of his nose, moving softly to his lips as she began their rhythm like a conductor of music, the rise and fall of their song one she alone would pace.

"You didn't lose me," she whispered, her lips close to his ear as he tried and failed to stop his eyes from burning.

She kissed away the tears that fell all the while picking up the tempo of their bodies, their song on the verge of climax. "You'll never lose me, Rev." She kissed his mouth, her body in fluid motion—a symphony of passion on top of his and all sense of purpose was lost to him.

It was only her.

It was only him.

He held her face in front of his as they joined in their ecstasy.

Her eyes ever so green.

Her breath ever so sweet.

Her heart ever so his.

CHAPTER 35
SYLVA

"You're much too hard on him, Heimlen."

He grunted, not in agreement, but in acknowledgement of her opinion. He dipped his toasted bread into the runny yolk on his plate, the brilliant yellow center spilling outward across the whole of it in a flood of gold.

"He still doesn't understand what it takes, Sylva. He hasn't accepted the truth of his situation, and he needs to."

She laughed, her smile genuine and youthful. "And would you have at only twenty-three, dear? Don't you remember what it was like in those days? You were young and free. Your burdens seemed too far away to pay attention to and your…vigor was almost unhinged." She drank coyly from her cup of tea, raising her eyebrows across the small table, daring him to deny her words.

They shared breakfast together each morning. They had done this for years in their own simple solitude. This was their one small commitment to each other, both knowing they could have little more than that.

Sylva would tell Heimlen of the ins and outs of the Fortress, who was doing what, and how things were fairing along.

After his Overseer had died, he had told her he didn't need a new one because he had her.

She was precious to him. She understood that.

She was necessary to him as well. All her sacrifices were given to the greatest cause she could think of—the continuation of Felgren, the training of channelers, the role of Barons, and the overall health of the forest and the people who lived there.

He smirked, shaking his head.

"What if you are approaching the subject in the wrong way? You are telling Revich that he is this and he is that and that everything lies on his shoulders."

"Because it does."

"I know, I know, but what if you spoke to him in a different manner? Not a Baron to his successor, but a father to his son? You might start by praising him first and go from there. You'll catch more flies with honey, darling."

"I don't need to catch him. I need him to focus. I need him to stop acting like a lesser man than he is."

"He is in *love*, Heimlen. Probably for the first time in his life—don't you remember what that is like? Think of the first woman you fell for within these walls. Surely you can remember that far back?" She grinned slyly, placing her cup onto its matching saucer.

She loved this set. Purple and blue violets adorned the handle, the artist capturing the detail of the colors so well. She kept them here, in the Baron's rooms, so that they could not be used elsewhere in the Fortress.

It was just for the two of them.

She took his cold, bare fingers into hers, his love of Felgren apparent on them. "All I am trying to say is that Revich has not yet had his first heartbreak. He loves wild and new, no holding back. She, on the other hand, is more cautious, but I can see her wanting to let go. Who knows what she endured in that dreadful city to make her so untrusting. You know she told me once that she was only ever allowed to light the fires in the rooms of the castle and occasionally ripen fruit. Can you imagine having all that power and nowhere for it to go?"

Heimlen placed his fork down across his plate, his other hand moving over hers and he smiled at her, but she didn't understand why it didn't reach his eyes.

"Yes, Sylva, my darling, you've told me that story before."

"Oh, well, maybe it serves as a good reminder for you. If you want her to be able to open up more of her magic to you, Revich might be a good way for her to be able to do so. Because if he can get her to understand her full potential…well, that means she is more useful to our cause, is she not?"

"You were always so cunning and beautiful, Sylva. My dear Sylva. What would I have been without you?" He kissed the top of her hand, squeezing it gently.

He loved her so well. He could only give so much, and she had understood that for many years now, watching him continue the legacy of Baron and develop his own legacy to be left behind.

She was glad to have been a part of it.

She had dedicated her life to the continuation of his and that was everything to her.

"Can you imagine? You'd have been lost long ago without me, Heimlen."

He smirked. "Are you ready, dearest?" He pulled his black leather gloves from his pocket, guiding them up over the hands that had just held hers.

She sighed and stood, nodding.

He did love her. He loved her as much as any Baron could love another.

"Yes. I am ready."

He whispered the words she had come to know well as she stood on the tips of her toes to reach his lips, "*Osculum Vitae*."

He kissed her, soft, sweet, familiar.

He must have been tired this morning. He took more life from her than usual and more quickly as well.

He held onto her arms as she felt herself growing weak, her ability to stay upright harder now that he needed her more often.

When their lips parted and he had taken what was necessary, she smiled up at him dizzily, his black eyes flecked with gray like the promise of a summer storm across the sky.

He lifted her onto his bed with his strong arms now fully anew with her strength. He unfolded the blankets and then covered her body as she curled into the scent of him in the sheets.

"Rest now, my darling Sylva. I will come and wake you before your duties at lunch." He kissed her forehead and brushed her cheek.

He really did love her.

He needed her.

He needed her just as much as she needed him.

CHAPTER 36
REV

"You look well today, Baron!" Revich greeted his mentor, giving him a hearty pat across his back as they walked to the lumen den.

"Yes, I slept well, Revich. And how fares the wild fae?"

"When I spoke to Karus this morning, she assured me her healing was progressing. I spoke to Moira yesterday, as you asked."

"And?"

"She was not very forthcoming, as you predicted. She did have one thing to say, though. Moira claims that light—particularly sunlight—causes the Blight to…regress? Have you come across this before?"

"Hmm. I have not. Shall we have a little experiment this morning, my boy?"

Revich raised his brows, unused to such a term of endearment from the Baron. "By all means, lead the way."

When they arrived at the Blight, reassuring their lumens with ear scratches, Revich could see the small patch of black vines that jutted out from the perimeter where Karus had stood the day before.

The morning summer sun shone down from the east, casting

long shadows across the forest floor, but somehow still, the Blight's shadow was darker.

Blacker.

Colder.

"Let's first try illumination magic."

Baron Heimlen held a gloved hand out before him, the silvery gray orb of magic he possessed floating above his hand as he mumbled, "*Illuminare.*" The orb began to pulse with his own heartbeat, growing in size as well.

He neared the edge and bent down, closer to the vines that created a thick barrier around the Blight. He moved his orb of magic closer, the pulse of it rising slightly as his heart beat quicker.

The silvery light illuminated the nest of vines, but they did not draw back into the abyss as Revich had hoped.

"It seemed too easy a solution," he sighed, squeezing Baron Heimlen's shoulder in reassurance.

"So it did. It's your turn, Revich. What can you do to produce sunlight on this spot?"

Baron Heimlen stood, his quickness surprising Revich. Since beginning daily training with Karus, he had seemed so weak.

"I was researching in Viridis last night and found something that might just work to act as sunlight." Revich inhaled deeply, focusing his magic, thinking of his purpose. "*Simulair Solum.*"

Just as it had happened in Viridis, beams of golden light spread from the very tips of his fingers. He posed them downward at the edge of the Blight.

The effect was by no means instantaneous, but he was determined to see something work. The simulated sunlight was warm on his fingers, the effect threatening to burn his skin if he held it any longer.

"Steady. Steady, Revich. Look—there!"

Baron Heimlen pushed aside a layer of vines with his gloved fingers, immune to the protruding thorns.

Revich squinted, the light bright in his eyes, but the evidence of his work was there was all the same. The blackened soil of the forest floor sizzled and withered under the replicated beams of sunlight, the inky layer retreating from the glow he produced, leaving behind a patch of brown earth. It was identical to the one he stood on outside of the abyss.

"You've done it!"

Revich let go of the spell, blisters forming at the tips of his fingers, but he hardly cared.

It had worked.

Small though the patch was, it was there still, before both of their eyes. The greatest of hope was restored in his chest as he heaved heavily, the effort of such magic draining him as he wiped sweat from his brow.

"How did you come across such an enhancement?" Baron Heimlen reached down between the vines, grabbing a fistful of rich, brown soil in his gloved hand, bringing it to his nose and holding it before them.

"After speaking with Moira last night, I headed straight to Viridis—to the Agricola Conduit Hall. I knew I had read books before about using simulated sunlight to grow crops in harsh springs and summers."

He pinched the soil with his blistered fingers. It was warm and smooth, healthy to his eyes, and he brought it to Rauca, letting her sniff his hands. She did so with enthusiasm, pausing a moment to lick the tips of his raw fingers before following the scent to where Baron Heimlen bent down, pulling the thorny vines back from the patch of new ground. She hesitated a moment, sniffing the vines before sinking her large snout into the hole the Baron created, rummaging in the dirt.

She sneezed loudly and Revich smiled. She looked to him then, whining in her high pitch, running to him joyfully, almost knocking him down as she managed to get her massive paws up to his shoulders, licking his face eagerly.

"Well, I think Rauca approves!"

Baron Heimlen's lumen joined into the revelry soon after, making the same sound of excitement as the Baron gathered more of the soil onto a wide strip of bark he took from a nearby tree.

"We must not become too encouraged yet. I will bring this soil back to the Fortress. Sylva has a knack for agricola magic. I'll see if she can grow anything from it, but—" He clasped a gloved hand across Revich's back, jostling him slightly, his smile reaching across his face. "You've done well today, Revich. I am proud of you. You've done this all yourself because that's all you need, my boy. That's all a Baron ever needs."

He repeated the line he had spoken to Revich often and though he couldn't agree, he grinned, allowing himself to bask in the praise of the only father he had ever known.

CHAPTER 37
KARUS

"How about this one?"

"Too orange."

"And this? Let me guess—too red?"

"Yes, but that one does make a nice paint. We use it to decorate our bodies on the longest day of summer."

"Sounds intriguing."

"Of course, you'd think so. No humans have ever seen the celebration, and besides, our singing would hurt your ears and our beauty melt your eyes out of their sockets."

Karus tilted her head back and laughed but not before seeing a small smirk creeping from the corner of Moira's lips.

"Something dark. A good show of my depression here. A reflection of its walls and all that."

Karus rolled her eyes and went back to the bouquet of flowers she had picked this morning. Moira had requested that she find her new attire that did not involve fabric or ribbons if she was going to have to stay in the Fortress to heal.

She had spent the better part of the morning in the forest searching for patches of flowers or bushes adorned in them so that Moira had a variety to pick from.

The faerie fascinated her. Her emotions and movements were so human-like at times and so foreign at others.

"What about this one?" She pulled out one of her favorites—a calla lily. The color of this patch had been the closest to black she had ever seen with a hint of a hue of purple.

"Yes. That one will do."

Transfixed, Karus watched as the faerie shimmied out of her ribbons and began to peel strips of the calla lily leaf into pieces, humming as she weaved them together with her long fingers. She braided them so quickly, Karus could not follow the pattern. Within only a few minutes, Moira was fastening the strips around her chest, her new clothing for her torso finished.

"I've never realized how perfect a calla lily is as a skirt."

"That's because you don't take the time you should to realize a lot of things," Moira sighed, stepping into the flower's single petal. "But, I suppose you are young. And you don't have much of a teacher, either."

"Can I ask how old you are?"

Moira licked the palm of her hand with a pointy green tongue and wiped her saliva across the flower at her waist. She did this several times, and finally, Karus's curiosity took over.

"Is that…is that some kind of adhesive?"

Moira's violet eyes looked up to hers and she nodded. "Yes, and thirty-seven summers. Thirty-eight by the end of this one."

"Oh. You don't count time in years?"

"Why would I count time in your years when Felgren does not follow them?"

"Good point."

"I would guess that my almost thirty-eight summers is equal to…I don't know, a good hundred of your years?"

"I see."

"Yes, that's a great estimate. Of course…well, do you know that seasons here are not the same in time outside of the forest? And… you know there are four seasons, right?"

"Of course I know there are four seasons."

"I cannot be sure of what you do and do not know, Karus."

"Well, knowing there are four seasons seems like an obvious thing an adult woman would know."

"I would think an adult woman would know a floral skirt when she saw one and how to avoid a bog monster, but you did not know those things, did you?"

"Knowledge is relevant, Moira. I would imagine an almost thirty-eight-summers-old fae to know what butter and flour is, but you did not."

"I see."

"Do you? We can learn from each other, you and I. We can be friends here. Our kind and yours can even work together to destroy That Which Consumes."

"Perhaps." She fluttered above the dresser, lifting off gently, her new calla lily skirt a lovely contrast to her sage skin. "What do you think?"

"I think you've done this before. And I think it will work for your time here perfectly."

Moira nodded, floating back down to the dresser and tucking her wings behind her. "Let's go to the kitchens then."

"The kitchens?"

"You can start our friendship by teaching me about butter and flour as long as it all turns into more of those cinnamon buns."

"You have flour in your hair."

Karus reached up to brush it away, but Revich's hands were already there, smoothing the streaks of white dust out of her chestnut locks.

"Baking lessons with Moira. Did you know that Lia uses her magic to quicken cooking times? It's very impressive."

"I did not know."

"What did you and Baron Heimlen do this morning?"

Karus and Revich were lying on the cool grass in the courtyard of Viridis, having agreed to meet there for lunch the night before. She leaned over his chest and held a fat, crimson strawberry above his mouth, teasing him by pretending to let him have a bite before taking it back and sinking her teeth into its juicy flesh herself.

"We discovered something that might have returned some of the soil to pre-blight."

Karus choked. "What! Why didn't you say something the moment you saw me?"

"I was easing into it."

"You were kissing me."

"Sounds like a good way to ease into something."

She sighed and bit into the rest of the strawberry, smiling at his scoff. "Nothing for you until you talk."

His grin was roguish, a single image that could lead to her complete downfall and she wouldn't even care.

"Last night, I searched these halls for something that could mimic sunlight as Moira mentioned. I had read before of such enhancements from agricola conduits. I figured there must be some way we could simulate sunlight if that's really what could repel the Blight."

"And you found it?"

"I did. *Simulair Solum.* It produces sunlight from your fingers." He held his up and she gasped at the raw blisters there. "But, it's not without its hazards."

She took his hands in hers, whispering words of healing, happy to see the blisters recede a bit as she gently kissed each one.

"This is a big discovery, Baron Revich. Possibly, with the combination of our power through Cosensian—"

"We're not ready to try that yet. Baron Heimlen has taken some of the soil to Sylva. She will attempt to grow something from it, and we will see if sunlight truly heals the forest."

"And if it doesn't? Isn't no blight better than anything else? We should go now. We should be out there trying Cosensian Magic together against the Blight instead of eating strawberries while the forest is consumed."

"I haven't had any strawberries yet."

"Here." She tossed one into his lap as she rose, dusting her thin skirts and packing up their lunch, uneaten as it was.

He stood and pulled her hair off her shoulder, trailing his hand down her back. "Karus. Baron Heimlen knows what he's doing. You don't need to go running off to the Blight right now."

"Yes, I do. We have a potential answer to this problem. Why would we just sit around waiting to see if something can grow from the healed soil when we could be fighting it?"

"Baron Heimlen is resting. He had more energy than usual this morning, but still, using his magic takes more from him each day. And we need him to get through this." He took her hand, kissing her palm and holding it to his chest. "Please listen. I understand how badly you want to destroy the Blight. I really do. And you are not the only one who wants this weight off our shoulders. But rushing into things isn't going to get us there. I do admire your tenacity. I find it quite attractive, honestly."

There was that damn grin again.

"Alright. We can eat—I guess. But I want to speak to Baron Heimlen myself when he wakes."

Revich kissed her forehead and pulled her into his arms, her head resting on his shoulder.

He had said he understood, but he didn't.

For now, she had another reason to destroy the Blight.

It had something of hers, and the emptiness in her pocket where the rhyzolm would usually hang heavily felt like a betrayal.

It was out there somewhere in the dark abyss, fallen out of her ripped pocket when she climbed over the tree to get to Moira.

She melted into his embrace, promising herself she would get it back. She told herself that by not telling him it was lost, she was protecting the man she loved.

CHAPTER 38
KARUS

"Can I help you, dear?"

Karus jumped. "Sylva! You startled me!"

She moved back against the door to Baron Heimlen's study, having just been about to attempt to unlock it with her magic. She wasn't even sure if that was something her magic could do.

"I'm sorry. If you're looking for Baron Heimlen, he is not in there." She smiled warmly. "Or are you looking for Baron Revich?"

"Oh. No, I just left him in Viridis. I am looking for Baron Heimlen, actually. Do you know where I can find him?"

"He is resting in his rooms, though I know that he is awake. Aren't you to meet him for training in an hour?"

Karus nodded, smiling. She wasn't sure how the Fortress could be run without people like Sylva or Pompeii to keep track of everything that needed to be done. She had enjoyed getting to know the woman and admired her love of Baron Heimlen after all her years under his reign as Baron.

"I wanted to speak with him before the training, actually. I was hoping to catch him alone."

"Ah, I see. Well, dear, I can show you to his rooms. He might allow you an audience, though Baron Heimlen is a very private man."

Karus watched with interest as her thin, gray magic encompassed the bundle of sheets she held. It lifted them over the staircase railing to deliver them a few floors down to a table in the foyer, but Sylva could not hold it for long. The bundle fell messily onto the table in a clump at least one floor below.

"Oh, goodness." Sylva giggled, looking down at the splay of white cotton. "I used to be able to do that."

"May I help?" Karus placed her hand over Sylva's cold fingers. Concentrating her magic into the aged woman, she grinned as Sylva's face lit with surprise, their gray and green essence swirling together in a dance of power.

Sylva tried again, this time with Karus's strength and the women watched as, in a haze of gray and green, the sheets were guided back into a neat stack and set upon the table, folded and crisp.

"That was lovely, dear. Thank you." She patted Karus's hand, her own having seen at least four times as many years as Karus. "I see what Baron Heimlen says is true then. You are so very gifted. And you've been doing well, practicing Cosensian Magic. He tells me that it is a talent not every conduit has."

"You are welcome, Sylva. And I'm not a conduit—not yet at least."

"Well, the trials will come before you know it. Time may move slowly here, but when you've found something to love, it seems to move swiftly as a hummingbird's wing."

"Has it moved swiftly for you, Sylva? Your time here, I mean?"

She placed a hand on the black stone rail and beckoned for Karus to follow her as she ascended the winding staircase. "Oh, yes. It seems like time has passed me by. If I hadn't lived it myself, I'd say I arrived at the Fortress only two decades ago instead of four. Much was different then, the people here, I mean. Besides Baron Heimlen, I believe I've been here the longest…and I know a thing or two about the locked doors of this place."

Karus's eyes widened as her mind swam with excuses.

"Not to worry, dear. I recognize in you a stubborn determination to see your goals through." She turned her head and winked. "I will say, Baron Heimlen's study is not a place I'd advise you to go breaking into. It is locked with a key, yes, but a phrase must be spoken aloud as well to enter. And before you go asking,"—she looked back again at Karus—"Baron Revich does not even know that. He will eventually, of course, when the study becomes his."

"I wasn't trying to break in or anything. I just…I was just curious. I realize how idiotic that sounds when I say it out loud."

"I understand, no need to be ashamed. There are all sorts of curious things in there. Giant tomes and beakers and bottles of who knows what? What's he doing in there anyway?" She laughed aloud as if she had told herself a joke—one that Karus felt she was meant to be left out of.

"Do you know how to get in, Sylva?"

"I do."

"But you won't tell me?"

"I would if I saw a reason for you to enter such a place, but I don't currently."

"Of course."

They continued their ascent in silence, Karus forgetting to count the number of floors up they had climbed to remember where Baron Heimlen kept himself when he rested.

Karus stood outside of the small alcove where Sylva had disappeared into. The Fortress had many secrets, yes, but Karus was surprised to discover yet another.

Behind the enormous painting of a young Baron Heimlen was a door to his rooms.

Apparently, Sylva was right, and he really did prioritize his privacy. The door had been there for the entirety of her time here, just a few floors down from the channelers's rooms in the tallest tower.

Voices murmured behind the slightly ajar painting. She assumed Sylva was trying to convince Baron Heimlen to see her. If his rooms were hidden and his study door locked twice, perhaps he was not interested in ever having visitors.

Well, except for Sylva and Rev.

She stepped back to look up at the painting again.

Memories of that first night in the Fortress—the first night she had met Sylva—entered her mind and she smiled.

She had been proud of herself, proud of her resistance to being brought here. She had known so little and had not yet fallen in love, nor had she been shown how well she could be loved.

It's funny, she thought while gazing up at the portrait of the man who now trained her, *life seems to go in circles, coming back to the same things over and over.*

The same stories are told, the same feelings are felt again. For now, her resistance would be in *leaving* Felgren.

She itched to get back to the Blight. She could just see it—standing there with the Barons at her side, using Cosensian Magic to kill it off for good. Then she could continue her training with Clairannia and Figuerah and become a conduit.

She missed them. She missed their laughter and their care for each other. She was only able to see them at breakfast each morning and occasionally at dinner.

She wanted so badly to finish off the Blight so that she could live a more carefree life here—training with her friends each day and loving Revich each night.

He had impressive ideas on how to bring more magic to Arcaynen Isle. He wanted to begin with the Hallow Marshes, bringing more lapis conduits there to aid in finding rhyzolms, bringing ease to the people who searched for them desperately to sell off at enormous prices. She wanted to help him, and she had realized that she wanted to be a part of this world of channelers and conduits in any way that she could. Maybe Sylva had wanted that, too.

Karus's gaze flickered up to the massive painting, done in brilliant oils. She studied Baron Heimlen as a young man. Now he was known as the Savior of Hyrithia and the most powerful man on the isle.

She knew history books wouldn't forget the first, but she wondered if that last title was still true. As Baron Heimlen's magic faded, Revich's grew stronger, and his ease into full baronhood looked easy.

The old Baron must have been slightly younger than herself when he came to the Fortress and stood for this portrait. What had he been like then? Exuberant like Revich or did he always keep a stern demeanor, taking everything so seriously? The man who had saved the largest city in Arcaynen from the Black Fever would likely have to be serious to accomplish such feats.

His eyes were grayer in the painting and his facial hair was trimmed down to a short blonde beard at his chin. His yellow hair was longer than it was now, and it hung at his shoulders in subtle waves. His features were so similar to the ones he carried in his current age, and she wondered if there was a giant painting of Revich somewhere in the Fortress she had not happened upon yet that would forever capture *his* youth.

She grinned, thinking of all the channelers who would come to see it when Revich was old and remark at how young he had been, yet another example of the circle of events they lived inside.

There was something a bit off with Baron Heimlen's portrait, though. As she studied it, she could not quite put her finger on what had caught her interest. She moved closer, tilting her head back and squinting her eyes.

It wasn't his face or his hair. It had nothing to do with the colorings and lines that were very different than the man behind the door. No, there was something tugging at her mind, some obvious revelation that she could not pull to the surface.

She studied the details harder. The clothes he was painted in were a little old fashioned for a Baron, but still recognizable as such. For the portrait, he had worn the customary dress shirt in a light cream color under a pine wool vest with five golden buttons fastened down the center. The cut of the vest was what gave away the time period as it was looser than the vests Revich wore now. His pants had been a similar shade, finely pressed and ending at his black boots, similar to the ones she had seen him wear in the present.

The young Baron Heimlen stood tall and posed with one pale hand cuffed on the front opening of his vest and the other resting against the large oak tree he leaned against.

And there it was.

The anomaly.

Karus looked away, her mind suddenly racing, attempting to make sense of something she had never thought much of before.

"Karus, my dear, Baron Heimlen will see you. Please, come in."

Sylva's soft, worn voice interrupted her thoughts and almost by instinct, Karus found her feet walking through the door of Baron Heimlen's chambers.

The rooms were brighter than Karus would have imagined, considering how dark the Fortress often was. A single window spilled cheery sunlight into the dark stone space, illuminating the rooms in contrast to the Baron she knew and the presence he emulated.

There were two rooms here that she could see. The first that she and Sylva stood inside was a sitting room of sorts with a small wooden table to the side of a green velvet settee. A massive sideboard stood against one wall that held all of the dining wear one could ever need. Karus realized she had never seen Baron Heimlen eat in the dining hall.

In confusion, she attempted to look elsewhere in the room, but her head was swimming, grasping at memories of her time spent with the Baron.

"Karus, Sylva has told me you wish to speak alone." He stood before her then, dressed in his usual black, hands in his pockets, and nodded to Sylva, giving her a smile Karus had never seen before. "Thank you, darling."

Seeing that it was a dismissal, Sylva nodded and grinned warmly at Karus, placing a hand on her arm before turning to leave, shutting the door and likely the painting behind her.

Karus's heart was a rapid mess. All thoughts of what she planned to say about fighting the Blight were lost since examining the painting. Her only focus now was recalling memories of each moment she had spent with him.

"Would you like some tea, my dear? You look shaken. What is it you wish to tell me?"

He moved past the door behind him, heading to the sideboard to pour steaming water into two delicate teacups. His movement revealed that the other room was a bed chamber, but Karus quickly glanced away to watch him.

He motioned for her to sit, placing a steaming cup of black tea before her, setting cream and sugar down on the table as well before exhaling loudly as he sat across from where she stood.

She sat, her eyes darting anywhere and everywhere at once, determined as she was to not let them rest on his hands.

No, she was sure of it. She had never before seen him without his black leather gloves.

That's what had been so unusual, seeing the light skin of Baron Heimlen's hands. There was something so strange about it, yet simple enough that she had never wondered why he wore gloves in every setting. He even wore them now as she joined him for tea in his rooms, and though gloves were of course not unheard of on the isle, wearing them indoors, especially at a mealtime, was indeed strange. Why did he never take them off? The longer she breathed, the more her stomach twisted, nausea overtaking her senses.

She finally let her gaze settle across the table. He brought a gloved hand to his cup, bringing it up to his lips to sip the steaming tea.

"Come, now, Karus, what is it that is bothering you? Did Baron Revich tell you of our discovery this morning?"

"He—he did, Baron."

"Did you wish to discuss it? I must admit, I am not at all surprised to see you. I figured you'd charge in here, demanding we go to the Blight right away and attempt to produce all the sunlight we can."

He chuckled lightly and she finally brought her eyes to his face. Question upon question swirled through her mind, and she attempted a steadiness to ask them.

"Yes. I said as much to Baron Revich, but…I wished to discuss something else."

He raised his brows, sipping more black tea, his gloved hand a contrast to the delicate white porcelain cup adorned in blue and purple violets.

"It's about Hyrithia."

"Oh? I would think you know more of the subject than I would."

"I mean about you and Hyrithia. Had you ever been there before? Before you came to take me?"

He narrowed his brows from across the table, setting his cup down on its saucer with a clink before answering. "Yes, I have been to Hyrithia on occasion. Why do you ask?"

"When was the last time before you arrived to bring me here?"

He shifted in his seat. "Many years before, Karus. The Baron of Felgren does occasionally meet with the leaders of the isle outside of the forest. We have duties to attend to with the settlements. Trade and conduit business as you can imagine. What are you leading to?"

"I realized I've never asked you how you negotiated my Offering with the Queen. It all happened so fast, I didn't have the opportunity to speak to her about it."

"So, you're wondering how I was able to convince her to get you here?"

"How did you hear of the Black Fever? Did you know about my presence in Hyrithia before or after the outbreak?"

He rose from his chair, clasping gloved hands behind his back, gazing out the window of the bed chamber. "You'd like to hear the story then, of how I cured the Black Fever and received you as payment?"

"I would."

"Then I will oblige you. It is just as much your story as mine, after all. One more event that connects the two of us, my dear. And, perhaps you will remember, I tried to tell you this very story on your first visit to Viridis." He turned to her and gave her a half smile. "You, of course, were not ready to hear it."

"I know Revich found me. I know that he used his rhyzolm to discover I was in Hyrithia. I want to know what happened next."

"Yes, that is what happened in the simplest of terms. You see, Karus, when a Baron uses a rhyzolm to find a channeler, it's not as if a beacon of light shines from their current place of residence. It's more of a feeling, deep within his chest, a pull to the general vicinity. When the said Baron gets closer, a face begins to appear with features becoming more distinct and prominent the closer he gets. It is then that we are able to tell if it is a man or woman we seek as well as their hair color, skin color, eye color, and so forth. Questions are asked around until we are able to discover a name to give an official Offering."

"But…you could not give an Offering to a resident of Hyrithia, not one who was born within its walls."

"No. Due to the Treaty, I could not just give you an Offering as you were. I also understood after discovering more about you, that you would likely decline one."

"So, the Black Fever gave you an opportunity—"

"It was months of letters with the Queen before the Black Fever fell upon your city. She refused to let you go, and I refused to back down from negotiations." He turned to her and smiled dimly. "It was a sorrowful affair, but my own good fortune when the fever spread through Hyrithia."

"Because you could cure it…for a price."

"Because I saw a way to bring you here. Now, that may make you think less of me, but I am a resourceful man. And still, it took almost three months to discover a cure. Do not think that I was not working with Baron Revich to help save your people, just as all conduits of the city were doing at the time."

"Revich helped find the cure?"

"He did. He worked as tirelessly as I did to bring you here. He has always understood the importance in you being brought here whether he believed you would be useful or not. And now we know that you are not just powerful, but have a connection to the Blight which we did not expect. In my eyes, it is just more evidence that you arrived just as you should, in the place you were always meant to be."

She looked down to his black gloved hand upon her shoulder as he stood behind her. A haunting chill ran down her spine as her stomach threatened to purge its contents.

His story made sense enough—but the timing still worried at her. Between the 'negotiations', as he had called them, and the Black Fever infecting the Prince just before he cured the city…

"When did the Queen finally accept your terms?"

"When her son was infected, of course. She held a strong front until then, weakened by the love of her child as most mothers are."

"How convenient for you—that her son was infected and she had to choose between his life or mine."

"I see it less as convenience and more of prophecy. You were meant to be here, and I was meant to be the one to escort you. I am thankful, in fact, that the Black Fever did not take ahold of you, my dear."

"Yes, it was random in its targets, never infecting a whole household, never any real connections to the victims young and old." Karus turned her head to look up at him. "An odd sickness. Had you ever come across such a thing before? Ever cured anything like it?"

He held a gloved hand to his chin, rubbing it in thought. "I have not in all my time as Baron. It was a strange thing, to be sure."

"Yes, very strange. And the way the sickness left the inflicted's fingers black and discolored along with their hands…even after being cured…" She looked down at her cup and shakily lifted it, her emerald conduit ring one more reminder of their connection. "I'll never forget the look of it."

A stillness filled the room. Karus sat stiff in her chair, unsure of her discovery, her motive, or her pursuit of answers.

His voice cut the silence in a low murmur, "You helped take care of the sick, did you not?"

"I did. I did what I could. I had no real ties to medicus magic, but I was able to help take some of the pain from those who suffered."

"Let us be grateful then, that you now have more purpose and use of your magic here in Felgren and that your talents are not wasted in a place that does not appreciate the use of them."

She wasn't sure anymore about where this conversation was going or where it had led to.

She feared what was underneath those black gloves.

The Black Fever was too convenient, too coinciding with his plans to bring her here. And its origin? As far as she knew, it was never found. Hopefully, the Queen had discovered more by now, but she couldn't shake the timing or the truth that the cure had given Baron Heimlen exactly what he wanted.

She refused to believe that Revich had anything to do with it. He would never cause harm to a mass of people, no matter how badly he wanted something.

She needed to leave Baron Heimlen's presence and think this over. She needed to speak to Rev.

"Thank you for telling me the story, Baron. I look forward to writing to the Queen at the end of the season when letters can be delivered. I hope they have discovered more about the Black Fever's origins so as to prevent its outbreak elsewhere on the isle."

"Indeed, I look forward to my own correspondence with the Queen. I am sure she is of great impatience to hear how your time here has fared. I will remind you, though, the Blight is not to be discussed outside of this forest. We don't want to cause a panic, now do we?"

Had his smile always been so menacing? The look on his face was full of authority and power. One she could never imagine on Revich's face, no matter how many years he had been Baron.

"No, no we do not. If you'll excuse me,"—she rose from the table, heading toward the door—"I'd like to freshen up before our training this afternoon and check on Moira."

"Ah, yes, the little faerie is doing well in your care, I hope?"

"Her strength returns quickly. It's a miracle she lived through the ordeal."

"Yes, the Blight seems to have no hesitation in taking what it wants. It's what makes it so very, very dangerous, Karus."

Her hand stilled on the door handle before her, unsure if he was really speaking of the Blight at all.

"I understand, Baron." She turned her head over her shoulder. "I understand that very well."

She left, hurrying past the painting, down the endless stairs into the foyer. If she was lucky, she would be able to find Rev before their training began. If anyone would believe her suspicions, she hoped it would be him.

CHAPTER 39
REV

"In some circles, it is said that before the first trial, there is another. Not having a formal name, nor formal rules, it is a sort of predetermination of a channeler's worth in Felgren.

Quite scandalous to history, but I will mention it here, as this is a book about the history of the trials and this, I would say, is history.

Indeed, the very first trial a channeler faces after their Offering, after being escorted to Felgren, is one of the heart. Can they accept Felgren as their home? As a piece of them they shall bring to all other things in life? That is the gist of this initial trial and there have been very few who have failed it, sent back to their homes in disgrace without much of a reason why.

This unusual trial is conducted solely by the Baron who gave the Offerings. The trial is given on his whim and to his liking. Past examples have included being able to let the channeler's voice echo in the wind, or identify a type of tree by mere touch alone.

Whatever the content of this trial, it is always performed before the channeler is introduced to Viridis—the Fortress and Felgren's great child that lies within both."

Not for the first time, Revich wondered who this author was. How had she known such information that was privy only to a Baron? Her insight and detail of the four trials was remarkable. He flipped back to the cover of *To Train a Conduit: A History of the Conduit Trials* by Thalia Lighton.

He'd never heard the author's name outside of this book he kept in their rooms. It was surprisingly helpful. His time was coming to conduct the conduit trials given to Karus, Figuerah, and Clairannia. By then, Baron Heimlen would be dead and his own reign as Baron official.

He stood to pace.

Pace and brood.

He did that more and more these days.

He must find a way to keep Karus away from the Blight for now. He knew well enough that nothing he could say could stop her, but maybe, just maybe, Baron Heimlen could convince her to keep her distance.

There was too much they didn't know. Karus around the Blight was too risky, even with both Barons there with her. Revich had had high hopes that Moira would divulge some important information that they were lacking, and, so it seemed, she had.

He rubbed the tips of his fingers, grinning at the remembrance of Karus's healing touch, the evidence of their sunburn faint.

Fuck, she was gifted.

She hadn't even begun her medicus lessons and she was able to heal him almost completely.

He wanted more than anything to rid Felgren of the Blight. The sooner that happened, the sooner they could live their lives together. There was so much to do in his Baronship that he often felt as if decades were never going to be long enough.

He had ideas and plans to streamline the trainings and bring more channelers at one time. The isle had its faults. There were holes in the system that it ran upon, but they could be fixed. They could be patched up with the help of more conduits, thus more opportunities to train and help the people who needed it most.

He had lived it firsthand. His village had all worked together to give what they could for him and the other orphans. So many orphans were made by the hardship that was rhyzolm mining, but it didn't have to be that way. Lapis conduits were the rarest, true, but if he could focus on finding more of them, if he could just train enough to help the people of his village who searched for the precious stone without magic…maybe he could prevent what had happened to him.

Being raised by a village kept him alive, but it did not keep him loved. If that was something he could prevent other orphaned children from experiencing, he'd use every last piece of power he contained to do so.

Pacing still, he found himself in front of the box he had carved for Karus. Smiling, he opened it, hoping to just hold the rhyzolm again, but as the lilting music played, he realized she must have it on her. The sound filled the room and the absence of her presence was heavy and obvious.

He sat on her side of the bed which was somewhat still tidy as she hadn't slept in it the night before.

Shame.

He loved waking next to her. She would be tangled up beside him, her bare skin so tempting to touch, her frazzled hair flooding her face and usually draped across his chest.

He should leave. It was going to do him no good to stay here and reminisce about the woman he loved to love. A long walk in the forest could possibly relieve some of his more anxious thoughts.

As he entered the foyer, he spied a swish of skirts leaving it, headed toward the dining hall.

He followed them, grinning, like a stalker of prey, hoping to catch up and startle her. A great joy of his since he loved to see her so out of breath in many situations.

She entered the kitchens through the dining room, and as he reached the door, he heard her speak.

"Lia, are there more cinnamon buns leftover from this morning?"

"Of course not, love."

"Alright, well, what breads do you have? My little fae friend demands more flour-based goods. And butter. Lots of butter."

"Aye, that I can get for you. Just sit right there and I'll gather the load."

"Thank you, Lia. And can I ask you a question?"

Realizing he was now completely eavesdropping, Revich turned to head back toward the hallway, hoping to catch Karus on her way to Moira. The question she asked next stopped him.

"Were you the cook here when Baron Revich arrived?"

"I was. I was here much earlier than that, too."

"How much earlier?"

"Oh, decades now, love."

"And Baron Heimlen? Were you here before or after him?"

Revich felt the pause in the woman's breath. Whether it was a true hesitation or a pause to remember, he couldn't tell which from outside of the door.

"Lia?"

"It was after. I cannot remember exactly how long, if that's your next inquiry."

He heard Karus laugh. "It was. The reason I ask is because I am curious to know about Baron Heimlen's power. I believe you know, but in case you don't, he was able to cure a terrible sickness that plagued Hyrithia, which led him to be able to bring me here and defy the contents of the Treaty. It just seems like powerful magic… to be able to cure something so deadly and swift."

"I know little of it. You're better off talking to Sylva in that case, she's close to Baron Heimlen, and after me, has been here the longest."

"This all looks lovely, thank you, Lia. I'll take it to her now and get out of your kitchen and out of your hair."

"Enjoy, love."

Revich sat on the dining chair, awaiting Karus's arrival.

"Oh, just one more question. Has Baron Heimlen always worn gloves?"

"What an odd thing to ask."

"It is. I just realized the other day that I've never seen him without them."

"I can't really say. I know that around the time you arrived, he stopped eating in the dining hall, preferring to sup in his own rooms, but as to gloves? I'm not sure I've ever noticed."

"Of course. Thank you again."

He listened to her steps on the short staircase to the door of the dining hall and watched her open it fully. "Hello, my darling. Just what are you up to?"

CHAPTER 40
KARUS

"Revich!" Her breath came sharp and she almost dropped the basket of bread. "What are you *doing* here?" She closed the kitchen door behind her and leaned back against it, settling her pacing heart with her hand across her chest.

"I followed you here, actually."

"Followed me? Why?"

"I happened to see you enter the dining hall and had plans to surprise you."

"I think you succeeded."

"However, I then overheard you having a conversation with the cook."

"Lia."

"And I was going to leave, not wanting to eavesdrop, but then I heard my name."

"You heard my conversation just now? That was rude of you."

"I agree, it was."

He stood then and walked a few paces toward her, quick as ever. His black locks fell into his face, and she resisted her usual urge to pull them back behind his ear.

"I do apologize. I should not have stayed to listen. But I did, and now I am quite curious about your inquiries, Karus. Why all these questions? And what's with the gloves?"

"I will tell you, but you have to walk with me. I need to get this basket to Moira before training starts. And if we don't hurry, we will be late. Again."

He took the basket from her hand and slid his fingers into hers, bringing them to his lips to kiss lightly.

"Don't think you're off the hook for eavesdropping. That discussion can wait, though."

"I look forward to you chastising me."

She rolled her eyes, his beguiling grin forcing her to look elsewhere as they left the dining hall and began their ascent up the unyielding black stone staircase.

She kept her voice low and close, nodding to the servants as they passed, going about their duties. "I spoke to Baron Heimlen after I left you in Viridis. Sylva showed me to his rooms."

"Behind the painting?"

"Yes. I didn't know that they were there or why they are hidden."

"Honestly, I have no idea either. I much prefer ours, away from all these stairs."

"Well, I realized something as I was waiting, looking at the ridiculously large portrait of him as a young Baron."

"Oh?" he mumbled through a mouthful of bread and butter that he had somehow managed to get to his mouth with one hand holding hers and the other holding the basket.

She took the basket from him and let it rest on the crook of her elbow, ensuring its contents would not be completely devoured before they reached the top of the staircase.

"I realized that something was strange about the portrait. He was much younger in it, yes, but he was also not wearing gloves."

"This is a very odd conversation."

"But that got me thinking," she continued, ignoring his comment. "Have I ever seen him without gloves? Doesn't he wear them at all times of the day, inside the Fortress or not?"

"Maybe he likes the feel of them."

"Or, as I concluded, he's hiding something. And that got me thinking about the Black Fever."

"The Black Fever?"

"Yes. You see, I don't know how much of the details you've been told, but the Black Fever is called such because the victim, once infected, is bedridden with a fever and the tips of their fingers turn black and are riddled with thin lines of markings that run down the length of them."

"Yes, I knew that."

"Even when the victim dies, they keep these markings."

"And if they survive?"

"Yes, if they survive as well. The Prince's hands were marred and discolored even when he was cured."

He squeezed her hand in acknowledgement. "And so, you're asking around to see if Baron Heimlen has always worn gloves. You suspect he has these black fingers—why?"

"I started to think—wasn't it extremely convenient that the Black Fever came to Hyrithia after the Queen had told him that she would not give me up? After he understood that I would never willingly leave?"

"Convenient, yes, but why would you think Baron Heimlen had anything to do with it? He would never cause something so destructive. He would not kill thousands of people, no matter how much he needed you here. Not to mention how much power that would take. To orchestrate something like that—to create such a deadly disease —I've never heard of such a thing. And what? He produced this disease and then caught it himself while also curing himself? That's ridiculous."

"But the timing—"

"The timing was advantageous, yes, but that doesn't mean—"

"Have you seen him without gloves, Revich?" She stopped on the umpteenth staircase landing, pulling on his hand wrapped around hers so that he had to face her.

"Sure, I have. I think blackened fingers is something I'd have noticed."

"Let me rephrase." Frustration seeped through her words, yet her body held no tension. She had much practice of that in her life. "Have you seen Baron Heimlen without gloves since my arrival in Felgren?"

He laughed. "It's not like that's something I would keep track of. I'm sure I have, or, if I haven't, I'm sure there's a different reason. This concern of yours is….unwarranted. I know Baron Heimlen much better and for much longer than you, and I can tell you, my love, that what he did was *save* the people of Hyrithia. He did not connive to kill them." He let go of her hand and rested his arms on the stone banister. "What real evidence do you have of such an evil deed? What has he done to make you think he would be capable of such a thing?"

He wasn't listening, not really, and this was not at all what she had expected from him. A quiet rage began to rise in her throat. She swallowed it, as she had been taught, and stilled her breathing. "How easily you forget, Revich, that he took me from my home as payment. I was the compensation the Queen had to pay in order to save her city—to save her son. He *forced* me to be here."

"And what would you have me say to that? That I wish it wasn't so? Of course, I do. Of course, I wish the circumstances of your arrival here were different. I wish those lives had not been lost, that the pain Hyrithia suffered was not an event that will be remembered for decades to come."

His voice was hard, his hands gripping the banister to the point of producing the whites of his knuckles. He turned to her then, his eyes black, his mouth thinned. "But I would not go back and give you up. The past is the past. Baron Heimlen did not cause the Black Fever, but he did find a way to bring you here and that is what matters. What matters is that you have the power to heal the forest. What matters is that you are loved and you are *home*. What matters is that you have found your place here, your place with me, and Clairannia, and Figuerah. We have a future here together and we can do so much, Karus."

He pulled her into an embrace, her arms hanging still at her sides. "Why do you linger on the past, when what we must look forward to is so much more important? You are here, and I am never leaving you. What's more important than that?"

She wanted so badly to accept his words, to focus on his words of confidence about their future—about the past. It would be so easy, wouldn't it? To ignore her intuition and let go of her feelings of mistrust. He said it would be alright and that she had no reason to worry.

Yet, something still churned in her stomach. There was a piece of the story that didn't quite fit into the box that held the events of her arrival to Felgren. Though she wanted to listen and believe every comforting word he said with that confidence she loved, she knew she could not let this go.

His lips brushed her forehead as he wrapped his arms around her waist. "We will get through this plaguing time, Karus. We must focus on studying the Blight. Once that is gone, we can look to the forward horizon as I take on my role as Baron." He chuckled into her hair. "Or when we take the roles as *Barons*. I see no reason there cannot be two at once always."

"But there's never been a woman Baron." She laid her head against his shoulder, inhaling the earthy musk of him.

"Well, there's always time for a first, my love." He began to sing then, softly, into her hair as they leaned against each other, halfway up to the tallest tower, halfway down to the entryway of the Fortress.

"So I will see you at dawn."

"So I will see you at dusk."

"Said the sun to the moon."

"Said the moon to the sun."

PART FIVE

SEVEN YEARS LATER

CHAPTER 41
KARUS

I can't escape the dark, but I can hear through it.

I can feel through it.

My heart beats at a slow pace, its rhythm steadying me.

Thump, thump.

Thump, thump.

My eyelids are heavy, and I try to lift them open. So very, very heavy.

I focus on what I can do.

I can breathe. Air fills my lungs and I know my chest rises, though I cannot see it do so.

I don't know how long I've been here, like this, breathing… sleeping? How long have I been asleep?

I hear voices, but they are too far, farther than I would need to make out what they are saying.

Who speaks nearby?

Do I know them? Am I safe in their presence?

What has caused me to lie here, imprisoned in my own body, unable to do more than breathe, and beat, and listen?

"Come now, Little Sprout, it is time for you to wake."

The voice is low and soft but does not echo through the place I am laying. It echoes in my thoughts, but it is not my own.

"It is time, Karus. You must wake."

"Who are you?" I reply, not aloud with my own voice, but inside my own mind.

"Who I am, you are not ready to hear, but who you are…that is what you must wake to. Come, open your eyes and see. Open your eyes and remember. It is time to wake. You have been asleep long enough to heal, long enough to rest. Long enough to replenish what you have lost."

"But, I cannot remember. I can't…remember what happened? And Viridis…what…what did I do to Viridis?"

The memory floods back into my mind, swollen and yet somehow sharp as teeth as my heart races—the sight of the tree. The state of the Blight fully encompassing every hall, every inch of the place I love. What happened? Did I cause all of that death? All of that decay of the place I longed to see again?

"You will remember. Your memories will return, but it is time to wake to them. You cannot continue on like this. You are a shell—a promise made, yet not fulfilled. Your journey will be a difficult one. You'll experience pain you do not deserve, but can bear nonetheless."

"I am afraid."

"Yes. You are afraid. But when has that ever stopped you? It is time to wake. Open your eyes, Little Sprout. Open your eyes and see."

Light floods into my consciousness as my eyelids flash open and I squint, the shock of it painful.

I am in my room in the tallest tower of the Fortress.

There is my desk, my dresser, my piles of books, though their subjects I cannot quite recall.

I hear the voices again just outside of my door. Three people are arguing in hushed tones.

No, a fourth is with them.

Should I lie here then? Should I pretend to sleep?

Or should I get out of this bed, open the door and say, *"Surprise! I am here! I am awake!"*

For some reason, that almost seems right as I feel a smile creep across my face and close my eyes once more.

Wouldn't they be surprised to see me like that, Clairannia and Figuerah? Yes, I know those voices. I could pick them out anywhere. And the other? That high pitch lilting is Moira, my dearest friend. She has done something for me recently.

What was it?

I open my eyes and frown. I should thank her, but why? She showed me something. Something hidden that should not have been.

And Revich.

He is there, just outside of my door. I feel as if I have not seen him in years.

Years, upon years, upon years, upon years.

Why has he been gone from my side for so very, very long?

I am suddenly hot.

I am suddenly thirsty. My heart hammers in my chest and I cannot breathe. Tears swell behind my eyes, my face is sweltering, I feel as if I am suffocating. My stomach churns in a desperate attempt at escape from its encasement in my torso, and I heave over the side of the bed, retching with little more than spittle resulting from my efforts.

"Karus?"

The door has opened and I feel a hand at my back. Another one has grabbed my hair and pulled it from my face, her touch light as I retch one more time over the basin near my bedside.

"Oh, thank the fungi! She's awake! Karus, just let it out. Someone grab a cloth or something."

"We've got this, Moira."

That was Figuerah. She's sitting beside me on the bed as I heave yet again into the basin of water. She is rubbing my back as we both watch yellow bile spew from my mouth.

It's so hot. My cheeks must be the color of strawberries in the summer. For some reason, that thought makes me want to laugh, but I don't.

My breathing quickens and a hand on the other side of me runs across my forehead.

"She's burning up. Moira, hand me that cloth there. No, the one on the dresser. Dip it in the pitcher first. She needs to cool down, Figuerah—yes, let's get this vest off her."

Before I can protest, Clairannia is wiping my neck with a cool cloth, and at the same time manages to help unfasten my vest with Figuerah.

"She was so cold before. We thought it best that she be in layers."

That was Moira again. When was before? Time races forward and I feel obliged to come with it, as much as I'd rather stop right now and just think.

"Do you think you're done, sweetheart?"

I lift my head, swimming as it is, and look into the gorgeous brown eyes of Figuerah.

Honey. There was always a bit of honey there in the flecks, and I smile before giving way to laughing.

"Figuerah?"

She grins, her face adorned in markings of gold paint, a ring attached to her nose. "Yes, love." She laughs. "Yes, it's me."

I fall into her arms, laughing, crying, joy protrudes from my chest and I swear I can see it. Joy is green, the color of the trees in Felgren on a cool spring day in a field of yellow blossoms.

I hold onto her and squeeze my eyes shut. My hand finds Clairannia's behind me and I hold onto it too, pulling it close to me. I feel her body cover my back and she whispers, "Karus. We've missed you."

I cannot imagine being as happy as this. I am reunited with the women who have been everything to me. At some point in time, I may not remember exactly when, but I know these two hearts held mine.

I cry in remembrance, I cry for all we've missed. And I cry knowing that they have left and I have stayed. What lives have they lived? What are they like now? Who loves them, and whom do they love?

I want to ask all of these questions, but I cannot. I cannot yet speak as Clairannia caresses my hair and Figuerah rocks us side to side.

I finally pull away, if only to see their faces again. Clairannia wipes the tears from my cheeks with the wet cloth and I laugh again.

"I want to know *everything*. Please, tell me everything I have missed."

"Goodness, girl, there is a lot to tell."

"And we will, but maybe you should get up? Get something to eat or drink? Through magic, I have been able to keep your heart steady and your belly full for a few days, but the real thing would be best for you."

Moira scoffs from the dresser where she sits hanging her legs over the side, swinging them as she often does. "Yeah, let's get out of this stuffy place. It smells awful in here."

I shake my head and stand, a little unstable at first, but I feel good on my bare feet. Clairannia hands me a cup of water, and I drink it down in big gulps, the liquid cold as it settles into my stomach. I wipe my mouth, my breathing slowing to normal.

I am wearing the skirts I used to wear as a channeler in training. They are a leafy green and light. My undershirt is untucked at the waist and loose. I unbutton the front a few times, trying to cool down further, pulling at the fabric.

It is still hot. I would like to leave.

I turn and walk toward the door, look up, and stop.

I cannot move, I cannot step even a single step further.

I cannot breathe, I cannot think.

I cannot *live*. It hurts too much.

I cannot.

Tears are streaming down his face in little rivulets, and they drop from his chin which I am surprised to find is covered in black hair.

He looks a mess, standing before me in my room, in front of my friends and yet, I still cannot move, or think, or be.

His hands are stuffed inside his pockets and he stands straight—tall? Taller than I remember?

No, it is just that his clothes are loose. They hang off his frame too much. His cream-colored shirt used to hug his arms, and his vest used to expand across his muscled chest as an adornment, not as a mere careless addition as it is now.

We stand there facing each other, and I believe we are the only two people in this world.

Were we always?

His eyes are sad, a mournful blue, the hue of the sky before the sunlight fully leaves it.

I shake my head.

"No," I whisper.

I pull my lips together tightly and bite down, hoping the pain will distract me from the utter agony I feel as I look at him, standing in my doorway.

He does not get to just stand there in my doorway.

"Karus—"

"No!" I yell it this time. I cannot pull up the memory, I cannot bear to see what has been hidden in my mind. I cannot see his betrayal that I know is there, its essence seeping into every part of him that I once loved. Every part of him I trusted to keep me safe, to hold my heart with his.

"Karus, *please.*"

The pain in his voice is so raw, I cannot hear it without my chest caving in. It will collapse under the pressure of all the air leaving my lungs.

I want to comfort him, to go to him as I listen to his pleas, yet my legs do not let me.

I am shaking my head again, short back and forths, my breathing is shallow and ragged. "What have you done?"

Tears, hot and heavy, run down my face. No longer are they produced from joy, from the happiness of being reunited with those I love.

These are tears of sorrow, a pain that is a dagger into my soul and I do not see how to heal.

I find my legs leading me to him. His scent hits me like a rock to the face, his warmth I could wrap myself in for days and never leave, even if it slowly suffocated me into a lifeless ball of skin and limbs.

I want to be that. I'd rather be that than this.

I grab at his chest and shake him. His arms are around me

immediately, smoothing over the expanse of my back where they always should have been.

Where they have been missing for years, upon years, upon years.

I shake him again and press my forehead into his chest. I cannot look at his face any longer.

"What. Have. You. *Done*?" I spit each word with great effort, unable to control the rage I feel swelling inside as my blood runs hot through my veins.

"I will tell you, Karus. I will tell you, my love, my life."

He pulls at the sides of my face, forcing me to look him in the eyes.

"I will tell you, and then…and then, you will understand your wrath."

PART SIX

SEVEN YEARS BEFORE

CHAPTER 42
KARUS

An orb of light hung above the three of them, growing in size. Silver, blue, and green, it seemed to war with itself on which color would dominate its surface.

Karus closed her eyes and pushed herself into it.

Well, first into Baron Heimlen, then to the orb. She imagined her magic flowing through his body and out of his upturned, gloved hand where the light floated high above their heads.

She peeked out of her right eye and grinned to see that it was mostly green. She opened the other and caught the gaze of Rev, who then closed his own eyes and she laughed when she saw the orb change to blue.

"We are working together, children."

Baron Heimlen's reproach came clear in the silence and Revich's body straightened, his eyes closed to focus as a proper successor to the Baron title would do.

"Hold here."

Karus sighed in a huff and closed her eyes again, letting the flow of her energy take on an even stream as she held onto Baron Heimlen's arm and Rev held onto hers.

They had been practicing for weeks and weeks and she was

losing her patience. Summer was already at its climax and still they practiced, neither Baron letting her near the Blight in that time.

It was difficult to keep her secret from Rev.

The rhyzolm was somewhere in the thick of it, and she had almost been discovered in her lies about the stone's whereabouts. But he never seemed to catch on to her falsehoods and for that, she felt the deep pangs of guilt.

On more than one occasion, she had thought about telling him the truth, but, selfishly, she could not bear to think of the disappointment on his face. And now she was so far into her sham that she also feared what he would think of her treachery, potentially losing trust in her.

No, it was better to find it and pretend the whole thing had never happened. She had kept up her farce for this long, she could continue as long as it took to get it back. Surely, it would find its way back to her, just as it had always done for Revich.

Sunlight almost blinded her behind closed eyes as Baron Heimlen used the Cosensian Magic to enhance the *Simulair Solum* spell.

He held it longer than usual this time before she felt a sudden chill on her face as the clearing's illumination vanished.

He fell to his knees, breathing heavily and Revich moved to his side, always a comfort to those in need of it—one of her favorite things about him.

Karus let go of Baron Heimlen's arm, of their connection, and took a step back. She hadn't forgotten her theory, nor had she seen him yet without wearing those damn leather gloves.

They had been civil to each other since that day in his rooms, but obviously avoided one another and it just bred more suspicions in her heart. She longed to enter his study, but, after several attempts on her own, she understood the power of having *two* locks.

She and Revich had argued about it a few times and had always left the disagreement at the same place they started it. He refused to see any merit in her theory, and she refused to let it go. They hung at an impasse, one she was determined to route her way.

"Karus, can you help me, please?"

Revich lifted the Baron's weight, pulling his arm over his own shoulder. She silently slipped under the other, and together, the three of them hobbled back to the Fortress. Thoughts of yanking his glove off then and there traversed her mind, but she wasn't sure she was so bold as that, especially in front of Revich.

"You called, Baron?" Pompeii arrived to greet them through the doors.

"Yes, help me get the Baron to his rooms, please."

"And call for Sylva," Baron Heimlen muttered as Karus slipped away to allow for Pompeii to bear his weight instead.

"I'll find her," she offered, withdrawing from the scene as the two able-bodied men lifted the other up the staircase. They had a long way to go.

She wandered into the kitchens asking Lia where Sylva might be, who directed her to the servants' quarters.

"It's the third door on the left, love," Lia instructed, wrist deep into dough that would become the evening's bread at dinner.

Karus had not wandered this far down into the servants' quarters and took her time. She happened upon a long corridor, black stone illuminated by sconces on the wall, flame flickering loudly. She found the third door on the left easily enough, but kept walking, counting nine in total on each side of the hallway, which ended in a tenth, larger door.

Backtracking to the third on what was now her right, she knocked. "Sylva? Are you there?"

The door opened in a flash, and Sylva was before her. "Is everything alright? Baron Heimlen—"

"He is asking for you in his rooms. Today's training was hard on him."

"Oh, *by the Blightress*, I thought you'd have worse news for me. I'll attend him right away."

She left as quickly as she had opened the door, hurrying off down the hallway with not even a glance back at Karus.

She moved to close the door, but stopped, thinking.

It would be wrong, wouldn't it? To search her room for the phrase needed to open Baron Heimlen's study?

She liked Sylva. Although, what she saw in Baron Heimlen was currently a great mystery. But that didn't mean she deserved to have her room ransacked by a channeler on a mission.

Sighing, she began to close the door, taking the small opportunity to glance around the room. There was a window near the simple bed, and upon the sill was a short pot, a red flower blooming in its soil. Her eyes glanced to the open book on the small desk in the corner, the quill spilling its ink all over the page.

Sylva must have been writing when Karus had knocked and, figuring it wouldn't hurt, she moved into the room to put the quill back in its pot to save the page from complete ruin.

She tried not to look down at the contents of the journal, but that was something her curiosity would never allow.

Among the pages that were lying open were tally marks. Tally marks and dates. The words *'For Felgren'* were sprawled in elegant script across the top. One was dated for the current day with a single mark underneath. The other, dated the day previous, had three.

She flipped back a few pages, convincing herself she was just trying to understand. There, two weeks ago, five tally marks and four the day before—*'For Felgren'* again scripted along the top of each page.

What was Sylva tracking and why?

She held the current ink blotted page with one hand and flipped back to the beginning of the book.

The date on the first page was six months ago when Karus had still been Ash'Arah and had just learned about the Blight. On average, it seemed there were about two tally marks a day. But as she continued to flip through the book, the marks rose in number each day, once even having as much as seven.

What was 'For Felgren'? There was no clear explanation for it. No notes on what she could be tracking. She looked to the small bookcase in the room to the right of the desk and saw that there were more journals. More dates and tally marks filling them up, more of that beautiful script—*For Felgren, For Felgren.*

Flipping through, she found the journal previous to the current and saw that it was dated near the time the Black Fever claimed its

first victim. Ten tally marks on that day with a note written below—
He almost died.

Karus frowned with even more questions streaming through her.

Who had almost died? And from what?

She shut the book in frustration, placing it back on the shelf, fixing the desk to look as if it had not been touched, even placing the quill back on the ink-stained page. Whatever she was tracking, Karus did not want Sylva to know she had seen and she turned to leave.

An eerie chill crept through her veins, and suddenly, like all intuition starts, she had the uncanny feeling that she *knew*.

She closed the door quietly behind her and moved with the swiftness of the one and only, Baron Revich.

She just hoped they were all there in Baron Heimlen's rooms, so that she had a reason to be there, too.

For she suspected she now knew the phrase that would allow her to enter his locked study. All she needed was the key.

HER ARRIVAL AT THE MASSIVE PAINTING LEFT HER OUT OF BREATH and she stopped to calm her chest, adjusting herself to look the part of a concerned channeler over her dear Baron's ailment.

Smoothing her skirts and tucking her braided hair back into the strands that wove around her head, she knocked loudly on the door behind the painting.

Pompeii answered and she smiled nervously, suddenly realizing she should have brought something of use like fresh water or food.

"I wanted to check on Baron Heimlen. He seemed more worn than usual, and I fear I might have pushed too much of my magic into him."

Pompeii understood things better than he had any right to, and raised one of his pointed eyebrows quizzically, turning his head slightly. But he gave her a soft smile nonetheless and stepped aside to let her through.

Baron Heimlen was sitting on his bed, the light of the afternoon sun streaming through the single window.

Revich was holding a cup of water and standing over him, concern across his features. Sylva sat beside him, her arm over his shoulder, rubbing his back and whispering words of comfort.

They all cared for this man. This Baron that she did not trust, nor believe.

"Is there anything I can do?"

Revich noticed her then, giving her his half-hearted smile. "I don't think so. He just needs rest. We pushed far today, and we had a lot of success. That was the longest *Simulair Solum* we've seen yet." He patted the Baron's shoulder and grinned.

"It was. I can hold it longer than that. I just need rest for now. But we will pick up in the morning."

"Perhaps we should skip the morning training, Baron. We can pick up again at our usual late afternoon time. Sylva, would you attend to him tonight and tomorrow, just to be sure he has what he needs? I can relieve you in a few hours."

"Of course, of course." She was busy, whispering something in the old Baron's ear which made him chuckle as he drank deeply from the cup Revich shoved in his hands.

Karus moved closer to the bed with her heart hammering so loudly, she was sure she'd be discovered.

"Here, let me help you out of your cloak," she mumbled, reaching out as Sylva began to pull it off his shoulders.

It was ridiculously easy. Much easier than she had dared to think and she did feel somewhat guilty, relying on their trust. She took the black cloak, her hand sliding seamlessly into the inside pocket where it wrapped around the black key she knew would be there after seeing it produced on more than one occasion.

She had forgotten he was there, Pompeii, as she slid the key into her own pocket and hung the cloak on the iron knob beside the door.

His smokey eyes, adorned in gold liner, stared at her and her cheeks burned red.

"Where are you off to, Karus?" His words were soft in the small sitting room, away from the people who cared for Baron Heimlen the most.

"I-I think I should rest a moment in our rooms. The efforts of today's trainings have drained me as well."

"Yes, you look…drained."

He said the last word with absolute acknowledgement that she looked anything but. Her cheeks were flushed, her eyes wild at her stolen artifact hanging heavy in her pocket.

She smiled as genuinely as she could and turned to leave. She refused to glance back to see if he was watching her, but somehow, something told her he was.

CHAPTER 43
KARUS

"For Felgren."

The click was the most welcoming sound. Karus exhaled in relief, swearing to never doubt her intuition again.

She smirked at her own cleverness, shutting the door of Baron Heimlen's study quickly behind her and placing the key back in her pocket. She would have to get it back into the Baron's cloak before he wore it the next day, but that was something for future Karus to worry about.

For now, she would pry. She would look for evidence of her theory. She had half hoped that when she had gone to steal the key, the Baron would be in his bed, sans gloves and everyone would be able to move on with their lives, but no. Of course, he hadn't been. Because as far as she knew, he never did take them off.

She lit the lantern at his desk with a snap of her fingers, sparking green in the dark, and began her search.

She started with his desk, pulling open drawers, finding them quite disorganized which surprised her, considering the cleanliness of his rooms. Inside were old quills, a few worn paintbrushes, and baubles taken from the forest—a pine cone here and an interesting rock there, she was surprised to see a sentimental side of Baron Heimlen. Shame rose from her chest, doing its best to question this invasion of privacy. She shoved it aside, inhaling deeply in the dark, musty room, refusing to stop what she had already begun.

There was nothing of interest in his desk except for a journal which was first dated around four weeks prior. It detailed all the training they had done.

She turned and began to search the bookcases, looking for more journals—anything written that could prove her theory. She slid between the desk and bookcases carefully, wondering how Baron Heimlen did so, and wondering why he had chosen this room as his study, considering its tight quarters.

Books on flora and fauna of Felgren were most of the subjects, with a few memoirs of the conduits who had left their writings behind.

There was nothing. Nothing of use to her, no obvious declarations of malice, no proof that he had created a disease so deadly, it killed thousands of her people. Her heart sank and that guilt she had shoved aside began to settle in her stomach like a stone.

She shook her head and kept on searching, unsure of how much time she had here, turning to the small table wedged between two of the bookcases. She'd noticed it the first time she had entered this study. It was odd and out of place, with beakers and jars cluttered atop its dusty surface. Picking up each jar, she read their labels: Danbury Root, Ashes of Sycamore, Petals of Crocus.

Karus knew there were potions and tinctures a trained conduit could make for ailments of the body, but she had no idea the Baron was so interested or skilled in doing so. That was typically what a medicus conduit did for their patients, not the Baron of Felgren.

She lifted one bottle to the light of the lantern. The glass was a dark purple and lacked a label. It was sealed with wax and from what she could discern, it contained sharp thorns from some kind of plant.

Confused and frustrated, she placed the bottles back in their spots, clearly marked with clean circles on the dusty surface.

Audibly exasperated, she turned and leaned back against the table, thinking about what she could ransack next.

The table moved slightly, rocking back and then forward again. Rocking?

Bending down to look at the legs, she found four small wheels at the base of each, covered by a small piece of wood, making them impossible to see without sliding to the floor.

She attempted to pull the table back toward the desk, but there was so little room, she could only move a few inches. Frowning, she bent down again, bringing the lantern with her.

Her heart jolted with fresh excitement. Near the top underside of the table, just to the right, was a keyhole.

Knocking her head, she ignored the bump that would surely produce itself in a few hours and scrambled in her pocket for the black iron key.

The click was loud, a resonating sound that this room likely knew well. She pushed on the door from under the table, but it was difficult, and she couldn't picture Baron Heimlen doing so each time he opened it.

Standing in front of the table, she began to push, realizing it was being used to open the hidden door fully, the long length of it turning to the left as the table fit through the new doorway.

Her steps on the stone floor in the dark room echoed. The lantern dimly lit the center of it, and she saw that a fireplace sat in the side wall, opposite the entrance.

She produced fire for it, her green magic speeding in haste to the wood, illuminating the room better than any small lantern could do.

It was cozy, really. Black furniture lay about including two cushioned chairs near the fireplace and another long desk at the side wall. More bookcases lined the large room as well as paintings that were hung along the walls in varying sizes. The subjects were... interesting.

Barely clothed women looked out from the portraits, each one wearing very little to cover their bodies and each one as beautiful as the last.

She counted seven in total with the final hanging above the fireplace, the largest of them all.

She knew that face.

A young Sylva looked back at her across the room, her eyes the same shade of gold, her lips just as wide and pink. Her hair had been between brown and blonde once, and seeing her face unlined was eerie in a way. A green sheet was draped across her breasts and torso, tucked in between her legs as she lay on a settee, her arm propping her head. Her face was lit in the most seductive arrangement of features as her other hand lay over her bare hips, casual and alluring.

She shouldn't be here.

This was a place where Karus was truly intruding. A place that was supposed to be Baron Heimlen's alone.

But she had gotten this far. She had discovered this room, and she knew well enough, nothing could stop her from searching it.

Breathing deep, she began at the desk, Sylva's seductive eyes following her across the room.

This was exactly what she had been searching for. She flipped through journals upon journals of Baron Heimlen's time at the Fortress, dating back across decades, filled to the brim with internal thoughts, successes, and woes.

The writing was often short, full of sentences like thoughts pulled out of his mind directly onto paper without much processing in between.

Bringing a stack of them closer to the fireplace, she sat and began to read. The journals had been neatly organized, the dates along the spine of each. She began with the one which contained his writings around five months before her arrival in Felgren, skimming the pages until her eyes picked up what she had been looking for.

"The Queen of Hyrithia continues to display an obstinance I have not the time for. In her correspondence,

which comes fewer and fewer these past months, I have found her weakness.

She keeps Ash'Arah close, but her son closer. She mentions him occasionally in an off-handed way, but I see through it.

I have found what I need. Viridis let me find it. Just more proof that I am on the right path. I will do what it takes to bring her here.

I will do it for Felgren. The lives lost will not be in vain.

I have not told Revich because he is likely to object. He has not had the decades of hardships that come with Baronhood, and I know that someday he will forgive me. Someday, he will understand that what I do is for Felgren. I will save it from this blight, and I will leave that legacy behind for him.

He will take up my mantle and he will praise my name to all others that come after him, my heroic deeds will be remembered."

Despite the growing fire, chills ran down her spine. She'd been right.

She stared at the page for a moment, the truth settling into her mind like a sore might on her skin, red and angry.

She'd rather be wrong. She'd rather have been wrong in a thousand arguments with Revich than learn that the man who had trained her, the man who had taken Rev under his wing, the Savior of Hyrithia…was a monster.

Rev hadn't known. He wasn't involved in the massacre of thousands.

She was thankful at least for that.

Desperate for more, she read on.

"The books Viridis gave to me about diseases have been helpful, but I need more. I need a way to create something powerful enough to kill the diseased, yet still controllable by my hand.

I cannot risk an infection on Ash'Arah, nor the Queen, and so I continue to search for something I can control.

The boy continues to be my eyes and ears in Hyrithia, watching Ash'Arah.

He has not seen her display a single bit of her magic but has confirmed with me that the rhyzolm pulses in his hands when she is near.

Through other sources, I have been able to identify those close to her. Thankfully, there are few, and she will be less likely to desire to leave Felgren and go back to them. She does sneak off with one of the guards occasionally. Hopefully, it's no more than a dalliance.

All of this information has given me hope. Once I have her here, she will make new friends, discover a love of Felgren and Viridis, and she will wish to stay. I have chosen two other channelers to join her. Their temperaments will compliment hers and I do not doubt they will grow in friendship."

He had known everything.

She'd been watched, studied, manipulated—all three of them had…and Revich?

In all of their time together, he had never mentioned he had spied on her for Heimlen. Not once in those moments of talking about their pasts in whispers in the dead of night did he confess what he had done.

Had he planned to keep that a secret forever?

She flipped through some more, looking for details on the Black Fever, a rage building with each entry she read, each line of confession by the keeper of this very room.

"I have done it.

The key was the Blight. With some of its thorns, I was able to reproduce a more potent, feverish disease detailed in a book from Viridis which disappeared as soon as I had the idea. I could not find it again, but no matter.

I will first create the cure, easy enough to do, I assume. I will then try the disease on myself, ensuring the cure works.

Once this is confirmed, I will send five of my spies one bottle each. Upon opening them, they will be inflicted, and I will be able to control the victims from the Fortress.

They will all have to be channelers. The only way I can control the diseased is through my rhyzolm. If the Queen still refuses to let Ash'Arah go, I will do what I must and inflict her only child. His magic is weak, but I have felt the pull toward him regardless.

I know she will then break.

Sylva will be of great help, as she has always been.

Revich has requested to stay longer, but I have denied him. If something were to happen to me, he *would need to be here, to continue on with my work and find another way to retrieve the girl."*

He had used the Blight to kill thousands.

Thousands of her people were dead because this madman was so determined to bring her here, and each of them had been a channeler. She had not known there were so many…and Prince Philius? He'd never once shown her magical capabilities.

She wished she had known what Heimlen was capable of because she would have come on her own. If she had understood, if someone had just explained to her the need, she would have left willingly.

Instead, mass graves of the victims of the Black Fever were shoved in too small a place in the grasslands outside of the city.

Bile crept to her throat and she rose from the chair by the fire to walk the room, breathing deep, trying to steady her shaking hands.

Revich didn't know.

Please, *please*, let her find that Revich still did not know.

How long had she been here?

Was Revich looking for her now?

She thought of taking the journals then. Shoving them into Revich's hands and saying *"Here! Here is all the proof you need that your mentor is a monster!"*

He'd have to believe her…but then what?

What would be the punishment for Heimlen's crimes? What council stood to judge the Baron of Felgren?

As far as she knew, there wasn't one. Which was part of why the Treaty was created all those years ago, to protect channelers and give them a choice.

If they could get this information to the Queen, she would have the power to detain him and put him on trial for his actions which led to the murder of her people.

All of the dead were stained on his hands. She knew the evidence must be there. The gloves, the careful way he spoke, lies flowing from his mouth as his heart had tried to give reason for them.

She'd never work with him again. She'd never help him destroy the Blight—she and Revich could do it.

But not him.

Never with him.

She grabbed a wine decanter on the table and threw it into the fire, the stack of journals falling to the floor, as the glass shattered and the fire flashed, flames hot and angry.

She welcomed the violence. She welcomed the rage.

Her emerald conduit ring glistened in the newly-fed firelight and she was tempted to throw that in too, wanting to be rid of everything and anything that man had ever given her.

Her magic swirled around it, sparking in short bursts at the tip of her forefinger, desperate to leave the containment of her body.

She could kill him. Instead of justice, she could give out his judgement herself. It'd be poetic coming from the woman he'd done such heinous deeds to get a hold of, the woman he'd stolen, manipulated, and lied to—pretending to care for her as a daughter.

Revich would be heartbroken when she brought him the truth. But she'd be there to help him heal. She'd stay by him, the only other soul who could really understand Heimlen's betrayal.

She hurried back to the desk, pulling the journal dated around the time of her arrival. She had to be sure the proof was not only in these journals, but there all along, discolored on the tips of his bare hands.

"I have survived, but barely. The cure was difficult to produce on myself in the state I was in. I took life from Sylva at least ten times that day, enough to correctly cast the cure on myself. She could not manage to do it alone.

It has left me with blackened fingers and black

veins running down my hands. I have since then tried to cure those as well, but in vain.

I wear gloves at all times now, unless in Sylva's presence, and yet, no one has noticed.

Revich talks of the girl often. I act as if he is helping me discover a cure for the disease they now call the Black Fever. He is concerned for her safety, and I wonder if he has grown in affection for her.

Indeed, I have not yet seen him take his work so seriously as when he believes her life is in danger. I know the sentiment well. But, as I tell him time and again, channelers will come and go from Felgren, but he will stay. And he will take what he is given from them and move on.

He never seems to like when I say this. It makes me worry about the Baron he will become."

"Bastard," she mumbled aloud, turning the page.

"He's not, really."

Karus looked up, seeing Sylva standing underneath her portrait, the stack of journals that had fallen now in her brittle hands.

Her eyes darting to the fire, Karus stood.

Sylva's eyes met hers and before she could take the fire from its setting, Sylva threw the journals in.

A billow of smoke flew from the fireplace as the journals were singed and blackened, even as Karus's magic withdrew the fire into a column of smoke.

"No!" She grabbed the journal from the desk and moved toward the fireplace, willing to burn herself to retrieve them if she must.

"Don't." Sylva held a silver knife to her own throat and Karus stopped in her tracks.

"I will do it, Karus. I will take my own life to preserve his."

"Why?"

"Why does any woman do what they do for a man? I love him. And I have come too far, we have accomplished too much together for it to end here."

Karus shook her head. Sylva was insane.

The smoke coming from the stack of journals caused Karus to move toward it.

"Stop!" Blood trickled down her neck as Sylva sliced her own skin in an unhinged attempt to save the Baron's legacy.

"Sylva…you don't have to do this. Everyone deserves to know what he has done. The harm he has caused, the murders he has committed. The world needs to know."

"The world cannot know. They will judge him before he has accomplished his goals, and I cannot have that. I will protect him with my life. Now, give me the journal."

Karus held it tighter to her chest. This was all she had to prove the truth she had suspected.

"If I don't?"

"Then I will be dead. And my death will be on your hands, Karus. They might even believe you did it."

"Not if I show them this. Not if they see how involved you were. Revich will believe me."

"Oh, will he now? Then why not hand me the journal, child, and he will believe you still. If he truly loves you, he will believe you. Isn't that how love goes?"

"What has he done to you? How have you ended up like this? Willing to take your own life to withhold the truth about him? Heimlen is a monster, Sylva."

"Do not judge me, girl. After decades of serving Revich, you will understand what it takes to love the most powerful man in Arcaynen." Her voice was venom and salt on the wound of betrayal inflicted on Karus.

She stepped forward, the journal held out in her hands.

Sylva sneered and took it, easing the knife off her neck, her wound still bleeding down into her dress.

"Thank you, dear. *Incendo.*"

They both watched the book alight with flame in Sylva's hand before she threw it to the smoking fireplace with the others.

"He will be so relieved."

"How did you know I was here?"

"Baron Heimlen is very astute, dear. After a short rest, he realized that you would not have come to check on him. Not after the conversation you had weeks ago about his gloves. And he knew well enough from me that you had tried to break your way into his study. He has always been very clever. But, so have you, Karus. I would never have guessed your suspicion of his gloves. When he first wore them at all times, no one batted an eye. Not one single person noticed, though he was so worried they would. And once all the new channelers arrived, we became busy again, and no one stopped to think about anything else."

"He has manipulated you, Sylva. You and everyone else here."

"Is it really manipulation if I fell into it willingly?" She gestured to her portrait above the fireplace. "We were once great lovers, the Baron and I. The love of his life, I'd say. But a Baron does not have time to settle down into companionship. Sure, there were others, but you can see where my portrait hangs compared to theirs."

Karus spoke softly, realizing with every second that Sylva was beyond repair, "What are the tally marks, Sylva? What does he do to you?"

She turned to Karus in surprise. "Oh, you little *sneak*. You found my own journals, didn't you? *That's* how you got in here. I see we've underestimated your willingness to be disloyal."

"*What are the tally marks, Sylva?*"

She cocked her head and smirked. "Those are the times that Baron Heimlen has taken my life and used it for his own. He'd be dead by now if it wasn't for me."

"But how? How can he take life from you?"

"There's an enhancement spell. A kiss. It takes some of my own life magic and gives it to him. It is how he stays alive, and I am happy to do it, no matter how much of mine is drained in the process."

"You're sick, Sylva. You need help."

"What I *need*, girl, is for you to do what you came here to do and destroy that blight. Then, Baron Heimlen is free to leave this world and let his legacy live as the Savior of Hyrithia and Felgren." Her eyes glazed over, and she smiled in her insanity.

Karus turned to leave having heard enough.

"Where are you going?"

"I'm going to find Revich. I'm going to tell him everything."

"Did you really believe me? Of course, he won't believe you without proof. Baron Heimlen has been a father to him, and you? You have been a distraction. He will see the truth of that someday."

"You're wrong. He'll believe me because he loves me. He will listen and hear the truth. We're not like you and Heimlen, Sylva. We are more than you ever were. More than Heimlen ever let you become."

CHAPTER 44

REV

Revich pressed a warm cloth to Baron Heimlen's head, blotting it around his face as the Baron turned in a fit of weary sleep.

They had worked too hard. He was fading too fast.

Not for the first time, Revich wished he could take on the role of Baron before Baron Heimlen passed.

But the magic didn't work that way.

The Baron of Felgren was just one. One sole person controlled the power that was given to him.

He didn't know if there really was a way to ever share it with Karus, but he was resolute in figuring that out someday.

Surely, he could at least control Cosensian Magic well enough to use it against the Blight. They had the spell. They had the power. They were so close. But he wasn't sure anymore that Baron Heimlen could survive it.

Why had the Baron refused to practice Cosensian Magic near the Blight? At first, Revich thought he was protecting Karus, but now? Now he wasn't as sure. The Baron and Karus's relationship was strained. They spoke few words together, and his suspicion was, it had to do with those stupid fucking gloves.

She was obsessed with them. All of their arguments circled around the same conversation, the same ridiculous theory she held about the origins of the Black Fever and the Baron's supposed role.

She didn't know him like he did.

And that was what he chose to tell himself as she continued to disbelieve him.

They'd argue and get nowhere with each other on the subject. But she was still there, every morning, every night, and he didn't care what exactly had brought her here.

She was here. And she would stay with him—he knew it in his heart.

He *could* do it, though.

He could pull the gloves off the Baron's hands now that he was asleep. It was a little strange, he admitted, that he wore them even to bed.

Baron Heimlen turned again and moaned slightly in distress. Yes, they had put too much pressure on his worn body, and Revich would gladly take the blame.

The Baron was nearing the end of his life faster than they had predicted, and soon, there would be no more time to practice. They'd have to act, regardless of if they were truly ready.

Rev put the cloth to the Baron's head once more, but his eyes shifted to the gloves again. For whatever reason he wore them, surely he would forgive Revich for taking them off. It was absurd that it was even a subject of so much discussion and argument.

His decision made, he threw the wet cloth to the bowl of warm water and gently, so as not to wake him, he pulled on the black glove that rose almost to the Baron's elbow.

As it slipped down his mentor's arm, his heart thudded through his chest, but sure of what he would find. He gently pulled on the finger holes, one by one, sliding them off each digit.

He sat still, the black leather glove clasped tightly in his hand, the Baron's fingers bare.

She'd been right.

All this time, her instincts were correct.

Heimlen's fingers were black.

The lines of the disease ran down the blackened tips in detailed patterns like the veins in a leaf.

His grip tightened on the glove, and in a fury, he ripped its twin from the Baron's other hand.

Heimlen lay there, looking frail and well past his prime, tossing in his bed, his blackened, ruined fingers a glaring evidence of the truth Revich did not want to face.

Excuses came.

He must have caught the disease somehow.

Creating the cure had given him the discoloration.

Maybe this was from something else entirely.

Then why would he hide it—why the secrecy?

It was possible he didn't want anyone to know of his deformity, but Revich doubted that. The Baron wouldn't be so vain.

There *must* be a reasonable explanation. There must be some way to explain why.

"Baron Heimlen," he whispered in his ear, rustling his shoulder harder than he had meant, he realized, as the Baron's eyes flashed open.

He put a hand on his head, rubbing his face and coughing while trying to sit up. "What time is it? How long have I been asleep?"

"Less than an hour. But I needed to wake you."

"What is wrong? Where is Sylva? I need her back here."

"I will find her, but there is something we must discuss."

Revich took the Baron's hand in his and held it up for him to see.

The Baron stared at Revich through his own discolored fingers before studying them himself. "Ah. I see curiosity got the better of you, Revich. Or Karus got the better of you, I presume."

"Tell me what this is."

"You know what this is."

"I want to hear you say it."

"Alright. But before I do, ask yourself, would you have had what it took to get her here? Would you have had the strength to do what I did to save this forest and this way of life? Tell me, Revich, would you have done it?"

"It's not true."

"That it is, and you cannot turn a blind eye to it any longer. I did it to save us all. We need her. Her magic is too great and the Blight too strong. The Queen of Hyrithia left me no other options."

"You *murdered* thousands of people. Women, men, *children*. No, I could not have done it. But you know that as well as I do."

"Revich. One day you will see how I saved this place. One day you will understand the sacrifice—"

Revich stood, throwing the gloves to the bed. "Don't tell me I will understand. I will not *understand*." His voice was venom spit between his teeth. "I *trusted* you. You were a father to me. And now? Now I see that you are a coward, unable to procure what you needed, so you chose instead to take the lives of so many for your own gains. I will never understand *that*. I will never be the Baron you have become." He turned to leave, his heart bleeding from his chest in utter despair of the truth.

"It will take her, Revich."

He stopped, the Baron's voice behind him blunt and full of conviction.

"Think this through, boy. If you tell her, she will refuse to work with me ever again. You know this. And without me, the Blight will consume her. It will find a way to take her. She is careless, she is rash. You will not always be there to pull her back out." He coughed violently, grabbing the towel on his bedside table. "You need whatever power I have left to finish this. Tell her after I am gone. Tell her the truth when I am dead, rotting in the ground. Tell her then what you have discovered. You cannot destroy this alone. You cannot destroy it with just her, and you know it. The Blight even now grows stronger as the colder seasons approach. It has already broken through the door to Viridis from the forest. You've seen it. You know I speak the truth."

Revich turned back to the Baron and watched him struggle to stand, holding onto the side of his bed, his discolored fingers gripping the dark wood.

"So, you can walk out of this door and tell her of your discovery. Tell her the truth and she will insist you fight the Blight right now.

She will insist she is ready. You know she will. But you need me. You cannot handle the burden of Cosensian Magic on your own."

"So, you'd have me lie to the woman I love? She deserves better than—"

"I'd have you save her. I'd have us all live to destroy what we are close to destroying. What we have worked for. I'd have those people not die in vain. I'd have my last few years as Baron not be for nothing."

He collapsed onto the bed, his breath short, his bare hands bracing on his knees.

Revich resisted the urge to go to him, to help the man who had given his life new meaning. The man who had taught him the Baronship, believed in him, loved him like a son.

"You betrayed me. You lied and you deceived. I'll never forgive you for it." He fought back the lump in his throat, choking on his next words. "But I will keep your secret—for *her*. For *now*. We go to the Blight tomorrow."

The old Baron looked up at him, about to protest.

"*Do you hear me?*" Revich darted before him with a cold swiftness. "We destroy it in the morning. I am ready, she is ready. So, get what rest you can. Your life ends tomorrow, Heimlen, and I will not mourn it."

CHAPTER 45
KARUS

She tripped at least three times rushing down the stairs, stumbling in her usual tangle of limbs if she tried to get anywhere quickly. She slid across the floor of the foyer, first checking on Revich's study before continuing to their rooms when she saw that it was empty.

She burst through the door, out of breath, her eyes a wild green, her heart racing with a secret she was desperate to tell.

"Rev!" She ran to his arms, and he lifted her off the ground, pressing her body to his with a force she'd not felt from him before. He buried his face into her hair, filling his lungs with the scent of her skin.

She lost her composure then, sobbing into his neck, the weight of what felt like the world pressing down on her shoulders. The knowledge of the man who had caused so much pain, so much death, was breaking her down, wounds flowing freely from his betrayal.

"I broke into his study. I found his journals. Sylva—" She sobbed, her breath catching on his shoulder, unsure of how to tell him about the man he had loved as a father.

"Karus. Please, listen."

He carried her to her chair by the fire, wrapping the green blanket there around her shoulders and kissing the top of her head.

He stood before the fire, his hands in his pockets. "I have discovered something you may not want to hear."

"I have as well, Rev. I don't—"

"Please, let me say this."

He turned to her, the light from the fire casting him in a dark shadow, his features hard and tight.

"What is it?" She rose and reached out to his face, her thumb brushing his cheek. He leaned into it, closing his eyes before speaking, steadying himself for whatever he was about to say.

"Baron Heimlen is dying. As we speak, life leaves him. In the morning, we go to the Blight. We destroy it. He will not live through it."

It certainly wasn't what she expected to hear when she'd found him. His look was grief, she realized. It was why she didn't recognize the emotions flitting across his face.

Heimlen was almost dead.

The bastard wasn't going to live long enough to face the consequences of what he had done.

She shook her head in disbelief, wondering if it was the right time to tell him. But he deserved to know. He deserved to know why they would not be destroying the Blight in the morning. He needed to know why she would never see Heimlen's face again, and she hoped he died alone and ashamed.

"I—I am sorry, Revich. I came to find you, to tell you—his gloves—"

"*There is nothing under his gloves, Karus!*"

She jolted, not expecting the rage directed toward her.

"I was there, just now, in his rooms. *There is nothing.* No black fingers, no abnormality of any kind—*you have to let this go.*"

"You…you saw him without gloves? You saw his fingers bare?"

"Yes. There is nothing. Let it go…please."

He turned back to the fire as she dropped to the chair, replaying what he had said.

Nothing? How could that be? He had written in the journals—

he had said that his fingers turned black and that he wore the gloves to hide it—just as she had suspected.

Revich was lying.

He was lying to her, but why?

He either claimed to see his bare hands and hadn't, or worse, he had seen the black tips…and lied.

"I am sorry I yelled. I shouldn't have. It's been a long day."

He bent down in front of her and she followed his gaze, her eyes struggling to see, her heart slashed through with his words. If she could see her heart now, she was sure she would see wounds—long cuts, open, and bleeding.

This was it. This was the truth that Heimlen had said all along. She had refused to believe that Revich would love her and leave her, but here was evidence that he could. If he could lie so blatantly about something so important, then he could leave her, too.

After all—all a Baron needed was himself.

She had forgotten that *she* had been told that, as well.

And the Queen had been right.

Because this pain was agony.

The pain of his lie, his betrayal of their trust, was more than she had the strength for. He protected Heimlen and lied to her.

It was the third betrayal she had discovered tonight, and it came from the first man she had ever loved.

"I…I need some time alone. To think." Her voice left her lips monotone, empty of emotion.

"Alright. I'll go."

"No. I'll go. I—I need to walk."

She rose from her chair and swept past him, careful not to touch him. She could not touch him. She'd never touch him again.

"I'll see you at dinner?" he called, watching her leave, his voice hopeful.

"Yes. I'll see you…"

She opened the door and shut it quickly behind her before the tears fell, before *she* fell to the floor, covering her mouth so that the sound of her sobs could not reach him.

CHAPTER 46
SYLVA

"I was only able to save part of this one."

Sylva handed his journal over, its pages charred black, but some of the entries were still readable.

"At least you were able to do that. Was anything else burned?"

"Just the journals. And I believe she broke your favorite decanter. I am so sorry. I felt like I had to. I know you planned for Revich to see them after your death. And I should have been more careful with my journal, but, I thought you were…"

"It is alright, Sylva, dear. You did your best. We did not count on the pieces falling together for her so quickly."

"She is cleverer than I realized—and more willing to connive as well. Do you think she has told him already?"

"I would guess so. I suspect the two of them will burst into my rooms any moment now."

"With hand ties?"

He laughed heartily, shifting his cloak up on his shoulders.

"How will you get her to go with you to the Blight now?"

"Easy. I'll tell her the truth."

"Oh, my darling, she will never believe you."

"Ah, but you have helped on that front, Sylva, darling. There is proof in my journal that I do not lie. Why would I write lies in my journal, believing she would never find them? Look, here."

He opened the blackened pages and pointed to a more recent entry, one written not long after Revich and Karus's relationship had steered toward romance.

"*I don't like where this is going. I know he's likely to give up everything for her and that cannot be.*

Her purpose is elsewhere. She is needed for something far more important than holding Revich's heart.

And his heart bleeds. Profusely. Like a wound that has never healed.

I gave him everything. Saved him, gave him purpose in life and natural talents, and still, he wants more. He's always wanting more. I am afraid it will one day be his downfall.

I am afraid of what I leave behind and wonder if he is up for the challenge of Baronhood as it has been for centuries.

But I needed him.

I could not find her, hidden as she was somewhere on the isle. But her forthcoming was told to me in whispers among the trees, upon the wind across my cheeks.

What do I leave behind as I begin to leave this world?

I must be harder on him. I see that now. My heart has softened to him too much. I must give him my strength as it leaves my body.

I will not leave behind a weakling.

I will not leave behind a blight, wreaking havoc on this place that has flourished for centuries.

I will not go down in the books in Viridis as the Baron who let it all slip away, destroyed all because he was too soft.

I love him like a son.

And I understand his want of her. I too, have wanted Sylva for decades now, but I have understood my role here and she hers.

Ash'Arah is not that.

She cannot be kept around for decades, she cannot be kept around to live.

Her power has one use.

And that is to destroy the Blight with my direction, my focus.

And I know that this will consume her. The fight will consume all who are present.

She and I will not survive the encounter.

But I must harden Revich, so that when he discovers our bodies, he will."

"Oh, Heimlen."

Sylva fell into his arms, and he held her shaking body, whispering to her softly, "We knew this day would come, Sylva. And here it is. By afternoon tomorrow, I will be dead, and so…so will you, my darling. But it is for Felgren. It is for this place we swore to protect and love. We are but two shining stars in the night sky, doing our part to keep the world alight."

She pulled her face away from his chest to look into his eyes. His black and gray eyes that she would never see again after this night, and she sighed. "We have done it. We are almost there. I am sad to think I will not live to see the forest return to its great beauty. I will not see the flowers bloom once again."

"I will ask that they bury you under the ash tree grove where you loved to dance while the fall leaves fell."

She nodded and grinned, her last tears falling down her cheeks. "Kiss me, darling, take what I give to you, and don't forget what I have done."

He smiled and held her face in his hands.

She could die in this moment. Before he even cast his spell, she could float away into the clouds just seeing him gaze at her like this.

A pounding at the door interrupted her haze and a single voice yelled, "Heimlen! Let me in!"

Karus? Alone?

She looked to the Baron for instructions, and he nodded.

Opening the door, Karus fell through, barely catching herself, her hair flying wildly around her tear-streaked face in dark, bronzed strands.

Her eyes were rimmed red and the brightest shade of green as her magic hummed around her in wisps of smokey trails.

"We're leaving. We're leaving for the Blight *right now*. Get your things, say your farewells—we go."

"Where is Revich?"

The Baron's tone was not to be unanswered. She knew it well, the venom that could seep from his words.

"*The Baron of Felgren* is in his rooms. He—he does not know about what happened in your study."

Baron Heimlen's eyes lit with the hardness she had seen before. "He has betrayed you then. That is why you storm in here, isn't it? You were going to tell him, and instead, he told you lies."

"*You are all liars.* Every one of you." She took a moment to wipe her sleeve across her nose, reddened from sobbing. "And as soon as the Blight is destroyed, I am taking Clairannia and Figuerah back home with me. They'll never train under Revich when I've told them the truth. He can go find new channelers." Her voice broke and she took a moment to swallow. "There will be new women to lie to. But Felgren deserves to survive. You and I will see to that."

"And we don't need Revich to do this?"

She flew to him then, her hand slapping across his face. His blackened fingers caught her arm in a grip Sylva knew well before Karus could hit him again.

She wrenched her arm away as if burned. "You *know* we don't. You know what I am capable of. You know that we have been ready for weeks, and yet you stalled. Why? What were you waiting for?"

"I was waiting for this. I was waiting for *you* to realize you are ready. Look down, Karus. You can hardly contain your magic. It flows around you in abundance."

They all looked to her boots, emerald tendrils of power trailing up her skirts, bright and strong, almost tangible.

"You cannot hold back when we are there. You cannot hesitate even once, and yes, I never planned for Revich to be in the final battle against the Blight. He would be nothing more than a distraction to you."

Her eyes wide, she spoke in unhinged amusement, "Well, it's your lucky day. And your last. We go—*now*—before the dark settles in."

He turned to Sylva, taking her hands in his, placing them at his chest. "So, we go, my darling."

"I understand. I have always understood. Kiss me."

She saw Karus jerk forward as if she could stop them before he whispered, "*Osculum Vitae,*" his lips pressed into hers.

Sweet, succulent.

She let him take it all, everything she had left, knowing he would need it. He would use it before he himself perished this night.

It was so beautiful, her life leaving her body and flowing into his.

They were finally one.

They were finally able to be together.

Forever and for always.

CHAPTER 47
KARUS

She could not mistake the irony.

Months ago, he had brought her into Felgren, and now? Now, she brought him to the place where he would leave it.

She laughed aloud, a little mad herself after watching Sylva's lifeless body drop to the floor just minutes before.

The shock of the last two hours was beginning to wear on her soul, but she found strength in the greenery around her, the soft touch of the breeze, the scent of the summer heat floating warm and heady in the evening air. The haunt of night bloomed in the little time they had left with the sun's gaze along the horizon.

The sun was leaving her home, and soon, so was she.

But it would return shortly, and she would not.

She didn't doubt Clairannia and Figuerah would want to go with her. She must find a way to say goodbye to Moira as well…and as for Revich?

She swallowed. Hard.

As for the Baron of Felgren, it was best she leave without speaking to him again. He would get over it. He would move on, no doubt becoming the Baron that Heimlen had always wanted him to be.

She grabbed her hair hanging on her shoulders and pulled, squeezing her eyes shut for just a moment while she composed her pain.

"What causes you to laugh, Karus?"

She heard him speak from somewhere behind her. He kept his distance as they neared the edge of the Blight.

She ran her fingers under her eyes and then called over her shoulder, "I was just thinking, Heimlen. You escorted me here, and now, I'll escort you out."

She mirrored his chuckle. After all, in a way, she would become a killer, too. He would die from this task. Revich was right about that and she would be sure of it. Heimlen could not survive it, and the only reason he was still standing at all was because he just drained a woman's life from her body.

Karus shook her head again.

Focus.

She let her gaze fall past the Blight, into the setting of the sun.

She'd always loathe dusk now.

How could it not forever serve as a reminder of what she was forced to do—due to circumstance, due to a duty she hadn't known most of her life?

The sun left the sky in a last goodbye, not in an endearment of love for the moon. It left the sky cold and dark.

Promises, promises.

"Here. Here is close enough."

Heimlen stood at the edge of the Blight beside her, the great abyss barely illuminated now by the waning orange glow.

"But shouldn't we step further—"

"No. We cannot risk it taking you before the spell is released."

She nodded and inhaled fully.

"Are you ready, Karus?"

She studied his face. She was the last one who would ever see him alive, and yet, she felt no sympathy, no pity. He had meticulously chosen all of this, the seeds of his plans coming together to bloom into this very moment. He got what he wanted.

All she really felt as she stared into his black eyes was rage—a rage that rattled through her bones, distracting her from the pain of her bleeding heart.

"I'm ready."

"Do not let go of my hand. No matter what you feel, do not let go. This is our only chance, Karus."

"Do you remember what I said to you, before you guided me into the portal that day?"

He stared at her for a moment, not in recollection, but in a strange praise she did not wish to see. "I do. *'The more you try to bind me, Baron, the less of me you'll have.'* I have taken those words to heart, believe it or not. I did everything I could to lessen the bind on you here. You were free to roam, free to study, free to live, Karus. I gave you that. Do you think Clairannia and Figuerah were let along so loosely? I spoiled you. Gave you everything you needed to feel safe here. To feel loved here. And I'd do it again. Because here we are. Your purpose is about to be fulfilled and I have seen to it well."

She shook her head in disbelief. "You murdered *thousands.*"

"*I saved Felgren.* The forest is worth tens of thousands of lives. You have no idea of its power, its use here on the isle. There are things even Revich has yet to know about this forest, and I would kill every last citizen of that city to save it."

He was a monster in fine clothing.

He was an evil dressed in black, posing as a man of strength and good will.

"Well," she laughed madly, "what's one more life then?"

He didn't respond.

He held his blackened fingers out toward her, and she took them into hers, binding their fates, binding their pasts and futures.

Karus closed her eyes and let herself fly.

She imagined unloading her pain, her anger, her aching chest that had been bleeding inwardly since she had left Revich's side.

She imagined she was flying above the blackened trees, touching each one to give them back the life that had been stolen.

Heimlen's hand squeezed tighter as she pushed all of herself into him.

He wanted her magic?

Fine. He'd get it.

"*Karus.*"

It came out low, like a warning, but she'd never heed a warning from him again.

"Karus, I can't hold this."

She opened her eyes to see him engulfed.

The orb he would use to mimic the sun had grown to the size of a boulder and was barely hovering above the ground.

The green tendrils of her magic were wrapping around his body, squeezing his torso, his legs. A cruel smile lit her face as he lifted his head in pain, more of her power wrapping around his throat.

"Say it. You have what you need. Say it and be done."

"I…I ca-nnot sp-peak."

How disappointing he was.

The once most powerful man on the isle struggled under the weight of the magic *she* wielded.

"Then give it to me. Give me your power and I will do it, if you cannot."

"N-no. It h-has to be m-me."

"THEN DO IT!" Her scream echoed through the forest as the last slip of the sun fell beyond the horizon of trees.

"L-let g-go."

She willed his throat to breathe and loosened the tendrils on his chest.

He gasped in the night air while she urged her magic into the orb.

The ball of green light illuminated the Blight below them. The inky vines crept along the forest floor quickly, like the slither of a snake stalking prey. They wove around her boot, lacing up her skirt, pulling her forward toward the abyss, welcoming her back, the Blight's heart pounding in the warm night.

"*SIMULAIR SOLUM!*" he roared beside her, the spell resonating throughout the grove of trees, dead and alive.

The Blight around her waist recoiled instantly as the orb of magic shone bright as the sun at midday in summer.

The effect was instantaneous—the light bursting through the

mist of black death, the unnatural growth of it sizzling away from the ground and trees it desecrated. The vines fell back, receding before them as they walked forward together, hands still clasped, stepping onto the newly healed earth.

They walked over bones, now clear of putrid death, and over fallen branches once clutched within the vines' dark embrace.

"HOLD! IT'S WORKING! HOLD, HEIMLEN!"

She pushed into him further as they began to run, the ebbing black disease loud in its destruction. Like the sound of burning flesh, it popped and crackled in every direction—anywhere the light touched its withering corpse.

They ran and ran, no longer hindered by the vines of death. No longer stumbling on pieces of decayed forest.

The light made it too difficult to see how far the spell reached. But the constant echo of renewed earth resounded throughout the forest, no doubt reaching the Fortress itself. If anyone there wondered where they had gone, they no doubt would know by now.

The renewed soil fell away softly under their boots as they slowed.

She knew he was breaking.

He collapsed a moment later, even as she held onto his hand and pushed more of herself into him.

"I have done all I can."

"It is not enough!"

"You must take it now, Karus. Take it and finish what we started."

Realization shook her core.

He was going to die and leave her here to finish the job. It wouldn't end with him—it would end with her.

It would end with two lives, not one.

"You *bastard*."

"Do you see now, Karus?" he choked, his knees sinking into the soil, as the massive orb of sunlight fell dangerously low to the ground, the sound of decay still hissing all around them. "You could never be together because you were meant for more. Revich could never join us in this task. He is meant to become Baron and you…

you were meant for this. I have done what I could to prepare you, train you into a different kind of conduit, Karus. And this—" He nodded to the orb of sunlight. "This is your trial."

He couldn't do this.

He couldn't leave her without finishing what he had started. All he'd needed was her power, all he'd needed was what she channeled from the forest, not her *life*.

Never her life.

She shook her head and spoke through gritted teeth, *"I will not die for you, Heimlen."*

He smiled, his body falling back onto the fresh earth of the forest floor, one arm outstretched still, holding what was hers to take. "Then do it for Felgren, Karus. Die a conduit. A conduit of light."

With the last of his strength, he lifted the simulation of the sun toward her, its glow blinding. She could barely see him as he pulled his discolored fingers from hers, disconnecting their magic, his life leaving the shell of his body, and she was alone.

So very alone.

It was heavy.

So very, very heavy.

She grunted in agony with the weight of the sun she now carried, as hot tears ran down her glowing face.

Everything she had, every last part of her soul would have to be forced into this light.

It grew to enormous size as she stumbled forward, finally having a proper conduit to light the world with its brilliance. The Blight still withered, the vines still hissed in recession, much further now— hundreds of acres away—but loud and echoing among the trees. She tried not to focus on how dense the simulated sun had become as it engulfed the forest, growing still, her green tendrils of magic expanding with its golden core.

In moments of great suffering comes great clarity.

And she understood she had to let go. If she wanted to save Felgren, she must fade to keep it from fading. It would take all of her power, her memories, her love. Everything she was would be needed and used to keep the sun aglow and destroy what she had been brought here to destroy. Memories flashed through her mind like the spokes of a wheel spinning on its axle as she made her decision.

She remembered the pear tree she had burned to ashes in the Queen's garden, the nights she listened to her stories, often sliding into bed with Prince Philius to giggle under the sheets before falling into a child's careless sleep.

She remembered climbing the rocks along the ocean shores, once slipping, her hand caught by Geyrand. That was the first time she had really noticed his quiet smile—it hit her differently then. Her nights with him had been reckless, she had used him to explore everything she could think of, their bodies consuming each other purely for pleasure.

She remembered the Queen's face as she declared that Ash'Arah would be used as payment for the cure, the tears running down her worn cheeks in the setting sun.

She remembered the dress she wore into the Fortress for the first time. Dark green, hanging off her shoulders, yet tight on her waist, black beading woven in intricate designs all across her breasts. It had been complex. It had been *her*.

She remembered Clairannia and Figuerah, their excitement uncontainable next to her resistance, and yet they had accepted her anyway. For the first time, she had been accepted as an equal and loved as a friend, admired for her spirit and her wit. She had been one of them, a part of something special for the first time in her life, and they had loved her for who she was, not for who she was supposed to become.

And she remembered Revich.

As blisters opened on her hands and face, her conduit ring brilliantly illuminated on her finger, she remembered the man she loved.

Images of their most intimate moments settled into her skin as warm as his lips had felt on hers.

Her attraction to him had been immediate, and though she fought it off fairly well, using sarcasm and sharp replies as a shield to his charm, she had given in finally, watching him waist deep in that pond—both of them vulnerable and free.

Rev.

Yes, she remembered him. The man whose heart she'd held, the one who'd offered to hold up hers, never questioning her light, but basking in the warmth of it instead.

The one who had taken all her faults and fears and laid them out bare saying, "*Yes, I see these, and I love you. Not regardless, not in spite of them. I just love you. All of you.*"

Why?

Why the lies, the deceit?

She'd never get to know. She'd never be able to ask the sky who held her. She was going to die here in this forest, the place which had given her new life, a new beginning, and an understanding of the woman she was.

The woman she wanted to become.

The woman she'd never get to see.

Karus was tired.

She fell to her knees, her strength waning as she bore the weight of her duty, pushing the fingers of one hand into the healed soil, extracting every ounce of power she could to continue. She watched as her long, unbound hair turned white in pieces of brilliance, illuminated and blinding from the sun she held.

She screamed, holding on just a little longer. The end of her torment drew nearer.

And as her memories continued to fade, like the wisps of smoke from an extinguished flame, the bluest of eyes she had ever seen flashed in her mind, and then…nothing.

She remembered nothing as she heard a name upon the night-kissed breeze.

Karus.

Karus.

Karus.

CHAPTER 48

REV

The branches that cut his cheeks were sharp as knives, and the roots that snagged on his legs were relentless in their efforts to stop him.

But he ran on.

Like he would never see her again, he ran on.

Like he'd never hear his name on her lips, or feel the brush of her hair across his chest, he ran on.

He bounded over fallen trees in his path, over rocks and bushes, ignoring the sudden shock of power—the sudden gasp as his head filled with clarity, with knowledge bound to the Baron of Felgren, intruding into his thoughts with a question he would not yet answer.

It could only mean one thing. Heimlen was dead.

But he ran on.

His way was lit. She lit the sky like the sun she was and he knew he had minutes, seconds, to get to her.

Sylva's dead body had lain on Heimlen's floor, and the journal had been open to the most disturbing of entries.

He should have stopped to listen. He should have heard what she had come to say to him, but his own fear had muddled his thoughts. Heimlen's lies had weaved through his mind and held strong, even when his instinct had been to tell her the truth—a truth she must have discovered for herself, as his gloves had been cast aside next to Sylva's corpse.

"KARUS!"

He took everything he had and pushed forward, the lungs in his chest likely to burst at any moment, but it didn't matter.

He ran on.

He could see her silhouette underneath the giant sun as he heard her scream.

"KARUS!" he boomed again, but nothing was as loud as the sound of the Blight recoiling into the ground, the crackling of its demise echoing through the trees it left bare.

"KARUS!"

He was almost there, and she was almost gone.

He saw Heimlen's body as he neared hers.

He watched, pushing further, not letting his legs give out just yet as she kneeled, one hand lifting the sun, one buried into the dark earth.

There was only one way to save her. The only way he could think of.

He slammed into her body, forcing her to the ground as he covered hers with his completely.

The *Simulair Solum* was broken instantly and the dark fell upon them into absolute nothing.

He gasped heavily into her hair, his eyes adjusting to the lack of light as he rose to see her. Red blisters broke her cheeks and lips, white streaks of hair framed her head.

"Karus, can you hear me?" He straddled her and shook her shoulders. "Karus! Open your eyes! Please!"

Her lids blinked rapidly and her chest began to heave heavily as he tilted his head back to the night sky, thanking Felgren for letting her live.

"You did it! Karus, it's gone—you've done it!"

She blinked a few more times, turning her head to look around before setting her gaze upon him.

As he reached down to hold her, she scrambled backward out

from under his legs, across the newly healed soil, backing into a fallen tree.

"Who—who are you?"

"What?"

"I said, who are you? Where am I?"

Confusion crossed her face.

"Karus, I—it's me. It's Rev. You've done it, you've destroyed the Blight."

She shook her head profusely and grabbed the sides of her hair. "*No, no, no, no, no.*"

The air around them grew sharp and cold, chilling his bones further as he watched her rocking back and forth beside the tree, a different scent of decay in the breeze.

"It's okay. It's going to be okay. I love you. I'm here, I won't let anything hurt you anymore."

Her scream pierced through his ears.

"Karus! Stop!" he yelled over her cry of anguish, his words unheeded.

The snow came next, thick and frozen, slicing across his face in a flurry of a late winter blizzard. In seconds, the ground was white, and she stopped her scream, holding her legs to her chest, sobbing into her knees.

"Karus! Baron Revich!"

He heard their call behind him and they rushed to her side, their dark hair flecked with patches of snow.

"Karus, we're here. It's okay." Clairannia sat next to her, pulling her shaking body into an embrace.

"What happened? What's going on?" Figuerah's eyes were wild with fear, her chest gasping and she shook him, his gaze never leaving Karus on the hard ground.

He shook his head, finally looking to her face. "She doesn't know me. She doesn't know who I am."

"*What?*"

"She asked who I was and then…and then she screamed. Snow started to fall, and she…she doesn't know me, Figuerah."

"*Revich*. Get yourself together. We need to get her back to the Fortress. Baron Heimlen is *dead*. We need to get his body back, too."

She turned to kneel in front of Karus, brushing her hair back, lifting her face. There was no recognition. No realization crossed her features, and tears ran down her broken cheeks as she looked around wildly, sobbing in uncontrollable heaves.

He stepped forward, falling on his knees in front of her.

"Karus…*please*."

She pressed her back against the tree, panic crossing her face as her eyes darted between the three of them—between the three people who loved her most.

She bent her head back, looking up into the night sky, swirls of snow falling upon her face. Her eyes lulled as she fainted, her head tilting to the side.

He saw it coming and caught her in his hands, both women looking to him now for guidance.

Looking at the new Baron of Felgren.

"Figuerah, call the lumens. They can carry Heimlen's body back to the Fortress. Pompeii will know what to do from there."

She was up in a swift moment, her fingers pressed into her mouth and a high-pitched whistle pierced the muffled fall of snow.

"Clairannia, I need you to assess if anything is broken. Does she need treatment immediately?"

"Her pulse is strong and her breathing seems within a normal range."

Clairannia pulled Karus's feet out from underneath her body and bent each one, pulling her skirts up to look for blood or obvious bone. She examined her arms and chest next before hesitating, touching her hair, shaking her head at the streaks of white throughout.

"It looks like nothing's broken. My guess is…she has suffered something traumatic enough to cause"—she gestured around—"all of this. And she needs rest."

"Thank you."

He slid his arm underneath Karus's knees, pulling her torso to his chest with the other.

"The lumens are here!" Figuerah called to them and moments later he heard the pounding of their massive feet.

Parvus ran straight for him, sniffing at his rider's skirts and hair, whining in protest.

"Aren't you going to carry her on one of the lumens?" Figuerah asked, petting the beast's head in a reassuring calm.

"I'm going to carry her back to the Fortress myself."

"I don't think—"

"I don't need you to think. I'm doing this. Please do what I've asked, and get Heimlen's body back to the Fortress. I won't be far behind."

Figuerah shook her head and bit her lips, her disagreement on his decision evident. "If you're not back within ten minutes of our arrival, I'm sending Parvus after you."

He nodded and adjusted her body, beginning his long walk, stepping through what was once the Blight, now barren earth covered in a dusting of snow.

He grasped her tightly while she slept, telling her stories of how he had fallen for her, how he had known he would love her forever, ignoring still that buzzing question of power in his head.

And somehow, he knew.

He knew this was him, holding her for the last time.

PART SEVEN

SEVEN YEARS LATER

CHAPTER 49
REV

"I carried you back to the Fortress, the snow still falling. Winter had begun."

Karus stood there, just out of my reach through the entire retelling of events that tore through me like claws beneath my skin, leaving marks that I could not see. She stared into my eyes, and I held her gaze—even though it hurt. My shame in my betrayal of her trust haunted me each day, but I would not look away from her now.

"We tried everything, love. You couldn't remember and you'd panic, ending in a screaming rage before passing out again."

I glanced at Figuerah who moved to Karus's side, sliding her painted hand into hers just as I longed to do.

She turned her head as Clairannia spoke next, and I squeezed the rhyzolm in my pocket.

"We stayed as long as we could, longer than any conduit had before. You just never knew us. And finally, we left. Checking in on you from time to time through Rev, occasionally staying at the Fortress to see if you'd recognize us."

Moira piped in from the dresser, "You seemed to know me best. We don't know why, but you didn't mind me hanging around so much, so…I took care of you. We made new memories until you were able to hold onto them and live a normal life. Well, as normal as it gets in the Fortress." Moira fluttered in front of her face, grabbing her chin in her tiny hands as she always did, making Karus laugh. "Glad to do it, too. You did so much for Felgren…and me."

Karus spoke finally, "But, the Blight. It isn't gone. I've seen it, and it has poisoned Viridis, but…worse."

Figuerah squeezed her hand tighter. "As best we can tell, what you did was push it back. It has struggled to grow as quickly since then. If you had held the sun long enough…maybe it would be gone, maybe not, but you wouldn't have survived." Figuerah nodded toward me. "He saved you, Karus."

Her gaze met mine again and I held it, waiting.

Seven years.

Seven years, I waited to see recognition in those emerald eyes. And I smiled, my lips trembling.

I knew she knew me.

"I'd like to speak to Revich…alone, please."

We studied each other as I moved aside, the two women and the most vexing of faeries passing by me and out of the room.

"It's almost dinner, so we'll gather something to eat. Meet us in the dining hall when you're done?" Clairannia paused at the door, glancing between the both of us.

"Sure," I acknowledged, nodding once, unwilling to break my gaze.

Karus waited until the footsteps faded, staring at me all the while, thoughts flickering across her face in flashes.

She bit her lower lip.

I clenched my jaw and swallowed.

This wasn't going to be easy.

"I'd like to see our rooms, please."

I raised my brows in surprise. "Sorry?" I choked out.

"I'd like to see our rooms, the ones we shared."

"Why?"

"I think it will help. I have these memories. But they're all mixed up, tangled in a web of thoughts and I…I think seeing will help me sort them out. Just like when Moira showed me the Blight—it helped me remember that I was angry."

"I don't want you to see our rooms and get angry."

"I don't think I will—I…I'd just like to see them. Please, Rev?"

I blew air out through my lips slowly.

"Alright. You can look around and then we go straight to the dining hall, promise?"

She laughed lightly. "Promise."

CHAPTER 50
KARUS

I closed my eyes and entered the room.

I imagined what it would have looked like seven years ago. There had been a gigantic bed in the middle, bookshelves along the furthest wall, two chairs before the fire—one blue, one black, and a door to the left as you entered, leading to the washing room and an enormous tub.

He stayed behind me, shutting the door.

I opened just one eye first, getting a quick glimpse.

I laughed and covered my mouth. It was like I had never left. Everything was in its exact place, just as it was seven years before when I told him I'd see him at dinner.

It was easier then, for me to rearrange the memories. Some were still fuzzy on the inside and some were crystal clear as if they had happened yesterday.

"I haven't changed much," he muttered, pouring a cup of water from his side table and bringing it to me.

"Have you changed *anything*?" I teased, drinking the cool water quickly and fully, stepping nearer to the fireplace.

"*Incendo,*" he murmured, bringing it back to life. I placed the empty cup on the mantle, stretching my fingers out over the fire, wiggling them as the flames danced in reaching patterns.

"I don't spend a lot of time here, honestly. It's never felt right."

He didn't say, *"Without you."* But it hung there between us as I turned to him.

"I can only imagine your pain, Revich. I understand now, when you said you suffered. I believe you. I know you did. I know you still do."

He shook his head, looking down at his boots, his hands shoved into his pockets. The old memories of him mixed with the ones I had made in my time of forgetting.

"I don't remember you being so quiet. But in all the memories I have of you recently, you'd hardly say more than a few words to me. Why is that?"

His head leaned back, not in annoyance, but in a desperate attempt to hold his composure.

"Do you mind if we sit?" He pointed to the blue chair. "This one was always yours and—"

"That one was far less comfortable, but you insisted on using it. I remember."

He grinned in a half smile and sat, just as I did, both of us leaning forward, arms on our knees, faces a mere foot apart.

"When I would try to…talk to you…you got worse. My presence and voice especially set you off. And after a long time of trying and failing to get anywhere, it was Moira who lovingly told me I should shut my mouth more often around you and see if you'd come any closer."

"That sounds like something Moira would lovingly say."

"Yes, well, it worked. You slowly would at least let me be near without falling to pieces. Eventually, we realized that you had lost the rhyzolm somewhere, and I finally felt like I had a purpose. Something outside of the Baronship that I could pursue to help you." He pulled his hand through his hair, rubbing his neck and I grinned.

I remembered loving when he did that.

"I thought maybe, just maybe, if we found the rhyzolm, you'd remember something. Anything. And so, we all looked for it. For weeks we were all out there, searching blindly." He paused and chuckled, looking at me with admonishment. "I realized you had lied to me, you know. I know that you must have lost it that day in the Blight when you saved Moira. I found the hole ripped in your skirt that you had attempted to mend yourself. I wish you had told me then. Would have helped narrow down where to look."

"But that's where you ended up looking? Where the Blight used to be?"

"Yes. We searched day after day, and I held onto hope that it would come to me, as it always had before. Before I had given it to you. But it wasn't mine anymore. I knew it was more likely it would find its way back to you, so..."

"So, Moira and I would walk through the forest every day and you would hope that I would come across it."

I remembered that new spring day, talking to Moira about the harsh winter, enjoying the scent of the fresh spring rain from that morning. I remembered my hand sliding over the stone buried in the wood of the fallen tree. Yes, it had finally come back to me.

"It also gave me an excuse to talk to you. I had to keep to the script. If I ever diverged, Moira noticed you would leave tired and irritable. She kept me in line as best she could."

"I can't believe how much she did for me." I shook my head in wonder.

"I think she resented it a little at first. But then she became everything to you. Your only friend in the world, and I think she enjoyed the attention, honestly. I know I would have."

He smirked and pulled the rhyzolm from his pocket. It seemed to hum facing me and he held it out for me to take. "Don't lose it this time, deal?"

I took it from his hands, nodding, and the electricity I felt as my fingers brushed his, sent a tug to my lower torso. Something stirred that I had not felt in ages.

My cheeks flushed and I sat back in my chair, crossing my legs tightly, spinning the stone in my hand. The same feelings of joy, and love, and companionship raced through me just like the first time I had discovered it weeks ago.

He sat back as well, placing a hand over his mouth. "Can I ask you something?"

"Hmm?"

"Why did you hide it from me? From Moira? Why didn't you tell either of us you had found the stone?"

I thought about those first days of waking. My thoughts had been so muddled and hazy, confusing, like I was grasping through murky water for any sign of life.

"I didn't want you to take it from me. When I held this stone I felt —*I feel*—alive. I feel happiness and love, and I feel like I belong somewhere. I couldn't risk that feeling leaving. So, I hid it. And every time I rubbed its surface, I woke a little more. You could see it. I realize that now. You took me into Felgren on those little walks. That helped, too."

"Those walks were for me more than you. I saw you changing slowly and I was impatient. I thought, if she lets me near her more often, that's a good thing. That means she'll…" He swallowed hard. "That means she'll let me talk to her, touch her even."

"*Revich…*"

He stood, moving in front of the fireplace, staring down into the flames. "Wait. Just…wait. I have some memories to untangle, too."

I shoved the rhyzolm into my pocket and watched him stand there for three minutes, four. He wiped his eyes at one point and I couldn't sit there any longer.

"Rev?" I stood and touched his shoulder. He turned his head toward mine, tears falling down his cheeks into the shadow of hair on his chin.

"The bluest eyes I ever did see." I beamed, brushing strands of black waves from his face, tucking them behind his ear.

He cleared his throat as I wiped the tears away, moving close enough for our bodies to touch. "Karus? Would you like to go see the nitor moths?"

I tilted my head back in mirthful laughter, easing myself into his arms as he wrapped them across my waist. "Absolutely not." I stood on the tips of my toes and pressed my forehead to his, leaning into his scent.

I remembered *this*.

I remembered these moments between love and lust at the threshold of intimacy and desire.

"I'd rather be here. I'd rather stay." I inhaled, long and slow. "Stay and remember."

"Karus," he whispered near my lips, "I don't know if..." He slid his hand up my back and I shivered, the familiar touch causing my hips to sink into his. "...If we should do this so soon."

I paused, my lips over his, feeling the heat from his breath. "Should we wait another seven years?"

I heard him swallow and he let out a stunted laugh, smiling. "If that's what you needed, then yes."

"And you, Rev? What do you need?" I pulled on my skirts and lifted my leg up onto the chair behind him, his hand leaving my back to follow it, tugging on the other so that he could lift me.

I wrapped my legs around his waist, holding onto his shoulders, looking into his eyes as they filled with black and blue, a mixture of a midnight sea.

He laid me on the bed, hovering over my body as I pulled him down.

"*Karus.* Is this really what you want? Is it really you?"

I pulled a hand through his hair, resting it on the base of his jaw. He took my palm and kissed it lightly, trembling. The touch so familiar, so loving.

"A heart for a heart, remember? That's what you promised me. You said that I could have it. I am your stain, the part of you that lingers. And all these years later, I've come back to you. I've come back to claim what you've given me."

His mouth was over mine in an instant, and I felt his hot tears drop onto my face. "*I've missed you.*"

I could not get enough. His mouth, his breath, his very soul that I longed to meld forever with mine until I could not distinguish the two.

He tangled his hands through my hair, sinking his hips into me, our bodies seeking each other's touch like we had been starved of that which made life worth living.

He became ravenous with each of my soft moans and kissed his way down my neck, stopping a moment to fill his lungs with the scent of my skin, and I arched my back, pleading his name in a need I remembered well.

He left, working his way down to my chest, his impatient fingers tearing at my shirt, exposing my breasts where he took his time, caressing them in turn, his mouth hot and scraping over each point, kissing the underside as he moved his lips down my stomach. He unfastened my skirts, rising only to pull them off my hips, my feet still bare from hours before.

He returned to my lower belly, skimming his hands up my sides, and I ran my fingers through his hair knowing my ecstasy was moments away from being fulfilled.

His hands lifted me up, grabbing ahold of my backside before beginning his devotion to the very center of me.

His tongue lay wide and hot at first, and I cried out, pulling his head closer still, lost in my own desire for more. He knew where to lick, where to suck, where to be soft, and I relished in knowing he hadn't forgotten this part of me.

He took his time, my hips moving to his rhythm eagerly, as our pace met in unison and sweat trickled down my back. I propped myself up onto my elbows so that I could witness what he did to me.

So I could watch how he undid me.

It was pure pleasure, the escape from reality I could only imagine sharing with him, and as I reached my peak, he stayed, enjoying every bit of his efforts before lifting his head, grinning like he held the world in his hands. He swiped a thumb across his mouth, a wicked grin left there as he licked it clean.

I pounced, pushing him off the bed and onto the rug in front of the fireplace, straddling his body with mine, dripping with sweat and the sweetness between my legs.

Buttons flew across the room as I clawed at his shirt, needing to get to his skin, needing to feel his warmth against me. He reached up to kiss me more and I allowed it, pulling at the buttons on his pants, guiding him to his knees so that I could shove them down and off his legs completely.

He sat, back to the fire, pulling from my lips to look into my eyes, and for a moment, we held each other's gaze in a serene disbelief.

He swept my hair to the side, his thumb brushing my cheek. "You are so beautiful."

I grinned, sliding myself onto him easily in a gasp, my hips beginning a rhythm, slow, steady. He groaned as I moved over him, guiding my hips with hands that dug into my skin.

"Oh?" I breathed, reciting what we had already confessed to each other in this very room years before. "And what does that make you?"

He kissed me, hard, in a welcoming pain, his tongue inviting me into a moment of time only we two shared. I picked up the pace of my hips, rolling over him, our pleasure building together.

"It makes me never want to lose you again." In one swift turn, he had me on my back, catching my head in one hand, tangling his fingers in mine with the other, our bodies never separating in the movement. The flames from the fire reflected in his eyes as he resumed our rhythm, my legs open wide, begging for all of him to fill me.

"I can't lose you again, Karus."

I couldn't hold on much longer, not while he slid in and out of me like that, and my body loosened, desperate to let go with every pulse to our rhythm.

"Then don't," I whispered, breathless as he grabbed the side of my face, pushing his mouth back onto mine, his tongue sweet as ripe melon on a summer day.

We ended there together in cries of passion, two lovers separated by time and memories, returning to our old ways right where we belonged.

CHAPTER 51

REV

"Do you think we've learned our lesson?" Karus whispered to me, her head on my chest, one glorious long leg sprawled across my waist in a possessive hold. Her finger traced the liberum mark on my wrist, her touch light and caressing. Our bodies lay bare next to the fire as it crackled and sparked.

"Hmm?"

I had felt myself drifting off, the events of the day exhausting me, physically and emotionally, but I wanted so badly to stay awake. If I was awake, then it couldn't be a dream—a nightmare, haunting me as it always had. I had dreamt time and again of holding her while she was away. While she had forgotten me, I could not escape her. And I didn't want to.

But it had been torture.

Those dreams of her, of us, together like this.

I was glad she couldn't see my face.

"I was just thinking…we said we'd meet them in the dining hall for dinner, just like I had promised all those years ago." She lifted her head to look at me, biting her lip. "And, if you remember, I never showed."

"If you keep doing that, I'll bar the door so you can never leave it."

"Keep doing what?"

"Biting your lip. It's tantalizing."

She chuckled and stretched her body against mine.

Yes, this was torture.

"We should probably go before they come pounding at the door. It wouldn't be right, would it? To stay here all night? I'm much older now, after all. Surely, I've matured in that time."

She kissed my chest in short, quick brushes and I struggled not to touch her. If we were ever going to leave this room, I shouldn't start touching her.

"Can I dress you?"

"What?"

"Can I dress you? Pick out what you'll wear to this evening's dinner with my closest friends? I must present you to them, and say, *'Hello, this is my lover, the Baron of Felgren—isn't he lovely?'*"

My chest heaved in laughter and I caught her by the waist, lifting her over my torso, running my fingers down her bare hips, tracing my favorite lines of growth there. "And what would you have the Baron of Felgren wear?"

She lowered her bare chest down on mine, and I stirred in exquisite torment, lifting a hand to her chestnut hair streaked with white.

"I'd have you wear something that fit, Baron Revich. Your clothes are too loose these days."

"I…I don't have much of an appetite, honestly."

"Hmm, I see. And these dark circles under your eyes?"

"I don't sleep well, either."

She touched my face, understanding what I couldn't say.

For seven years I couldn't eat, couldn't sleep—I had barely lived, a shell of a man, broken, but never losing hope.

That I held onto.

It kept me sane most nights, though there were plenty I'd gone mad, delirious, finding myself climbing all those damn stairs to her room, sitting outside of it, facing her door. The knowledge that she was near had been enough to keep me together for just one more night.

"I'm so sorry," she whispered, her eyes a field of green clover that covered the forest floor. "I should not have left you that night. I should not have left this room without telling you what I knew."

"Don't say that. It's not your fault. I was a young fool. I thought only of myself and what I was desperate to keep. I should have been honest with you. I should have listened to what you were trying to say—recognized the pain on your face." I brushed a hand across her forehead. "Instead, I listened to a man I knew was a monster. He convinced me to lie, convinced me that if I told you, we would never defeat the Blight and it would eventually take you from me. I was so afraid of losing you, Karus, and he played off that fear. But I lost you anyway. And you paid for it with years of your life...gone."

I pulled myself up, holding her hips over mine. "I don't deserve you. I didn't then, and I don't now."

Her eyes swelled with tears as she cupped my cheek.

"If I had been there, maybe we would have destroyed it completely. If I'd been there, maybe it wouldn't have been too much for you. I could've shared in your burden, I could've—"

"You could have *died*. Just like Heimlen. For all his faults, he cared about you living to become Baron. He knew the fight would claim his life, just as it would have claimed yours, just as it almost claimed mine." She shook her head. "No. Don't do that to yourself. Maybe it wasn't my fault, but it wasn't yours, either. We don't need to look for someone to blame, and if we do, we blame him. He was wrong in so many ways. He hurt you, manipulated us both. He took advantage of your loneliness, Rev. He took Sylva's life, he took thousands of others." Her eyes turned dark and the anger there was raw.

I bowed my head to her chest. "For years, I wondered. I wondered how I didn't see it—all the signs, all the manipulation. I was blinded by his charity. He'd given me something I'd never had —a purpose to live, a father. And then he gave me you, and I...I should have wondered as you did. I *should* have seen that it didn't add up, that the Black Fever was too convenient, too easy a way to get you here, but Karus, I didn't care.

"I watched you, you know. In Hyrithia. He sent me to learn about you, to see what ties you held, the relationships you clung to. It felt like…like I was watching my future take shape. Like bringing you here was going to be the greatest thing that ever happened to me, and I didn't care how you got here, I just wanted it to happen. I wanted to introduce myself. I wanted you to meet me, just a man visiting your city. I wanted you to know me before I knew you'd hate me."

She lifted my head and placed her lips on mine with a kiss so sweet it hurt. "How——" She cleared her throat. "How did you know I'd hate you?"

"I had watched you enough to know that it was going to be a fight to get you to accept your training. You had a home, you had friends, a lover, a mother. I knew you'd be angry. I knew it would take time to get you to see why you were needed here."

"You knew about Geyrand?"

"The guard?" I grinned, kissing the tip of her nose. "Of course, I did. I watched him watching you. And I saw on more than one occasion how you touched him, teasing. I figured you two were… intimate."

"Yes. Yes, we had been friends for years before…before we became that."

"Well, I figured he was likely the most difficult obstacle to over-come. I had no way of knowing if you were in love with him or not. If you were, the fight was going to be unwinnable. Thankfully, he didn't seem to be what was holding you back. You'd have mentioned him on occasion, but you never did."

"What did you tell them? Where do they think I've been all this time?" She rose from my lap, headed toward my wardrobe, rifling through the clothing there. I admired the view.

I stood and stretched, my body feeling more like my own again.

"Actually, that's something I was going to tell you before…"

She turned her head, pulling a shirt down from its wooden hanger. "Before you became distracted?"

"I'm always distracted around you."

She smirked, finding pants in a drawer and bringing them to me. "These should work."

She pulled the shirt over my arms, tugging it over my chest, concentrating on the buttons. "So, what did you tell them?"

"I told them you were dead."

"What!" She stopped, her mouth open in shock and I grabbed her hands.

"I had no choice. I couldn't tell them you were here, training still. The Queen and the Prince had already asked to see you several times, and obviously, I couldn't let them do that. They'd have seen how lost you were and would have tried to take you away. And that was not going to happen."

"They think I'm…dead?"

"They do. I told them there was an accident, that you had taken on too much, had tried too hard to work a magic enhancement, and it took your life. Clairannia and Figuerah agreed it was best to convince them of this lie."

She sniffed, her eyes glazing over as she worked at my buttons. "I can't believe they think I'm dead. We need to tell them. All of them. We have to explain."

"We will. We will right all of this. Of course, we will. Later." I kissed her, pulling her face close to mine, loving her as I was destined to do. "We'll tell the whole isle about what you did, if you want. But for right now? For a little bit of time at least, I don't want to share you. I just want to keep you, hold you. I want to love you, Karus. Can I have that? Just for a little while?"

She wrapped her arms around my neck and nodded. "For a little while, Baron Revich. Just for a little while."

CHAPTER 52
KARUS

Our days passed us by.

We hardly noticed time moving at all, making up for the seven years we'd lost.

We didn't leave, really. Once, maybe twice, when I'd convinced him to love me in his study. I'd been insatiable there, before the massive windows that lit the room in sunlight, looking out into the densest part of the forest.

I had wanted to change my memories, shape them into something more than a place where I had been told to go each day, to talk to a man I barely knew or understood. I wanted to combine my past seven years with what I now thought of as my future.

I'd made it out.

I'd found my way through the fog of my mind, and as more and more memories returned, I found myself panicked at times, afraid of falling back into confusion, afraid of drifting through the days like a feather on the wind, never knowing where to land.

He had nightmares, too.

He'd wake in our bed, sweating, his heart pounding, and I'd be there. Finally, I was there, whispering to him that he was safe, holding him to my chest, letting him know I'd found my way back and I was never leaving again.

He'd shake, holding me, kissing me as if he'd never get to again.

Yes, he had suffered.

And I realized that, in a way, I had been protected from my own pain. I had been forced into a state where I couldn't feel it. I couldn't live, but I couldn't succumb to anguish either.

But he did.

Seven years.

I wondered how it had changed him. Surely, it had.

I saw glimpses of it, watching him. He smiled less, moved slower.

And I wondered how I could return him, if it was possible or even fair to try.

I stayed with him, never leaving his side, never allowing myself to step away more than a few minutes at a time, knowing that he wasn't ready.

We eventually left our nest, Pompeii having been our caretaker for at least two weeks, but the duties a Baron held could not be pushed aside any longer, and people were beginning to wonder if he'd given up his title.

The poor channelers were confused, allowed to roam free, and thankfully, Clairannia and Figuerah had stepped in, letting us take our time together.

They had become conduits.

They both had passed the trials, which I had learned from Revich, had been the first he had ever conducted and he didn't even remember giving them.

"I was just a shell in those days, two years in, unable to do more than what I was told to do."

"But you managed to get the trials together?"

"Yes, but I had help. Lots of it. It wasn't fair for Clairannia and Figuerah to be stuck here. They loved you still, but they were ready to move on. To begin their lives as conduits. And so, they did."

"A medicus and iumenta conduit." I grinned brightly, so very proud of what they had become, what they had made themselves into.

"That's right. When it was time to search for more channelers, I didn't know what to do. The rhyzolm was still missing and I refused to use another."

"Then how did you find them?"

"I asked around. I left Felgren a few times, looking for people with potential. It worked. I've trained two other conduits since you've been gone. And this group now, well, they've only just begun their training."

"But Viridis…how do they study?"

"We use what we have. What we've taken out of Viridis over the years. I've called for books throughout Arcaynen as well and they've arrived. Not nearly as many as in Viridis, but we make do."

I perked up, my eyes brightening. "I want to help. I want to do what I can to help train them. I want to pick up where I left off and complete the trials."

I didn't tell him what Heimlen had said that night. He had said fighting the Blight was my trial. He'd said I had become a conduit.

But, even though I knew Heimlen was right, and I understood more than anyone the power I held, I wanted it from Revich. I wanted to go through the trials, just as any other channeler would have. I wanted to experience the same tests, pass them, and make it official.

He sighed heavily. We were sitting in our chairs, pushed close together, my bare feet tucked in under his legs, keeping them warm as I read through one of the books I had brought from my room in the tallest tower.

The Language of Magic, a Guide to Speaking With a Conduit's Soul by Seraphyn Antynn.

It was the same one that had revealed my true name, and I was glad he had saved it for me. I wasn't sure how, but he had been able to retrieve some books from Viridis before the Blight grew to where it was now.

I wanted to see it again. I wanted to go back there, more prepared to witness all that was lost, and maybe I could try again.

Simulair Solum.

I was feeling stronger, as if my magic was slowly returning to what it had been.

He reached over, my feet still tucked under him, and pulled my chair even closer, my knees bending as the black and blue fabric almost touched.

"I think that's a great idea—you completing the trials, but…I've been meaning to ask you something."

I set my book down gently on the floor and folded my hands in my lap. "Yes," I answered, shrugging. "Whatever you want—yes."

He snickered, shaking his head, rubbing his hands down my calves, pushing my skirts back to my waist, kissing the tops of my bare knees. "I don't think you should give in so easily."

"Oh, really? Because I do."

"You're giving me a lot of power here, Karus, and I'm tempted to take it."

I leaned forward and took his hands in mine. "Do you really think my answer will be no? That I'll deny you whatever you're asking for? I'm powerless, Baron Revich. I love you. You've caught me in your charms, and I have no desire to escape." I laughed, loving to see him surprised still at what I'd say.

"Alright. Be my companion then. Let's make it official. You and me. We'll show the world our love. We'll be bonded by magic, we'll have babies, and memories, and we will fill this fortress with joy, and light, and all things good. Our love will filter through the trees, and we will do this together. You and me."

It wasn't what I expected to hear.

"Barons can't have companions."

"Barons can't be bound by love, either, yet here I am."

"But—"

"But we make the rules. We decide our future, not some history books, not some tradition that doesn't apply to us." He pulled me onto his lap, leaning back into his chair, running his fingers through my hair.

"We write our *own* history. We change Felgren—the isle—for the better. No more loneliness. No more single soul to reign over the most powerful place in this world. I want to share it with you. I want to live this life with you, not as a conduit who stayed, not as a servant I keep around, but as my equal, my life companion."

My breath was soft above him, looking down into the face of the man I loved, who I'd never willingly leave again. "I…I don't even know what to say…"

"Technically, you've already given me your answer."

His smile was something else. The way it had always captured me, even in the days I had convinced myself I found it annoying—I was trying my very best to resist it. It had never really worked.

"Yes, then. My answer is still yes. I'll live this life beside you. You'll never have to bear it alone."

He took my hand and slid my conduit ring onto my forefinger. "I have kept this safe for you, holding onto hope that you would wear it again."

I smiled down at the brilliant emerald, rubbing its surface gently. "I'll remember it like this, then. I'll remember it as something you gave back to me. I'll remember it as my promise to be yours, Rev. Through whatever comes next, I'll shine for you, and you'll be the sky that holds me."

I kissed him, both of us smiling, holding each other, no pressing worries of the world able to seep into our embrace, no concerns on the obstacles we would have to face, no fear of the future—the one that would rear its head soon enough.

No, for that moment, there was nothing else in the world but him and me.

A Baron and his companion.

The most powerful man on the isle loving the most powerful woman.

EPILOGUE

KARUS

I wove the clover through the stems, admiring the light pink hue of the tiny petals. The delicate nature of its blooms was a contrast to the hardiness of clover. It grew in a field of white, pink, and green. So much green now covered this place.

I sat, cross-legged in my white, gauzy dress. Somehow, Lia had been able to get the stains of the Blight out from its fibers, something I'd never thought possible, and I was thankful for it.

I loved this dress, loved this forest, this life I saw as mine to live, mine to take.

Parvus lay beside me and Rauca paced nearby, sniffing through the field of green, walking the perimeter. She still insisted on coming with us, even when Revich wasn't around.

It had taken a lot of effort on my part to remind him that I was a free person with a free will, and if I wanted to walk in the forest alone, I was going to do so.

At first, he came each time. Then, as his duties took precedence, he insisted Moira go with me. I obliged, soaking in new memories of us walking through the trees together, this time with a better understanding of all she had done for me.

Eventually, I convinced him that I would be fine alone. I had shown him how my powers returned to me, stronger each day, and I, admittedly, used my other powers over him to get what I wanted. Quieting his objections with a kiss, a whisper of his name, my teeth over my bottom lip. These were things I knew he couldn't resist—at least not very well, and I wore him down eventually. I understood his fear, but I would not indulge it.

The field of clover was my new favorite, proof that Felgren could take back what the Blight had destroyed. It lay right in the heart of what once was all death and decay. The boundaries of the Blight were still hundreds of acres away from this place. The field was a new promise that we could fight what now plagued Viridis and return it to its beauty.

I finished the crown of clover and placed it on Parvus's head. He looked up at me, sniffing the air, his fuzzy, brown-tipped ears flicking, attempting to shake it off.

I laughed, patting his graying snout, taking the crown from his head and placing it upon my own.

"Well, you look like a prince to me!"

He panted, his giant pink tongue lolling to the side of his mouth, slobber dripping down to his leg, and I rubbed his belly.

His ears perked suddenly, and his head turned, sniffing the air, pulling himself to his feet.

"What is it, boy? What do you see?"

I rose as well, his head meeting my elbow and I stroked it in a reassuring calm.

He bolted, racing ahead, the field of clover laid out far before us as the first droplets of a spring rain began to fall on my face.

I raced after him, which was difficult to do. Lumens are fast, not to mention giant, and I soon realized that by the time I caught up to him, I was going to be soaked through.

I turned my head, looking for Rauca, but I didn't see her flash of white coat anywhere.

"Parvus!" I yelled across the field, the sound of thunder distant, but a promise of downpour from the graying sky nonetheless.

I saw his form, far ahead of me before it fell. It disappeared, and I stopped in my race to reach him, stunned.

I picked up my pace again along with the skirt of my dress, a new ring of mud tracing across the bottom. I heard his high whimper of pain ahead.

As I reached the place he had disappeared, I slowed, suddenly aware that I had not known this field for long and that I should be careful in my assumption of it.

Before me was a wide, dark hole, a contrast to the bright green of the leaves of clover, but a mirror to the blackening sky above.

"Parvus!" I bent over the edge, looking down, the air rising from it rotten and putrid.

He whimpered again about ten feet below me, lying at the bottom, roots from trees once grown there climbing down the earthen walls of what looked like a massive tunnel.

Rauca's white and black body lay there, too. Her leg was bent at an odd angle, and my stomach churned as I rose from the edge, ready to run for help.

A figure approached their bodies, bending down inside the hollow ground, assessing the massive wolves.

Her figure was thin and tall. A black dress, long and trailing with sleeves that ended at her wrist, clung tight to her body. Her stark white hair flowed long down her back, curled at the ends, and a reflection of her light skin.

Her head held a crown in a ring of gold that shone in the dark cavern. A pattern of flowers I could not distinguish adorned the sides.

"I think their legs might be broken, poor things."

Her voice was soft and low, a voice I'd heard before and one that I was not likely to forget. A voice that had spoken to me of waking, one that I had never heard aloud.

The woman stood then, her head slowly rising to the light as I stared down at her over the fissure in the field, my pulse rising even more.

She was beautiful.

Her eyes shone bright, the iris iridescent and reflective in the light above her. Her nose was long and thin, almost ending at a point, and her lips were red as blood as her grin grew across her face in a charade of pleasantries.

"Who are you?" I whispered, unsure if I had spoken aloud.

"You know who I am, Little Sprout." The woman cocked her head slowly, her gaze piercing, the flicker of varying colors in her eyes like the wings of a faerie flying across a sunlit sky, and she answered, "I am the one they call the Blightress."

A BARON OF BONDS
BOOK 2 IN A CONDUIT OF LIGHT SERIES

Find out more about this series here! Join my newsletter for new releases, character art, and giveaways! If you enjoyed this book, please consider leaving a review wherever you like to review books. Happy reading, dears!

ACKNOWLEDGMENTS

I would like to acknowledge how challenging it is to see a book to completion. Not just the writing (which wrecked me), but the editing and the formatting, the commissioning of a professional editor and cover artist (mine were fabulous), and the marketing—showing this thing to the world that I love and want others to love, too. I could go on with the many challenges, but I find that authenticity and clarity are essential to me as an author and essential to me as a human.

This was fucking hard.

And it was so worth every tear, elevated heartbeat, and grimace I endured to get this story into your lap. Thank you, readers, for giving this book a chance, and if you enjoyed reading this story and would like more, please consider leaving a review so it can find its way into other hands.

There are a few people I need to acknowledge in the creation of this book.

First, my alpha readers were phenomenal in this process. Thank you Memaw, Kate, and Kelley, my own found family, my very own cheerleaders who experienced this book chapter by chapter, twist by twist, and shared an experience with me that is unforgettable.

To my beta readers: ya'll were essential in this process, thank you for reading something totally random and providing feedback.

Alysh Kay, you have been the biggest fan of my writing since fifth grade, and I must say, without your encouragement for my stories, I would probably not have made it this far.

Reed, you have pushed and cheered for me through this entire journey, and I am forever thankful for you in my life. You kept my battery going and your antics and jokes lifted my sails on windless days.

My little loves, W & V, I know you are small and the world is bright. I hope that you continue to look to the horizon each day with joy and if you cannot, I hope I can be there to remind you that clouds do not last forever.

Lastly, to everyone who has/is experiencing depression: I know something of what it is like to live each day in an endless fog with little memory of the day before, nor the hope that is tomorrow. I will say this: I hear you, I feel you, I acknowledge what you're going through. I made it out and though there are days I am afraid to fall back in, I am more thankful for each breath, each laugh, and each memory I get to keep now that I know what the darkness feels like. You are loved, you are worthy of great things, and I promise, you have strength still inside. I wish you better days, I wish you times of healing, and I wish you love.

ABOUT THE AUTHOR

Chelsey Ann Tompkins was born a storyteller, specializing in tales of love and soulful romance. Her adolescence was spent reading countless historical romance novels, along with the classics by Jane Austen. However, *Jane Eyre* will always remain her favorite. When she is not dreaming up heartbreaking romance stories, you can find her brewing yet another vanilla latte, taking her kids to the park, quilting, or indulging in the blissful silence a bubble bath provides. She resides near Seattle with her husband, two children, and an old kitty named Marjie.

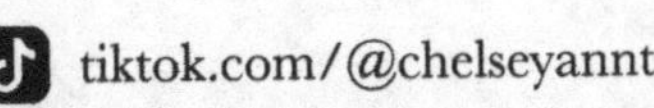

tiktok.com/@chelseyanntompkins

instagram.com/chelseyanntompkins

www.ingramcontent.com/pod-product-compliance
Lightning Source LLC
Chambersburg PA
CBHW011846300726
48970CB00009B/2673